PROTECTING ADDISON

SEAL OF PROTECTION: ALLIANCE
BOOK 5

SUSAN STOKER

CHAPTER ONE

Ricardo "MacGyver" Douglas rolled over and glanced at the clock on the small table next to the bed. It was half past three in the morning, and he was wide awake. And the reason was sleeping next to him in his bed. Rolling his head the other way, he looked at his wife.

His *wife*.

That was still so weird to say. Well...to think. He'd been married to Addison Wentz for a month now, and he'd honestly been surprised when she'd said yes to his proposal. It wasn't romantic. They weren't in love. It was strictly a wedding of convenience for them both. He needed her to help him care for three children he'd rescued during a mission, and she needed him for the health insurance she could get from the Navy as his wife.

He hadn't thought much about what would happen after he'd brought her and her twelve-year-old daughter to his home, but he should have. Things were pretty crowded in his small house. He bought it when he'd first moved to Riverton, California. It had three bedrooms, which seemed positively huge when it was just him. He'd had plenty of room for his hobby of tinkering with electronics and building things from random metal, plastic, and ceramic crap.

Now that there were five additional people living under his roof—four of them children—he'd had to clean up his house, put most of his stuff in the garage, and somehow make a comfortable home for the three orphans from Ukraine he hoped to adopt...as well as a wife and an almost-teenager.

Ellory, Addison's daughter, was in one room with Yana, who'd recently turned five. The boys—eight-year-old Artem and seven-year-old Borysko—were sharing the other room. Most mornings, MacGyver found Yana in the queen-size bed in her brothers' room, snuggled between them. It would take time for her to feel safe in her new environment, and the child psychologist the kids were seeing had told him to not make a big deal out of the sleeping arrangements.

But it was his *own* sleeping arrangements that had MacGyver waking up at the ass crack of dawn every morning. Rolling onto his side, he stared at the woman in his bed.

It was one thing to have a marriage of convenience...to marry Addison for practical purposes on both their parts. It was another to realize, too late, that he was head over heels for the woman.

He'd always wanted what his parents had. A loving relationship. His mom and dad openly adored each other. It often embarrassed MacGyver when he was a young kid. They were always holding hands and kissing. But before long, his dad became his role model. He went out of his way to make sure his wife was safe, happy, and protected. He stood up for her if a sales clerk was rude or if someone disrespected her. MacGyver had grown up with a desire to be just like him, which was part of the reason he'd joined the Navy. He wanted to protect those weaker than him. Protect his country. He hadn't planned on being a SEAL, but here he was.

Blinking sleepily, MacGyver continued to study his wife. Addison Wentz—no...Douglas now—was beautiful. Tall, with curly auburn hair that never stayed confined in whatever barrette or scrunchie she tried to tie it back with. Her forest-green eyes were too serious most of the time. She carried a lot of worry and responsibility on her slender shoulders. From the first moment they met, MacGyver had wanted to take away some of the worry she seemed to be drowning under.

But underneath all the crippling responsibilities, Addison was a funny, caring, and beautiful woman. One MacGyver was drawn to. He loved that she was the same height as him. He hadn't even realized he was attracted to tall women until Addison. He could look her in the eye without stretching his neck, she was the perfect height to wrap his arm around her waist comfortably, and when they'd hugged after being pronounced man and wife, he found out exactly how well their bodies lined up.

And lately, he couldn't think of anything else.

Including now. Which meant his dick was hard...as it was every morning. At thirty-three, he'd thought his days of spontaneous morning wood were past him, but he'd been wrong. Sleeping next to Addison, smelling the lemon lotion she used every night before she came to bed, feeling the mattress move ever so slightly when she shifted positions...it all made MacGyver hyper-aware that the woman he wanted more than he was ready to admit out loud was just inches away.

But they had a deal. In exchange for access to healthcare for Ellory, she'd help him care for Artem, Borysko, and Yana...and help make him look like a better candidate for adoption. That was the extent of their marriage.

Addison had given him no reason to think she wanted anything from him other than what he'd already provided —protection and safety for her daughter.

MacGyver inhaled deeply, then slowly let out his breath. Even though his cock throbbed and it was physically painful, he did his best to ignore his body's reaction to the woman in his bed. He'd never do anything to make her uncomfortable around him. Not purposely. For two full weeks, he'd actually slept on the floor in his own room, just because he could tell she was uneasy sharing the bed.

MacGyver felt ten feet tall when she'd finally decided it was silly for him to keep sleeping on the floor every night. He didn't like that the change of heart was largely because she felt bad for being comfortable in bed, while he was on the hard floor. He'd slept in worst places, and had told her as much, but he had to admit he was happy to be back in his own bed.

But now he woke up every morning, dick as hard as his previous sleeping surface, about an hour before his alarm went off. Part of the reason he needed help was because his days as a Navy SEAL started early. Far too early for the three kids under his care. And getting up even earlier because of Addison? Exhausting.

However, that was his new normal.

Besides, being a father was even *more* exhausting...and MacGyver loved every second of it. Seeing Artem's eyes

widen when he tried Lucky Charms for the first time...
Borysko's enthusiasm when he came home from school
excited about something new he'd learned...the relief and
pride at seeing Yana gaining weight between her first
doctor's appointment, and the one she'd had the day
before.

The kids were blossoming, and MacGyver knew it was
partly because of Addison. She was wonderful with the
kids...caring, patient, and compassionate.

She sighed in her sleep and rolled over onto her side,
facing him.

MacGyver held his breath. Lord, this woman was so
out of his league, it wasn't funny. He was bossy, a loner, and
a nerd from his head to his toes. He'd rather spend time
alone in his garage, tinkering with his inventions, than be
social...even with his SEAL teammates, who were as close
to him as brothers.

Addison was a bright shining light, and he was...What
was he?

MacGyver smiled. He was the power source behind her
light. The nerd behind the scenes keeping her plugged in.
Kind of like the guy in *The Wizard of Oz*. The one who ran
around behind the curtain fiddling with this, messing with
that. Keeping things going.

It was a silly thought, but one he rather enjoyed.
MacGyver would gladly stay behind the scenes, supporting
those he loved, letting them have the limelight.

"What time is it?"

Blinking, MacGyver realized that Addison had woken
up...sort of. She sounded still half-asleep. A pang of
tenderness hit him hard. "Too early to be up. Sleep, Addy."

Her lips twitched into a slight smile. "I've never had a
nickname before."

"Do you mind? I started calling you that without even asking if it was all right. I can call you Addison," MacGyver told her quietly.

But she shook her head. "I like it."

"Okay."

A beat of silence settled between them. Then she asked, "What's on tap for you today?"

"Working out, as usual. Then I'll come home and shower and help with breakfast. I can take Artem and Borysko to school if you can get Ellory and Yana."

"Of course."

"I should be home early. We have a few meetings, but Kevlar told us yesterday that we should be done by three."

"Cool."

"You? What do you have going on?"

"I have three cakes to make."

"Three?" MacGyver asked incredulously.

"Yeah. I said yes to a last-minute cake because the woman was desperate."

"You don't need to say yes to everyone anymore," he reminded her gently.

Addison's green eyes were steady on his. MacGyver loved this. The intimate feeling of talking in the dim light of the early morning. When the kids were asleep and it was just them.

"I know. I mean, I forget sometimes that I don't need to squirrel away every penny just in case. Have I thanked you today?"

MacGyver shook his head. "Don't. You've thanked me more than enough. We're moving on."

"I just...what you've given Ellory and me...it's...it's more than you'll ever know."

MacGyver reached out and ran his hand over her head,

smoothing her bedhead hair away from her face. He loved touching her, didn't get the opportunity to do it enough. Her eyes closed as he caressed her. It was all MacGyver could do not to lean forward and kiss her. His desire for her was a physical ache. But he didn't want to do anything that might scare her, or make her think he was going to take something she didn't want to give freely.

"If you weren't here, Artem, Borysko, and Yana would probably have to be sent back to that hellhole where I found them. So you're giving me, *them*, more than you know as well."

She smiled at him. A lazy, sleepy smile that MacGyver would give anything to be on the receiving end of every day for the rest of his life.

"What masterpieces will you be creating today?" he asked, changing the subject back to the cakes she'd spend the day baking.

"Elsa from *Frozen*, *Jurassic Park*, and a fiftieth anniversary cake."

"You'll take pictures?" MacGyver asked.

She chuckled. "You've already seen my Elsa cake."

"Don't care. I'm in awe of what you can do with flour, eggs, sugar, and frosting."

Addison's smile widened. "It's not that big of a deal."

"Are you kidding? You're a true artist, Addy. What you do...it's impressive as hell. Not only do you make cakes that should be featured in some decorating magazine—wait, is there such a thing?"

Addison giggled. "Probably."

"Anyway, not only are you a freaking artist, you're helping families make memories. And that's something that's more important than anything else."

"Ricky," she murmured.

A bolt of heat shot through his chest down to his cock, making that appendage throb all the more. He loved hearing his nickname on her lips. He'd been given the moniker MacGyver because of his ability to put together gadgets to assist him and his SEAL team when they needed it the most. But there was something so intimate about hearing Addy call him by his childhood nickname.

"I mean it," he told her. "Growing up with four siblings meant we were always having birthday parties, and my mom went out of her way to make every one special, even with store-bought cookies and cakes. But you making the masterpieces that you do, which not only look amazing but taste good too? The memories for those kids and adults will stick with them forever."

"Thanks," she said softly. "Depending on how Ellory feels this weekend...do you think...would you mind..." Her voice trailed off.

"Of course I wouldn't mind," MacGyver said immediately.

"You don't even know what I was going to say."

"Doesn't matter. If she wants to do something, I'll make it happen."

Addison stared at him for so long, MacGyver felt uneasy. He couldn't read what was going on behind those green eyes of hers.

Finally, she continued, her words rushed and strung together as if she was afraid he'd say no. "She asked if I'd talk to you about showing her how to jump-start a car. And change a tire. And maybe show her something you've made while on a mission that helped save the day."

Joy swamped MacGyver. "Of course I will. It'll be my pleasure." His mind raced with things he could show her that wouldn't be too dangerous. "How's she doing?"

Addison shrugged. "Okay for now. We'll see how the new medicine she's taking works out. We've tried so many combinations of things, and they all seem to work at first, then the inflammation comes back."

Ellory had Crohn's, a form of inflammatory bowel disease. It didn't usually hit children, but she'd started having issues about four years ago. Her symptoms began with cramps, fevers, fatigue, and an extreme amount of weight loss, mostly because eating was so uncomfortable. She'd been in the hospital a lot, had a ton of tests, none of which were cheap, and was still dealing with the horrible symptoms to this day.

MacGyver had learned a lot about the awful disease, and he was relieved that she'd be able to get more care, now that she was covered under his health insurance. The fact that the girl wanted to spend time with him made him feel good. *Really* good. It was only a matter of time before her teenage years hit and she'd probably want nothing to do with her nerdy stepfather.

Addison yawned then and gave him a sheepish little smile.

MacGyver wanted to kick his own ass. Here he was, having a conversation they should've had later, over breakfast. She needed her sleep. Addison worked her ass off now that she had three more kids to look after. She worked all day, baking and decorating cakes, and he was being selfish by wanting to talk.

"Sleep, Addy. We can talk more at breakfast."

"I like talking to you," she said.

It was too dark to know for sure, but MacGyver could swear he saw her cheeks darken with a blush. "I like talking to you too. But it's the middle of the night. You need your rest."

"So do you."

"Don't you know? SEALs are immune to needing something so inane as sleep," he joked.

She smiled...then did something that blew MacGyver's mind. She reached out and put her hand over his on the mattress. Then she closed her eyes and sighed.

MacGyver didn't move. Not one inch. The warmth from her hand seeped into his. It was kind of pathetic how excited he was over the small touch. But it was the first time since their wedding ceremony that she'd voluntarily touched him.

MacGyver wasn't tired anymore. He watched Addison's breaths deepen as she fell back asleep. He had no idea what the future held for them, but he had no illusions. There was no way Addison would stay married to him. Not long term. This was a mutually beneficial arrangement. Eventually, she'd find a man she wanted to spend the rest of her life with. And while it would gut him, MacGyver would let her go. He wanted her to be happy more than he wanted to force her to stay with him.

But in the meantime, he'd be the best father he could be. The best husband. He'd make sure Addison wanted for nothing and was treated the same way his dad treated his mom. With Respect. Love.

MacGyver watched her sleep for as long as he could before turning and shutting off his alarm a few minutes before it was set to sound. The last thing he wanted to do was wake Addison again. He eased out of bed and went into the bathroom to change into his PT clothes. Then he went back into the bedroom, hesitating before walking out the door.

Taking a deep breath, he padded over to Addison's side of the bed. She'd turned onto her back and was sleeping soundly. He pulled the blankets higher, making sure she was covered. Then he leaned down and kissed her forehead with a barely there caress.

MacGyver stared at her for a moment more before turning and striding to the door.

CHAPTER TWO

Addison Wentz, now Douglas, smiled as she put the plate of pancakes on the dining room table. Artem's and Borysko's eyes widened at the size of the stack, while Yana was more interested in combing the hair of the Barbie doll she held. Unfortunately, Ellory was having a flare that morning, so she was still in bed in her room, hoping she'd feel better by the time she had to go to school.

Every time her daughter cried with pain, Addison wanted to take her place. She'd gladly suffer every one of the symptoms in place of Ellory if she could. Crohn's was a horrible disease, especially for a young child. Her daughter was dealing with an illness that would never be cured. She'd have to deal with the ramifications of Crohn's her entire life. It sucked.

And now that she was in seventh grade, the bullies had decided her daughter made a good target, to boot. She was underweight and hadn't really started any kind of growth spurt because of malnutrition. She simply wasn't eating as much as a growing girl should, and it showed in the percentile for her height and weight compared to other girls her age. Crohn's disease made eating many foods difficult, if not impossible. That made her a target at school.

She also had the same red hair as Addison. It was beautiful, but anything different, anything that made you stand out in middle school, was never a good thing. Addison had found that out the hard way when she was Ellory's age too.

"All for us?" Artem asked.

His question brought Addison back to the present. "Yes. All those pancakes are for you. But don't feel as if you *have* to eat them all. When you get full, we'll save the rest for a snack after school." When she'd first met the children, they'd all stuffed themselves to the point of being sick every time they were presented with food. It had taken a while, but it was finally sinking in that they weren't in a food shortage situation, as they'd been in the bombed-out city where they'd lived back in Ukraine.

"Yana, you need to put down your doll and eat some breakfast," Addison said gently but firmly.

"Barbie," she said, holding up the doll proudly.

The little girl wasn't as proficient with English as her brothers, as the boys had some schooling before war had broken out in their country. Yana had been too young, and therefore had only learned what she'd picked up from Artem and Borysko. She could understand much more than she could speak, but after only a few short weeks in a special program for children with English as their second language—which took place after her regular mornings in kindergarten—she was picking it up quickly.

"Yes, I see. Barbie is pretty. But you need to eat," Addison repeated, putting a pancake on a plate and squirting some syrup onto it before pushing it toward the girl.

Yana looked over at her brothers, who were happily

shoveling bites of pancakes into their mouths, and picked up her fork.

Satisfied the kids were eating, Addison went back into the kitchen to clean up the dishes she'd used to make breakfast and to start prepping to bake her first cake. As she worked, she thought about earlier that morning.

Specifically, the kiss.

She hadn't been fully asleep when Ricky had gotten out of bed to get ready to go work out with his SEAL team. She'd felt the mattress dip as he rose and opened her eyes just in time to see his sculpted backside disappear into the bathroom.

The man was built—and the more she was around him, the more Addison wanted him. He was everything she'd always dreamed of in a partner. And the way he treated Ellory? That was the icing on the cake.

When she'd first met him, she was immediately attracted to Ricky. Then, oddly, they'd started running into each other more and more around town...at gas stations, coffee shops. When he ran into her and Ellory at a local diner, and ended up at their table, her daughter instantly liked him. But their relationship was still pretty much an acquaintance. Friendly but impersonal.

Until one day he went away, gone on another mission, then came home with three kids in tow...and asked her to marry him for their mutual benefit.

As crazy as it might seem to others—after all, they'd never so much as dated—she hadn't hesitated to say yes. After years of hospital stays and ER visits for Ellory, Addison was one medical bill away from being homeless, and Ricky desperately needed her help with the kids he'd suddenly found himself parenting.

They were a month in, and true to their arrangement,

Ricky hadn't once made any kind of sexual move toward her...much to her dismay. Being friend-zoned sucked, but she'd brought it on herself. She was too shy to let him know that she wouldn't mind being more than friends, more than married in name only. The last thing she wanted to do was ruin the good thing she had. She'd do *anything* for her daughter. Absolutely anything to ensure she had the medical care she needed. And if that meant living with the man she wanted more than she could remember wanting anything else in the world, and *not* touching him, she'd do it.

But this morning...it was the first time they'd shared such an intimate moment. Ricky went out of his way not to crowd her. Not to touch her without her permission. But this morning, in the dim glow of the nightlights he'd plugged into every outlet in his room, he'd not only brushed her hair back from her face, but he hadn't pulled away when she'd spontaneously put her hand over his.

And then that kiss...

After she'd heard the front door shut behind him, Addison hadn't been able to stop herself from reaching between her legs and pleasuring herself as she fantasized about pulling down the sweats he wore to bed every night and showing him without words how much she wanted him.

"Addy, milk? Please?" Yana asked from the table. The kids had immediately picked up on the nickname Ricky had given her, and she loved it.

Shaking herself out of the fog of memories, Addison went to the refrigerator and grabbed the gallon of milk. She refilled the little girl's cup and topped off Artem and Borysko's while she was there. She'd just turned to go back to the fridge when the front door opened.

"Ricky!" Yana yelled, jumping off her chair and running for the man Addison couldn't stop thinking about.

He caught Yana mid-leap and lifted her above his head, making them both laugh. He carried her to the table and put her back in her chair. "Doesn't look like you've finished breakfast, little one. How many pancakes have you eaten already, Borysko?" he asked.

The little boy smiled and said proudly, "Four."

"Don't talk with your mouth full. It's impolite and gross," Ricky scolded gently. "What about you, Artem?"

The other boy chewed furiously, then swallowed before saying, "Six."

"Wow. You going to have room for the amazing lunch I'm sure Addy's made for you?" Ricky asked.

Both boys nodded eagerly. There was nothing they liked more than mealtimes. Addison smiled from her spot in the kitchen. She was leaning against the counter, watching Ricky with the children. He was so good with them.

Before she could brace herself, he turned and walked toward her. Remembering what she'd done after he'd left that morning made Addison's cheeks heat. She forced herself to look him in the eye as he came into the kitchen.

To her surprise, he leaned in and kissed her cheek.

"Morning," he murmured, before turning to the coffee that Addison had brewed earlier. "Mmmmm, hazelnut?"

Addison swallowed hard and managed, "Yeah."

"You spoil me. Us." His voice lowered. "What fun do you have planned for their lunches today?"

Addison smiled. "I got some new cookie cutters, so their sandwiches are shaped like dinosaurs today. The cookies are naturally dinosaurs too."

"Decorated?" he asked.

"Is a cookie a cookie if it doesn't have icing on it?" she retorted.

Ricky chuckled. Then leaned toward her and whispered, "Any chance there were extras?"

He smelled like he'd been working out. Like sweat. He even had sand stuck on the side of his cheek. And it took everything within Addison not to throw herself at him. It was going to kill her when the adoption went through and the kids were old enough not to need a nanny. Because why would he keep her around when he didn't need her anymore? This fantasy she was living of the happy family would end. She had to keep that in mind. Try not to get any more attached than she was already.

"Of course," she told him with a small smile. "I know how much you like my cookies."

"I love your...cookies," he said.

Addison felt as if she imagined the small pause in his statement. Because of course they were talking about cookies, right?

"Hi, Ricky."

Addison turned at the sound of her daughter's voice. As did Ricky. He stepped toward her and pulled her into a bear hug, lifting her up. That was just one more thing Addison loved about this man. He didn't shy away from showing her daughter physical affection. And she drank in his attention like she was dying from thirst and he was a tall glass of water. Much like her mom did.

"How you doin' this morning?" he asked, putting her down but keeping his hands on her shoulders.

Ellory shrugged. "I'm okay."

"That bad, huh?" Ricky said, not letting her lie about how she was feeling. "You need to stay home today?"

Addison had asked her the same thing earlier.

"No. I'm okay."

"You want to eat anything?"

"No," Ellory said again.

"Okay, but if you aren't feeling better by lunch, call your mom. You can't go all day without getting some nutrients in you. She can bake some chicken for you. Maybe you can try a banana and a protein smoothie this morning?"

Addison's heart melted. Ricky had learned so much about Crohn's since they'd gotten married. He'd researched for hours online to find out what foods were best for Ellory and what to do when she had a flare.

"Okay," Ellory said, hugging Ricky once more before heading to the fridge.

Addison should've been surprised at her daughter's acquiescence. After all, she'd suggested Ellory have a smoothie not twenty minutes earlier but had gotten an unequivocal no in response. But when Ricky suggested it, she was all for it. Addison would've been irritated if she wasn't grateful that *someone* could get her daughter to eat. She was underweight and needed all the calories she could get.

"Ricky?" Ellory said, turning away from the fridge.

"Yeah, El?"

"You stink," the almost-teenager said bluntly.

Ricky laughed. "Yeah, well, that's because Kevlar thought it would be fun for us to do burpees in the sand this morning. I hate those with a passion." Then he growled and hunched over and stomped toward Ellory with his arms out, as if he was some sort of sand monster.

Ellory screeched and yelled, "Stay away from me, smelly-man!"

Ricky laughed. "You weren't telling me to stay away a second ago," he said.

"Whatever."

It was such a teenage thing to say, Addison couldn't help but chuckle. "Don't forget to fill your water bottle before you leave. And drink as much as you can throughout the day."

Ellory rolled her eyes once more and mumbled again, "Whatever, Mom." Then she took her smoothie and banana, went to the table and sat next to Yana and Borysko, and immediately began talking to them about school.

Addison was grateful her daughter had taken so well to the children. She could've been resentful they were taking some of her mom's time and attention away from her, but she wasn't. She seemed happy they were there, and grateful for the distraction they gave her from the constant pain she was in most of the time. And while Addison had been afraid she'd hate having to share her room with a five-year-old, to her surprise, Ellory seemed to love having Yana around. She was a huge help with the kids, if nothing else by keeping them occupied. Artem and Borysko loved to talk with her, loved to practice their English, and Yana was content to play with her dolls with Ellory.

"You good?" Ricky asked, bringing Addison's attention back to him.

"Yeah. Why wouldn't I be?" she asked, genuinely curious.

"Because you're cooking for six now, running kids around everywhere, still working full time, and doing all the laundry, cleaning, *and* dealing with the state when they unexpectedly show up to check in on the kids."

"I'm fine," Addison told him honestly. "Why? Is there

something I'm doing that I shouldn't be, or not doing that I should be?"

"No!" Ricky said almost forcefully. "This...it's just a lot. And I want to make sure you're okay with it all. I don't ever want you to feel as if I'm taking advantage of you or not doing my part. I want this to work, Addy. And it won't if you don't tell me when you're unhappy."

There. That. Only one of the reasons he was such a good man. And would make some woman an amazing *real* husband one day. "Honestly, I'm fine. You do a lot, Ricky. You do all the grocery shopping, you work full time too—in a much more stressful job than I have, I might add—and when you're here, you do as much as possible to help out."

"Well, if there's anything else I can do, please let me know. I don't ever want you to feel as if you're the only parent."

"I don't."

"Good. Now, I need to shower. I have it on good authority that I stink," Ricky said with a small chuckle.

"It's not that bad," Addison blurted, then immediately blushed.

"Glad you think so," he said. Then he shocked the crap out of her by leaning in and kissing her on the cheek once more.

She could smell the coffee on his breath before he turned and took his cup with him and walked out of the kitchen. He stopped by the table and touched each of the younger kids on the head, saying something in a low voice that Addison couldn't hear. He squeezed Ellory's shoulder before disappearing down the short hall toward their bedroom.

Once he was gone, the electricity in the air seemed to

dissipate. It had always been like that when Ricky was around. He lit up whatever room they were in and made everything seem so...exciting. It should've been exhausting, but instead it was thrilling.

By the time Ricky returned, he was freshly showered and wearing his blue naval camo uniform. It was all Addison could do not to jump him right there and then. There was just something about his uniform that made him even more attractive than he was before...and that was saying something.

"Better?" he asked Ellory, holding his arms out, as if for her inspection.

To Addison's amusement, Ellory walked up to him, leaned in, and sniffed. Then she pulled back and smiled. "Better," she agreed.

Ricky laughed and pulled her against his chest for another long hug. Then he took hold of her shoulders and looked down at her with a serious look on his face. "You sure you're okay to go to school today?"

"Yeah."

"You don't hurt?" he asked.

"I didn't say that," Ellory said with a shrug.

Her response made Addison's heart ache. There was nothing worse than knowing your child was in pain and not being able to do anything about it.

Ricky obviously felt the same way, because he frowned.

But Ellory being Ellory, she patted his chest and said, "But it's not awful today. I'll be all right."

"You take your meds?" Ricky asked.

"Of course."

The girl had a litany of medicines she took to try to keep her Crohn's under control. Antibiotics, an anti-inflammatory, an acid-reducer, and an immune system suppressant to reduce the swelling in her intestines. Addison hated that she was so young and taking so many medicines, but they really did seem to help. Besides, the next step was surgery, which wouldn't cure her but might keep the worst symptoms at bay for a while. But the thought of anyone slicing into her baby was abhorrent.

"Right. If things get bad, don't hesitate to call your mom or me," Ricky told her.

Ellory rolled her eyes. "I know."

Her daughter was growing up before her eyes. Addison didn't know whether she should reprimand her for being disrespectful or laugh at the exasperation in her tone.

"I know I'm not your father, but I care," Ricky told her seriously.

Ellory tilted her head as she stared at the man in front of her. "Why?"

"Why do I care?"

"Yeah. Like you said, you aren't my dad. And you haven't known me or my mom very long." Her voice lowered, so the three other kids couldn't hear. Addison herself had to strain to hear what she was saying. "And I know you married my mom so she could have insurance for me, and you could have a babysitter for the others. So...why do *you* care if I hurt or not?"

Addison's gut clenched. She hadn't really wanted Ellory to know the circumstances behind her marriage, but she also didn't like lying to her daughter. So when Ellory approached her one night, wanting to know why she'd married Ricky when they hadn't even dated, Addison was completely honest. Well...as honest as she could be, leaving out the part about loving the man.

"I did *not* marry your mom for those reasons alone," Ricky told her.

Addison held her breath.

"Yes, us being married made things easier in regard to you getting the healthcare you need. And yes, having her here is a tremendous help with Artem, Borysko, and Yana. But I married your mom because I like and respect her. We've actually known each other a while now, and there wasn't anyone else I even considered marrying."

It was kind of a non-answer, but it still made Addison feel warm and gooey inside.

"Do you love her?" Ellory asked almost nonchalantly.

The warm feeling disappeared in a puff of smoke. She wanted to rush over to where her daughter was standing with Ricky and laugh off her question. She both wanted to hear his answer and was terrified of it at the same time.

His gaze lifted at that moment and met her own. Addison swallowed hard as she stared back. He only looked at her for a heartbeat, but it felt as if something momentous happened in that short span of time.

"Your mom is one of the most generous, talented, and beautiful women I've ever met. She would do anything for you, for her friends. She puts everyone else first, even if it means she goes without. She's got more love in her little finger than many people have in their entire bodies. I would bend over backward for her. I'll protect her, and you, with every breath in my body. And before you ask why again, it's because she's got a pure soul. And she makes me a better man. If that's not love, I don't know what is."

Addison felt as if she was going to pass out. People had told her she had pretty hair, that she was lucky she had such a slender frame, that she was nice. But what Ricky just said? It floored her. He hadn't come right out and said he loved her, but obviously he'd satisfied Ellory. Because she nodded.

"Okay?" Ricky asked.

"Okay," Ellory told him.

"No more talk about doubting whether I care about you or your mom, all right?"

"Yeah."

"Will you help get Yana ready for school while I talk to your mom real fast?"

"Sure." Ellory spun toward the table and held out her hand to the little girl. "Come on, Yana. Do you want to wear your Elsa shirt or the Little Mermaid?"

"Elsa!" Yana practically shrieked.

Ellory laughed and headed down the hall toward their room hand-in-hand with the little girl. Artem and Borysko had finished putting their dirty dishes in the dishwasher and ran down the hallway more rambunctiously than the girls had, pushing and shoving each other to try to be first to get to their room to grab their backpacks.

Addison knew she and Ricky only had a couple of minutes before the kids would be back, and they'd all have to leave to get to school on time. She held her breath as Ricky walked toward her.

"I'm sorry."

Addison frowned, her brows furrowed.

"I didn't mean to overstep there. I just…I hate thinking of her in pain. I hope you aren't offended by what I said."

That wasn't what she was feeling. "Offended? No, not at all."

"Good. I respect you, Addy. So damn much. You've stepped into this role without any hesitation. Taken on me and the kids as if you were born to it. I couldn't do this without you. Most of the time I feel completely out of my element. I can shoot my way out of a dangerous situation, MacGyver my way out if I'm trapped, and basically kick ass when it comes to anything related to the military or electronics. But three kids? I don't know what I was thinking. Am I doing the right thing? Would they be better off in their own country, surrounded by their own culture?"

Addison reacted without thinking. She stepped toward Ricky and put her hand on his arm. "You're an amazing father. Artem looks up to you so much. I don't know if you realize it, but his eyes are always on you. He watches you, and whatever you do, *he* does. This morning, you told Borysko not to talk with his mouth full, and Artem, who'd been doing the same thing all morning, immediately chewed and swallowed before he spoke.

"And Borysko, he's blossoming under your care. When I first met him, he was shy and looked to his brother for reassurance. Now he's gaining confidence and actually making some decisions on his own. And Yana has you wrapped around her little finger." She smiled. "She's also so darn smart. And I can't even begin to express everything you've done for Ellory. You're doing the right thing, Ricky. I promise."

His shoulders relaxed, as if he'd needed to hear her words. Addison wanted to kiss him so badly, but she refrained...barely.

"And you?" Ricky said with a grin. "Do you regret marrying me?"

That was an easy question. "No."

"Good. You ready to be seen with me in public?"

"What?"

"Public. You know, outside this house? Since we got married, we haven't done anything together. Some SEAL friends of mine are having a get-together. I thought we could go."

Addison licked her lips nervously. It wasn't that she didn't want to be seen with Ricky in public. It was more a self-preservation thing on her part. The more she integrated into his life, the more it would hurt when he got permanent custody of the kids and decided he didn't need her anymore. She was aware those kinds of thoughts didn't paint Ricky in a very flattering light, but she didn't think he'd want to be with her if and when he no longer had to.

He took her silence for a refusal and hurried to continue speaking, to try to convince her. "It's an informal thing. Wolf and Caroline never had children, but they love their friends' kids as if they were their own. They have these get-togethers all the time so they can get their kid fix. It'll be crazy. The kids are older now but they still run around like hooligans. The grownups sit around and drink beer or sodas and catch up with everyone's lives. It's laid-back and a chance for everyone to talk about stuff other than work."

"Of course I'll go," Addison told him, reluctantly giving in.

"Yeah?"

"Yeah."

"Good. Everyone's gonna love you."

"You *have* told them that we're married, right?" she asked a little hesitantly.

He looked confused. "Of course I have."

"Oh." For some reason, Addison thought he was keeping their marriage a secret.

"My team knew the day after it happened. They weren't thrilled with me for not inviting them, but they also understood that it could be overwhelming for you and

Ellory. They've been bugging me to introduce them ever since. And of course, the ones with girlfriends have let them know about us, and now I'm also being badgered by Remi, Wren, Josie, and Maggie too."

Addison knew all about his SEAL teammates. Ricky had no problem talking about them. It was obvious he respected and liked them a hell of a lot. Which wasn't exactly a surprise, since they went into life-or-death situations together. She'd heard all about how he'd come to meet Artem, Borysko, and Yana in Ukraine, how scary their situation in the war-torn country had been, and how they'd come to be in the States because Borysko was shot when Ricky and his teammate and Maggie were rescued. The story was frightening. Hearing about what Maggie had been through was equally terrifying.

Addison wasn't anything like what she imagined Maggie to be, and the thought of having to figure out what to talk about when she met the woman scared the crap out of her. But she was Ricky's wife, and she knew that came with certain obligations. So she'd go to this get-together, do her duty, then hopefully not have to do it again for a long while.

"Anyway, it'll be great. It's a potluck, so we'll have to come up with something to bring, but we can worry about that later."

Addison smiled. Now *that* was something she could take care of without any issues. "I can make something," she told him.

"Are you sure? I figured you bake so much for work that you wouldn't want to do it for this. We can stop at the grocery store on the way and grab some cookies or something from the deli."

Addison widened her eyes and gasped in mock outrage.

"Store-bought cookies? Over my dead body!" she exclaimed dramatically.

Ricky chuckled, and the smile on his face transformed him from handsome to drop-dead gorgeous. "Right."

"When is the thing?"

"This weekend."

Addison nodded. "Okay."

"Are you saying that because you think it's what I want to hear, or are you really okay with going?" Ricky asked.

He was so astute it was almost scary. "I'm a little nervous, but these are your friends. I want to meet them. And it'll be good for Ellory and the others to hang out with new people."

"Great. I'll let Wolf and Caroline know. And the girls too."

"The girls?"

"Wren, Josie, Remi, and Maggie. They've been driving me crazy, texting and wanting your number. Is it okay if I give it to them?"

"I guess. But I don't have a lot of time to be on the phone," Addison warned him.

Ricky didn't look concerned. "They're text people. It's their preferred mode of communication. You can respond whenever you have time."

Addison relaxed a little. She hated talking on the phone. Many times she didn't know what to say and those awkward silences made her cringe. "Okay."

"Okay."

They stared at each other for a beat, and Addison could've sworn that he was leaning toward her before Artem and Borysko burst into the room, arguing with each other in Ukrainian.

"English," Ricky called out gently.

Mid-argument, the boys switched to English. It was still a bit broken and stilted, but they were getting better by the day. It was astonishing how fast they were picking up the language.

Any intimate moment she and Ricky might've had was lost as Ellory and Yana joined the others. Addison quickly grabbed her purse and headed for the door with Ricky and the kids. She would drop off Ellory and Yana, as their schools were close together. Ricky took Artem and Borysko. They were currently going to a private school for kids who were learning English as a second language. They were the only ones there from the Ukraine. Most of the kids spoke Spanish, but there were a few who spoke Farsi, Korean, Tagalog, and even one little girl who was from France.

The kids ran to the vehicles to get themselves strapped in. After Addison locked the front door behind her, Ricky touched her arm. As she turned to look at him, he was already leaning in to kiss her. His lips brushed against hers in a short, chaste kiss. It took everything in Addison not to reach up and trace her lips reverently.

"I'll touch base at lunch. See how everything's going. If you need anything in the meantime, don't hesitate to text me. I'm in meetings most of the day, but nothing so important I can't get away to talk if you need me."

He always made it clear that if there was any kind of emergency, he'd be there for her. It was comforting. Addison had gone through too many health scares with Ellory by herself not to realize what a gift Ricky gave her with his reassurances. "All right."

"Want me to bring anything home for dinner?"

"No. I'm going to make chicken for Ellory, since she's

having a flare. I thought I'd make lasagna for everyone else. That all right?"

"I can't remember the last time I had homemade lasagna. That sounds perfect. But I hate that Ellory has to have bland food while the rest of us eat pasta."

"I know, but she's used to it. And more importantly, she doesn't miss the rich food that we can eat. She knows it'll just make her feel horrible later."

"Still. That sucks," Ricky insisted.

"It does."

He sighed, then nodded. "Have a good day, Addy."

"You too."

He smiled at her, then stepped away and headed for his Explorer. The boys were already in the backseat with their seat belts on.

Four. That's how many times Ricky had kissed her today. Three more times than he ever had before. The one and only other time had been their wedding day. She had no idea why he was suddenly so affectionate...but she liked it. A lot.

He waved at her once more before he pulled out of the driveway and headed down the street. Addison backed out and headed in the opposite direction.

All in all, her life was going really well. Which worried her, because in her experience, just when things were going well, life seemed to throw her a curveball.

Hoping she was past that, she concentrated on the traffic. She had two girls to get to school and three cakes to bake. She had no time for curveballs.

CHAPTER THREE

"I still can't believe you're married, man," Safe said with a shake of his head.

The SEAL team was sitting in a small conference room waiting for their commander to join them to discuss their next mission.

"Right? I mean, we haven't even met this chick," Flash complained.

"So? *You* aren't married to her," MacGyver told his friend.

"I know, but we want to make sure she's good for you."

MacGyver snorted. "Good for me? She's way out of my league. If anything, *I'm* not good enough for *her*."

"Now that's bullshit if I've ever heard it," Kevlar said. "You're the best of this bunch, MacGyver."

"Hey! I resent that," Smiley bitched.

Everyone laughed.

"But since you're all so concerned, I'm bringing her and the kids to Wolf's house this weekend."

"Awesome!"

"Sweet!"

"About damn time!"

Everyone seemed excited that they were finally going to get to meet the mysterious woman he'd married.

"How are Artem, Borysko, and Yana doing?" Preacher asked. He'd been with MacGyver when they'd met the children in the Ukraine. He'd seen firsthand their horrible circumstances, and was the only one of the team who'd had any inkling of MacGyver's plan to marry Addison to help gain custody of the kids. Of course, he was as surprised as everyone else that it happened so quickly after they'd gotten home from that mission.

"They're good," MacGyver said. "I spoke with Artem and Borysko's teacher the other day, and she said she's never seen kids learn so quickly. And their math skills are way above normal for kids their age."

"That's great. So they'll take after their dad," Blink said. "Since you're a genius when it comes to engineering stuff."

"I don't know about that. But I'm relieved. I was afraid they'd been so traumatized by what happened to their parents, their village, all of it, they wouldn't be able to settle in," MacGyver said.

"Their sessions with the psychologist are going all right?" Safe asked.

"Yeah. I don't know all the details, but the woman says that mentally and emotionally, they're healing well."

"And Yana?" Blink asked.

"She's adorable," MacGyver told them. "This morning, she was totally decked out in her Elsa gear."

"You're spoiling her," Kevlar warned.

"Yup," MacGyver said, with no hesitation and a huge smile on his face. "I sure am."

"They're lucky," Smiley said.

"No. I'm the lucky one. I never really thought much about being a father. It wasn't anything I particularly aspired to be. But now? I can't imagine my life without them," he said.

"I can't wait," Preacher said. "I know Maggie isn't that far along, but I'm more than ready for that baby to get here."

"It has a bit longer to marinate," Flash reminded him.

"I know. And that sucks."

Everyone laughed again.

"Any plans for you guys to have kids?" Flash asked Kevlar, Safe, and Blink.

"We want at least three," Blink said. "With hopefully one set of twins, since they run in my family."

"We also want them, but Wren and I are enjoying our time together for the moment," Safe said.

"Famous last words," Smiley said with a chuckle. "You say that, and then—BAM. Preggo."

Everyone talked over each other, agreeing.

"Kevlar? What about you and Remi?" Flash asked.

"Yeah. We want at least one. Maybe more. We might adopt, like you, MacGyver. Maybe take in a foster. A kid who needs someone to love him or her."

"With all the time you spend volunteering with the Girl Scouts, I can see you with several little girls," Safe told him.

Kevlar smiled. "Yeah."

"Right, so everyone wants kids except me," Smiley said. "They're smelly, loud, and take up way too much time."

"You might change your mind when you meet some-one," Kevlar said. "I didn't think much about kids until after Remi and I got together."

"I don't think so. I mean, I like other people's kids, but I don't really want any of my own."

"What if you find a woman who wants, like, ten kids?" Flash joked.

"I'd like to think that when I *do* find someone who can put up with my grumpy ass, that we'll be on the same page about something so important. If we aren't, I'm not sure I'd fall in love with her in the first place."

"I don't think it works like that," Kevlar said seriously.

Smiley simply shrugged. "Honestly, I don't think it's going to be an issue anyway. I have a feeling I'm going to be the single one of our bunch. I'll be the annoying uncle who takes all *your* kids and teaches them bad words, how to do doughnuts in a parking lot, how to sneak out of their houses, and how to shotgun a beer."

"That's it, you are officially not allowed anywhere near Artem or Borysko. Or my daughters, for that matter," MacGyver said.

"Daughters," Flash said with a shake of his head. "It's so hard to wrap my head around any of us having children. And an almost-teenager? It's mind-blowing."

Everyone nodded.

"How's Ellory doing? She's got that bowel thing, right?" Safe asked.

"Crohn's disease, yeah. And she's okay. Today wasn't a good day. She puts on a brave face, but I can always tell when she's hurting. It sucks, because there's nothing any of us can do to make it better."

"But now that she can get consistent healthcare, that'll help, won't it?" Kevlar asked. "I mean, that's why Addison married you, isn't it?"

For some reason, his friend's words hit MacGyver

wrong. "Well, she wouldn't have married me if she didn't like me a *little*...at least, I'd like to think that."

"Of course she wouldn't," Preacher agreed immediately. "Look, I'm not an expert on women, not even close. But it wasn't as if marriage was her last resort. You told me that you offered to help pay for Ellory's treatments even if she didn't marry you."

That was true. After MacGyver had asked Addison to marry him, he'd promised that even if she said no, he'd still help with Ellory's medical care. He'd met the girl several times and genuinely liked her. He couldn't stand the thought of her not being able to get the help she needed because Addison couldn't afford it. Yes, he needed help with the kids, but he never would've pressured Addison to do anything she didn't want to do.

"We're hoping the doctors at the base hospital will be able to regulate her meds so she doesn't have so many ups and downs. Her doctor has scheduled an upper GI series to see if he can spot anything new on the scans," MacGyver told his friends.

"Ugh. That's where she has to drink that nasty stuff that'll make her insides light up when she goes through the machine, right?" Smiley asked.

MacGyver couldn't help but laugh a little at that. Before meeting Ellory and reading up on Crohn's, he probably would've described the procedure the same way. "Yeah. She drinks a mixture with barium in it, and it'll make her GI tract light up in the x-rays."

"And that'll help figure out what's wrong?" Kevlar asked.

"Well, the doctors pretty much know what's wrong, but it'll pinpoint where the inflammation is and maybe how to help relieve the pressure."

"Sounds like you have a plan. And the other kids are doing good. How are *you* doing?" Kevlar asked.

Glancing at his friend, MacGyver frowned. "What do you mean?"

"You've had a lot thrown at you in a very short period of time. Three traumatized kids—one of which is still recovering from being shot—an almost-teenage step-daughter, a new wife, a full house...it's *a lot*. How are you dealing with it all?"

MacGyver took a moment to really think about his friend's question. To his surprise, he realized that while he felt as if he was busy every moment of the day now, and he didn't have any of the free time he used to have to tinker with his electronics and junk at home, he wasn't unhappy about any of it. "I'm good," he said with a small shrug.

"Really?" Safe asked.

"Really," he confirmed. "I work hard all day, then go home and Yana runs toward me yelling my name, as if it's been years since she's seen me instead of hours. Artem and Borysko talk over each other in their eagerness to tell me about their day, what new words they learned. The house smells like food that Addison's been cooking for dinner, and the baked goods she makes for us are the icing on the cake, literally. And when I can make Ellory smile through her pain, my day is pretty much made. I go to bed every night exhausted but...fulfilled. Which is an amazing feeling."

"Damn, I think I'm jealous," Flash mumbled.

"Happy for you," Kevlar said.

"Thanks."

"Can't wait to meet Addison," Preacher said. "Is she ready for the girls?"

MacGyver snorted. "Is anyone *ever* ready for the girls?"

"They aren't that bad," Kevlar protested, defending his wife and the others.

MacGyver simply raised a brow at his friend.

"Okay, they can be a lot, but it's just because they're so eager to make friends. To make others in our circle feel welcome."

"I warned Addy that I was going to give you guys her number to pass on. We'll see tonight how she feels about the unofficial-official SEAL welcome to the team," MacGyver said.

"It'll be fine," Safe said confidently.

"Maggie already told me that she'll be so happy to have someone to talk to about her pregnancy, you know, since Addison's had a baby of her own. She's super nervous and she's still only in her first trimester," Preacher said.

"I'm sure Addy will be happy to talk to her about her experiences," MacGyver reassured his friend.

The door opened and their commander strode into the room, a stack of papers in his hand and a small frown on his face. He looked serious. It was obviously time to get to work.

MacGyver usually had no problem switching gears in his head from his new family to work. But today, no matter how hard he tried to focus completely on the mission they'd likely be leaving for in a few weeks, Addison wasn't far from his mind. He wondered what she was doing, if the girls had texted her yet, how the cake decorating was going, if she'd heard from Ellory. It was a buzz in the back of his mind. Not *fully* distracting him from the work at hand, but sort of like being under a thick, fuzzy blanket on a cold winter's day in front of a fire. Comforting. Soothing. Heart-warming.

He had no clue a family could be such a grounding

force. And Addison was the person holding them all together. Of that he had no doubt. Yes, the kids enjoyed being around him and loved when he arrived home each evening. But Addy was the one who kept them on track. Feeding them, waking them up and getting them ready for bed...the glue that held them all together.

And MacGyver had no clue how to let her know that he wanted more than a marriage of convenience. The last thing he wanted was to mess up what they had. If he moved too fast, he could scare her. Or make her back out of their agreement. He needed to go slow.

He'd let down his guard this morning and hadn't been able to stop himself from kissing her—four freaking times. It was less than he wanted and more than he should've done. But he consoled himself with the reminder that she hadn't pushed him away. Hadn't asked him not to take such liberties. Granted, the first kiss, she'd been asleep. Then he'd caught her by surprise the next two times. But that last one, when his lips had touched hers...It had taken all his control not to grab her around the waist, pull her against his body, and kiss her like he'd dreamed of doing. Long, hard, and deep.

His commander cleared his throat loudly, and when MacGyver looked at him, he realized he'd spaced out there for a moment. He nodded at his superior officer and pushed his carnal thoughts about his wife to the back of his mind. Okay, maybe she *was* fully distracting him. He needed to concentrate. And he couldn't do that if he was thinking about how good Addy would feel against him, under him.

Jesus. There he went again. He was like a teenage fucking kid again. Unable to think about anything but sex.

When and if the time was right, he'd let Addy know how he felt about her. How he *really* felt about her.

It was difficult not to simply say "yes" when Ellory had asked if he loved her mom. Maybe someday he'd be able to say the words to Addy's face. To let the world know exactly how he felt about his wife. That he hadn't married her simply to make it easier to adopt Artem, Borysko, and Yana. But for now, he'd bide his time.

First, they needed to get through the party at Wolf's house, then Ellory's medical procedure, then their first deployment together, meeting his parents and siblings, and whatever else might arise. If all that went okay, he'd slowly begin letting Addy know that he wanted a real marriage. That he wanted to hold her against him all night, instead of simply sleeping beside her. That she meant more to him than a means to an end.

No mission had ever been more important than winning Addy. Than making her his wife in all the ways that mattered.

* * *

Addison wiped her brow with the sleeve of her shirt and smiled at the cake she'd just finished decorating. Two down and one to go. Baking the cake was the easy part; making sure it looked perfect and was just what the client wanted was the more difficult job. The most rewarding part was the gasp of delight that her customers let out when they first saw their cakes. It made all the hard work worth it. And when they shared pictures of their cakes on social media? That was validation of the blood, sweat, and tears she put into making each one perfect. It also didn't hurt that she usually got a few inquiries from each post from potential new clients.

And Ricky's kitchen made her job so much easier. She'd made do with her kitchen in the apartment she'd shared with Ellory. But Ricky's kitchen was a baker's dream come true. She had double the counter space, so she could spread out and do more than one thing at a time. There was room for a blast chiller, which was vital to help cool cakes fast, so she could get them decorated in half the time it had taken her in the past. The first cake was already in its box on the counter, waiting for pickup, and the second would join it shortly.

Addison felt happier than normal today. Maybe it was the orgasm she'd started the day with, maybe it was the kisses she'd gotten from her husband, or the way her daughter had leaned over the backseat before she'd gotten out of the car at school to say she was glad her mom had married Ricky.

Or maybe it was the way her phone kept vibrating on the counter next to the cake she'd just finished decorating.

As Ricky had warned, the "girls" had texted her as soon as they'd gotten her number. She'd been added to a group text with them all, and the amount of exclamation points that had been used so far was amusing. Everyone seemed genuinely happy that she was joining them that weekend.

Each woman had introduced herself and shared a little about what they did for a living. Addison had reciprocated, warning them that she wouldn't be able to text a lot as she had three cakes to bake today. No one seemed offended, and to prove it, the texts continued throughout the day. When the girls took breaks from their own work, they would check in with everyone else. Say hi. Ask what everyone was planning on bringing to the potluck that weekend.

Remi took the time to give Addison an abbreviated history of Wolf and Caroline. Who they were and how the SEALs knew them.

Addison felt included and welcomed. She couldn't remember a time when a group of women had been so friendly.

She'd almost always been the odd one out. In both elementary and high school, she got picked on a lot because of her height and hair. Seventh grade was when the worst of the bullying had started for Addison, the so-called popular clique taking great delight in tormenting and making fun of her. It had been hell, and she'd felt like an outsider from that moment on. Which was why she was so worried about Ellory, with her daughter going through the same thing.

But Remi, Josie, Wren, and Maggie made all those old feelings disappear in one afternoon. With their constant texting, joking, and easy banter, Addison felt as if she was already best friends with the women. Of course, she could be disappointed when she met them in person this weekend, but she hoped not.

A couple of hours later, just as she was finishing her last cake, her phone rang. It was Ellory. Wiping her hands on a nearby towel, Addison quickly answered.

"Hey, El."

"Mom? Can you come get me?"

"Of course. Are you all right?" Addison didn't hesitate to pull off her apron and head around the counter toward her purse. Ellory wasn't the kind of kid to lie about whether she was sick or not. She actually loved school.

Loved learning. So if she asked to come home, something was wrong.

"I just don't feel good."

Her daughter didn't sound like herself. There was more going on...and Addison's belly clenched with concern. "I'm on my way."

"Thanks. Bye."

Addison stared at her cell for a beat before putting it into her pocket. Ellory was curt on the phone. She never hung up like that. Her worry ramped up even more. The only other time she'd heard her daughter act like this was right before she'd ended up in the hospital for a week. The pain had been so bad, she hadn't been able to stand or walk, and the doctors had ended up giving her some hard-core pain pills as they did test after test to try to figure out what was wrong. That was when she'd first gotten the Crohn's disease diagnosis.

She prayed Ellory was all right. That she wouldn't need to go back into the hospital. She drove way too fast on her way to the school and parked haphazardly before hurrying into the building. Ellory was waiting in the nurse's office, and after Addison signed her out, she followed her mom silently to the car.

"Talk to me, El," Addison said in a low voice.

"I'm okay. I just want to lie down," Ellory replied.

Addison frowned. It wasn't like her not to talk about her pain. From the first time she'd been diagnosed, they'd talked about everything and anything. Even the embarrassing stuff. The bloody diarrhea, the black stools, the cramping, the gas, the constipation—all of it. So for her to not want to talk about what was really bothering her now was...concerning.

As soon as Ellory sat inside the car and put on her seat

belt, she bent forward, holding onto her stomach as she did.

For the millionth time, Addison wished she could take the pain away from her daughter.

"Mom?" Ellory asked. She hadn't sat up, was still hunched over with her arms wrapped around her stomach.

"Yeah, sweetie?"

"Why are people so mean?"

Addison's stomach dropped and she pressed her lips together. She, more than most people, knew how horrible that felt. How it made her dread going to school every day. How she'd gone out of her way to avoid certain hallways and kids. She absolutely *hated* that Ellory was now going through the same thing.

"I don't know, honey. Because they feel inferior in some way, so they have to take out their feelings on others? Because no one ever taught them common human decency? Because they're simply rotten people? I don't know that there's a good answer to that." Her response felt inadequate, but she wasn't sure what else to say. She had no answers for her daughter. None that would make her feel better, at least.

Ellory didn't respond, and Addison didn't push. She wanted to go back to the school and find the girls who were harassing Ellory and shake them. But confronting them would make Ellory's situation worse. She knew that firsthand. Her own mother had talked to the principal, and he'd contacted the parents of the girls making fun of her. Which had only made the girls double down on their harassment...they were just more careful not to do or say anything where adults might witness it.

Her daughter sniffed, and the small sound shattered

Addison's heart. "What do you need from me?" she asked quietly.

"Nothing."

The one word broke Addison's heart even more. She'd started asking her daughter that question when she first got sick. When she felt helpless to know what to do, she'd ask that question, and Ellory would tell her what she needed. A backrub, lying with her in bed until she fell asleep, reading a book to her, a favorite stuffed animal... Now, none of those things would help.

"Okay, honey. If you think of anything, let me know."

"I will."

The rest of the ride home was done in silence, and when they arrived, Ellory shuffled into the house and went straight to her room.

Addison put her purse down on the counter and stared at the cake she still needed to box up. It was one of her best creations. The fiftieth wedding anniversary cake was three tiers with a cascade of fondant flowers winding down the side from top to bottom. The flowers had taken hours to make the day before—and a full twenty-four hours to dry—and Addison had been so proud of how they'd turned out.

But as she stared at the cake now, the accomplishment felt hollow in the face of something far more important, and her vision blurred with tears.

There was nothing she could do for Ellory. Not with her health, not with the bullies at school. She felt as if she was failing as a parent, and she had no idea what to do.

Her phone vibrated against her hip and with a sigh, she pulled it out of her pocket. Seeing it was Ricky on the other end, she answered. "Hey."

"What's wrong?"

Addison was surprised by the concern she heard in his voice...and that with only one word, he'd picked up on her distress. "Nothing."

"Don't do that. Talk to me, Addy."

She sighed. "I just got back from picking Ellory up from school."

"Shit. She had a flare-up?"

"Yeah, I think so, but it was more than that. She didn't tell me what happened, but those girls who've been picking on her were obviously at it again."

"I'll talk to her when I get home."

Addison bit her lip. She didn't know how to say what she *wanted* to say without hurting his feelings.

"What? Spit it out, Addison."

How could this man read her so well after such a short period of time? And when they weren't even in the same room? She had no idea, but she didn't hate it. "It's just that...she's about at that age where she doesn't want to talk about *anything*. We have a very close relationship, and she doesn't want to talk to *me* about it, even though I went through the same thing with bullies. I just don't want you to feel bad if she won't talk to you."

"I fully admit I have no experience with teenagers. Or almost-teenagers. But maybe talking to an outsider will help her open up."

"Maybe," Addison said skeptically.

"I'm not going to say or do anything to make the situation worse," Ricky told her.

"I didn't think you would," Addison told him, honestly shocked he'd even think that. "She respects you. Loves having you around. You've given her something I couldn't give her in a million years."

"What's that?"

"A positive male role model. I know you aren't her dad, and you probably haven't realized it since you didn't know her very well before, but she's opened up a lot since we've moved in. She talks more. Smiles more. If you'd be willing to talk to her, I'd be grateful."

"Of course I will," Ricky said without hesitation. "Ellory is a beautiful person. But more than that, she's tough as nails...just like her mother. She'll get through this. Promise. Did you get your cakes finished?"

The change of subject was abrupt, but Addison was glad. His words hit her hard. She'd always thought her daughter was strong, but hearing her feelings validated by Ricky felt really good. "Yeah. I just have to box up the last one and get it ready for pickup."

"How did it turn out?"

"Good."

Ricky chuckled. "Which means it fucking rocks. Sorry...freaking rocks. Take a pic and text it to me? I want to brag about my wife's decorating skills."

"Whatever," Addison told him, secretly thrilled. "How's work been?"

"It's work. I've had two meetings, and now I'm headed out to give a pep talk to the wannabe SEALs who are about to start Hell Week, then it's on to another meeting."

"So you're going to scare the hell out of them by sharing all the worst things you've had to do on missions?" Addison joked.

Ricky chuckled. "Pretty much. Don't want anyone thinking this SEAL thing is a walk in the park. You need me to pick up anything on my way home this afternoon?"

"No. I think I'm good."

"All right. If you think of anything you need, just shoot me a text."

"Okay."

"Addy?"

"Yeah?"

"You're an amazing mom. Ellory idolizes you. And Artem, Borysko, and Yana aren't far behind, and they've only known you for a short time. You're doing a great job with all of them. I'm in awe of you."

Addison's eyes teared up again. There were so many times she felt as if she was failing. Trying to earn enough money for Ellory's medical bills, figuring out what she could eat that wouldn't irritate her condition, and now with the three little ones, trying to interpret their needs, which were so different from her daughter's because of their experiences. It was a lot. And hearing Ricky say he thought she was doing a good job meant the world to her. "Thanks."

"You're welcome. Don't forget to send me a picture of that amazing cake. I can't wait to see it. I'll see you in a couple hours. If you need me, yell."

"Okay."

"Bye, Addy."

"Bye."

When she hung up, Addison felt better. Nothing had been resolved. Her daughter was still hurting, physically and mentally, she still had to get this cake boxed up so the man who ordered it for his parents could pick it up and transport it safely...and she still needed to make dinner, pick up the kids from school, and return the texts she was still getting from the other women in Ricky's circle. But amazingly, the responsibilities didn't sit so heavily on her shoulders anymore.

CHAPTER FOUR

MacGyver looked around the dinner table and marveled anew at the direction his life had taken. Never in a million years would he have believed someone if they'd told him two months ago that he'd be sitting around his table with four kids and a wife. It was chaos, and he couldn't imagine going back to the way things used to be.

"I no like spelling," Artem pronounced firmly.

"You *don't* like spelling," Addison corrected gently. "Why not?"

"It is hard," Artem told them.

"It is," she agreed. "I was terrible at it when I was your age. And I can understand why you don't like it. English is a hard language to learn, even as a native speaker. But you're doing so well, Artem. I'm so impressed with how smart you are. Just do your best with that spelling. That's all we can ask."

MacGyver watched the little boy sit up straighter in his chair at Addison's praise.

"I best in class at math," Borysko bragged, obviously wanting to be recognized as well.

"I'm not surprised," Addison said with a small smile. "When I helped you with your math homework, you got every question right."

"Red!" Yana said, pointing at the plastic placemat under her plate.

"Yes, good!" Addison said. "What color is this?" she asked, pointing to her shirt.

"Blue!"

"And this?" she quizzed, pointing at the milk in the cup in front of the little girl.

"White!"

MacGyver smiled as his wife took turns talking with each of the children, praising them, challenging them, mothering them. He'd made the right decision to ask her to marry him, he knew that down to his very core. And not only because of how good she was with the kids. She balanced his life. Before Addison, he'd stay at work as long as possible, then come home and tinker with some contraption before working out and going to bed.

Now he hurried home as soon as possible so he could help her with dinner, and so he could spend time with the kids...and Addison. She was easy to be around. Easy to talk to. She never raised her voice to the children, never got upset when something was spilled or if the many toys he'd bought the kids were strewn all over the living room.

The more he was around her, the more he *wanted* to be around her. It was a novel feeling for MacGyver. In the past when he'd dated someone, the longer they went out, the more he learned about each woman, the less he wanted to hang out with them. But not Addison. If he could, he'd spend all day by her side. He was fascinated by how talented she was with her cakes. She should be working in some fancy hotel or bakery. Not working out of his house. But he was lucky she was. They all were.

Looking over at Ellory, he saw her smiling slightly at her new siblings...but she was pushing the grilled chicken her mom had made especially for her around her plate, not really eating. It was clear something was on her mind, and it was time to see if he could do or say anything to help her.

"Ellory, you want to come out to the garage and help me with something?"

"Sure," she said eagerly.

MacGyver pushed his chair back and picked up his plate. He leaned over and kissed the top of Addison's head, unable to keep his hands...or rather, his lips...off her. "Thank you for the amazing lasagna. You cook as well as you bake and decorate."

She blushed a little, and he vowed to compliment her more often.

"Me too?" Artem asked, standing up next to his chair.

"Next time, buddy," MacGyver told him gently. "You have homework, and after that, Addison was going to let you all watch an episode or two of *The Magic School Bus*."

"Yay! All right!"

MacGyver and Ellory brought their plates into the kitchen and put them into the dishwasher, then headed for the garage.

"If you don't feel up to doing anything, we can just sit in the backyard," he told her.

"I'm okay. The nap this afternoon helped," Ellory said.

MacGyver nodded. The girl knew her body and how she was feeling better than he did. He trusted her to let him know when and if she'd had enough.

He opened the garage door and winced when he

turned on the light. He really needed to work on cleaning the space so they could put their cars inside, but it was filled to the gills with the stuff he'd moved out of the house to make room for everyone. There were wires and plastic piping, old batteries, more tools than any one man could ever need in a lifetime, wood scraps, and things he'd found in junkyards that he thought one day he might be able to do something with. In short, it was a tinkerer's paradise.

"Hmmmm, where to start," he mused.

Ellory chuckled. "I have no idea how you find anything in here."

MacGyver shrugged. "Honestly? Me either."

They both laughed. It was nice to see the girl smiling. He went over to one of the two chairs in the middle of the chaos and sat, gesturing to the other one with a tilt of his head. "Sit. You know, most people would look around this room and think it's a bunch of junk. And individually, I guess it is. But there's more to it than meets the eye. Kinda like what I do."

"Being a SEAL?"

"Yeah. Many people think being a SEAL is about strapping a bunch of guns to our bodies and shooting first and asking questions later. Or that we go around stabbing people and blowing crap up. And yes, we sometimes have to do that stuff, but more often than not it's about using our brains to figure out different situations. To decide how to infiltrate enemy lines without being seen or heard. To rescue hostages without any casualties. To figure out how to get out of tricky situations with a minimum of fuss."

"So you have to be super stealthy," Ellory said.

"Yeah. For example, years ago, SEALs didn't have any kind of way to communicate silently, and thanks to an astute consultant, he realized that American Sign Language was a perfect way for us to talk to our fellow SEALs without saying a word. Such a simple solution, but genius at the same time. From that moment on, every class of SEALs learned signs that would be appropriate to our job."

"Smart," Ellory said with a nod.

"Yup." MacGyver leaned over and picked up a paper-clip that was lying on the ground. "See this?"

"Uh-huh. It's a paperclip."

"Right. But it's also a key. A lock pick. A lightweight pulley. An electrode that can be used to make an audio signal with a phone. You can unclog a bottle of dangerous chemicals with it. Make a light with pennies and this paperclip. It can be a magnetic compass. Or just twist it into a fun shape to entertain a toddler who might be crying hysterically."

Ellory looked skeptical.

"Anything around you can be used in an emergency. The trick is recognizing the junk as the tools they *can* be."

"This is why your friends call you MacGyver, isn't it? Because of that old show with the weird guy who magi-cally gets out of impossible situations with things like that stupid paperclip."

MacGyver chuckled. "Teenagers are so hard to impress these days," he said.

"We're realists," Ellory countered. "Besides, everyone has phones. We can just call for help."

"That's all well and good...when you *have* your phone. But what if you don't? What if you forget it and you go for a walk and fall into a deep hole in the ground?"

"First of all, I never forget my phone. It's surgically

attached to my hip," Ellory sassed. "And if I fell into a hole, I'd just shimmy my way up."

"Ah, the chimney-climbing technique. Yeah, that's one way, but that's harder than you think," MacGyver told her. "Especially if you're injured. You could also move dirt from the sides of the hole to the bottom, and eventually raise the level of the bottom itself. That would take a long time though. And the risk of getting dehydrated and weak is huge.

"But take stock of what you have. Your clothes, shoelaces, shoes themselves. Anything can be used to help you dig, or give you traction, or even to make some sort of flag that you can throw up and out of the hole to let others know you're there. Or to trap water if it rains. There are a lot of things you can use or do to help yourself."

"That makes sense."

"The important thing is not to sit there and feel sorry for yourself. Use your brain. Nine times out of ten, there's something around you that can help in whatever situation you find yourself in."

"Will you teach me how to make a bomb out of nails, a battery, and that paperclip?" Ellory asked.

He burst out laughing. "No. But we can start with how to change a tire, how's that?"

Ellory rolled her eyes, but nodded.

MacGyver got up and opened the garage door. "I'm thinking we should use your mom's Bug as a test subject, since that's the car you'll most likely be in that gets a flat tire."

"Your car is immune?" Ellory asked with a smile.

"Smartass. No. But if we get a flat tire while we're in *my* car, there's no way I'd make you change it."

"Because you're the big bad Navy SEAL, and a guy, and you don't think a girl can do it?"

"No. Because the day I sit around and watch someone I care about do work that I'm perfectly capable of doing myself, is the day my human decency card is taken away."

Ellory stared at him but didn't say a word.

"But if you're with me when I get a flat, I would certainly welcome your help in fixing it."

"You wouldn't want me to just sit in the car and wait for you to do it?"

"Only if that's what you want to do. The thing is, Ellory, I'm not the kind of man who likes to sit on the sidelines. Whether it's watching your mom cook us dinner, or doing dishes, or laundry, I want to help. Or if I see one of my teammates struggling with something, or their girlfriends or wives, ten times out of ten I'll try to help find a solution for whatever's happening. Be it if my team's held captive in a foreign country by terrorists, or I'm at the grocery store and see someone haranguing one of the cashiers for no good reason. I'll always speak up. Always do what I can to help."

He could see the wheels spinning in the girl's head, but he didn't give her time to respond. "Come on, let's get the jack out of the trunk. I'll show you where it is, how to get the spare out, and how to change the tire."

MacGyver didn't actually *show* Ellory anything, he made her do it all. In his experience, that was the only way to learn something. At one point, Addison stood in the front door, shaking her head at the sight of her perfectly good tire sitting on the driveway as Ellory tightened the lug nuts on the spare she'd put on in its place. Then she smiled at MacGyver and went back inside.

It felt good that she was checking on them, and that

she trusted him with both her daughter and her vehicle. MacGyver knew how much Addison loved her little VW Bug. It wasn't the best car to have when you had four kids, but he'd never encourage her to get rid of something she loved so much. If push came to shove, MacGyver would buy her an SUV or minivan.

"Like this?" Ellory asked, bringing his attention back to what she was doing.

"Yes, exactly like that," he praised. Then he took a deep breath and brought up what he'd wanted to talk about all evening. "Your mom said you had a tough day at school today."

He thought there was a fifty-fifty chance that she'd blow him off. Or get mad that he'd even brought it up. But to his relief, Ellory sighed. She didn't stop what she was doing, which was part of the reason he decided to teach her how to change a tire tonight, he wanted her hands to be busy, a distraction.

"People are jerks."

"Yup," MacGyver said easily, hoping if he didn't fill the silence, she would.

And it was a good bet. Ellory kept talking.

"As if I can help it that I have Crohn's. Or that my hair is red. Or that I'm short. Just because Chrys has boobs already and flaunts them all the time by wearing tight shirts, and I don't, it doesn't mean that I don't like boys."

MacGyver felt way out of his element, but he forged ahead. "So Chrys is picking on you."

Ellory turned away from the tire and sat back on her heels. "Yeah. And she's gotten Hilary, Mariah, and Nikki to do it too. Nikki and I used to be friends in elementary school, but now she does whatever Chrys tells her to. It's as if all the good times we had mean nothing. And she told them some of the stuff I go through because of my Crohn's, so now whenever I walk by, they make fart noises and pretend that I stink."

MacGyver's hands curled into fists. Kids could be horrible to each other. Yes, some people insisted it was just part of growing up, but he disagreed.

"I don't know what to do to make them stop," Ellory said, looking down at her hands. "I know stuff about Nikki. About her parents' divorce. She told me about it when we were still friends. I've thought about getting even, telling everyone all about how her mom worked at a strip club and her dad was screwing around with his secretary. But that feels...mean."

"She's being mean to *you*," MacGyver said as nonchalantly as he could.

Ellory looked up at him. "I know. But Mom has always said to take the high road. That stooping to someone else's level of meanness makes me just as bad as them."

MacGyver's heart warmed. He already thought Addison was amazing, but her daughter's words just solidified that a little more. "She's right. So what else could you do? Let's brainstorm here. Could you go to a teacher or principal?"

Ellory snorted. "And be a snitch? That would make it worse."

"Try to talk to Nikki and let her know how much she's hurting your feelings?"

Ellory shrugged. "Maybe. But I think she's probably enjoying being part of the popular crowd too much to change."

"Change schools? Homeschool? Beat up this Chrys person? Get a boyfriend, someone who's big and tall and can protect you? Or a girlfriend to do the same? Surround yourself with your other friends? Avoid them?" MacGyver threw out as many suggestions as he could. Honestly, he wasn't sure what was the right thing to do in this situation, and he struggled to find a way to help this little girl on the cusp of womanhood.

"Beating Chrysanthemum up would feel amazing," Ellory murmured.

"Wait, wait, wait...Chrys's full name is Chrysanthemum? Seriously? And she's making fun of *you?*" MacGyver asked incredulously.

Ellory giggled. "Right?"

"Seriously, what were her parents thinking?"

"Ricky?"

"Yeah, hon?"

"Next week we have Career Day at school. I heard my homeroom teacher talking with the gym teacher about how they were having a hard time coming up with new and interesting people to come in and talk to the students. Do you think...would you...You probably don't have time and it's stupid, but—"

"Yes."

"Yes?" Ellory asked.

"If you're asking if I'd be willing to come in and talk to your classmates about being in the Navy, about being a SEAL, the answer is yes. And not only that, but I can get the rest of my team to come in as well."

"Really?"

"Really. And if this Chrysanthemum chick dares to even look at you sideways, I'll make sure she knows that would be a *very* bad choice on her part."

"Thank you!" Ellory said with more enthusiasm than she'd shown all night. She jumped to her feet and hugged MacGyver hard. "This is gonna be great! Chrys was bragging all about her cousin who worked on a submarine and how amazing he was, but I've seen his picture. He's short, fat, and kind of ugly. You and your friends are hot, and everyone is gonna be *so* jealous that I have a DILF!"

"A what?"

"Oh, um…never mind. Tomorrow, I'll talk to my homeroom teacher and see if she thinks it would work. I hope it does! And I'll let you know what time they'd want you there and everything. I don't think you'll be allowed to bring any of your guns or knives though."

"Wasn't planning on it," MacGyver said with a small smile.

"Okay. Oh, I can't *wait* to rub this is Chrys's face! And Hilary, Mariah, and Nikki's too. I'm gonna text Sara and let her know my stepdad and his SEAL friends will be coming!" The girl spun around and headed for the house. She already had her phone in her hand, her fingers flying over the screen.

Looking at the carnage on the driveway, MacGyver could only snort-laugh. Looked like it would be up to him to take the spare tire off Addison's car and put things back to rights.

He'd just taken the spare off and was picking up the regular tire when Addison walked out of the house.

"Everything okay inside?" he asked with a furrow of his brow.

"It's fine. Homework is done and everyone is watching *The Magic School Bus.* Everyone except for my daughter, who just came into the house looking happier than she has all day. What happened?"

As he worked on putting the tire back on her car, he asked, "Did you know one of the girls at school is named Chrysanthemum? Who names their kid that?"

Addison chuckled. "That's what I thought the first time I heard it. Interesting names are all the rage. Apparently they were twelve years ago, as well."

"Well, the flower bitch has been bullying Ellory. And getting her bitch followers to do the same. Flashing her boobs and making fun of Ellory for not having any yet. And worse, picking on her for things she can't control. She and her posse are making farting noises as Ellory walks by them in the hall."

"I don't think you can call twelve-year-olds bitches," Addison said.

"I can when that's what they are," MacGyver told her. He tightened the lug nuts, making sure they were snug and secure before standing to face Addison.

"I knew she was being bullied, but I have no idea how to help or what to do to stop it."

"I'm not sure anything *can* stop it. Kids normally learn from their parents, and Chrysanthemum's parents are obviously twatwaffles of the highest order. They're probably stingy with tips, and the type who yell at clerks in stores and blame all their problems on others," MacGyver said.

"Right. So why was Ellory smiling so huge when she came in?"

"Because her big bad stepdad and his Navy SEAL friends are going to come in and talk to her classmates next week for Career Day."

Addison blinked. "You are?"

"Yup. And I'm going to have Ellory point out this Chrysanthemum bitch, and I'll make sure she knows that if she continues to bully my daughter, she's going to have to deal with seven pissed-off SEALs...and their girlfriends. Oh, maybe I can have Wolf and his crew join us. If there are a dozen of us glaring at her and making it clear we aren't impressed by anything she says or does, while gushing over Ellory and her friends, maybe she'll get a damn clue."

Addison laughed.

"What? I'm not kidding."

She stepped into his space, and MacGyver held out his grease-covered hands so as not to get her dirty. Addison put her hands on his shoulders and leaned into him. "I know you aren't. And I can't think of anything I would've liked more when I was Ellory's age than to have you and your friends stand up for me and flex in front of my entire school."

"I'm not going to flex...much," MacGyver said.

Addison laughed again. "So you aren't going to give a sample of the PT you and the others do? Burpees, sit-ups, pushups?"

MacGyver grinned. "Good idea. I do have a question though."

"Yeah? What's that?"

"What's a DILF?"

Addison's eyes widened, and she almost choked on a laugh. "Seriously?"

"Yeah. Ellory said everyone was going to be jealous that she had a DILF. I know a lot of military acronyms, but that one I've never heard of."

"Right. Um, well...there's no good way to say it, so I'll just tell you straight up. It means 'Dad I'd like to fuck'."

MacGyver blinked. Then he smiled. Huge.

"I can't believe you aren't freaking out," Addison said. "Why aren't you freaking out? I think *I'm* freaking out a little."

"Dad," he said reverently. "I mean, I know we entered

this marriage thing as a business relationship, and I'm not *really* her dad, but—"

"You're more of a dad than she's ever had. Even when her bio-father was around for the short time after she was born, he wasn't ever much of a dad. In the month we've been married, you've more than earned that moniker."

"What happened with her dad?"

Addison sighed. "I loved him. Thought he loved me. Thought that we would end up getting married after Ellory was born. But he pulled away, couldn't be bothered with dirty diapers and crying. He left, and when I tried to find him, I couldn't."

"I know someone who could track him down in a heartbeat...if that's what you want."

"No. I mean, we're doing okay. And why would I want someone who turned his back on us without a second thought?"

MacGyver was proud of this woman. When she struggled with money, with Ellory's health scares, she could've hired a private detective to find her deadbeat ex and at least make him help monetarily. But she hadn't. "Well, for the record, she's an amazing young woman. You've done an exceptional job raising her on your own to be kind, smart, and friendly."

"Thanks," Addison said with a shy smile. Then her smile slowly faded as she looked up at him.

"What? What's wrong?" he asked.

"I just...you're so good with her. We're so lucky to have you in our lives. I don't know how it happened, but I'm grateful."

"I don't want your gratitude," MacGyver growled.

She blinked in surprise at his harsh tone and took a step back.

MacGyver snatched up the shop towel he'd grabbed in the garage before changing the tire and quickly wiped his hands clean. Then, without pause, he wrapped an arm around Addison, pressing his hand to the small of her back and pulling her close. He buried his other hand in her hair, holding her against him with a firm grip. If she made the slightest move to step away from him, or if she struggled in the smallest way, he would've let go. But instead, she seemed to melt into him. Her hands clutched his shirt at his waist and she licked her lips as she stared into his eyes.

It was all MacGyver could do not to kiss the hell out of her right then and there. They were standing face-to-face, and he wanted to bend her backward and take her lips with his own. But he forced himself to stand still.

"I know this marriage wasn't what you wanted," he told her. "But that doesn't mean that I don't care about you and your daughter. That I don't want what's best for you both. Someone bullying Ellory is as much my problem as it is yours and hers. I'll bend over backward to make things right for her, and for you. And it's not because I'm grateful you helped me out of a tight spot with the kids. It's because I care about you, Addy. I wouldn't have married you if I didn't. And because this is what people who are married do. They look after their spouse and kids. They help with the shopping and chores. They wipe runny noses, clean up puke, and talk to the kids when they're struggling. The last thing I want for any of it is your gratitude. All right?"

"All right. But can I say something?" Addison asked.

"Of course."

"You might not want my gratitude, but you have it anyway. You have no idea how many nights I sat up worrying about how in the world I was going to be able to give Ellory the medical assistance she needed. How I was going to afford her medications. The tests she needed. I would've given up anything, done just about anything, to give my daughter what she needed to thrive. Then I met you. And you became my friend. You were supportive even before you met Artem, Borysko, and Yana. Just being around you made me feel more positive. Hopeful that things would work out. And I didn't marry you just because of Ellory. I would've figured something out. Somehow.

"But it wasn't a hard decision to say yes to you. I saw the kind of man you were—the kind of man I want around my daughter. Teaching her. Volunteering to go to her school to talk to a bunch of preteens about your job, not because you think they want to know, but because you want to show her bullies that she has some of the baddest Navy SEALs at her back. That's priceless to me. You don't want my gratitude? Tough. You're getting it."

MacGyver's hand tightened in her hair, and he had to consciously force himself to relax.

"Okay."

Addison grinned. "Just like that? No other comments?"

"Nope."

"You're a pushover," she said, still smiling.

"Just with you," he said, not lying in the least.

"I have a question."

"Shoot."

"My car's gonna be all right to drive in the morning, right?"

MacGyver chuckled. "Of course."

"Okay. Then I should get back in and check on the kids."

"Right." But MacGyver was having a hard time letting go.

They stared at each other for a beat, then his heart sped up as she leaned in. She kissed him, brushing her lips against his. When she pulled back, her cheeks pink, she smiled.

"Don't be too long out here, because I made some cookies today and we're going to have them with frozen yogurt when the kids' show is over."

"I'll be in soon," MacGyver said as he forced himself to let go of her.

She smiled at him once more, then headed through the garage to go back inside.

Despite his attempts to clean his hands before touching her, there was a faint black handprint on her shirt at the small of her back, and MacGyver couldn't stop the satisfied smile from widening his lips at the sight of his mark on her. He'd tell her when he got inside so she could put the shirt in the wash before it stained.

Turning to the car, he lifted the spare to put it back in the trunk. He wasn't sure he'd done much of anything tonight, but he'd enjoyed spending time with Ellory...and of course the kiss from Addison had shown him that she wasn't exactly immune to him. He loved spending time with her, and maybe, just maybe, she felt a fraction of the same way about him. A man could dream.

CHAPTER FIVE

"Careful with that, Ellory. Don't drop it."

"I won't!"

"Borysko, don't point that fork at your brother. If you fell, you could stab him with it. And, Artem...stop antagonizing Borysko."

"What does that mean?" Artem asked.

"It means egging him on. Making him want to poke you with that fork because you're teasing him on purpose. Yana, you can't bring twenty Barbie dolls to this picnic. Choose three. That's it."

MacGyver couldn't help but smile as he watched Addison wrangle their kids. It was always like this when they tried to leave the house. They had the school routine down, but anything else seemed to be chaos. Addison handled it, and them, like a pro. He stood by the front door, holding it open, patiently waiting for everyone to file out and to his Explorer.

Ellory was holding the container of cookies that she and Addison had decorated last night, and he held the cake—which had morphed from a simple circle to a multitiered masterpiece, complete with a ship on a fondant ocean, buttercream waves, and a zodiac boat with little people inside. Honestly, MacGyver had never been so impressed. Yes, she could make a mean Elsa or Little Mermaid cake. Even a recent dinosaur cake had been out of this world. But watching her bring his world to life out of sugar and an icing bag had blown him away.

Yana padded toward him, holding up the three dolls she'd chosen to come with her today. "Ricky?"

"Yeah, sweetheart?"

"Look! I had doll before." Then she said something in fast-paced Ukrainian that MacGyver obviously couldn't understand.

"She said she had a doll back in Ukraine. It looked like these but wasn't so nice. But she misses her," Artem said, translating for his sister.

The little girl had her lower lip out in a pout, looking like she was about to cry. MacGyver squatted down so he was eye level with Yana. He balanced on the balls of his feet, holding the precious cake carefully with one hand while cupping Yana's cheek with the other. "I'm sorry about your other doll."

The little girl leaned her head against his hand for a moment before straightening and nodding. Then she looked down at the trio of Barbies in her hands. Addison had found what had to be some previous little girl's collection at Good Will the other day. He'd tried to convince her that she didn't need to shop at the secondhand store anymore, but old habits were hard to break. And he had to admit that the gleam of delight in Yana's eyes when she'd seen the box full of dolls and clothes and other accessories had been worth it. She now had Black, Asian, and white dolls, and she played with them equally.

"Pretty," she said happily, holding up a dark-skinned doll with a natural-looking afro.

"Yes, she is," MacGyver agreed.

"Pretty!" she repeated, holding up the Asian doll with long, sleek black hair.

"Yup," MacGyver said, as he slowly stood up. But Yana wasn't done. She waved the last doll, a Barbie with long red curls. "Pretty. Addy."

MacGyver looked up and met Addison's eyes. "Yeah, she's as pretty as our Addy, isn't she?" he said.

He didn't hear Yana's response as her brother took her hand and led her out the door, because his concentration was locked on the woman in front of him. She looked a little frazzled. Had a small stain of something on her shirt —probably jelly from helping Yana get their breakfast ready that morning—her hair was already coming out of the barrette she'd used to pull it away from her face, and he could see nervousness in her eyes. And to him, she was beautiful.

"I'm sure we're forgetting something," she said as she came toward him. "I forgot how hard it was to get little kids ready for a social outing. Ellory's gotten much better at leaving without having to do a million things right before the door opens."

"If we've forgotten something, it's not a big deal," MacGyver reassured her. "Come here."

Addison frowned a little as she stopped in front of him and tilted her head to the side, as if asking what was up.

"Before we go, before things get crazy, I just wanted to say something."

"Things aren't already crazy?" she asked with a small laugh.

"You haven't seen anything yet," MacGyver told her. "I

just want to let you know how proud I am of you. You've accepted everything that's been thrown at you with a grace that's incredibly rare. I know things haven't been easy, but you've made them look that way. I'm proud to have you at my side today. Everyone is going to love you. Try to relax and enjoy the day."

"I will. I just...I'm nervous," Addison blurted.

"There's nothing to be nervous about."

She snorted. "Ricky, these are your friends. Your team-mates. If they don't like me, that won't be a good thing."

"They're going to like you. Hell, they *already* like you. Yes, they were surprised that we got married, and they're irritated at *me* for hogging you all to myself and not intro-ducing you to them yet. But I've told them all about how talented you are at baking and decorating, how well your business is doing, how perfect you've been with the kids, about Ellory and how she's struggled with her illness, and how you've taken such great care of her. All you have to do is be yourself. Because you're perfect exactly the way you are."

"Ricky," she whispered.

He couldn't stop himself. It was becoming more and more difficult to hold back and not show this woman how attracted he was to her, despite his warning to himself to go slow. And while he might be able to keep from blurting out that he wanted more than a marriage of convenience, he absolutely *couldn't* stop himself from leaning forward and kissing her. It was another mere brushing of their mouths, nothing passionate, but he still felt it down to his toes.

"Come on, if we dally too much longer, Artem will start the car and drive *himself* to Wolf and Caroline's house."

Addison giggled. "He would, wouldn't he?"

"In a heartbeat. That kid is too smart for his own good." He put his hand on the small of Addison's back and followed her out of the house. He waited until she'd locked the door and put her keys into her purse to wrap his arm around her waist. They walked side-by-side to his car, and MacGyver found himself unable to keep the satisfied smile off his face.

This was what he'd always dreamed of—a large family, chaos and all. He vowed then and there not to do anything to mess it up, and to protect these humans with everything within him. Nothing and no one would hurt them... or take them away from him.

* * *

Ricky had told her not to be nervous, but Addison couldn't help it. She so wanted his people to like her. She was out of practice socializing with others. She'd gotten used to hanging out with Ellory, and only talking to others when her business demanded it or when she was talking to doctors and nurses in the hospital about Ellory's condition.

This was as different as night and day. These people were Ricky's friends. The men who kept him safe when they were deployed. The women who loved them. Fellow SEALs who were retired and who her husband looked up to. Mentors. And *their* wives, who had already been through countless missions and had perfected the role of Navy Wife.

She felt like an imposter. Yes, she was married to Ricky, but it wasn't a real marriage...except, it felt real enough to her. Not as real as she wanted, but other than the intimacy she craved like a druggie fixated on their next hit, she felt as if she was a true wife.

But then again, she hadn't been through a deployment with Ricky yet.

He helped out a lot around the house with the kids. Artem, Borysko, and Yana were thrilled to see him when he got home every night. He helped with homework, watched TV with them, helped with chores, supervised the brushing of teeth and tucked everyone in.

Could she do it by herself? Yes, she'd done it with Ellory, but she was one child. Having three young kids all asking questions and needing her at the same time, without Ricky there to help, seemed overwhelming.

The time was no doubt coming when he'd be sent off on a mission. Addison figured she'd find out soon enough if she was cut out to be a SEAL wife. She hoped so. She wanted to make Ricky proud. But she was also scared that she'd mess up. As well as the three kids were doing, they still had occasional setbacks psychologically. Borysko had nightmares, Artem sometimes wet the bed at night. Yana would get a thousand-yard stare that concerned Addison greatly.

And today she was meeting some wives of veteran SEALs who'd dealt with missions and kids and all manner of challenges, and seemingly managed it all perfectly.

The one thing that was making her less stressed about this get-together was her text group—Wren, Josie, Maggie, and Remi. They'd been messaging her nonstop since Ricky had passed her number on to their men. They were funny and friendly, and it felt as if she'd known them forever. But still...talking to someone via text and in person were two completely different things. It was possible they wouldn't actually click at all. That they'd meet and things would be awkward.

"Breathe, Addy," Ricky said as he pulled up to the curb. There were cars lined up all along the street, and the sheer number of people who were going to be here today suddenly hit Addison, making her stress levels rise all over again.

Everyone unclipped their seat belts, and Borysko helped Yana get out of her car seat before they all climbed out of the SUV. They were collecting the cookies and cake when a child's voice rang out.

"They're here!"

Chuckling, Ricky looked toward Wolf and Caroline's house. There were several people standing on the front lawn chatting. Including a bunch of children.

Two boys ran toward Ricky and his family, with a girl following behind.

"Hi! I'm James."

"And I'm Matthew."

"Come on, let's go play!" James exclaimed excitedly.

When his kids hesitated, Ricky said, "Go on. It's okay."

That seemed to be all the trio needed, his reassurance.

Ricky said quietly to Addison, "Those are Benny and Jessyka's kids. They're older than ours, but I think they'll get along just fine."

Addison nodded as all the kids headed toward the house, and Ricky called out, "Watch your sister!"

Artem turned, looking confused. "Yes. Why would we not?" Then he took Yana's hand and turned back around.

"Hi. I'm Taylor," the girl who'd come to meet them said. "You're Ellory, right? My mom told me a little about you. You're in seventh grade? I'm a sophomore."

Ellory nodded a little shyly.

"Want to come hang out? Taylor Swift's latest concert is streaming, we can watch it if you want to. Caroline said we can use the TV in the basement."

"I'd like that. Thanks," Ellory said.

As the two girls wandered toward the house, heads tilted toward each other, chatting away as if they'd been best friends forever, Addison asked, "And who was that?"

"Dude and Cheyenne's daughter. I don't know her very well, but I'm impressed with her so far. See? Things are going to be fine," Ricky said. "Come on. Let's get this cake and the cookies inside. I can't wait for everyone to freak over how amazing this cake is."

Addison rolled her eyes, but she was tremendously relieved that so far, at least the kids seemed to be comfortable.

They'd barely stepped onto the lawn before a woman with shoulder-length brownish hair, walking hand-in-hand with what could only be described as a silver fox, stepped toward them.

"MacGyver!" the guy exclaimed, leaning in and giving him a one-arm man-hug.

"Careful, man, you don't want me to drop this cake. Trust me, it's going to knock your socks off. Not only because it looks like a masterpiece, but because it's the best cake you'll ever eat in your life."

The woman smiled at Ricky's over-the-top bragging and smiled at Addison. "Hi. I'm Caroline. And this is my husband. The guys know him as Wolf, but I call him Matthew. Don't worry about remembering everyone's nicknames and real names. It can get confusing really fast, since we all call the guys different things."

"Oh, I already know that. I call Ricky by his name, but

most everyone else calls him MacGyver. And I've noticed the same thing with his teammates," Addison said, shaking the other woman's hand.

"Right, then you already fit in perfectly. I can't wait to see this cake! MacGyver's been bragging about it on his group chat but wouldn't tell the guys what it is. Everyone else is inside or in the backyard. Come on, and I'll introduce you after we drop your stuff inside. And I'll warn you now, it looks as if there's enough food for eight hundred people, but trust me, it'll get eaten. I learned years ago that we can never have enough."

Addison took a deep breath and smiled at the older woman. She'd built Caroline up in her mind as being some sort of untouchable and cold matriarch. Probably because Ricky had told her the story about how she'd earned the nickname "Ice." But instead, she seemed...normal. Almost plain in looks, but with a personality that made her sparkle.

She glanced at Ricky. "You want me to bring the cake in?"

"Nope. I've got it. You go with Caroline. I'm sure the other women are eager to meet you."

Addison figured as much, but hearing confirmation from Ricky made her nervous all over again.

"MacGyver, you're stressing her out. Shush," Caroline scolded. Then she hooked her arm with Addison's. "Don't listen to him. I mean, yes, everyone *is* excited to meet the woman who has our MacGyver wrapped around her little finger, but they aren't going to pounce on you the second you enter the house. Though, we can't wait to hear how you two met, and all about how Artem, Borysko, and Yana are doing. They looked great the few seconds I saw them before they raced by with Jess's kids, but when we heard about everything they've been through, it hurt *all* our hearts."

Caroline kept talking as she led Addison away from Ricky. She looked back once, and Ricky gave her a small chin lift and a smile. His reassurance was all she needed to take another deep breath and attempt to relax. These were his friends, the people who meant the most in the world to him, other than his blood family. She was in good hands... she hoped.

* * *

Four hours later, Addison was having the time of her life. She'd met so many people and children that her mind was spinning. Caroline hadn't lied about the names being confusing. She was just grateful that she'd already known both the real names and nicknames of Ricky's teammates.

She was currently sitting in the backyard with Remi, Maggie, Wren, and Josie, watching the kids play. From the second she'd met the other women, she felt a kinship. It was a little odd, but Addison felt the same way when she'd met Ricky, and that had turned out all right. No, more than all right. Going outside her comfort zone and befriending him had ended up changing her life, and Ellory's life, for the better.

"Girl, that cake was ah-may-zing!" Remi exclaimed for what seemed like the tenth time.

"I have no idea how you made that water look so real," Wren gushed.

"And those little people in the boat? I thought they were plastic at first," Josie agreed.

"You're very talented," Maggie agreed quietly.

Addison blushed a little. She'd received so many

compliments on not only the way she'd decorated the cake, but how it tasted, that it was getting a little embarrassing. "Thanks, you guys."

"Why aren't you working in some sort of shop or something? I mean, if you don't mind me asking," Remi said.

"Well, I'm not sure I'd really make any more money, and I'd be required to be there for set hours and wouldn't be able to pick and choose the projects I want to do. As it is now, I get requests online for cakes and a rough idea of what people want. I'm able to filter through and pick the ones I want to do, based on my available time and experience. And...with all of Ellory's health issues, it wouldn't work out anyway, me working full time outside the house. Being on my own, I can take the time to go to her appointments. If there's an emergency, I can drop everything to be at the hospital with her."

"Vincent told me a little about her condition," Remi said. "I have to admit that I didn't know anything about Crohn's disease."

"Me either," Maggie agreed. "It sounds horrible."

"It is," Addison agreed. "I feel so helpless when she's hurting and there's nothing I can do."

"It's rare that kids her age get it, isn't it?" Wren asked. "I researched it a little so I wouldn't sound like a doofus when we met."

The thought that the other woman had gone out of her way to try to learn about Crohn's meant a lot to Addison. "Yeah. Which is why it was so hard to diagnose her. The doctors thought it was just about everything else before they finally decided it was Crohn's. We're just starting to get to the point where we're figuring out how best to treat her, but of course there are always wrenches in the plan.

Just when we think she's good, she'll have an especially bad inflammation."

"That sucks," Josie said.

Addison agreed.

"She's a great kid," Remi said. "So polite. And the way she helped Yana with her cake earlier was adorable. I hate that she wasn't able to have any herself."

"I felt bad about that myself for a long while, that she couldn't eat a lot of the sugary stuff kids love. But I'm so proud of her for learning what triggers the inflammation. I don't think she even misses it most days anymore. And yes, she's a huge help with Yana and the boys."

"How are they all doing?" Maggie asked. "Things were...they weren't good over there. If you could've seen how they were living. In the ruins of buildings, scrounging for food and water. It was heartbreaking."

"They're okay. They have their moments where they miss their home and their parents, and when they struggle with the culture here, but the fact that they're together helps a lot, I think. How are *you* doing?" Ricky had told Addison all about what happened in the Ukraine. How Maggie had been kidnapped by her ex-boyfriend, a high-ranking naval officer, who'd used his connections to have the SEAL team of her *new* boyfriend, Preacher, almost leave her in the country in the middle of a war zone.

"I'm good," Maggie said, one hand resting on her belly unconsciously. "Tired, but I feel really amazing, considering I'm growing a human inside my body."

Everyone laughed.

"I need to pee what seems like every ten minutes, and I'm starting to get weird food cravings, like peanut butter and pickles. What's up with that? I mean, pickles I get, that seems to be the stereotypical pregnancy craving...but with peanut butter? I gross *myself* out sometimes."

"I wasn't too bad with wanting weird things in my first trimester, but in the second? I was an eating machine," Addison said. "Bananas and ketchup? The most delicious thing ever back then. Now even thinking about it makes me want to puke. But one thing that I ate just about every day for three months was tomato and mayonnaise sandwiches. I can still eat those today."

The others laughed.

"I'm scared," Maggie blurted.

"Of what?" Wren asked, her brow furrowed in concern.

"Everything. Of the actual birth; I know it's gonna hurt and I'm not a fan of pain. That my baby won't be healthy, of Shawn being gone when I go into labor, of screwing this kid up...pretty much *everything*."

"I think that's probably normal," Josie said.

"I know, but I can't stop thinking about all the things that might go wrong," Maggie said, her voice hitching.

Addison scooted her chair closer to the other woman and put a hand on her arm. "I didn't know I was pregnant with Ellory for four months. And in the meantime, I was still going out to bars, drinking, being around people who smoked...so when I *did* finally realize I was knocked up, I freaked. I thought I'd hurt the baby for sure. Even when the doctor told me that everything looked fine, I didn't really believe him. And I was dating at the time, but still pretty much on my own. My boyfriend didn't seem to have much interest in anything to do with the pregnancy. That should've been a clue, but I was still living in a fairytale land where we'd end up happily ever after.

"Anyway, I *can* tell you that the fears in your head are way worse than reality. The drugs they have these days for birth are really good, which cuts down on a lot of the pain, and one thing I've learned is that even if your baby isn't completely healthy, you'll still love them just as much as if they were. Of course, my baby wasn't a newborn when I learned that lesson. But I love Ellory even more today than I did the moment she was born, when I thought she was perfect.

"And you aren't going to mess your kid up. Because you and Preacher are...you're good people. From everything I've heard from Ricky about you guys, you're going to be amazing parents. And if Preacher and the guys happen to be gone when you go into labor, I'll be there for you."

"Me too," Remi said immediately.

"And me," Wren chimed in.

"And of course me too," Josie agreed.

"It'll suck if Preacher misses the birth of his baby, but being present at the actual birth doesn't make a man a good father. It's how he acts after they're here," Addison said.

"You're thinking about MacGyver," Remi said knowingly.

Addison nodded. "Yeah. He didn't have to take in Artem, Borysko, and Yana. But he did. And you should see him with them. He's...it's as if he's known them his whole life. He knows when to be strict and when to let them be kids. He loves them for who they are, even when they make mistakes, or pee in the bed, or leave their stuff everywhere."

"I take it Ellory's bio-dad wasn't like that?" Remi asked. But as soon as the question was out, she shook her head and said, "Sorry, no, ignore that. It's none of my business."

"It's okay," Addison said. "And no, he wasn't. He was annoyed by her crying, he never once changed a diaper. It was more a relief than anything else when he broke things off shortly after her birth. At least then, I could stop trying to rely on him to do things, only to be disappointed every time he let me down."

"I'm sorry," Remi said.

"Don't be," Addison said with a shrug. "I think we've done all right."

"You've done more than all right," Wren said quietly as they watched Ellory play with Yana in the yard. They were playing Ring Around the Rosie over and over and over, and Yana screamed with laughter every time they "fell down" at the end of the rhyme.

They continued to watch the kids play for a beat before Remi said, "So...Vincent told me that MacGyver asked if they'd all come to Ellory's school for Career Day next week."

Addison nodded. "Yeah."

"He also said something about DILFs?"

Everyone roared with laughter. Addison couldn't help but remember the look on Ricky's face when she'd told him what that meant.

"Ellory is thrilled that she'll have some hot Navy SEALs that *she* knows there. She's been having an issue with bullies. Because of her hair and her size...because she's not hit puberty yet, and of course because of the Crohn's. Kids are cruel, especially twelve-year-olds."

Cheyenne happened to come outside right when Addison was talking and said, "I can't stand bullies. Career Day, huh? Any chance Faulkner and the others can come too? I mean, if Ellory is excited about showing off one team of SEALs, maybe having two will be even better?"

"Really? That would be great. Ricky mentioned something about talking to your husband's team about it.

Although I'll have to contact the school and see if it's okay," Addison said.

"I mean, I know our guys are older, and maybe they'll seem like old farts to the kids," Cheyenne mused.

"Old farts? Have you seen your husband lately?" Wren asked with wide eyes.

"Uh...yeah. Last night. When he stripped me naked and tied me to the bed and did all sorts of—"

"Right. TMI, Cheyenne," Remi said with a laugh.

Cheyenne didn't seem embarrassed at all. Addison thought it was refreshing and awesome that she and her husband still had what sounded like a very active sex life.

"Let me know what the school says. I'm sure Faulkner and the guys can do something like challenge your younger men to some sort of competition. That way, they'll *all* get to show off."

"You think that will make the bullies back off Ellory?" Maggie asked.

"I have no idea. Maybe? I don't know what else to do though," Addison said with a frown.

"I guess MacGyver can't go to school and be all big and bad and threaten the mean girls, huh?" Remi said.

Addison couldn't help but chuckle. "No, but he wants to. He wasn't happy when he heard about what Ellory's been going through. I have no idea why kids are so damn mean."

"If my kid is a mean girl or boy, I'll yank them out of school so fast, their head will spin!" Maggie exclaimed. "No kid of mine is going to be the reason someone else's child is hurting."

"Though, it's really no wonder the girl who's mostly responsible for the bullying is the way she is," Addison mused.

"Why?" Wren asked.

"Because her name is Chrysanthemum."

"No, it's not!"

"You're kidding!"

"Holy crap, seriously?"

Addison giggled. "Not joking. That's really her name. Although she goes by Chrys."

"Now I feel a little sorry for her," Maggie said.

"Addy, pee!" Little Yana had approached when they were talking.

Addison started to stand, but Cheyenne shook her head and said, "I've got her." She held out her hand to the girl and said, "I think I saw a cookie leftover. After you use the bathroom, maybe we can grab it before the guys can steal it."

"Cookie!" Yana exclaimed happily, as she took Cheyenne's hand.

Addison was surprised all over again at how trusting the little girl was. How well she'd taken to the strangers she'd met today. But right before she and Cheyenne disappeared inside, Yana looked over her shoulder, back toward where her brothers were playing. Artem paused to wave at her, letting her know everything was all right.

She was adjusting well, but some things—like relying on her brothers to keep her safe—were obviously deeply ingrained in her psyche. Which wasn't a bad thing. The thought of how she would've felt if she'd been separated from them hurt Addison's heart.

Two hours later, Yana was zonked out in Ricky's arms in Caroline's living room, and almost everyone had left the party except for Cheyenne, Dude, their daughter Taylor, and Addison and her family.

Her family.

Those two words were foreign, and yet they sounded so right in her head.

Artem and Borysko were at the table, having another snack. They could definitely pack in the food, but since they'd been deprived for so long and were active, growing boys, Addison wasn't worried. She was sitting next to Ricky and Yana, while Caroline and Wolf were across from them on a love seat. Dude was in an oversized chair with Cheyenne draped across his lap. Ellory and Taylor were in the basement, watching a movie.

Addison was tired, but in the best way. The day had been better than she could've imagined. She'd been nervous and worried to meet Ricky's people, but everyone was welcoming and so darn nice to both her and their kids. It felt as if she'd finally found what she'd been looking for her whole life. True friends.

"So...I don't know about the rest of you, but I feel as if the day was successful," Caroline said with a smile.

"It was perfect," Wolf countered, leaning in to kiss his wife's forehead. The obvious love the couple shared was beautiful.

"Thanks for inviting us," Ricky said.

"Of course. The more the merrier. And I mean that. Ice and I may have made a conscious decision not to have kids, but that doesn't mean we don't love them and don't love having them around. We just like being able to send them home too."

They all chuckled.

"You guys good?" Wolf asked Ricky, sounding serious. "You need anything? Food? Clothes? Bedding?"

"We're good. Thanks."

"Any word on the adoption?" Cheyenne asked.

"Not yet. Tex got us emergency approval to be foster

parents, but there are still a lot of hoops to jump through before we'll be allowed to adopt. Visitations, psych evals, interviews with people at work, things like that," Ricky said.

"Well, it'll be fine," Dude said firmly. "Anyone who's around you all for more than a minute or two can tell that you're meant to be together. Those kids are in good hands."

"Thanks," Ricky said. "On that note...before Artem and Borysko eat Wolf and Caroline out of house and home, we should probably get going."

"Already?" Caroline said with a pout.

Addison couldn't help but laugh. "We've been here for hours."

"I know, but the house is going to be so quiet when you go. You know, if you wanted to have Ellory sleep over sometime...maybe when Taylor is here, since they're getting along so well...we would love that."

"That sounds awesome," Dude said. "We could have the house to ourselves." He raised and lowered his eyebrows suggestively at his wife.

Cheyenne smacked his arm but giggled.

"Really?" Addison loved the thought too. Her parents lived too far away for her daughter to have a close relationship with them. Ricky's parents were closer, but she still wasn't sure she'd be comfortable letting Ellory be a few hours away from her. Of course, it would be up to Ellory if she wanted to have a sleepover at Caroline's house, but based on what she'd seen today, Addison was pretty sure her daughter would love it.

"Of course, really. She's a doll."

"All right. We'll see what the future holds," she said diplomatically.

Everyone stood, and Caroline went to the basement with Cheyenne to get the girls. Dude and Wolf went over to the table to sort the boys out. Ricky leaned into Addison. "You good?"

"I'm great," she said with a huge smile. "Everyone was so nice."

"Told you," he said with a smirk.

"Yeah, you did." Addison couldn't even be irritated by his smugness. He'd told her that everyone would love her and it seemed that they had. Her cookies and cake were a huge hit, and all the men and women, and kids for that matter, had been laid-back and friendly.

"At least the kids will sleep like logs tonight," Ricky said as he took her hand in his.

His fingers wrapped around hers felt so natural. As if they held hands every day of their lives. The truth was, this was the first time, and Addison had a feeling the memory would be burned into her brain.

Ellory came upstairs with Taylor, and they hugged each other before saying their goodbyes. The boys' eyes were drooping, but they dutifully said their thank yous to the adults before heading out of the house.

They weren't even halfway home before everyone except for her and Ricky were sound asleep in the car. The silence was comfortable, and Addison soaked in the feeling of contentment.

At the house, Ricky picked up Yana, still asleep, and Artem and Borysko headed straight to their room to change for bed.

"Mom?" Ellory said when Ricky left with Yana to put her to bed.

"Yeah, sweetie?"

"I had the best time today. Taylor was awesome. So

nice, even though I'm younger than she is. We have a ton in common. And is it true that her dad and his team might come to Career Day along with Ricky and his friends?"

"Yeah, if it's all right with the school. I'll call them on Monday to make sure."

"Sweet!"

"Are you hungry? You didn't eat much today."

"I'm fine."

"Your belly feel okay?"

Ellory shrugged, and Addison frowned. Usually when her daughter didn't immediately say she was fine, it meant she was anything but and was trying to downplay her pain level.

"Ellory," Addison warned.

"I'm not a baby anymore," she said with a sharp bite to her tone. "I'll tell you if it gets bad."

"I know you're not a baby. I just worry about you."

Her daughter took a deep breath. "I know. But I'm fine. You can't worry about me for the rest of my life."

"Who says?" Addison said with a chuckle. Then she reached for Ellory and pulled her in for a long hug. "I love you, kiddo. I'm very proud of the young lady you're becoming."

Ellory blushed and nodded. Then she pulled away and headed to her room.

Addison sighed. She missed the days when Ellory was content to snuggle against her for hours at a time. She had to face the fact that she was growing up.

Thirty minutes later, the kids were all zonked in their beds, sound asleep after a long, fun day. It wasn't too late, but Addison found her own eyes drooping.

"Why don't you head to bed too?" Ricky suggested. "I won't be too far behind you."

"You don't mind?"

"Of course not. You don't have to stay up just because I do."

"All right. Thanks for today. It was awesome."

"*You're* awesome. Good night."

"Night."

Addison headed to their room, spending some time in the en suite before climbing under the covers and thinking about how fun their day had been, how wonderful everyone was...how she'd stressed so hard for nothing.

She was half asleep when Ricky came into the room a short time later and climbed under the covers on the other side of the bed. That was why she didn't really think about what she was doing when she rolled closer to him and wrapped her arm across his chest.

"Addy?" he asked softly.

"Hmmmm?"

He was silent for a moment. Then... "Nothing. I'll see you in the morning."

"M'Kay."

That night, she slept better than she had in months. Snuggled up next to the man she respected...and was beginning to think she couldn't live without.

CHAPTER SIX

As MacGyver stood in front of a class full of seventh-grade boys and girls, he was still thinking about last weekend. Like he had been for days now. He hadn't expected Addison to curl up against him when he'd come to bed after the get-together at Wolf and Caroline's house. The day had gone so well, and he'd felt good about where he and Addy stood. But when she'd wrapped her arm around him and sighed in contentment, it was all he could do not to roll over until she was tucked beneath him.

He wanted her. In all the ways that a man wanted his wife. She was an amazing mother, a hard worker, kind, compassionate, and sexy as all get-out. He was half hard every time he was around her now, which was a lot. It was getting difficult to hide his constant erection, but the last thing he wanted to do was put her off or pressure her into doing something she wasn't ready for.

Because if Addy was intimate with him out of a sense of obligation or duty, or because she felt as if she owed him in some way, it would destroy him.

"How many bad guys have you killed?"

The question came from one of the boys. MacGyver let Kevlar handle that one. It wasn't as if they hadn't been asked inappropriate questions in the past, but it was always a little uncomfortable.

"Did you really have to kneel in the ocean for hours and hours while you were freezing to death?" another boy asked. He'd obviously seen a movie or a documentary on BUD/S training.

"Yup. It wasn't fun, but do you know why we were asked to do that in our training?" Safe asked. There were some brave kids who tried to answer the question, but eventually Safe explained, "It was to toughen us up. When we're on a mission, if we get cold or hot, or if we get hurt, we can't just stand up and call a time out. There's usually no one around to help us but our teammates. We have to work through things that are uncomfortable in order to complete our tasks."

The kids in the class were enthralled with the presentation, which made MacGyver feel really good. If they could inspire just one child today to want to serve their country when they grew up, it would be time well spent.

The presentation for the current group of kids ended, and they shuffled out of the classroom. Wolf's team was in another room; there'd been so much interest in the SEAL teams that the school had told Addison they'd be thrilled if another group came to talk to the kids. Apparently, they were a larger draw than the accountants, doctors, and engineers. Although, the pair of veterinarians was giving the SEALs a run for their money. But MacGyver thought they'd cheated by bringing along not only a dog and cat, but a sloth they'd been caring for as well.

While they waited for the next group to enter, Smiley

approached MacGyver. "I'm going to bug out early, if that's okay," he told him.

"Why would I care?" MacGyver asked.

"Well, this is your girl's thing. I didn't want you to be upset if I left early. It's not because I don't care. This has actually been fun and kind of interesting. It's just that I want to get an early jump on the weekend. I'm going to go to Vegas one last time to see if I can find Bree."

MacGyver knew how much finding the mysterious woman meant to Smiley. Bree Haynes had been sold by her boyfriend to a sex trafficker—the same man Josie's deceased ex-boyfriend's family had tried to sell *her* to. Blink and Smiley had freed Bree from the man's car, but in the ensuing drama, the woman had disappeared. Smiley had been almost obsessed with finding her ever since...but he hadn't had any luck.

"You're giving up?" MacGyver asked.

Smiley shrugged. "I don't know what else to do. Where else to look. Tex has been helping me a little, between more important jobs. But her apartment was cleaned out, she hasn't used her cell or credit cards, and he can't find any trace of her. She was either found by her ex or she left town. I'm hoping for the latter."

MacGyver frowned. "You need help? I can go with you."

His friend chuckled. "Right, because you don't have anything going on here."

He shrugged. "I admit my plate is kind of full, but if you need help, you know I'll drop everything to do what I can."

"I appreciate it, but I'm probably on a wild goose chase anyway. If Tex can't find her, I don't know what makes me think *I* can. It feels pretty useless driving around the city, looking for a woman I met just once. Hell, I probably wouldn't even recognize her if I *did* see her again."

MacGyver wasn't so sure about that. Smiley was one of the most observant men on the team. No one had seen him so serious about anything as he was finding this Bree person. "All right, but if you need us, you know all you have to do is ask."

"I know. And I appreciate it. Has the bitch been through yet?"

MacGyver smothered a grin. He knew exactly who Smiley was talking about. "I don't think you're allowed to call a kid a bitch," he told him, even though he'd said the same thing when Ellory had first told him about Chrys.

"She's bullying Ellory for things she can't control. She's getting her friends to turn on her too. She's making that girl miserable. I can call her a bitch if I want."

"Well, hopefully she'll figure out that being a mean girl isn't the path she wants to take," MacGyver said diplomatically.

"With a name like Chrysanthemum, I wouldn't bet on it," Smiley muttered, before stepping away to speak to Kevlar. Just as a new batch of kids started to trickle into the room, Smiley headed for the door.

MacGyver really hoped he found Bree. She'd obviously struck a chord in the usually taciturn and unemotional SEAL, and MacGyver could only hope that wherever she was, she was all right.

"Ricky!"

Turning, he saw Ellory rushing toward him. He opened his arms and was pleased when she walked into them without hesitation, giving him a big hug. "Hey, El."

"You guys are a hit," she told him quietly. "People are talking about you and your presentation all over school.

And they can't wait to see you in action after lunch, when you and Wolf's team give a demonstration of some of the stuff you do, outside in the square!"

MacGyver smiled. They'd set up a small obstacle course in front of the middle school, and they'd brought the gear they usually wore while on a mission, minus the weapons, to show the kids.

"Cool," he said.

"She's here," Ellory whispered. "Chrys. I tried not to get in her group, but since our last names both start with W, I usually get stuck with her."

The first thought MacGyver had was that if she changed her last name to *his*, Douglas, she wouldn't have that problem anymore. But it was way too soon for that.

"She been giving you problems today?" he asked quietly.

But Ellory simply shrugged. "No more than usual."

Which meant she was.

"Okay, kids, everyone find a seat so we can get started," a teacher called out.

"Gotta go," Ellory told him.

MacGyver nodded, but hugged her again before letting her go.

Once everyone was seated, Kevlar started his spiel once more. They had it down pat now, since this was their fourth time giving the presentation today. He talked about the history of the Navy SEALs, their motto, *The only easy day was yesterday*, then each of them gave an entertaining story about Hell Week. After the basics were covered, they opened the floor for questions.

Many of the things the kids asked were the same questions others had asked in previous sessions. But when a girl who could only be the infamous Chrysanthemum—based on Ellory's description of her—raised her hand, MacGyver straightened.

"You guys are all so big and strong," she said with a smile. "Were you all athletes in high school and college?"

It was a ridiculous question, but maybe not so much for a twelve-year-old. MacGyver was eager to answer.

"We're all strong because we've worked *very* hard to get this way. Muscles don't grow overnight—neither do brains. You have to train both. And to answer your question, I was small in high school. I was probably the kid you'd like to make fun of...skinny, short, and nerdy. I played the trombone in band. I was bullied a lot. By kids who thought they were smarter, cooler, better-looking than I was. You know what my bullies are doing today? One is a drug addict; another is a businessman who made a lot of money, but went to jail for tax evasion; and the third guy— the one who bullied me the most—is grossly overweight and has had four heart attacks.

"Just because someone isn't an athlete or doesn't meet society's standards of 'beauty,' doesn't mean they aren't going to be someone important or successful. The person you bully today, might end up being the paramedic who shows up at your door in the future when you call nine-one-one because your baby is choking. Or is the next Taylor Swift or Lady Gaga. But even if they aren't...even if they don't end up famous, or rich, or a Navy SEAL... doesn't mean they aren't good people contributing good things to society. These men standing next to me? They'd be my best friends even if we weren't SEALs. I can count on them to have my back no matter what. Whether I run out of gas on the interstate, need a couple bucks to buy a hamburger, or if I'm pinned down by enemy fire and have no chance of escape unless they risk their life to help me.

"You're all young. You have your entire lives ahead of you. You don't have to be an athlete or popular to be successful. You just need to be a decent person. Do what's right. Be the kind of teammate you'd want to have at *your* side if everything in your world went to sh—um...went bad."

He wasn't being very subtle, but MacGyver didn't care. He was just about finished with his little speech when he thought of something else he wanted to say. A warning of sorts.

"Oh, and being an athlete isn't always about being the biggest or strongest person in a crowd. It's often about knowing proper defense. I'm teaching my own wife and kids to stand up to anyone who might try to harm them. It's not about violence, just as being a Navy SEAL isn't all about shooting up the bad guys. Being a SEAL is about standing up for yourself and your country. Not backing down when the bullies who are in charge of other countries decide to flex their muscles. At home, that means when someone at a store or a bar decides to pick on my wife—or a kid in the neighborhood or at school picks on my children—I want them to be able to defend themselves."

Again, not subtle, but MacGyver wanted Chrysanthemum to get the message. He was going to start that evening, teaching both Ellory and Addison basic self-defense moves. While he didn't condone violence, if things continued the way they were for Ellory, the torment could *turn* violent. Bullies loved when people were afraid of them. That went for leaders of countries as well as seventh-grade girls.

The presentation continued, with other kids asking questions, and soon their time was up. Chrys didn't look at

Ellory as she left the room, and MacGyver was taking that as a win. Time would tell if what he'd said sank in for the mean girl.

Ellory came up and gave him another big hug before she left the room, whispering, "Thank you," against his chest before pulling away and following after her classmates.

MacGyver saw the tears in her eyes, and he hoped like hell he'd done the right thing.

"Good job, man," Blink told him when they were alone once more. They had one last group before their demonstration outside. "I'm thinking you might have made her think a little."

"I hope so. I mean, she's too young and pretty to be such a meanie-head."

Flash overheard his comment and burst out laughing. "Meanie-head?" he asked.

"Hey, we're in a school. Can't exactly say what I'm thinking," MacGyver retorted.

"True."

"You didn't play the trombone in high school," Safe said with a small chuckle.

"Nope. And I *was* on our football team. We won a state championship too," he bragged. "But I didn't think that would help Ellory's case any, so I embellished a bit."

"I was in band," Flash said. "I played clarinet. And I was in theater. I was bullied all the time, but I mostly ignored the assholes. Except the one time, when I was cornered by three guys."

"And?" Kevlar asked, when he didn't finish his story.

"I beat the shit out of them, and no one ever bothered me again," Flash said smugly. "So you're right, MacGyver. It's not about being big and strong. Those karate lessons I had when I was little paid off. Self-defense for *all* our women isn't a bad idea."

"Our women? You don't have a woman," Preacher said with a grin.

"Well, being around all you guys has to rub off on me at some point," Flash said with a smile. "Maybe I'll find one by osmosis or something."

He was being ridiculous, but MacGyver could hear something in his friend's tone. He might act like he didn't care if he had a girlfriend...but being around couples all the time might be making his friend a little weary.

Kevlar shared a loaded look with Safe, then the two men pounced on Flash and began to gyrate against either side of him.

"Hey! What the hell are you doing? Stop it!" Flash exclaimed, trying to push his friends away, with no luck.

"Cooties! Girlfriend cooties! We're getting them all over you. Maybe it'll attract a woman," Safe told him.

Everyone was laughing hysterically, and it didn't help when the next batch of kids entered the room and found two big men basically dirty dancing against a third.

Getting through the presentation was difficult, as everyone kept giggling and it was almost impossible to keep a straight face. When it was over, and they met up with Wolf and his team, everyone laughed all over again when they tried to explain what was so funny.

The rest of the day went by without a hitch. The obstacle course was a huge hit with the kids and it was fun to watch them try to navigate it. Even the biggest boys had problems finishing, and MacGyver loved that it was ultimately a girl who outperformed everyone else.

Then the students got to try on the armor the SEALs wore, check out the scuba gear and wetsuits they used for underwater missions. Watching them attempt to lift the forty-pound packs and walk around was hilarious.

All in all, it was a good day. MacGyver had enjoyed himself, and not only because he'd gotten to speak his mind to Ellory's main bully. He had no idea if it would make a difference or not, but the gratitude in his stepdaughter's eyes was all the thanks he needed.

He was in a great mood—which made the phone call he got when they were packing up the gear and obstacle course a total shock.

The number on his screen read "unknown." Normally he didn't answer those kinds of calls because they were usually from spammers, but for some reason, his gut told him to pick up.

"Hello?"

"Is this Ricardo Douglas?"

"Yes, who is this?"

"My name is Samantha Price, and I'm with Child Protective Services. We understand that you're in the process of attempting to adopt three children from the Ukraine. As you probably know, our office is swamped with cases and we recently began working on yours, and some irregularities in your case have come to our attention. Therefore, while an investigation is ongoing, the children have been removed from your care."

"What?" MacGyver barked, his blood running cold.

"They have been picked up from their schools and are being interviewed as we speak."

"You can't do that. Are they okay? What have you told them?"

"They're fine, sir."

"When will you be done? When can I come and get them?"

"They'll be placed with a foster home until this matter can be investigated thoroughly."

"Are you fucking kidding? We *are* their foster home. My wife and I. You can't just take them away from us."

"Actually, we can, Mr. Douglas," Samantha told him. "We need to make sure they're in the best possible place for them. And it doesn't look good when soldiers take three kids from a war-torn country without permission, and without even trying to place them with a family from their *own* country first."

"Sailors," MacGyver corrected automatically. His heart was breaking. The kids had to be so confused and scared.

"What's happening?" Kevlar asked, hurrying over to his side, obviously hearing MacGyver's distress. The rest of his team hovered nearby.

"Can I see them?"

"Unfortunately, no. Not right now. Maybe after initial interviews have taken place and recommendations have been made. We're working as fast as we can on this, sir. I know it's distressing, but we want what's best for the children."

"No, you don't," MacGyver said between clenched teeth. "You have no idea what those kids have been through. What they've seen and done. You know who does? Me. Because I was there. They're in a good home, with a mom and dad who love them, with a sister who would do anything for them. They're getting food and water without having to scrounge for it. They're in school. I have no idea what *irregularities* you're talking about, but no one will love those kids as much as my wife and I do. What's best for those kids is for them to be brought home. To *their* home."

"As I said, we're looking into things and will be in

touch soon. They're in good hands, Mr. Douglas. Don't worry."

Then she hung up.

She fucking *hung up* on him! MacGyver was furious. And terrified.

"What? What's happening?"

"They took Artem, Borysko, and Yana. They're interrogating them and putting them in another foster home! I don't understand."

"Did someone call about them?" Safe asked.

"No clue. She just said they're backlogged and just now getting around to our case, and some 'irregularities' came up and they're investigating. Yana is probably terrified. What if they don't let her see her brothers? If they put her in a different home than them? Shit!" MacGyver closed his eyes. He could feel his blood pressure rising. Then his eyes popped open. "Fuck. How am I going to tell Addison? She's going to be devastated."

"Come on," Kevlar said, grabbing MacGyver's arm. "I'm driving. Flash, call Tex. Get him on this. Blink, notify the commander. Safe, can you and Preacher pack up the rest of this stuff?"

"On it."

"I'll call the commander right now."

"Of course."

MacGyver let his friend lead him to his Subaru, feeling sick as they pulled out of the school's parking lot. He heard Kevlar talking to someone as they drove, but he couldn't concentrate. All he could think about was how scared his kids had to be. It wasn't until they pulled into his driveway, Safe's Jeep Wrangler pulling up behind them, that he even realized where they were.

Wren and Remi got out of the Jeep and hurried over to

Kevlar's car. He was glad for the reinforcements, but at the moment, all he wanted was to see Addison.

He hurried to the door and unlocked it, stepping inside, followed by his friends. The smell of chocolate was almost overwhelming. Addison had been busy baking gluten-free brownies for a unique brownie cake for a customer. He'd heard all about it this morning.

"Ricky?" she called out from the kitchen.

All of a sudden, MacGyver didn't want to be there. Didn't want his wife's day to be ruined, the way his had been. But it was too late to back out now. She came into view from the kitchen/dining area—and stopped when she saw him and the others standing in the foyer.

The smile on her face disappeared as she asked, "What's wrong? Is it Ellory? The kids?"

MacGyver didn't know how to tell her.

"Ricky?" she said, her lower lip trembling.

Shit, he couldn't drag this out. "Ellory's fine. It's...it's the kids. CPS apparently thinks something is hinky, how they came to be here. They picked them up from school and are investigating."

"*What?*"

MacGyver took a deep breath. "They aren't coming home. Not tonight. I'm not sure when. CPS is putting them in a different foster home until they figure things out."

"Together? Or separate?"

"I don't know."

He'd expected Addison to be distraught. To cry and fall apart. But he'd underestimated his wife. It shouldn't have surprised him, really. She'd been to hell and back with Ellory. Why he thought she'd crumble now was beyond him.

"Right. They're going to need clothes. And Yana will want her Barbies. Maybe not all four hundred and twenty-three that we've bought her, but some. And Artem and Borysko will want the books they've been reading. They all need their things. Who do we contact to get their things to them? And what are we doing about getting them back? Whose ass do we need to kick that this happened in the first place?"

Taking a deep breath, MacGyver realized this was exactly what he needed. His wife's practical nature...and her anger simmering just under the surface. She wasn't happy about what happened, but since they couldn't just snap their fingers and change things, she was doing what she could to move forward. To get their kids back.

He stepped toward her and yanked her against him. She let out a small *oof* as she fell forward but didn't hesitate to wrap her arms around him, to hold him as tightly as he was holding her. He felt her breath hitch, but then she controlled herself.

She pulled back just enough to look him in the eye. "What do we do, Ricky?"

Just then, his phone rang. MacGyver ignored it. But whoever was calling immediately called back. Thinking it might be CPS, telling him they'd made a mistake, he reached into his pocket and pulled out his cell. Once again the number said "Unknown."

"Hello?" he barked into the receiver.

"What the absolute fuck? This is bullshit! Fuckers fucked with the wrong fucker. How *dare* they fucking pull this shit! After all those kids have been through? I have no idea who thought it was a good idea to fuck with you, but I'm not going to fucking stand for it. You'll have those kids back before the end of the day tomorrow, or my name isn't

Tex fucking Keegan. I didn't fuck up the paperwork. Some asshole must have a stick up his ass, but I'm going to find out who it is and twist that motherfucking stick until it's a permanent part of his body. Thinking it would've been better to leave those kids in that country, at the mercy of a fucking system that's already overwhelmed with orphans, is fucking ridiculous! And it's not as if you and Addison aren't going to make sure they know about their heritage. Fucking fuckers fucked with the wrong people! Sit tight, MacGyver, your kids will be home before you can fucking blink."

The connection cut out, and MacGyver slowly took the phone away from his ear.

"Was that Tex?" Kevlar asked.

He glanced at his team leader. "Yeah."

"I could hear him from all the way over here. I don't think I've ever heard him say the word 'fuck' so many times before. He's usually pretty stoic and calm."

"Yeah," MacGyver said again. For some reason Tex's absolute fury made him feel better. A hell of a lot better. A pissed-off Tex wasn't a good thing, at least for whoever his ire was aimed at. He now truly believed that Artem, Borysko, and Yana would be back as soon as possible. It sucked that they'd most likely have to spend the night in a strange place, but if Tex said he'd fix things, he'd fix things.

"Ricky?" Addison said.

"Tex'll get 'em home."

"Should we get a suitcase put together for them? They really do need their things...pajamas, books, dolls...familiar stuff."

"I think we need to let Tex do his thing."

Addison didn't look convinced. It was another thing he loved about her. That she worried so much about the kids.

"Did someone report us? Or them? How did this happen?"

"I don't know. But again, Tex will figure it out."

"Okay."

MacGyver turned around to face his friends. "Can you give us a second?"

"Of course. You want us to go?" Kevlar asked.

"Addy?" MacGyver asked.

"Um...they can stay."

"We'll be in the kitchen," Remi said.

"But don't worry, we won't touch anything," Wren reassured Addison.

She smiled slightly at that.

"You want me to go get Ellory when school is out?" Kevlar looked at his watch. "Half an hour, right?"

"Yeah. Would you mind?"

"Not at all. I'll be sure to flex extra hard so if any of her bullies are around, they'll see." Kevlar clapped MacGyver on the shoulder. "Be back soon."

When they were alone in the foyer, MacGyver said, "I'm so sorry."

"About what?"

He wasn't sure. Just that he hated the idea that Addison might be hurting because of him. If she hadn't married him, she wouldn't have gotten close to Artem, Borysko, and Yana. But then again, if she hadn't agreed to marry him, he probably wouldn't have been able to keep them either. His mind was spinning.

Addison leaned in and put her forehead against his. As they were the same height, it was easy for her to do. Her hands were at his waist, and his were at hers. Their breaths mingled as they stood there. It was an intimate position, and just what MacGyver needed.

"Do you think they're all right?" she whispered.

"Probably scared and confused."

"Yeah. I wish I knew what happened so we could keep it from happening again."

"Me too. And Tex will determine what went wrong. I'm guessing he'll do what needs to be done to make sure they're never taken away again."

"This Tex guy sounds kind of scary."

"He's a teddy bear."

Addison snorted and lifted her forehead from his. "Are you all right?"

"Me? Yeah, why?"

"Because. I know how much those kids mean to you. I love them, yes, but the three of you...you have a special bond. One that was formed in that bombed-out city. This had to have hit you hard."

MacGyver closed his eyes for a moment. She was right. It blindsided him. He hadn't been able to function after that call. If Kevlar hadn't been there, taking control, he wasn't sure what he would've done. "They're so innocent. They didn't ask for their country to be bombed. For their parents to be killed. To be on their own so young, trying to survive. If we hadn't been there...if we hadn't taken shelter in one of their hiding spots..." His voice trailed off.

"But you *were* there. And now they're here. With us."

"Addison?"

"Yeah?"

"If things don't work out, if Tex can't work his magic... if the kids have to go back to Ukraine...I'm not going to hold you to our marriage. I mean, I'll stay married to you so Ellory can have the healthcare she needs, but you can stay here at the house and I'll find an apartment."

"What?" Addison gasped, sounding shocked.

"We both know this marriage happened because of those kids. And if they aren't a factor anymore, it doesn't feel fair to make you stay with me."

Addison straightened. "Seriously?" she asked, sounding pissed now.

"Well...yeah."

"That's *bullshit*, Ricardo Douglas."

MacGyver couldn't help but actually *like* that his wife got pissed when he expected her to be upset, maybe even crying. Not that he wanted to make her angry, either.

"Yes, we got married to make it easier for the kids to stay with you, but I don't want you to leave. And do you think Ellory wants to lose you? No. She doesn't. She loves living with you. Having you teach her stuff I couldn't in a million years. She's more interested in the crap in your garage than she is learning how to bake or cook. If you're looking for a way out of this marriage, then just come out and say it. Don't use those kids as excuses."

"You think *I* want out?" MacGyver asked. It was his turn to be shocked.

"Don't you?" Addison challenged.

Frustrated over the events of the day, with feeling powerless to help Artem, Borysko, and Yana; pissed that the government—a government he'd given his blood, sweat, and tears to—had dared take away three of the most important things in his life; upset that the woman he loved thought he didn't want her...

MacGyver thrust his hand into her hair and pulled her toward him.

He kissed her. Hard.

Her lips parted in shock, and he took advantage, plunging his tongue inside and aggressively taking posses- sion of her mouth. He wasn't really aware of what he was doing until he heard her moan. Then he realized her fingers were clutching the material at his chest, and she was leaning into him, giving as good as she got.

What started as a ridiculous attempt to allay some of his frustrations became so much more. His need for her went from one to a thousand in a heartbeat, even as the kiss gentled, becoming more about showing her how much he cared than an act of domination.

They were both panting by the time he reluctantly pulled his head back. His hand was still tangled in her hair, and she was still leaning against him. Her fingers flexed against his chest.

"I don't want out of this marriage," he said, unsure what else to say in the charged moment.

"I don't either," she whispered.

"Do I need to apologize for that kiss?"

"If you do, I might get violent."

MacGyver smiled. The day had started out well, went to shit, and now, amazingly, was looking up again. Tex would fix whatever snafu had taken his—their—kids away, and if he was reading the situation right, the woman he'd wanted for months seemed to return some of his feelings.

It was his turn to rest his forehead against hers. "This marriage may not have started out in a conventional way, but I like you, Addy. A lot. Enough that the thought of you leaving makes me feel as if I'm a green SEAL on my first mission. Itchy. Nervous. Panicky."

"Then it's a good thing I'm not leaving," Addison said quietly.

"Ever?" he blurted. "Sorry, ignore that."

"Ever," she agreed. "As far as I'm concerned, this is a real marriage."

His cock twitched, and since he was plastered against Addison, she had to feel what her words did to him.

She pulled her head back, but otherwise didn't move away. The smile on her face was shy...and pleased. "I mean, we *do* have four kids and are sleeping in the same bed."

"You think someday you might want to do more than just sleep?" MacGyver couldn't have stopped the question if his life depended on it.

"Oh yeah."

The longing in her voice almost had MacGyver throwing her over his shoulder and hauling her to their room right that second. The only thing that stopped him was Remi's voice coming from the kitchen.

"Addison? There's something beeping in here!"

"My brownies," she told MacGyver.

"Go. Don't let them burn."

"Okay. Ricky?"

"Yeah, hon?"

"You really think they'll be back tomorrow?"

"I do."

"Okay. I trust you." Then she put a hand on his cheek and leaned in once more. This time the kiss was chaste, but MacGyver still felt it down to his toes. Addison smiled at him, then headed into the kitchen.

He had no choice but to let go of her, even though he didn't want to. When she was gone, MacGyver leaned against the wall and closed his eyes. He could feel his lips tingling, and his fists opened and closed at his sides, the silky feeling of her hair still echoing in one, and the other remembering how perfectly it fit in the curve of her waist.

He had no idea what was to come, but married to Addison, he suddenly knew he could overcome whatever life threw at them.

* * *

Addison had no time to contemplate what had just happened. Her emotions were seesawing all over the place. She was terrified about what was happening with Artem, Borysko, and Yana. Hated that they were probably scared and wondering why they were with strangers. She was also pissed at the system that had taken them away in the first place. It wasn't as if they were being abused in their home. If someone needed to look into the legalities of the kids being in the US, they could've done that without taking them out of their current home.

And then there was Ricky. Never in a million years would she think they would've ended up making out in their foyer. But it had been good. No, it had been great. Life-changing. This relationship was a dream come true for her. Sure, it wouldn't be easy, and they'd probably have some rocky times ahead, simply because of how they'd started out. But he was worth fighting for. She knew that without a doubt.

"Are you all right?" Remi asked as soon as she entered the kitchen.

Addison donned an oven mitt to take out the brownies. They were a tad bit overdone, but nothing a little more icing wouldn't fix.

She put the pan on the stovetop and turned to her new friend. "Yeah, I think so."

"Tex is amazing. Josie told us all about him. How he tracks SEAL teams and other special forces guys all the time when they're on missions. Blink had a tracker in his underwear, and that's how they were rescued from that prison in Iran."

"Really?"

"Uh-huh. And Caroline and her friends have all directly been helped by him over the years too," Wren said. "If anyone can light a fire under CPS, it's Tex."

"That's good."

Remi tilted her head and lowered her voice. "Did something else happen when you and MacGyver were talking?"

Addison felt herself blush, and she nodded. She wasn't sure about telling all her secrets to these women, but she liked the idea of having such close girlfriends. "He kissed me," she whispered.

"Yeah?" Remi asked with a grin.

"Wait, you guys are married. You haven't kissed before?" Wren asked in confusion.

Then Addison found herself telling them about her marriage of convenience, and how, despite sharing a bed, they were more like roommates than man and wife.

"So, this is good," Wren deduced, when she was done explaining.

"I think so..."

"Girl, you should see the way that man looks at you. It's definitely a good thing," Remi said firmly.

Addison hoped so. She really, *really* hoped so.

CHAPTER SEVEN

"Mom?!"

The second Ellory entered the house, she was hollering for Addison.

She turned from the tower of brownies she'd made into a cake and hurriedly wiped her hands on a towel before Ellory ran into the kitchen.

"Is it true? Did they take Artem, Borysko, and Yana? Are they coming back? What happened?"

Addison hugged her daughter tightly. It was times like this when she was reminded that she was still basically a child herself. She was visibly overcome with worry about her brothers and sister.

"It's true. But they'll be back. Hopefully tomorrow. Ricky has a friend who's helping us cut through the red tape."

Ellory's eyes filled with tears. "Why'd they take them away? Did they not think we were a good enough family for them?"

Addison's heart broke at that question. She hated

seeing her daughter in pain, and while this wasn't a physical pain, it was still hurtful.

"Come here, El," Ricky said, putting his hands on Ellory's shoulders and turning her to face him. He knelt down on the kitchen floor so he was eye-level with her. "Honestly? We don't know what happened. But *no one* is going to break up our family. Your mom and I will fight to get Artem, Borysko, and Yana back where they belong. Sometimes in life, things don't go the way we want, but we don't give up. We keep fighting for what's right and fair."

"Like me having Crohn's," Ellory said with a sniff.

"Exactly. It's not fair, but none of us are just going to shrug our shoulders and say 'oh well,' right?"

"Uh-huh. Is it because they were taken out of Ukraine without any paperwork?" Ellory asked, with far more insight than Addison expected.

"I'm guessing yes. Obviously, it's illegal for people to be transported to another country without the proper permissions and paperwork. But it wasn't as if we had a choice."

"Because Borysko was hurt," Ellory said with a nod. She wiped her face and nose on her sleeve.

"Exactly. And as soon as we could, your mom and I took the necessary steps to make it legal for them to stay here."

"You got married," Ellory said.

"Well, not exactly. We filed the paperwork with the Navy and the country, to grant them asylum, and then we did what we could to make the decision for them to stay with us easier to make."

"By getting married," Ellory repeated.

"Yeah," Ricky agreed with a shrug.

"If they get taken away forever, will you and my mom get divorced?"

Ricky's gaze met hers, and he let out a little huff of laughter. "No, Ellory. Your mom and I aren't breaking up. No matter what."

"Promise?"

"Well, I don't know what the future holds, but I can promise you this...I'm going to do everything in my power to make your mom never, ever want to leave me. I'm going to give her—and you, Artem, Borysko, and Yana—the best life possible. I'll be the best dad and stepdad I can. How about that?"

Ellory nodded. Then she turned and looked up at Addison. "Can we have a party when they all get back? I think they'd like that."

"Sure," Addison agreed without hesitation.

"Okay. Mom, you should've seen Ricky and his friends today. They were awesome!"

Addison used to be surprised by her daughter's abrupt change of topics—and moods—but she'd mostly gotten used to it. Ricky stood and leaned against the counter.

"That's right, I forgot with all the other stuff happening. How was Career Day?" Addison asked.

Remi, Wren, and Kevlar had gone into the living room, giving the trio a little privacy, but they returned to the kitchen eagerly when they heard the subject change.

"We flexed and proved that we were the biggest, baddest guys in the school," Kevlar joked from behind his wife. He'd stepped up against Remi's back, putting his arms around her waist and pulling her back so she was leaning against him.

Remi rolled her eyes. "Oh yeah, like that's hard when

you outweigh everyone and are older than them by decades."

"Don't make it sound like I'm an old man," Kevlar complained.

Addison chuckled at her friends' banter.

"The SEAL sessions were the most popular," Ellory gushed. "Everyone wanted to meet them, and when they did the obstacle course after lunch, even the old SEALs were impressive."

Addison met Ricky's gaze and suppressed her laughter as much as she could. "Oh yeah?" she asked, encouraging her daughter to continue.

"Yeah. But the *best* part was when Ricky gave Chrys a smackdown."

"What?" Addison asked, somewhat alarmed.

"Not physically, just verbally. She asked a dumb question, and he came back and told her to her face that bullies were stupid and told her to go listen to the song 'Sk8er Boi' by Avril Lavigne. Oh, and he's gonna give us self-defense lessons so if she tries to sic her girl posse on me, I can kick their butts. It. Was. *Awesome!*"

Addison raised her brows as she looked at Ricky in surprise.

"I'm gonna go clean our room so it'll be ready for Yana when she gets home. I want to set up her Barbies so they're all waiting for her." Then Ellory turned and hurried out of the kitchen, toward her room.

"Um...want to put all that in plain English for me?" Addison asked Ricky.

He chuckled. "That wasn't exactly how it went," he protested.

"I don't remember any mention of Avril Lavigne, but he did basically say that the nerds of today could end up being very important people in the future. He made some really good points that hopefully the flower chick will take to heart," Kevlar explained.

"I'm not holding my breath," Addison muttered.

"I want to get in on those self-defense lessons," Wren said eagerly.

"Me too!" Remi agreed, looking up at Kevlar. "When can we start?"

"As soon as you and the others can make the time," Ricky told her.

"Sweet!"

"I'll call Josie and Maggie. Wait, Maggie can participate even though she's pregnant, right?" Wren asked.

"Of course. We'll just be careful about what she does," Ricky said.

"You guys good?" Kevlar asked. "I want to get home and touch base with the commander, and maybe even Tex. Want to give him some time to calm down a little though. Don't think my tender ears can handle any more of those f-bombs he was throwing out."

Ricky glanced at Addison. "We good?" he asked.

"I think so. I need to finish this brownie cake, then start something for dinner."

"Pizza. I'm thinking a movie night with the three of us on the couch together is called for."

Addison agreed. She was still feeling a little raw, and the house would feel super empty tonight without the other kids. "Sounds good."

"You want company tomorrow for your coming-home party?" Remi asked.

"That would be nice."

"When I call Josie and Maggie about the self-defense lessons, I'll let them know we're all getting together over here tomorrow night. But if anything changes, if you don't think the kids are up for it or if you need a quiet evening at home with just the family, let us know. We won't be offended."

"Thanks. We'll play it by ear. As much as you guys say this Tex guy is good, I'm not as confidant things with CPS will move quite so fast," Addison said a little hesitantly.

"Tex isn't just good. He's the best. If he says the kids will be home tomorrow, they'll be home tomorrow," Kevlar said firmly.

Addison walked everyone to the door, along with Ricky. He thanked Kevlar for picking up Ellory and for the ride home. His teammates had already arranged to get his Explorer from the middle school and return it to him later.

Soon it was just the two of them, standing in their foyer again. Addison felt a little nervous about what would happen with Artem, Borysko, and Yana, but having Ricky at her side helped. A lot.

"Did you really tell Chrys off?"

"It probably went over her head," Ricky said with a nonchalant shrug. "But I couldn't stand there and not say anything. She's pretty, and she knows it. She's already learned that she can use her looks to get attention and praise. And that the meaner she is, the more attention she gets. I doubt what I said will change things much, but maybe it'll make her think twice about continuing to harass Ellory. If nothing else, our girl will learn to hold her own, and she'll be able to ignore her in the future."

Ricky standing up for Ellory meant the world to Addison. She wanted to kiss him again. To show him without words how much he meant to her. But she had a cake to finish, a pizza to order, and a daughter to check on to make sure she was handling the latest crap life was throwing their way all right.

"Have I told you lately how glad I am that we met?" she asked.

Ricky smiled. "No. Not today at least."

Addison grinned. "I'm glad we met," she repeated.

To her surprise, Ricky stepped toward her and pulled her roughly against him. Her hands braced on his chest as she looked at him in surprise.

"Meeting you was the best thing that ever happened to me. And I'm not just blowing smoke up your ass. I wake up feeling excited about each day, rather than ambivalent. The house always smells delicious, I'm always laughing now, and I have no worries that you'll be able to handle whatever comes up while I'm deployed."

Addison frowned. "Is that coming soon? You leaving, I mean?"

"Probably."

"What do I do if CPS decides to take the kids away while you're gone? Or if they have some sort of major psychological relapse? You're their whole world, Ricky. Without you, I'm not sure they'd do half as well as they're doing now."

Ricky laughed, and Addison blinked in surprise. She was kind of offended that he was laughing at her fears.

He must've read her dismay in her expression, because he sobered and shook his head. "I'm not laughing at you, sweetheart. I'm laughing at the fact you think I'm the reason the kids are doing so well. Addy, *you're* the one who feeds them, plays with them, helps with most of their homework, fixes their lunches, and a million other things. Sure, they'll miss me, but they aren't going to blink when I'm gone...because you're home with them."

Addison wasn't so sure. Yeah, she did her part to help take care of the kids, but they'd bonded with Ricky while he'd been in Ukraine in a way that couldn't be replicated.

"You're an amazing mom," he went on. "You've taken on three kids who barely speak English and are learning a new culture. All while dealing with a preteen who has a chronic illness. And if anything happens while I'm deployed, you call Wolf. He'll do whatever's necessary to make sure you're all taken care of. Better yet, I'll give you Tex's number, you can call him directly. But I have a feeling after this colossal screwup, no one will dare even think about removing our kids from our care again."

"I know dealing with deployments is a part of being a military wife...but I don't think I'm going to like it," Addison admitted.

Ricky smiled again.

"What? That makes you happy?" she asked, feeling frustrated.

"No. But I don't want to leave you or the kids. And knowing you feel the same...I've never had that. Never had anyone who cared if I left or came back."

"I care," Addison told him.

"And that's why I'm smiling," Ricky said. He licked his lips, and his gaze locked on her own. "May I kiss you?"

It was Addison's turn to smile. "You're asking this time?"

He looked a little sheepish as he met her gaze. "Yeah. I realize that I haven't exactly gotten your consent before kissing you, both earlier and recently."

"You have my permission," Addison said seriously. "Anytime, anywhere, any way you want to touch me. You can."

His pupils dilated as she stared into his eyes. "Don't say that unless you mean it," Ricky warned.

"I mean it. I don't know what will happen with us in the future, but I'm done lying to myself...and you. I want you, Ricky. Sleeping next to you every night has been torture."

He groaned—and moved quickly. Wrapping an arm around her waist, he bent forward, leaning her backward until he was basically holding her up.

"Ricky!" she exclaimed, grabbing his arms. "Don't drop me!"

"Never," he breathed. Then he lowered his head.

Addison forgot all about the fact that the only thing keeping her from crashing to the floor was Ricky's arms around her. All she could think about were the electrical impulses shooting from where their lips met, throughout her entire body. Trusting him to hold her up, to not drop her, made the kiss even more powerful somehow.

"Ewwwww, gross."

At Ellory's words, Addison felt Ricky smile against her lips. He stood upright, bringing Addison with him, but didn't remove his arms from around her.

"If you're done smooching, can one of you come help me move some furniture?"

"What in the world, El?" Addison asked.

She shrugged. "I just thought that since Yana likes to go into Artem and Borysko's room and sleep in one of their beds, maybe I'd try pushing our beds together. I know I'm not like her brothers, but maybe it would make her feel better to have me closer."

Addison's heart melted. Her daughter was awesome.

"I'll help. Your mom needs to finish up that brownie cake," Ricky said.

"Thanks." Ellory spun around and headed back toward her room. But she turned at the last minute and said over her shoulder, "Don't start smooching again or you'll never get that cake finished!" Then she giggled and walked out of view.

Addison thought she should be embarrassed, but she couldn't muster the feeling.

"Soon," Ricky said in a serious tone. "I'm gonna make you mine in more than name only." Then he kissed her hard and fast before following behind Ellory.

Addison stood in the kitchen and tried to get her libido under control. The man was lethal...and he was all hers.

Sighing, she turned back to her brownie cake creation. She had to hurry now if she wanted to be finished by the time the woman who'd ordered it arrived for pickup. And as worried as she was about Artem, Borysko, and Yana, she was going to need that night of snuggling on the couch with Ellory and Ricky.

* * *

Later that evening, while the classic movie *Pretty in Pink* played, MacGyver sat between his girls and let his mind wander. Ellory was sound asleep against one side of him, and Addison wasn't too far behind her daughter. Holding the two of them seemed like a dream. How he'd gotten so lucky to be the one to look after them was a mystery.

There he'd been, minding his own business, living the life of a single Navy SEAL, and the next thing he knew, he was a father of four with a wife he could barely keep his hands off of. He was a lucky son-of-a-bitch, and he knew it.

And as much as he loved this—all the bonding with his girls tonight, and another serious talk they'd had about bullies—he desperately missed Artem, Borysko, and Yana. MacGyver wondered if they were all right. If they were scared...

Of course they were. They'd been taken from the only home they knew here in the US, didn't know if they'd see the people they'd come to rely on ever again.

He had no idea what happened. If someone had made a complaint against them, or if someone in some office somewhere had taken offense to the kids coming into the country illegally on the military transport plane. Their foster parent application had been rushed through the system, thanks to Tex, and it was possible a mistake had been made somewhere. But he doubted it. Tex didn't normally make mistakes.

"They'll be okay. We'll make sure of it," Addison whispered from next to him. His arm was around her shoulders, and she was snuggled into his side.

"Yeah," he agreed. She was right. Together, they'd do whatever was necessary in order for the kids to feel safe once more. He leaned in and kissed the top of Addison's head. The feelings he had for her were almost overwhelming. He wasn't sure how Kevlar and the others did it. How did they go on missions, knowing they were leaving behind the most important people in their lives? The thought of leaving her to wrangle four kids by herself felt incredibly selfish and cruel.

"I only have two cakes to make tomorrow. I'm going to get up early to start, well before Ellory leaves for school. I want to be done by mid-morning, so I can be ready whenever the kids come home. They'll probably be hungry, so I'll make a large lunch, just in case they're home early. If they don't get returned until the afternoon, we'll have an early dinner, then they can eat junk during the welcome-home thing. I need to go to the store and get some finger foods, and we need more milk. Ellory's running low on chicken too. Oh, and I want to do a load of laundry, so they can sleep on clean, fresh-smelling sheets tomorrow night."

MacGyver smiled as he stared blankly at the TV. There he was, worried about Addison being able to handle four kids, but it seemed she more than had things under control. "Okay. Let me know what you want me to do."

"Your job will be to reassure the kids that it wasn't *us* who sent them away. That if someone takes them again, we'll do whatever we have to do in order to get them back. Wait, don't say that, it might make them worry about it happening again. Just love them, Ricky. They're going to need that most of all."

"You don't have to tell me to do that, hon. That's the easy part."

"Yeah," she agreed.

It wasn't long before Addison fell asleep against him as well. MacGyver hated this damn movie, but he didn't move to grab the remote because that might've woken up one of the girls. Instead, he sat very still, the arm that was around Addison going numb, but he didn't care. He loved being a pillow. Loved the trust they showed in completely lowering their guard with him. This was what he fought for. What men died for. To keep their families safe and happy.

Closing his eyes, he rested his head against the back of the couch and eventually fell asleep himself.

CHAPTER EIGHT

Tex was as good as his word, and at two o'clock the next day, a white CPS van pulled up in front of the house and Artem, Borysko, and Yana leaped out and ran toward MacGyver. He'd gotten a heads-up on when they would arrive and received permission to leave work early to be there. Of course, his entire team had wanted to come too, along with their women.

So it was a full house that met the kids and welcomed them home. It seemed as if they'd been gone for weeks instead of a single day.

Yana cried when MacGyver picked her up and held her, and Artem and Borysko didn't look very steady themselves. To his relief, his friends all backed off after welcoming the trio, giving them some space to greet the kids privately.

MacGyver went to his knees in the grass and put Yana on her feet, including the two boys in his huge hug.

"They tooked us," Borysko said, tears in his eyes.

"They did not tell us why. It was scary," Artem told MacGyver.

His heart broke. "I know. I'm so sorry. I did everything I could to get you back as soon as possible."

"Why did they take us?" Artem asked.

"Honestly? I don't really know. All I can assume is that it may have something to do with how you came into the US. Someone obviously thought things weren't legal and proper. But I promise you that I have friends who are making sure this doesn't happen again."

MacGyver hated the look of skepticism on both boys' faces. They'd been let down too many times already in their short lives, and he wished he wasn't another person adding to those feelings...even inadvertently.

"It was not because you decide you no want us?" Artem asked.

"No!" MacGyver said loudly. He took a deep breath to try to control his emotions. "I want you. All three of you. You saved my life back in the Ukraine. But even before that, something between us clicked. I felt as if you were meant to be mine. To come to the States and live with me and grow up to do amazing things. You'll never know how sorry I am that you were taken away without a word from me. I didn't know that was going to happen. I swear. And when I found out, I did what I could to get you back as soon as possible."

Artem nodded. Then his little lips quirked up. "The lady who pick us up was very nice this morning. Asking many times if we were okay. She seemed...I do not know word."

"Nervous? Anxious? Worried?" MacGyver suggested. He'd noticed the woman was being overly solicitous when she'd dropped off the kids. Had apologized for the mix-up several times and swore more than once that the kids had been well taken care of. He suspected Tex had put the fear of God into several people at CPS. He appreciated the men and women who did the job, because it had to be emotionally and physically stressful, but he wasn't ready to forgive anyone who was involved in taking his kids away from him.

"Yes!" Artem said happily.

"Well, you're home now, and Addy and I have arranged for a little party. She's made your favorite foods, a special cake just for you guys, and Ellory has been fussing over the decorations."

"A party? For us? We have never had party," Borysko said, his eyes big in his face.

"Just for you," MacGyver told him. "I'm so glad you're home," he added, feeling emotional about holding these three kids in his arms once more.

"Home!" Yana said. She had tear tracks on her face, but MacGyver was happy to see her smiling again.

He felt a touch on his shoulder and looked up to see Addison standing behind him.

"Addy!" Yana shouted, pulling away from MacGyver, circling around him to hug Addison. She snuggled into her, then lifted her head and said, "Cake!"

Artem and Borysko also hugged Addison.

"Yana is right. She smells like cake," Artem said with a smile.

Addison laughed. "That's because I've been in the kitchen making an extra-special cake for three extra-special children I know."

"Us?" Borysko practically yelled.

"Yes."

"We go inside now?" Artem asked.

"Yeah, go on. Remember to thank everyone for coming to your party," MacGyver coaxed.

"Yes! Will!" Borysko said, then the three kids hurried for the front door and their party.

MacGyver slowly stood. "There are going to be some difficult times for them when the excitement dies down," he said sadly.

"Yeah, but we'll be here for them. We'll make sure they understand that what happened was an anomaly," Addison said, slipping her hand into his and leaning against him.

MacGyver immediately put his arm around her waist. He loved being able to touch her like this freely and without wondering if she thought he was overstepping some imaginary boundary. Now that she'd told him that he could touch her whenever he liked, he found he couldn't keep his hands off her.

Last night, when the movie was over and they'd woken up on the couch stiff and sore, he'd walked Ellory to her room, then joined Addison in bed. She hadn't hesitated to curl into him, and this time she hadn't been asleep. Last night wasn't the right time to show her how attracted he was to her, but that moment was coming. Of that, he had no doubt. And the anticipation was both a blessing and a curse.

But one thing MacGyver knew was that he'd never take this woman for granted. In his eyes, she was Super-woman. She stepped up without any complaints. Working her ass off for not only her business, but to keep their household running smoothly and with as much love as she had in her heart. He couldn't have chosen a better woman to marry. Their marriage of convenience was quickly turning into his dream relationship. Who would've thought?

The afternoon was full of laughter and way too much sugar. The kids stuffed themselves with the special cake

Addison had made for them. By the time everyone went home, it was past seven o'clock.

"All right, anyone have homework they need to get done?" MacGyver asked.

Artem and Borysko looked at him as if he had three heads.

"We have party. No school."

But MacGyver shook his head. "The party's over. Things are going back to normal now. And that means chores and homework. How can you expect to get smarter if you don't do your school stuff? Go grab your backpacks and we'll see what's in there," he said in his no-nonsense tone.

Thirty minutes later, Ellory was sitting next to Borysko, helping him with his English homework, and Addison was with Artem, watching him do some math problems. MacGyver was on the couch with Yana in his lap, reading a book out loud to her.

He took a moment to sigh in contentment. For a moment there, he thought he'd lost this. That somehow the kids he'd learned to love as if they came from his own loins would be taken from him. But here they were. All under the same roof. Happy and healthy. Maybe a little more cautious about their immediate futures, but he hoped that would fade sooner rather than later.

He owed Tex big time. The man didn't like to be thanked. Hated it, in fact. But he didn't care. MacGyver would somehow show his appreciation in a way the former SEAL couldn't complain about. But how did you thank someone for saving your family?

Bedtime was a little rough. Yana had a meltdown, and Artem and Borysko seemed to be afraid to turn off the light. But finally, after reading three books and making a huge nest of blankets and pillows on the floor of the boys' room that all three kids and Ellory settled into, all was quiet.

Feeling more exhausted than he had after some of the missions he'd been on, MacGyver fell into bed.

"Whew," Addison breathed as she lay next to him.

MacGyver didn't hesitate, he reached over and pulled her closer. She came willingly. Her head rested on his shoulder as she sighed in contentment.

"I'll talk to Yana's teacher in the morning. Let her know what's going on. It might be a good idea if you do the same when you drop off Artem and Borysko."

"Of course," MacGyver reassured her.

"It feels right."

"What does?"

"Having them home."

MacGyver couldn't agree more. "Yeah. Is this gonna get easier?"

"What?"

"Raising them."

Addison chuckled against him. "No."

"No?"

"Nope. These *are* the easy years. When they actually like their parents and want to be around us. They don't mind school, there aren't many bullies. Learning is fun and they're easily entertained. Wait until they get to be Ellory's age. Hormones will kick in. Zits will happen. Little things will ruin their lives forever. Social media. Texting. Phones. It's gonna be hell."

MacGyver laughed. "Can't wait."

"Yeah, me either."

Surprisingly, they were both sincere.

"One of these nights, when we have more energy, I'm

gonna show you how happy I am to have you at my side for this adventure," MacGyver said.

"So...like in fifteen years or so?" Addison joked.

MacGyver chortled. "Let's hope it's sooner than that."

He felt Addison scoot a little closer. Her arm went over his abs and she moved her head slightly to kiss his chest. "Yeah," she agreed.

Once again, MacGyver found himself holding his wife as she fell asleep against him. It was quickly becoming his favorite thing in the world. He had a brief vision of her doing the same thing, but after he'd exhausted her by making love to her over and over.

He fell asleep within minutes with a huge smile on his face.

Addison was surprised when their lives fell into a normal rhythm very quickly after the excitement of the kids being removed by CPS. Tex was attempting to fast track the adoption and, amazingly, after only a few hiccups, Artem, Borysko, and Yana settled back into the routines they had before.

Her cake business was booming and she had to make a hard decision to limit the number of orders she accepted. Ricky had sat her down one night recently and said that she was working herself to exhaustion, and he wasn't willing to stand by and watch her do it anymore. Between the kids and baking, she'd reached her limit.

So she'd backed off to a maximum of two cakes a day, and she found she actually enjoyed the more reasonable pace. Decorating had become a chore, and now she was liking what she did once more. Only making one or two cakes a day also freed up some afternoons to run errands, meet up with the other women—which had become one of the highlights of her week—and participate in school activities when they came up.

Things had been going so well, Addison was able to put in the back of her mind the fact that Ricky and his team would be deployed soon. They'd been preparing for a mission for the last four weeks, and the countdown was on. He couldn't say exactly when they'd be leaving, but he'd begun talking to the kids about him being gone for a while, making sure they understood that it was a part of his job and that he'd be back.

Addison didn't want to think about how lonely she'd be without Ricky there. He was a huge help with the kids. Was a very hands-on dad. They'd all miss him tremendously when he was gone.

And somehow, even though it was obvious they both wanted to move their relationship forward physically, they hadn't found the time or energy to do anything about it. Addison was certainly enjoying the kissing and snuggling they did. But she was also getting frustrated. It felt as if just when they made the decision to go for it, something always happened to put a kink in her plans.

Borysko getting sick and vomiting all over his bed, which necessitated them cleaning him up and stripping the bedding. Artem having a nightmare. Yana crying about something she couldn't articulate very well. It was all a part of having kids, but exasperating all the same. She wanted her husband, and she was starting to contemplate shipping all four kids off to Caroline's house for that sleepover she proposed, just so she could have some uninterrupted time with Ricky.

Some of her favorite moments were right before Ricky

got up to head to base for PT. She'd gotten in the habit of waking up right before his alarm, and they enjoyed a few minutes of quiet conversation before he had to get up and she went back to sleep for a couple of hours.

This morning was no exception.

"You awake?" he whispered.

Addison nodded against him. As usual, she was plastered against his side. Sometime during the night, one of her legs had hitched over his thigh, and she could feel almost every inch of his hard body against the length of hers.

"I'm worried about Ellory's appointment," he admitted.

Addison was too, but she did her best to allay his fears. "It's just a meeting to discuss the results of the upper GI test they did and the bowel rest program the doctor wants to try."

"I know, but I don't like the idea of her not being able to eat."

"I think she's actually looking forward to it. You know she's been in more pain lately. Even when she eats exactly what's on her approved list, she still has issues. This will be like fasting. She'll get the nutrients she needs through the special drinks and hopefully no painful cramping or diarrhea."

"I hate this for her."

"Me too. But honestly, I think most of the time eating is very stressful for her. Because all she can think about is how that food is going to make her feel later."

"What about at school? Will she be made fun of even more for not eating?"

Addison loved this man so much for being so worried for Ellory. "She's going to spend the lunch hour in the library. It's already been approved. You know how much she loves to read. It's a win-win in her book."

"The flower chick hasn't been messing with her...more than usual, that is, has she?"

Addison chuckled at his nickname for Chrysanthemum. "Ellory claims she hasn't. Ever since she used a few of the comebacks you taught her...which I'm not sure was the best idea, but since they seem to be working, I won't scold you too much."

"Hey, all I said was that when she insulted her, to come back with creative and unexpected responses. To confuse her. Like when Flower Girl said that she was smelly, and Ellory shrugged and said, 'Good thing I'm nice.' And when she told her that she's skinny as a stick, our girl just smiled and said, 'At least I'm not ugly. And I can always gain weight to change.' Classic."

Addison did her best not to laugh. "I'm just glad their encounters haven't turned violent."

"If they do, Ellory will wipe the floor with her," Ricky said smugly.

He'd had a few self-defense lessons so far, and Ellory's self-confidence seemed to increase after each session. While Addison wasn't a fan of her daughter using violence to solve any kind of problem, she wasn't so naïve to believe it could never happen.

"So...doctor's appointment today, then what?"

"I only booked one cake today, so then it's back here to get that done. Afterward, Yana has her meeting with the child psychologist, Artem and Borysko have soccer, I need to go grocery shopping, and in case you haven't noticed, the dirty clothes are taking over this house."

He chuckled. "I'll put a load in before I head out this morning."

"Thanks. Any word on when you might be leaving?"

He sighed. "Soon. That's all we know right now."

"Okay."

They were both quiet for a moment. Then Ricky moved, gently pushing her onto her back and hovering over her. The nightlights they had in the room gave off enough glow for her to be able to see his face.

"Ricky?"

"You told me that I could touch you anywhere, anytime. Does that include now?" he asked.

Addison's breath hitched in her throat. She couldn't speak if her life depended on it. So she nodded.

His fingers brushed her hair back from her face, trailed down her cheek to her collarbone...then down her chest. Her nipples immediately hardened under the loose tank top she was wearing. But he didn't stop there. His hand continued downward until it was resting on her belly.

"You are so damn beautiful," he said reverently. "Every time I look at you, I have to wonder what the hell you're doing with me." His finger slipped under the waistband of the sleep shorts she wore.

Addison held her breath.

"Okay?" he asked.

Again, she could only nod.

"I want to make you feel good. Give you an orgasm. Will you let me?"

"You think you can?" The words popped out without thought. She cringed.

But Ricky simply smiled. "That sounded like a challenge."

"It's just that in my somewhat limited experience, men aren't always good at being able to do that."

"It's a matter of following a woman's cues. How she

rolls her hips. What motions make her moan, what makes her thighs shake uncontrollably. How about this...you let me give it my best shot, and if I suck at it, you can tell me 'I told you so' afterward. Okay?"

Addison was breathing hard. It was all she could do not to push him onto *his* back and have her wicked way with him. But if he wanted to finger her to an orgasm, who was she to complain? At the very least it would feel nice. At best, she'd be extra relaxed to start her day. "Okay," she whispered.

"Lift your hips," he ordered.

She did, and he had her shorts over her hips and down her legs before she could blink. "Spread for me. Yeah, like that. Stay there. Don't move," he ordered.

His hand covered her pussy, and she couldn't help but jerk a little under him.

"Easy, Addy. I've got you."

"It's been a while," she admitted.

"For me too. It might take me a moment to get the hang of this again."

"Are you going to be late for PT?" she couldn't help but ask.

"Don't care. Now hush."

His fingers moved, lightly caressing, learning the feel of her. Then he flattened his hand over her, his fingers resting on her pubic area and his thumb right over her clit. He started out with a light caress, eventually adding more and more pressure.

Watching his face as he studied her, as he caressed her, was as intimate a thing as Addison had ever done. Everything he was thinking was reflected there. He licked his lips, frowned in concentration, smiled, and sighed in contentment when her juices flowed.

"That's it. I've got you, Addy. Relax and enjoy."

Oh, she was enjoying, that was for sure. Ricky knew exactly what he was doing. He'd pay attention to her clit for several moments, then move lower, his fingers dipping inside her body, before moving back to her clit.

When he shifted above her and straddled her thighs, she looked up at him in surprise. "I need both hands," he said.

Looking down, Addison could see his erection under the boxers he wore to bed. He used to wear sweats, but lately he'd paired down to the boxers. She could feel the hair on his legs against her thighs, and it made her arousal ramp up all the more.

Ricky shifted again, moving so his knees were now on the *inside* of her thighs, forcing her legs to open wide.

"Okay?" he asked, pausing in his ministrations.

"Okay," she confirmed. Addison felt very exposed, and she was grateful the only light in the room came from the nightlights. Then his thumb moved back to her clit, and she couldn't think any more. She reached down and grabbed hold of his forearms. Not to stop him, but to have something to hold on to.

"That's it. I've got you. You're perfect. I can't wait to see this pussy in the light. See your red pubic hair mesh with my dark. You're so wet, hon. And you smell delicious. I wanna taste you. Would you like that? My lips on you? That's it, rock those hips. Show me what you like."

Addison felt like she was having an out-of-body experience. The man between her legs was playing her like a maestro. He was using one hand to strum her clit, and the other was spreading the wetness leaking out of her body.

She jerked as he eased a finger inside her.

"So tight. You're going to strangle my cock when you

take me. It's gonna feel amazing. That's it, squeeze me. You feel so damn good. Let's see if I can find...there? No, apparently not. Here...?"

Addison wasn't sure what he was looking for, but what his thumb was doing to her clit felt so good, she couldn't concentrate on much of anything else.

But when he twisted his hand and added another finger inside her body, she jolted almost violently when he touched something deep within her.

"Ahhhh, there it is."

He sounded smug and so proud of himself, but all Addison could do was feel. It felt as if he had a shock stick or something inside her. It was almost painful, but so damn good.

His fingers began moving faster, pumping in and out, touching whatever that spot was inside her over and over.

"Ricky!" she exclaimed.

"Shhhhh, don't wake the kids," he warned with a little laugh.

Horrified that they might be interrupted, Addison slammed her lips together and did her best not to moan too loudly.

"Come for me, sweetheart. Don't hold back. Give it to me."

She had no thought of holding anything back. She couldn't. She was putty in this man's hands. Her thighs began to shake, just as he'd talked about. Looking down her body, she saw that Ricky was staring between her thighs with a...reverence...she'd never seen on a man's face before.

Then before she was ready, her body seemed to detonate from the inside out. She let out a little squeak, and her entire body seized up. She bore down on his fingers as every muscle tensed. The orgasm he'd wrung from her felt as if it had changed her irrevocably.

His fingers stilled inside her as she pulsed against him, and it wasn't until she let out a moan of protest that his thumb ceased its movement over her clit.

She felt as if she'd just run a marathon. Her breaths came out in harsh pants as her heartbeat almost out of her chest. All she could do was lie bonelessly under him with her legs spread wide open.

"One taste to tide me over," Ricky murmured, before he dipped down.

Addison felt his tongue glide from her slit to her clit, licking her copious juices. Then he sat up and licked his lips, as if he'd just had the most decadent dessert imaginable.

"So damn good," he said. He leaned over her, his hands at her shoulders, his cock hard and throbbing against her still extremely sensitive pussy.

"Good morning, sweetheart," he said huskily, before doing a kind of push-up and lowering himself to kiss her. Addison could taste herself on his lips, and surprisingly, it turned her on more rather than embarrassing her.

One of her hands tried to circle his cock. She wanted him. Inside her. Now. She was going to die if she didn't feel him deep inside her body right this second. But he caught her hand and brought it up to his lips.

He kissed her knuckles and said, "No time. I really need to get to work."

The whine that escaped wasn't something Addison was proud of, but she couldn't hold it back.

"Soon," he whispered. "When we make love, it won't be anything that's hurried or rushed because either of us have to be somewhere. I'm going to want to take my time.

Once I get inside that hot, wet cunt, I'm not going to want to leave. The way you squeezed my fingers? Yeah, I can't wait to feel that on my cock. Sleep, Addy. You have a long day ahead of you. Let me know how the meeting with Ellory's doctor goes?"

She immediately nodded. "Of course."

"Good. I'll start the laundry and see you at breakfast."

Then he kissed her forehead sweetly and climbed off her. But not before Addison saw how the front of his boxers were tented.

"I can take care of that before you go," she offered.

But Ricky simply smiled. "Again, if you touch me, I won't be able to get out of this bed. I'll take care of it in the shower. Won't take more than thirty seconds." Then he winked at her and headed for the bathroom.

The orgasm had done what he'd intended, made Addison feel mellow and tired. She heard the shower come on and, like he said, not a minute later, the water shut off. He appeared over her not too long after that, dressed in the T-shirt and shorts he wore to work out with his SEAL team.

He leaned over her and kissed her once more. Long and deep. By the time he pulled back, Addison wanted him all over again.

"Love seeing you like this in our bed. Sleepy, sated, and greedy for more," he murmured.

Then he turned and disappeared through the door. Addison knew he'd poke his head in the other rooms, checking on the kids before heading out for PT. She heard the washing machine start up, and then she knew no more as she fell back asleep.

* * *

Later that day, Addison could still remember the feel of Ricky's fingers moving in and out of her body. It was unsettling because she usually wasn't so...aware of her womanly parts as she went about her normal everyday activities. She was sitting in the waiting room at the hospital on base, waiting to see Ellory's doctor. Her daughter was on the other side of the room, playing with a kid who was probably around two or three. Addison had no idea why the toddler was there, but her mom looked relieved to have someone else entertaining her son for a few minutes.

Addison was lost in her own head, recalling what had happened that morning, when she heard someone saying her name.

"Addison? Addison Wentz? Is that you?"

Looking up, she saw the face of someone she never thought she'd see again in her life.

Her ex.

Brady Vogel.

Seeing him was a shock. Never in a million years did she think he'd ever be back here in Riverton. He'd left right after telling her that he wasn't cut out to be a father, but he'd be sure to send money to help out. She'd never heard from him again.

And now here he was.

He wore a pair of scrubs with a name badge attached to his hip. He quickly sat in the chair next to hers and smiled as if he hadn't simply left her high and dry to raise their child on her own. He'd been twenty when they'd met. She'd been twenty-three. They were both so young. So damn young. But still, by the time Ellory was born, he'd been twenty-one, and more than capable of stepping up and being the father Ellory needed...and a man Addison could lean on. But that had ended pretty quickly. He'd found out that having a baby around wasn't all fun and games, and that was that. He was gone.

"Brady," she said.

"It's so good to see you. You look great. I see that red hair of yours hasn't toned down at all, huh?"

She resisted the urge to roll her eyes. "Are you a doctor?" she asked, not sure what he was doing here.

"Oh, no." He laughed a little too loudly. "I'm a domestic attendant."

Addison barely resisted the urge to snort. "A janitor."

"Well yeah, but it pays really well. Especially in health-care. You'd be surprised by how many people turn up their noses at cleaning a little blood or other bodily fluids. I'm surprisingly immune to the sight of poop these days."

That was especially ironic, considering he used to gag when Addison changed Ellory's diapers.

"What are *you* doing here? Wait, are you sick?" he asked.

"No. I'm here with Ellory," Addison said, gesturing across the room where her daughter was still playing with the toddler, oblivious to the fact her biological father was in the same room as her for the first time since she was a month old.

His head turned, and the way his eyes widened was almost comical. "Holy crap. She looks exactly like you. What is she, like eight now?"

"Twelve," Addison informed him, the irritation easy to hear in her voice. The fact that he had no idea how old his own daughter was shouldn't have been such a surprise to her, and yet it was.

"I want to meet her," Brady said.

Immediately, Addison's stomach tightened. She wasn't

ready for this. And she definitely wasn't going to spring Ellory's father on her out of the blue. She'd just opened her mouth to tell him that now wasn't the time when she was saved by a nurse coming into the waiting room, calling Ellory's name.

"We have to go, sorry," she told Brady as she stood, not feeling sorry at all.

"Wait—"

"Can't, we have an appointment."

"Can I call you?"

She wanted to say no. That he hadn't shown any interest in his daughter for twelve years, and she didn't see why now would be any different...but the fact of the matter was, the man *was* Ellory's biological father. If her daughter wanted him in her life, that was up to her. But within boundaries that Addison put in place. She wouldn't allow Ellory to get hurt. Not with everything else she had to deal with.

She reached into her purse and pulled out a receipt and a pen, quickly scrawling her number on the back. "Here's my number. Text me later so I have yours, and we'll talk about it."

"Great! Thanks. It was good to see you, Addison. You really do look great. Maybe we can go out for dinner or something and catch up."

"Sorry, I'm married. Talk later."

It felt amazing to be able to say that to her ex. To not have to make up an excuse about why she didn't want to have dinner with him. Addison hurried over to where Ellory was waiting in the doorway with the nurse. She looked back before the door shut behind them and saw Brady staring at their daughter. He had a look in his eyes that she couldn't interpret, but she didn't have time to think too much about it; she needed to concentrate on Ellory and her appointment.

But for some reason, an uneasy feeling settled in her gut. Brady hadn't been the best boyfriend, and he was obviously a horrible father. She reluctantly had to give him credit for immediately asking to meet his daughter. She had no idea what would happen in the future in regard to him and Ellory...but like everything else in life, she supposed she'd just have to hang on for the ride.

* * *

"How'd it go?" MacGyver asked when he saw Addison's name on his caller ID.

"The visit with the doctor...good. He went over the results from the upper GI. She's going to start the bowel rest protocol today. Liquids first for a few days, then lots of high protein, high but good fats and low to no fiber. If that doesn't help alleviate some of her symptoms, we'll see about extending the fasting."

"Is that healthy?" MacGyver asked worriedly.

"We'll monitor her closely. And she'll need to go in to see the doctor for blood tests regularly. The main concern is her weight."

"Right. So...what else happened?"

"What do you mean? How do you know something else happened?" Addison asked.

"You said that the visit with the doctor went well, indicating that something else didn't?" MacGyver said.

She sighed. "It's not something I want to talk about over the phone."

"Are you all right? The other kids?" MacGyver asked urgently.

"We're fine. I just ran into someone from my past today, and I want to talk to you about it. Later."

"Okay. Are you sure you're all right?"

"I'm sure. How's your day been? Any more word?"

MacGyver knew Addison was going to ask that. And he wished he had a definite date when they'd be headed out on their mission to the Middle East, but tensions were high there these days and the Navy had a lot of irons in the fire. So things were pretty fluid right now. But the truth was, the entire team was ready. They'd studied and researched and trained and were ready to head out to take down the HVT, the high-value target they'd been tracking. He wasn't a good guy, and no one would be sorry when he was gone.

"Soon, sweetheart. That's all I can say right now."

"Okay. Anything in particular you want for dinner?"

MacGyver adored this woman. He supposed it was partly because she'd been a single mother for so long, but she could go with the flow so easily. He had no worries about leaving her behind when he was deployed. Well, no worries about her being able to handle four kids, a business, and keeping her sanity. He definitely worried about her well-being, but he did that every time he left her side. It was an odd feeling, one he'd never had about anyone before, but after talking with Kevlar, Safe, Blink, and Preacher, he realized that it was simply a part of loving someone more than you could ever imagine loving another human being.

Love.

He *did* love Addison. The feeling had been there from the start, when he'd asked her to marry him, but it had grown exponentially since then. Every day he'd spent with her, the more he'd gotten to know her, the more sure he became that she was the perfect woman for him. Now he just had to figure out how to make her love him back the same way. That was the rub. He had no idea how to accomplish that.

"Ricky? Dinner?"

"Sorry, no. Whatever you make, I'll eat."

"Liver and onions?"

MacGyver almost gagged simply at hearing the words. "Um..."

She let him off the hook and giggled. "Kidding. I know how much you hate that stuff. I haven't forgotten the story you told me about having to choke it down while at a dignitary's house overseas. How about hamburgers?"

"Sounds perfect. Addy...are you really okay?"

"Yeah. Thanks. And we'll talk tonight. Promise."

"Okay. Have a good rest of the day and let me know if you need me."

"I always need you, but I think I'll manage."

His dick twitched at her words. She had no idea what she did to him. Then she giggled again...and he figured that maybe she *did* know, and was enjoying the power she had over him.

"Killin' me, Addy," he said.

"Just keeping you on your toes. See you when you get home. Be safe."

"Always. Later."

"Bye."

It was a struggle not to end their conversations with "I love you," but the last thing he wanted to do was freak her out, so he'd keep his feelings to himself...for now. But after this morning, after feeling her come apart under and around him, MacGyver felt better that he could *show* her how much she meant to him, at least, even if he couldn't say the words yet. There was no going back after this morning. Not after feeling how wet she got for him. Tasting her.

Smiling, MacGyver headed back up the stairs to the conference room he and his team were using today. They had a few more things to go over and then they'd be done for the day. There was nothing he wanted to do less than leave the country, now that things with his wife were finally progressing physically, but he'd waited this long. He could wait a little longer to make Addison his in every way.

CHAPTER NINE

Later that night, after the kids were in bed, Addison knew it was time to talk to Ricky about Brady. She didn't want to. She still had an uneasy feeling about her ex coming back into her life so suddenly. She couldn't put her finger on why, but things had been going so well with her, Ricky, and their family, she couldn't help but think Brady's arrival would shake things up...in a not-so-good way.

"Come here," Ricky said from the couch, holding out a hand to her.

Addison walked over and let him pull her down next to him. She leaned into him, feeling some of the stress of the day dissipate a little. Being with him always did that for her. She was an independent woman, had been a single mother for over a decade, and yet having someone to lean on, to talk through stressful situations, was a gift she didn't truly appreciate until now.

She decided to not beat around the bush, but to come right out and tell Ricky what happened at the hospital. She sat up a little and said, "Ellory's biological father was at the hospital today."

"*What?* Are you joking?"

Okay, maybe just blurting that out hadn't been the best way to break the news to Ricky. He was obviously shocked, but surprisingly, he sounded pissed too. "No. We were waiting to be called back when he approached me."

"Was Ellory there too?"

"Well yeah, but across the room. She didn't see him or hear what we were talking about."

"What did he want? Where has he been all this time? Did he apologize for leaving you high and dry with an infant? For not sending you any of the money he promised?"

"Um...no to the second two questions, and I don't know where he's been. He seemed just as surprised to see me as I was to see him. I guess he's working there. At the hospital. He's a janitor."

"And? What did he want?" Ricky asked, his hazel gaze boring into her own.

"He said he wanted to meet Ellory. I'm assuming he wants to get to know her."

At that, Ricky stood up and began to pace. "*No.*"

"Ricky, he's her father."

"Is he?" he countered, stopping and staring down at her. "Was he there when she cried in the middle of the night? How many diapers did he change? He didn't send you a dime, Addison. He up and left without one back-ward glance when she was a month old. And *now* he wants to be a part of her life? That's bullshit."

Addison shouldn't have been surprised at his animosity toward her ex, and yet she still kind of was. But that just showed what a good man she'd married. He'd been a father for such a short time, and yet he was more a father to her daughter than her biological dad had ever been.

"Ricky? Sit. Please," Addison said, patting the cushion next to her.

She saw him take a deep breath before he returned to her side.

"I know. I thought all the same things as you. But he *is* her biological father. What kind of mother would I be if I didn't allow her to at least meet him?"

"Smart?" Ricky bit out.

Addison sighed. He was making this extremely difficult, but she understood. She did.

"Sorry, I'm protective of her," Ricky said, running a hand through his hair. "And you. I don't like this guy. I know I haven't even met him, but what kind of man up and leaves his girlfriend right after she gives birth to his daughter?"

"A young, immature one?" Addison asked with a shrug.

"That's no excuse. There are plenty of fathers out there who are young, or younger than your ex was, who have stepped up. They haven't abandoned their children. I just question his motives. He could've reached out at any point. Why now? Was it really a coincidence that he saw you today? Did he know you were here in Riverton the whole time? Was *he* here? Wait, is he married? Does he have other kids?"

"I don't know."

It was Ricky's turn to sigh. "Right. So what now?"

"I guess I need to sit Ellory down and talk to her. Tell her that her biological father lives here in town and wants to meet her. We can play it by ear after that. She's a smart kid. If he has some ulterior motive, she'll sense it. But if he's genuine about his desire to get to know his daughter, I want that for her."

"You gonna ask for child support?" Ricky practically growled.

"No."

"You should."

"Here's the thing, if he starts giving me money, that gives him more of a right to see Ellory. If things don't go well, I don't want her to be *forced* to see him. Yes, he could always take me to court, but I don't see him doing that."

"You don't know the person he is now."

"True. But still, I don't want or need his money."

"What do you need from me?"

That right there was one of the many reasons she loved and respected this man. It was obvious he wasn't happy about Brady coming back into their lives, but he was willing to support her while they navigated this new wrinkle...and that meant the world to her.

"There's no way I'll let him be alone with her, at least to start. Will you come with me when we meet with him?"

"That's a given. There's no way *I'd* let you guys go by yourselves. What else?"

"Help me watch her? Look for signs that she's meeting with him because she thinks it's what *I* want, or something else is wrong. Listen to her if she wants to talk about it? I'm not sure she'll talk to me about how she's feeling."

"I can do that. How are *you* doing with this?" Ricky asked.

"It's not really about me."

"Of course it is. This is a man you once thought you'd spend the rest of your life with. You had a baby with him. And then he up and left, and now he's back out of the blue. Do you still have feelings for him?"

"What? No! *Hell no*. I'm a completely different person

than I was when I was in my early twenties. Besides, why would I want him when I have *you?*"

Ricky smiled. "True."

"Big bad Navy SEAL or a deadbeat dad...no comparison," Addison said.

"Hey...hear that?" Ricky asked, tilting his head to the side.

Addison frowned. "No? I don't hear anything."

"Exactly. The kids are asleep. With luck, they'll stay that way. Whaddaya say we head to our room?"

And just like that, Addison clued in to what he was hinting at. "Yes."

"Yes?" Ricky asked.

In response, Addison stood and held out her hand to him silently.

He stood as he took her hand, and then he was leading her down the hall to their bedroom. He shut the door firmly behind them and turned to face her. "Be sure, Addy."

"I'm sure," she told him, feeling anticipation flow through her veins.

"Go ahead and use the bathroom first," he said, his gaze glued to hers.

Addison backed away from him toward the bathroom, only turning around once she was through the door. Inside, she took a deep breath then quickly used the bathroom and brushed her teeth. She was finished in minutes, more than ready for what was to come.

Ricky was standing where she'd left him. In the middle of the room, staring at the door behind her as if he was afraid she'd turn back around and slip out the bathroom window or something.

"All done," she said, feeling a little awkward.

Ricky finally nodded and on his way past her, stopped to kiss her temple before continuing into the bathroom.

The second the door closed behind him, Addison spun toward the dresser. She pulled out her sleep shorts and top and whipped off her clothes. She made it under the covers just as the bathroom door reopened.

To her surprise, Ricky walked out completely naked. Addison had a feeling her mouth was hanging open, but she couldn't help it. She'd seen the man wearing only his boxers, but *nothing* could have prepared her for the sight of him without a stitch of clothing on.

He was sexy, stacked, and intimidating.

She was a thirty-something mother. Yeah, she was tall and slender...but almost *too* slender. She'd always wished she had more curves. The last thing she wanted was to be worrying about what she looked like right now, but she couldn't help it when she was faced with Ricky's utter perfection.

He didn't hesitate to walk to the bed and pull back the covers. He climbed in and scooted over to where Addison lay frozen, leaning on an elbow next to her.

"Hey," he said softly.

"Hey," she returned.

"We don't have to do this if you aren't ready," he told her, obviously reading her body language.

"No, I want to. I just...Ricky, you're perfect."

He snorted. "Hardly."

Addison licked her lips nervously.

One of his hands rested on her breastbone in the middle of her chest. "Breathe, Addy. Let me make you feel good. We can just do what we did this morning. There's no pressure here. None. Understand?"

And just like that, her nerves dissipated. This was

Ricky. The man who didn't blink when he had to change pee-covered sheets. The guy who patiently read the same book four times in a row to Yana because she demanded it of him. Who volunteered to go to Ellory's school for Career Day even though he and his team were in the middle of planning what was probably a very dangerous mission to some far-flung spot in the world. Who stood up to Ellory's bully. Who refused to leave three orphans in a war-torn country. Who got married not only help those kids, but because he knew she needed insurance for her daughter.

Ricky might have a body sculpted by hours upon hours of working out and doing dangerous things, but it was his heart that she was in love with. Even if this man gained a hundred pounds and had a beer belly, he'd still be the only man she wanted in her life...and in her bed.

Putting on a brave face, she sat up and pulled her top over her head before lying back down. This was the first time she'd bared herself to him, and she couldn't help but hold her breath.

But she shouldn't have worried. Ricky's pupils dilated so wide, she could barely see the hazel ring around them. Then he lowered his head.

As he covered one of her breasts with his hand, he sucked her other nipple into his mouth.

Addison let out a small, muted cry of pleasure and arched into him.

He didn't mess around, he sucked and nibbled and licked her nipple until it was so hard it almost hurt. Addison's belly clenched with desire, and she felt her pussy gush with excitement.

"Ricky," she murmured, tangling her fingers into his hair, holding him to her.

He shifted, moving to her other nipple. His five o'clock shadow lightly scraped the sensitive skin of her chest as he pleasured her. She could feel his erection against the side of her thigh and it was heady knowledge. She, the woman who'd been made fun of for being too flat, too skinny, too tall, too redheaded, too freckly, was turning on this amazing man. He could have any woman he wanted, she knew that without a doubt, and yet he was here with *her*.

Ricky lifted his head and met her gaze with his own. His hand replaced his mouth and he played with her erect nipple even as he stared down at her. "I want to go slow, but I don't think I can," he told her.

"The kids might wake up," Addison breathed. "Fast is good. Because if you stop now, I might have to kill you."

He chuckled but didn't seem in any rush to move things along.

"Ricky?" she asked, holding onto his biceps with a nervous grip.

"Shhhh," he murmured. "I'm memorizing this moment. The moment I make love to my wife for the first time."

Her pussy spasmed.

He shifted until he was kneeling at her feet. "Lift," he ordered.

It was like deja vu from this morning when he'd taken off her sleep shorts. This time, he yanked them down her legs with much less finesse than he had before. Then he shuffled forward on his knees, forcing her legs wider.

Looking up at him, Addison felt her heart thumping hard in her chest.

"I love your freckles," he murmured, his gaze roaming up and down her body.

"It's a good thing," she joked. "Because when I get too much sun, they seem to multiply tenfold."

"One of these days, I'm gonna kiss every single one," Ricky told her, using his finger to trace over the spots around her breasts.

"Ricky," she whispered.

"Yeah?"

"Please."

"Please what?" he asked with a grin.

He was messing with her, and Addison couldn't decide if she was irritated or amused. She took matters into her own hands—literally—and reached down to wrap one around his erection.

He inhaled sharply, then shuddered. Even though he was hovering over her, Addison felt as if she had all the power in that moment. He braced himself over her with a hand at her shoulder and used the other to pinch one of her nipples.

To her amazement, Ricky's cock hardened further as she stroked him. A bead of pre-come formed at the tip and she used it to help lubricate the head as she continued her ministrations.

"Fuck, Addy, wait a second," Ricky begged suddenly, swallowing hard.

She froze, not sure what was wrong.

He sat up and took her hand off his dick and placed it on his chest. "I don't have any condoms," he told her.

Shit. She hadn't even thought about protection. Which was stupid, because she'd already gotten pregnant once even when she *had* used protection.

"I'm so sorry. I never...I didn't think...*Fuck*," Ricky swore. He closed his eyes and took a deep breath. Then his eyes popped open and he looked more determined than ever. "It's fine. I can still get you off."

"I do," Addison blurted.

"What?"

"I have condoms," she told him, feeling the hot blush on her cheeks. "I bought them last week. I don't know why, I just...it seemed like it might be a good idea."

"You're a fucking genius. Where?" Ricky asked.

Turning her head, Addison nodded over at the dresser. "Top drawer. Right side."

Ricky was moving before she'd even finished speaking. He wrenched open the drawer where she kept her socks and smiled as he held up the box.

"You even got the right size. Extra-large."

Addison rolled her eyes. The truth was, she'd had no idea what size to get, but with the erection she'd felt against her leg now and then, she'd had a feeling he'd need the bigger ones. She'd been right too.

Condoms went flying when he tore the box open hastily, but his grin never faded. He had a packet in his teeth when he climbed back over her. He pushed her legs open once more, then ripped the little foil.

Addison watched as he rolled the condom over his erection. She much preferred for him to be bare, but as she wasn't on any birth control right now, and four kids was plenty for the moment, thank you very much. She didn't dare make the offer for him to forego protection.

"I'm not going to last long once I get inside your hot, wet pussy, so we need to make sure you're ready to take me." And with that, Ricky rested his hand on her belly, like he had the other morning, and his thumb immediately got to work strumming her clit in the way he'd learned she liked best.

It didn't take long for Addison's desire to ramp up. Ricky's other fingers were covered in her juices as he used them to prepare her to take him by gently pumping in and out of her pussy.

"That's it, hon. Come for me. You're almost there."

She was. Clamping her lips together, Addison exploded.

* * *

MacGyver had never seen anything as beautiful as his wife squirming and coming under him. Her chest was blotchy red and her nipples were rock hard. She didn't have very big tits, but he'd discovered they were extremely sensitive. He mentally vowed to make her come simply by playing with them...later.

Now, it was all he could do not to plunge between her soaking-wet folds and take her the way he'd dreamed of for weeks.

He loved the way her thighs shook as she came. How her belly visibly clenched. How tightly she squeezed his fingers with her cunt and how she gushed for him.

MacGyver was an idiot for not having condoms, but like the amazing, organized businesswoman and mom she was, Addison had taken care of that for them. Looking down at his cock, he wished he could rip off the rubber and take her bare, but there was no way he'd disrespect his wife that way. Until they could sit down and have a talk about babies and birth control, he wouldn't risk an unplanned pregnancy.

Addison was still twitching with pleasure when he notched the head of his cock between her legs. Biting his lip, he reached for the legendary control he had while on the job. But no mission had been as difficult as waiting for Addison's consent.

She didn't make him wait. Her legs rose and she rested her ankles on his shoulders.

"Please," she whispered, her green gaze boring into him.

"Hold on," he said in a hoarse voice. Then, with one steady thrust, he was balls deep inside her.

They both gasped. MacGyver had never felt anything as pleasurable in his entire life. He'd had sex many times, but nothing had ever felt like this. He was eye to eye with Addison, and seeing the red flush of her chest expand up her neck and down over her tits was fascinating and intimate.

"Move," she ordered.

But MacGyver shook his head. He couldn't. If he moved, he'd come. He had no doubt about that. The pleasure of being inside her was that intense. He felt like a virgin.

Then his wife smiled up at him and tightened her inner muscles.

A spurt of pre-come shot out of his dick.

"*Fuck!*" he exclaimed.

"That's the goal," Addison sassed.

Sitting up, holding her legs on his shoulders, MacGyver knew he needed to do something to distract her. To torture her as badly as he was being tortured at the moment. He managed to reach between them and began to stroke her clit once more.

She jerked in his grasp and moaned. But the joke was on him, because as he tried to torture her with bliss, he was actually only hurting himself. Her inner muscles contracted and released once, then again as he ramped up her pleasure. She was basically fucking him from the inside out—and he was done holding back.

Moving her feet from his shoulders, he wrapped them around his back, then leaned over her once more. She stared up at him as he began to thrust. In and out. In and out. In a steady rhythm.

Addison hooked her ankles together at his ass as she held onto his biceps. Her body inched up and down the bed as he took her. Her tits weren't big enough to sway with their movements, but he could see them shaking as her entire body jerked against the mattress with his thrusts.

He could do this. Make it last. Make it good for her...

Until she moved a hand between them and stroked his cock as he pulled out of her body. Then he lost it, and began fucking her hard and fast.

They both groaned, and MacGyver felt Addison's hips push upward into him on every downward stroke. His balls slapped against her ass with each thrust, and he could smell sex on their bodies and on the sheets. Every sense was engaged with making love to her, and he couldn't remember anything that had ever felt better than being with his wife.

To his surprise, her legs began to shake. She was coming again. Damn, was that the third time? He loved that his wife was multiorgasmic, it would make future lovemaking sessions even more exciting.

But her orgasm meant that every muscle in her body seized, which made it more difficult for him to push in and out of her pussy. And that made him lose the control he'd been holding on to with every ounce of strength he possessed. She made him weak as a kitten—and he fucking loved it.

Even though he was on the cusp, his orgasm still surprised him. He began to come on an outstroke, and when he pushed all the way back inside Addison, he fully let go. A too-loud grunt left his lips, and it felt as if he'd been pulled inside out. He kept coming, filling the condom to the brim. And yet his cock still twitched.

"Holy fuck," he said as he collapsed on top of Addison, catching himself at the last second so he didn't crush her.

She giggled, and the sound reverberated through him. He actually felt it around his softening dick, which was still lodged deep inside her body.

Lifting his head, MacGyver stared down at the woman who owned his heart and soul. There was sweat at her temples and her face was red. She was smiling up at him as if he'd just given her the moon and stars.

"Hey," she said softly.

Without thought, MacGyver lowered his head and kissed her. He couldn't believe he hadn't done that before now. His head moved from side to side as he tried to find the best angle. Her hand tangled in his hair as they kissed. It was a kiss filled with promise. Hope. Love.

He lifted his head and stared down at her once more. This time, she gave him a lazy smile.

"Thank you," MacGyver blurted.

"I think that's my line," she returned.

But MacGyver shook his head. "No. You giving that to me? Giving me *you*? I'll never forget it. Making love to my wife...it was...I have no words."

"Ricky," she breathed.

"Say it," he ordered.

"Say what?" she asked.

"That I'm your husband." He didn't know why he needed to hear Addison say that he was her husband...but he did.

"I didn't know my husband was such a stud," she joked.

Her words settled in his soul. He was a husband. *Addison's* husband. He belonged to her as much as she belonged to him. It felt amazing.

Moving slowly, he eased himself to the side and grimaced when his cock slipped out of her. He went into the bathroom and took care of the condom and wet a washcloth with warm water. Then he brought that into the bedroom and smiled at Addison's blush as she cleaned herself.

He stepped back to the bathroom, throwing the washcloth into the sink before cleaning himself a bit. Reluctantly, he put on his boxers, knowing he'd made the right decision when he saw that Addison had donned her top and sleep shorts. He didn't hesitate to pull her against him when he was settled back under the covers. With a sigh, he kissed her forehead, honestly speechless at the moment.

That had been...life-changing. He'd been in love with Addison before tonight, but now that he knew how compatible they truly were? He was going to do everything in his power to make sure she never wanted to leave him.

They had some hurdles ahead of them. His deployments, her ex, Ellory's Crohn's disease, the adoption process...but they'd make it through. He'd make sure of it.

CHAPTER TEN

Addison was having trouble concentrating on her work. Smiling as she worked on the Batman cake she was making for a customer's six-year-old son, she thought about the last few days. She and Ricky hadn't made love since that first time, but he'd proven how good he was at oral sex, and she'd returned the favor. Nothing with him seemed awkward. Their time was limited to after the kids were all put to bed, and even then it was a crapshoot if Yana or one of the boys woke up and needed something. But they made the little time they *did* have count.

Standing up and stretching her back, her smile faded as her mind switched to a less pleasant topic.

Today after school, Ellory would be meeting her biological father for the first time.

To her and Ricky's surprise, she'd been excited to learn about Brady, even more so to know that he wanted to meet her. Addison was relieved but also cautious. She just hoped Brady would follow through, wouldn't just meet her once and then decide he didn't want to be a father anymore. That would crush Ellory.

Since Ricky would be going with them, Artem, Borysko, and Yana would hang out with Preacher and Maggie after school, here at the house. Their friends would pick the boys up from school while Ricky grabbed the girls.

The truth was, the closer the time came for Ellory to meet her bio-dad, the more worried Addison got. Time had a way of making things she hadn't seen back when she was in her twenties clearer. Brady had been impatient, concerned with outward appearances, and he didn't have a very high tolerance for any kind of behavior that was outside the norm. She just hoped that he'd changed over the years.

A few hours later, the woman who'd ordered the Batman cake arrived and gushed over how adorable it turned out. Addison was pretty pleased with it herself. She still had an hour or so before Ricky arrived home with Ellory and Yana, and she figured she should do something productive, like laundry or vacuuming, but she was too nervous.

She sat on the couch, then immediately got up. She couldn't stop wondering how today would go. Worries about how Brady could treat Ellory kept creeping in.

When her phone rang, Addison was glad for the distraction. Looking down, she saw Maggie's name on the caller ID.

"Hi, Maggie."

"Hey."

"Please tell me you aren't calling to cancel," Addison begged.

"Nope. Shawn and I will be there soon. I was just calling to check on you. See how you were doing. I know when we get there, we won't have much time to chat."

"Oh...I'm okay."

"We haven't been friends for long, but you can talk to me."

And with that, Addison found herself pouring out all her worries to the other woman. "It's just that...Brady wasn't reliable twelve years ago, and I have no idea what kind of person he is today. *I* can handle him being a jerk, but I don't want that for Ellory."

"You've warned her that things might not go the way she wants, right?" Maggie asked.

"Of course. But that doesn't mean she still isn't hoping he'll end up being the perfect dad."

"Right. So...what's the worst-case scenario?"

"Huh?"

"The worst case? If you think about what that might be, anything he actually does has to be better, right?"

Addison chuckled. "Right. Um...he's a drug kingpin who wants to use Ellory to run drugs?"

"Or he owns a circus and wants Ellory to move in with him and become his main act."

They both laughed. Addison took a deep breath. "Or he's a changed man, honestly wants to get to know his daughter, and they click and things work out just fine," she said quietly.

"Yeah. I'm hoping for that one," Maggie agreed.

"I appreciate you coming over to stay with the kids while we meet with Brady."

"Of course. I miss them. And since they already know Shawn and I, hopefully they won't be as nervous with you guys gone."

Addison had already warned Maggie that the three of them were still a little skittish when it came to being separated from her and Ricky. She didn't blame them, and they were working on building their confidence back up. "They're looking forward to hanging out with you guys," she said. "How are *you* doing? Everything all right with the baby?"

"So far, so good. I've been getting a little nauseous in the mornings, but I'm hoping this will be the worst of it."

Addison couldn't help but chuckle.

"Shit. I know, I know, it'll probably get worse. I just really *hate* throwing up. Seriously."

"I agree. So I won't tell you that when I was pregnant with Ellory, I had morning sickness for four months straight."

"No, I definitely don't want to hear that," Maggie said, sounding horrified.

"Well, if you feel up to it, I tried something new and made cake-batter brownies."

"I have no idea what that is, but it sounds delicious."

Addison smiled. "Oh, it is. It's a mixture of brownies that somehow looks and tastes like a cake."

"I don't care about the particulars, I just want it in my belly," Maggie joked.

Addison's smile faded. "Maggie?"

"Yeah?"

"I'm really nervous about today. I want to shield Ellory from any hurt, and I just have a feeling this meeting isn't going to go well."

"Of course you want to keep her from getting hurt, but that's not how life works. All you can do is teach her how to deal with disappointment, celebrate successes, and be there for her when things don't go the way she wants. And from everything I know about you, you already do all that. Just be there for her. Love her."

Her words made Addison feel better. "Yeah."

"If I'm half the mom you are, I'll consider that a success."

Addison was overwhelmed at her new friend's words. "Thanks," she said.

"You're welcome. Okay, I need to go and get ready to meet Shawn when he gets off work so we can go get the boys. You good?"

"I'm good," Addison confirmed.

"All right. We'll be there in half an hour or so. Don't worry. Whatever happens will happen."

"Am I doing the right thing?" Addison blurted. "I mean, by letting Ellory meet Brady."

"Yes. The last thing you want is her finding out later that she had the opportunity to meet him and you didn't allow it. No matter how things go, she has a right to meet her father. To make her own decisions about whether she wants a relationship with him or not."

"You're right."

"I know," Maggie said. "But that doesn't mean the decision is easy. He hurt you. And there's no guarantee he won't hurt his daughter. But you have to take that risk and deal with the consequences after."

"How'd you get so smart?" Addison asked.

"It's easy to be when I'm not in your shoes. If I was, I'm sure I'd feel differently. I'll see you soon."

"All right. Bye."

Addison hung up and realized she felt better. Maggie was right. If there was the smallest chance that Brady had changed, that he really did want a relationship with his daughter, she wouldn't stand in the way of that. It meant a new complication in her and Ricky's already pretty hectic life, but if things worked out, Ellory would have someone else who loved her. And that would never be a bad thing.

Deciding she had time to fold a load of laundry—she swore the damn clothes multiplied when she wasn't looking—she'd just finished putting the clean items away in dressers and closets when she heard a knock on the door.

It was Maggie and Preacher with Artem and Borysko.

The younger boy immediately ran forward when the door opened and hugged Addison tightly. He was the more clingy of the two boys. While Artem didn't offer a hug, he still looked relieved to see her.

"Hey. How was school?" Addison asked.

"Good," Borysko said. "I learn how to spell lasagna. It is strange word, but good in stomach."

Addison laughed. "Very true. Unfortunately, there are a lot of words in the English language that are spelled strangely. Artem? What did you learn today?"

"Girls say one thing, but mean different."

Addison sensed a story there. "Yeah?" she said, encouraging him to keep going.

He nodded. "Girl in class, she say she no like me, but when we outside, she want me to chase her. So I did. When I caught her, she kiss me! *Blech!*"

Addison, Maggie, and Preacher all laughed. "Yeah, girls can be weird about telling the boys they like that they *actually* like them," Addison told him. "How about you two go change. Then you can get a snack."

"Cheese!" Borysko yelled before running toward his room.

Artem was a little more subdued, but Addison knew how much he loved his snacks too. He smiled at her, then followed his brother just as a car pulled into the driveway. It was Ricky with Ellory and Yana.

Yana raced into the house, hugged Addison, then ran

to find her brothers. It was always the first thing she did when she got home.

Ricky's arm went around Addison's waist. "Ready?"

She nodded. Ellory had stayed in the car, waiting for them.

"She okay?" Addison asked.

"Excited. Nervous. But okay."

"Things will be fine here. Take as much time as you want," Preacher told them.

"Yeah, we'll just be stuffing our faces with your brownie cake thing," Maggie said with a smile.

"Wait, what? Brownie cake?" Ricky asked.

Addison smiled. Her man had the biggest sweet tooth...it was adorable.

"Come on, let's get this over with," she said, dragging Ricky toward the open door.

Maggie waved and Preacher gave them a chin lift before they shut the door behind them. Ricky's hand on the small of Addison's back felt good. To have him by her side was all the confidence she needed to put on a brave face for her daughter.

After she got in the car and put on her seat belt, Addison turned slightly to look at Ellory in the back. She looked...freaked out. No matter how nervous Addison was about this, she wanted the visit to go well. She needed to calm her daughter a little.

"Hey, how was school?" she asked.

"Fine."

"Learn anything new?"

"No."

Right. This wasn't going well. "Breathe, El. This is going to be fine."

"What if he doesn't like me?"

"How could he *not* like you?" Addison asked.

Ellory shrugged.

"El, listen to me. Are you listening?" Ricky said as he drove down the road.

"Yeah."

"Whether or not Brady likes you isn't the point of this visit. It's so you can meet him and he can meet you. You have plenty of time to build rapport. You're going to have to get to know each other. This is like a first date, they're almost always awkward. Just go with the flow. Besides, if he doesn't like you, it's *his* loss. Because you're an amazing young lady. Kind, smart, compassionate, beautiful, and strong as hell. Got it?"

Addison loved this man all the more for always sticking up for her daughter.

Ellory said nothing.

Turning back around so she was facing forward once more, Addison looked over at Ricky. His hands were tight around the steering wheel and his knuckles were white. He was as nervous about this as she and Ellory were. She suspected he was feeling uneasy about his role in Ellory's life. He'd settled into being her father as if he'd been born to it, and now another man—one who held the official title as her father—was coming into their lives. It had to be nerve-racking for Ricky.

Reaching over, Addison took his right hand from the wheel and held it tightly. He looked over at her for a brief moment, gave her a small smile, then turned his attention back to the road.

It wasn't long before they arrived at the café where they'd planned to meet Brady. There was a parking spot not too far down the street, and Ricky deftly parallel parked. Before long, they were entering the café.

Brady hadn't arrived yet, so they found a table near the windows—because the seating situation would be awkward in a booth—so they could see him when he got there.

"Do I look okay?" Ellory asked, smoothing her hair back.

"You look perfect," Ricky told her.

The waitress came over and Addison ordered waters for them all. Ellory was still fasting, so she wouldn't be eating anything, but it didn't seem as if she was interested in food right now anyway. Addison herself wasn't sure she'd be able to keep anything down with the way her own stomach was rolling with nerves.

Five minutes went by. Then ten. When fifteen minutes past Brady's scheduled time went by, Addison started to get mad.

"He's not coming, is he?" Ellory asked, her shoulders drooping.

Addison reached for her daughter's hand, holding on tightly when she tried to pull back. "Brady's always late," she reassured the preteen. "Seriously, when we were together, we didn't get anywhere on time. We'd always miss the previews of movies when we went to the theater, and everyone knows that's the best part. Hell, he was late for your birth, sweetie. He missed the entire thing, showing up an hour after you were born, strolling in as if he had no clue that he'd arrived late."

"Really? You aren't just saying that to make me feel better?"

"I'm absolutely telling you that to make you feel better," Addison said. "But it's also true. I should've remembered that about him and gave him a meeting time half an hour before we really wanted to meet."

Ellory nodded and sat up straighter.

Addison wanted to kill Brady. Couldn't he attempt to show up on time just this once? He had to know this was important to Ellory.

Just as she had the thought, she saw him walking toward the café. "See? There he is."

Ellory's head spun around, and she watched as Brady strolled down the sidewalk as if he didn't have a care in the world. "Oh, he's not very tall."

Addison suppressed a chuckle. She was a couple of inches taller than her ex, and while Brady wasn't exactly short, her daughter had obviously gotten used to her height, and being around Ricky and his friends, who were all at least six feet or taller.

Addison stood as Brady entered the small café, and he immediately saw her and headed toward the table.

Ellory was staring at her father as if entranced.

Brady leaned forward and hugged Addison before she could step back. It was an uncomfortable moment, as Ricky had stood with her, his hand on the small of her back as her ex held on for a beat too long.

"Good to see you again," Brady said when he pulled back. He held out his hand to Ricky. "And you must be the husband."

"I am," Ricky said, waiting a long moment before shaking Brady's hand.

Then her ex turned to Ellory.

"And you have to be Ellory. I'd know you anywhere. You have your mom's bright red hair. Can't miss that." He chuckled at his own joke. "Shall we sit?" he asked, not waiting for anyone to answer before pulling the fourth chair out at the table.

They all sat. It was awkward that he hadn't hugged his daughter, or even offered to shake her hand.

"So..." Brady said. "You're my daughter. I thought you might be taller by now. You're twelve, right?"

"Uh-huh."

"Your mom is a giant, and I'm no slouch. Wonder what happened to you."

Addison's belly rolled. This wasn't starting out well. "Puberty happens at different times for different people, Brady. She's only twelve, lots of time for her to grow."

"Right. So...tell me about you? What do you like to do? Where do you go to school? Are you in any activities?"

Ellory was hesitant at first, but she slowly relaxed, especially since she had her father's undivided attention. He'd turned toward her and was nodding and offering the appropriate responses to everything she said. He genuinely seemed interested in what she was telling him, which made Addison relax a fraction.

But Ricky was still as tense as ever next to her. Addison put her hand on his leg, trying to reassure him. That didn't seem to help at all. He was sitting ramrod straight, staring at Brady.

"Have you lived in Riverton long?" Ellory asked after a while.

"Been back here about a year or so. I've lived in New York City, Chicago, DC, Atlanta...but always missed the West Coast. There's nothing like being back in California. It just has a different vibe, you know?"

Ellory nodded eagerly. "I love it here."

"But it's good to get away, to see more of the world than one little corner. You ever been to LA? Or out of the state?"

Ellory shook her head.

"Pity. I'd love to take you to New York. Now that's a city that never sleeps. We could go to a Broadway play, eat some authentic New York bagels, see Times Square...you know, all the good stuff."

Ellory's eyes were huge in her face. "Really?"

"Yeah, really. And every kid should see our nation's capital. We could rent scooters and see all the monuments."

With every word out of his mouth, Addison tensed. For one, she wasn't yet willing to let Ellory go on trips so far away without her. But two, she had no idea if Brady really meant what he was saying or if he was blowing smoke up his daughter's ass. He'd been full of promises back when they were together. Promises he could never keep.

"Should we order?" Brady asked no one in particular. He raised his hand and snapped his fingers at a waitress who was across the room.

Addison winced. She'd forgotten that about him. He used to do that all the time, and it always embarrassed her. It was a rude thing to do and extremely disrespectful. Ricky's thigh muscle tensed under her hand. She gripped him tightly, hoping he wouldn't lose his cool.

The waitress came over to their table.

"We'd like to order. I'd like a bloody Mary, a double hamburger with cheese, and fries."

"I'm sorry, sir, we don't serve alcohol."

"Well, shit. Fine. A large soda then. Ellory, what do you want? Get anything. It's on me."

"Oh, I'm not hungry," she said with a shrug.

"Not hungry? How can you not be hungry? I was always starving after school. And you're skinny as a rail.

You should eat something. If you ever want to get curves, you have to eat."

"It's okay," Ellory said.

Brady opened his mouth to protest some more, but Addison intervened. "I'll have a small salad with ranch on the side, please."

"Nothing for me," Ricky said tersely.

"Great, so now there are two of you not eating. Whatever," Brady said.

The waitress left to put their order in, and Brady started talking about some of the people he'd met while he lived in New York. Addison hadn't heard of any of them, though he swore they were all famous movie stars. Ellory didn't take her gaze from her father. She seemed star-struck.

When their food was served, Brady couldn't keep from commenting once more on the fact that Ellory wasn't eating. He spoke with his mouth full, something else Addison had forgotten about the man.

"Seriously, why aren't you eating? Something wrong with you?"

Addison could see the moment Ellory decided to tell her father about her condition. She wanted to stop her, tell her to leave the explanation for another time, but it was her decision.

"I have Crohn's disease."

"What's that?" Brady asked, his burger halfway to his mouth.

"It's where my intestinal tract becomes inflamed and painful."

Brady frowned. "So what does that mean? You can't eat?"

"I can," Ellory explained patiently. "But sometimes it

hurts. Right now, I'm doing a new kind of treatment where I fast for a few days, then eat a little before fasting again. It's a way to empty out my system so I don't get cramps or any other symptoms."

Brady put down his burger. "So you're starving yourself?"

"No. I have these shake things I drink to get nutrients."

"No wonder you're so small and puny. You have to eat to grow, Ellory."

"Brady," Addison warned, not liking her ex's attitude. He hadn't been any kind of father to their daughter for even one day in the last twelve years, and why he thought it was appropriate to share his offensive opinions now was infuriating.

"What? I'm just saying," Brady said defensively.

Addison watched her daughter flush. She was sensitive about the fact that she had delayed puberty as a result of her Crohn's. She didn't need her father pointing it out. "Until you get to know Ellory better, you have no right to give her advice about *anything* going on in her life. But so you know, she's doing really well on this new treatment. Eventually, we'll reduce the days she rests her bowels in the hopes that her intestines will adjust."

Brady stared at Ellory. His gaze flicked from her face, to her torso, then back to her face. "Well, sucks that you can't enjoy things like this amazing burger and fries. They're delicious."

Addison gaped at the man. Ellory was used to not eating what others around her enjoyed, but to rub it in her face that she was missing out was just plain cruel.

"So, you're a janitor," Ricky said out of the blue. "You a contractor for the Navy then?"

Brady shrugged and took another large bite of his burger. "Yeah. Decided to try something new."

"What did you do before?" Ricky pressed.

"This and that."

"This and that meaning what?" He obviously wasn't going to let it go.

As if just realizing that Ricky was interrogating him, Brady put down his burger and wiped his fingers on a napkin. "Sorry, man. I don't feel like I need to tell you my life history."

"If you want to keep seeing your daughter, you will," Ricky said, his voice low and harsh. "Because if you think we're ever going to let her be around a complete stranger without us accompanying her every single time, you're dreaming."

"I'm not a stranger," Brady insisted. "I'm her father. Tell this Neanderthal he's being unreasonable, Addison."

Taking a deep breath, Addison said, "Actually, I'm interested in what you've been doing these last twelve years myself. I tried to find you after you left. You said you'd help with Ellory, then you disappeared as if into thin air."

Brady stared at her, then scowled. "I don't need this shit. Ellory, it was great to meet you. I hope we can talk again. But until your mom stops jumping down my throat and being unreasonable, I'm not sure that will happen. Maybe we can text or something. *If* she'll give you my number, seeing as I'm obviously a serial killer and all that." Brady sounded disgusted. He stood up abruptly and stormed toward the door.

Addison stared after him with a sigh. Yup, that was a pure Brady reaction. Twisting things so nothing was his fault. Blaming *her*.

Worried about what Ellory was thinking, Addison looked at her daughter. She'd turned in her chair to watch Brady storm out of the café, and now she slowly turned back around to face the table. She looked at his half-eaten meal, then up at Addison.

"Guess the food wasn't on him, was it?"

Addison practically sagged in her seat. There was disappointment in her daughter's face, but not anger at *her*. It was a huge relief.

"Guess not," Addison agreed.

"Ricky? Are you okay?" Ellory asked.

Looking at her husband, Addison saw that his lips were pressed together, and he was sitting stock still. "Ricky?"

He took a long, slow breath in through his nose, then let it out. "If you'll excuse me for a moment," he said, then stood and headed for the door.

"Oh no. He isn't going to hurt him, is he?" Ellory asked.

"No," Addison said...but honestly? She wasn't sure *what* Ricky was going to do.

* * *

MacGyver was pissed. Angrier than he could remember being in a very long time. How *dare* Vogel be so condescending to his own daughter. Constantly commenting on her height and weight. And when he'd found out she had Crohn's, he'd been incredibly insensitive. If the man ever wanted to spend another second with his daughter, he needed an attitude adjustment.

Jogging to catch up to Addison's ex, MacGyver called out, "Vogel," as he approached from behind.

Turning, Brady seemed surprised to see Ricky coming

up on him fast. "What do you want?" he asked belligerently.

Yeah, this was the man Ricky had sensed was under the fake interest he'd shown in Ellory.

"I want to know what your deal is," MacGyver said. "Why you're showing any interest in your daughter now when you haven't cared for the last twelve years. Hell, you've been in Riverton for a year, by your own admission. Why haven't you tried to look up Addison and Ellory during that time?"

"It's none of your business," Vogel told him.

"*Wrong*. It's one hundred percent my business. Ellory and Addison are living under my roof. They're my step-daughter and wife. And I protect what's mine."

"Do they know you're talking about them as if they're property? Or slaves?"

MacGyver couldn't help it. He laughed. "I know it's been over a decade since you've seen your ex, but I'm sure you remember enough to know that Addison is no one's property. She has a mind of her own, and I love it. And her."

Vogel rolled his eyes. "Whatever, man. I don't answer to you."

"Again—wrong. If you truly want to get to know your daughter, you absolutely answer to me. And when you get defensive and angry about a simple question regarding what you've been doing for the last twelve years, that makes me suspicious. Makes me wonder what you've been up to. I know people, Vogel. People who are all too happy to do an in-depth background check to protect those they care about."

"Are you threatening me?" Vogel asked.

"No. I'm telling you what's going to happen. If you've

got skeletons in your closet that'll hurt Ellory, I'll find them."

"Fuck you!"

MacGyver simply raised a brow. He really didn't like this guy. It sucked that he was Ellory's father, but he'd do whatever it took to protect his stepdaughter. Even if it made her angry. Even if she hated him for it. He'd gladly accept her ire if it meant keeping her out of danger.

"Fine. You want to know what I've done in the last twelve years? The same thing I do now. I've been a janitor. I didn't want my daughter to know because I wanted her to admire me. To look up to me. No one wants a janitor for a dad. Yes, I'm still a janitor here in Riverton, but working at the medical center on base is a step up for me. I earn a decent salary and benefits for the first time in years. That's why I didn't want to say what I've been doing. Happy now?"

MacGyver stared at the man in front of him. He sounded genuine. But he still had his doubts. "Ellory doesn't care what you do for a living. All she wants is to get to know her dad. Don't lie to her. She's smart. She'll figure it out, and then you'll lose her before you've even had a chance to get to know her. And stop commenting on her size. She's sensitive about it, and you constantly harping on it isn't helping endear her to you."

"Fine."

"And if I can give you more advice, do some research on Crohn's. It's something she's going to have for the rest of her life. She'll never grow out of it, there's no cure. You'll need to understand the ins and outs of the disease so you can help her if she needs it."

Vogel nodded. Then said, "Are we done here?"

"Yeah. We're done," MacGyver said.

"Am I going to get to see my daughter again?"

"That's up to her, not me."

"Bullshit. We both know you and Addison can keep her from me if you want. Don't make me get a lawyer."

MacGyver snorted. "Right. That's not happening. If you wanted to see Ellory that bad, you would've seen a lawyer long before now—*and* you would've been giving Addison child support. Prove that you're willing to do whatever it takes to spend time with your daughter, and we'll see what happens."

With that, MacGyver turned and headed back to the café. To his wife and Ellory, who were both probably freaking out.

Vogel said the right things...well, no. He said a bunch of not-so-right things, but his explanation of why he'd sidestepped telling them what he'd done for a living before moving back to Riverton rang true. MacGyver still didn't like the man, though for now, he had no reason to keep Ellory from talking to him. But time would tell.

* * *

Brady Vogel paced his small piece-of-shit apartment. Back and forth, back and forth, stewing in his anger. Today hadn't gone as he'd hoped. His bitch of an ex just *had* to bring her new husband, and he'd asked too many questions. Questions Brady wasn't willing to answer.

And not because he was *embarrassed*. He wasn't a goddamn janitor. Hadn't been a janitor for the last decade...but he couldn't afford to let Addison's husband actually follow through on that background check.

Because he was a con man. He made money off anyone and everyone he could. Men or women. Drug addicts, millionaires, old women who were desperate for a man, young men who trusted him to invest their money. You name the con, he'd done it.

He'd actually come back to California because he'd gotten connected with a new contact. A man who made more money than Brady had ever seen in his lifetime...and he did it by peddling human flesh.

He bought babies from desperate women who didn't want or couldn't care for their children, and sold them to families desperate to adopt.

He befriended runaways and "introduced" them to pimps who needed new employees.

Befriended sick men and women, old and young, with no families to protect them, and convinced them to give him medical power of attorney. The second they died, he sold their usable body parts to big corporations for thousands of dollars.

And Brady was lucky enough to become a small part of it. At the request of his contact, he volunteered at the free clinic downtown, which gave him access to people and information that helped the man's business. He noted the women who came in to give birth alone. Who were addicted to drugs. The sick and dying who were desperate for a friendly face. He passed all the information along to his associate, who in turn funneled money back to him.

Brady didn't feel bad about any of it either. He'd been conning people for too long to have a conscience. Hell, he'd felt no guilt abandoning his own child all those years ago. A kid was just something that would've gotten in his way and cost him money.

When he ran into Addison on base, it was a surprise—one he'd hoped to benefit from. If there was anything easier than swindling strangers, it was conning people he knew well. And for a minute there, he'd actually looked forward to meeting his daughter too. You never knew where opportunities might arise in his line of work.

But now? Not so much. She was *pathetic*. Puny. Looked too much like his ex. If something was wrong with her bowels, that meant she probably had shitting problems.

Despite what he'd told Addison, the worst part about his job at the hospital was cleaning up after people who lost control of their bowels. The fact that his daughter was one of those people disgusted him. Twelve years old and her intestines didn't even work right...

But he bet her *other* organs did.

He stopped pacing and stared into space, thinking hard. It was one thing to sell the body parts for someone who died of disease or old age. But the demand for organs and other parts from children was sky-high. People would pay hundreds of thousands of dollars for an undamaged child's heart. Or liver. Or eyes.

Desperate people did desperate things.

He knew that so well, considering what he did for a living.

The longer Brady thought about the day—about the asshole Addison had married, about his daughter and her disease—the stronger the idea in the back of his mind became.

He didn't want anything to do with his daughter. Didn't want to get to know her. He couldn't deal with the kind of issues she had. But...what if he could make some money from this situation?

Everything he did was about making money. Brady had no problem throwing anyone under the proverbial bus if it earned him some cash. And knowing his daughter would live a shitty life—literally—suffering from an incurable disease, made what he was thinking seem less...horrible.

He spent a few minutes debating with himself.

Ellory *was* his own flesh and blood...could he really do what he was thinking to his own kid?

But she was suffering. Crohn's seemed like a horrible thing. Surely she wouldn't want to live the rest of her life that way.

Bonus...it would piss off Addison's new husband. Maybe even devastate him. Hit him in a way a physical confrontation never could.

Brady screwed people over all the time, but it was a huge leap from taking an unwanted kid from one woman and selling it to another who was desperate for a child, or waiting for an old man to die so he could sell his organs, to selling someone he had a cellular-level connection with. Ellory had his DNA in her veins.

Could he really hand her over to his contact, knowing what would happen to her?

The answer was...yes.

Brady scrunched his nose. He was an asshole. But truthfully, he'd be doing Ellory a favor. No one wanted to live with a chronic disease. She'd help other children and be relieved of her pain at the same time.

The more he thought about it, the better the idea seemed. He'd sell his daughter to his contact, who in turn would get hundreds of thousands of dollars for her body parts, which Brady would also get a cut of. *He* wouldn't actually be killing her, which made him feel better in a twisted kind of way.

His idea was foolproof. He just had to play the game a little longer...something Brady was really good at. He'd conned people all over the country. It would be even sweeter to see the new husband suffer when Ellory disappeared.

He protected what was his? *Bullshit*. Brady was smarter than that asshole. Ellory was *his* daughter—and he'd do whatever he wanted with her.

The unfortunate truth was, she was worth more to him dead than alive. It was just a matter of playing the role of a lifetime to get what he wanted. Money. He could pretend to be a loving and doting father. It wouldn't be for long. Just long enough for Addison and the asshole to let down their guards. Then he'd be swimming in more money than he could imagine.

It was time to step up his game. The new con was on, and Brady couldn't wait for payday.

CHAPTER ELEVEN

Ellory was subdued the next few days, though Addison couldn't blame her. Things with her bio-dad hadn't gone exactly how any of them had imagined. But Ellory was a naturally positive kid, and before long she was back to her normal self. It helped that the fasting seemed to ease the symptoms of her Crohn's tremendously. Letting her intestines rest had done what the doctor hoped. Lessened the inflammation drastically, enough to let her eat without pain for a few days before going back to the nutrient-based drinks.

Artem, Borysko, and Yana had settled back into their routine as well, which was a relief. They seemed to be getting over the trauma of being taken away from the people who'd come to mean the world to them. Ricky's friend Tex had obviously done something, because Addison and Ricky had gotten word that their adoption of the trio was moving along at a faster pace than before.

Addison was grateful for the assistance, even while admitting that she and Ricky were in a place of privilege.

Most people who wanted to adopt kids had to wait much longer and the process was far more arduous.

And as usual, just when things seemed to be going well in her world, life had a way of intervening...making sure she knew at any time her circumstances could change on a dime.

Addison was in the kitchen, putting the finishing touches on the Minion cupcakes she was making for a birthday party at the local bowling alley. They were adorable, if Addison said so herself. She'd used twinkies cut in half on top of each cupcake, blue icing, and Smarties for eyeballs. Add in some black icing piped around the eyes to make glasses, a dab for an eyeball and a smile, and voila! Instant minion. They were easy to make, but more importantly, super fun and something Addison hadn't made before.

She'd just taken the last of the pictures she wanted to use for her website and social media when her phone rang.

Wiping her hands, she saw it was Ricky calling. She wasn't immediately alarmed because he called her all the time to check on her.

"Hey," she said with a happy lilt in her voice.

"Hey," Ricky returned.

She immediately tensed. He didn't sound like his usual easygoing self. "What's wrong?"

"We got word. We'll be headed out in the morning."

Addison swallowed hard. They both knew this was coming, but it was still difficult to hear. She did her best to not sound as sad and worried as she felt deep inside. "All right. What do you need from me?"

Ricky was silent for a moment, then he sighed. "You're amazing."

Addison frowned in confusion. "What?"

"I know this is hard for you. It is for me too. I don't want to go, but I don't have a choice. You have every reason to be freaking out. To be upset that I'm leaving. But instead, your first instinct is to ask what I need from you. I don't deserve you, Addy. The best decision I ever made was asking you to be my wife."

"Ricky," she protested.

"I'm serious."

"And the best thing I did was say yes," she returned. "We knew this was coming. Hell, you're a SEAL, being deployed comes with the territory. We've prepared the kids as much as we can, and as you've pointed out time and time again, I have a ton of people who can help with anything that comes up. I'm not thrilled you'll be away, and I'll imagine all sorts of awful things that you're doing while you're gone. But I have to have faith that you'll come home safe and sound."

"I will," Ricky said firmly.

Addison knew as well as he did that he couldn't promise any such thing. But she didn't call him on it.

"I'm just glad," he went on, "that we have a little advanced notice. The last couple of missions we went on, the asshole in charge didn't give us more than an hour. I can pick up all the kids from school today if you want."

"Are you sure?" Addison asked.

"Of course. It's not a problem. Anything else you need me to grab on my way home?"

Her heart melted. He was leaving in less than twenty-four hours on what was surely going to be a dangerous mission, if the intense preparations had been any indication, and he was asking *her* if she needed anything.

"No, I think we're good. I just went to the store today."

"All right, but if you think of anything, let me know," Ricky said.

"I just need you," Addison blurted.

"You have me," Ricky said calmly. "I'll call if anything changes. Otherwise, I'll see you in a few hours."

"All right. Be safe."

"I will. Later."

After hanging up, Addison closed her eyes and willed herself not to cry. This was what Ricky did. She was as proud of him as she could be. Crying over him leaving wouldn't help the situation. But she gave herself some grace, since this was the first time he was being deployed since they'd gotten together.

After a few minutes, she took a deep breath, wiped the tears off her cheeks, and got to work boxing the cupcakes.

* * *

MacGyver was torn. He was actually looking forward to this mission. They'd gone over every contingency and he was positive about the outcome. There was no way the HVT would slip away. It should be a straightforward assignment. Not exactly safe, but nothing the team hadn't faced in the past.

At the same time, he hated to leave his family.

He'd worry nonstop about how Addison was coping while he was gone. It was hard enough to be a single mother to one kid, and now she was responsible for four. She was amazing at it though. Strict, but not in an over-the-top way. She worked her butt off not only for her business, but to make sure each and every one of the children felt loved, safe, and cherished.

And MacGyver would certainly miss holding his wife

throughout the night. Yes, the lovemaking was amazing, out of this world, mind-blowing...but it was the intimacy of holding her, of talking about their days and their upcoming schedules, laughing together quietly in the dark, that he'd miss the most.

He hadn't known what he was missing before Addison. Kevlar, Safe, Blink, and Preacher had been so much happier since finding their women, almost too damn chipper in the mornings for PT, and now he knew why. And it certainly wasn't because they were getting more sleep. Hell, they were probably getting less, now that they had women to love each night. No. It was because they were more content. Because they had someone to share their lives with. It was corny as hell, but MacGyver understood that now.

And one additional thing he had that his teammates didn't was the joy of children. He was extremely blessed. Yes, it was stressful trying to make sure everyone had what they needed, emotionally as well as physically, but the reward was in every hug from little Yana. From seeing her face light up when she asked him something in English and he understood. When Artem proudly told them that he'd made a new friend at school. When Borysko understood his homework. When Ellory came home from school smiling after a pain-free day.

"I'm headed out!" Flash shouted from the hallway before sticking his head into the conference room they'd taken over for their mission prep.

"Sounds good. See you in the morning," MacGyver told him.

"Addison all right?" Flash asked.

And that right there was one of the many reasons why

he loved the men he worked with. "She's good. Trying to be brave, but she'll be fine," MacGyver told his teammate.

"She has Wolf's number, right?"

"Of course."

"And Tex's?"

MacGyver chuckled. "Yes. Definitely. Thanks for thinking about my woman. You ever thought about settling down yourself?"

Flash leaned against the doorjamb. "Not really. I'm not the kind of guy most women want."

"What? Why would you say that?" MacGyver asked.

His friend merely shrugged. "I'm just not. I've learned the hard way. I'm too nice. Too intense. Too smart. Too focused. Too quick to fall in love. Too good-looking, so that must mean I'm a man whore. I've basically heard every possible reason why I'm not long-term material. It's fine though. I like living vicariously through you and the others. I've already claimed dibs on being Preacher's manny."

"Manny?" MacGyver asked, smirking.

"Yeah, a male nanny."

"How come you haven't volunteered to be *my* manny?"

Flash chuckled. "Because I like babies. Your kids are old enough to not need me."

"They will always need their uncles. To spoil them. To play catch with them...or Barbies," MacGyver countered.

"True. Anyway, I'm good. Honestly."

"Well, if I've learned nothing else, it's not to count on anything staying the same," MacGyver told him. "Not too long ago, I was as single as you, and now I'm happily married with four kids."

Flash snorted. "I'm still not sure how that happened."

"You want to come over and hang with us tonight?" MacGyver asked impulsively.

"Nope. No way will I be the seventh wheel," Flash told him.

"You wouldn't be."

"Yes, I would. Enjoy the evening with your family, MacGyver. I'll see you in the morning."

"All right. But if you change your mind..."

"I won't. Later."

MacGyver glanced at his watch and realized it was later than he thought. He quickly closed his laptop and cleaned up the area. He was the last to leave, and he made sure there was no sign of the mess he and his teammates had made while making their final preparations for the mission.

He picked up Artem and Borysko from their school first, then Yana, and lastly swung by the middle school to get Ellory.

To his delight, she was in a very good mood. It was a relief that apparently Chrys had backed off picking on her, which went a long way toward improving the preteen's mood.

"I heard from my dad again today," Ellory told him with a huge smile.

"Yeah?" MacGyver wasn't thrilled that Brady had been texting Ellory, but he couldn't exactly forbid the man from talking to his daughter. Besides, it made her happy.

"Uh-huh. He said that when he lived in Washington, DC, he met the president once!"

MacGyver highly doubted that, but he nodded anyway. *He'd* met more than one president. He didn't brag about it; it was simply one of the many things he'd done.

"He's also been asking when he can see me again. Do you think Mom will set it up soon?"

MacGyver's belly rolled. He didn't even know why the thought of Ellory seeing her father again bothered him so much. He and Vogel hadn't hit it off, which was kind of an understatement, but he hadn't done anything that would make him or Addison outright forbid him from seeing his daughter again. They'd agreed to follow Ellory's lead in whether or not she was interested in furthering the relationship with her father. And it seemed she was eager to do just that.

"Ricky?"

"Sorry. I'm sure she will." This felt like as good a time as any to let the kids know he wouldn't be around for a while. "Although, I won't be able to go with you guys this time. You know that mission I've been planning? Well, it looks like I'll be headed out in the morning."

There was dead silence in the car.

MacGyver looked in the rearview mirror and met Artem's gaze.

"I'm gonna need you to step up, buddy. Help Addy with some of the housework, watch after your brother and sister...you do that anyway, but maybe keep an extra eye on them."

Artem nodded.

"And, Borysko, I want to know at least ten new English words you've learned when I get back."

"Okay, Ricky."

"Yana?"

The little girl refused to look at him. She was staring out the side window with a little pout on her lips.

"Are you mad, Yana?" MacGyver asked her softly.

He realized he should've waited to have this conversation until he wasn't driving when tears began to drip down her little face.

"Ricky, gun. Run. Sad!"

MacGyver wasn't exactly sure what she was trying to say. She understood English quite well now, but speaking it was another issue. She was working hard, but she still struggled.

Borysko asked her something in Ukrainian, and she answered in a flurry of words.

"She is scared you will get hurt," Artem translated. "Like Borysko did when we were in Ukraine."

Yeah, he definitely should've waited until he'd gotten home to let the kids know about his upcoming mission. He'd messed up, and he wasn't sure what to say or do to reassure the little girl who meant the world to him.

Thankfully, Ellory turned in her seat as much as her seat belt would allow and spoke directly to Yana. "Ricky will be okay. He's smart. And he has all his friends with him. You saw how good he is when he was in Ukraine with you. He'll come back before we know it. And my mom will take care of us while he's gone."

"Addy," Yana said with a sniff.

"Yup. Oh! I know, maybe she'll let us make a fort in our room! We can drape a sheet over the top of our beds using the brooms and a mop to hold them up, and we can sleep under there. Would you like that?"

"I want sleep fort too!" Borysko said, a tad too loudly for the small enclosure of the car.

The kids began talking amongst themselves, and MacGyver didn't even scold them for speaking in their native language. Usually he preferred them to use English, so they could practice it and so he could keep his finger on the pulse of how they were doing, but he was too grateful for the distraction to insist on it at the moment.

"Thanks," he told Ellory quietly.

"You're welcome."

"You're a good kid," he told her.

"I know," she said a little cheekily.

MacGyver chuckled.

"So you think Mom'll let me see Brady again even though you won't be here?"

The tension MacGyver had felt about Ellory seeing her father returned ten-fold. "I don't see why not," he said as calmly as he could.

"Can I be honest?" Ellory asked.

"Of course. I prefer it."

"I haven't made up my mind about him. My dad. I can tell he's trying to be cool, but it feels as if he's trying a little *too* hard sometimes. Like, how did a janitor meet the president? That seems weird to me. But why would he lie about it?"

"Because he wants to impress you," MacGyver told her. "He wants you to like him, and people sometimes stretch the truth to accomplish that. Even adults."

"Have *you?*"

MacGyver immediately shook his head. "No. I want you to like me too, but I don't want to make stuff up in order for that to happen."

"I like you," Ellory said without hesitation.

"Good."

"Have *you* met the president?" she asked with a grin.

MacGyver returned the smile. "Twice."

"The same one?"

"Nope, different ones."

"Cool."

MacGyver shrugged. "It wasn't as cool as you might think. There were secret service people everywhere, and both times we just lined up and he went down the line and shook our hands, then he was gone. That was it. I didn't even get to speak to him."

"It's still cool."

"Yeah, I suppose it didn't suck," MacGyver agreed. "I have the pictures that were taken somewhere. You know, if you want me to prove I'm not lying. That was part of the thing...we got our picture taken shaking the pres's hand."

Ellory's eyes got big. "Really? I'd love to see them!"

"I'll dig them out. But it'll have to be after I get home."

"You're going to be all right, aren't you?" the preteen asked quietly.

"Yes. You were right in what you told Yana. I have my team at my back. We've prepared—hell, *over-prepared* for this mission. We'll be fine."

"Okay."

"You'll keep your eye on your mom for me? I know she'll worry about me, you, the others. She takes a lot on, and I'm afraid this first deployment will be really hard on her."

"I will. Maybe I'll wait to see my dad again until you get back. So she doesn't have to worry about one more thing."

MacGyver wanted to agree that she didn't need the added stress, wanted to encourage her to wait. But that wasn't fair. "I don't think it'll hurt to see him again."

"I'll see what Mom thinks," Ellory said.

MacGyver was inordinately proud of this young lady. She was growing up quickly and already very mature for her age.

He pulled into the driveway and cut off the engine.

Artem and Borysko helped Yana climb out of her car seat and they all headed into the house. As usual, the smell of baked goods hit MacGyver's nose as soon as he entered, along with something garlicky and savory.

"Cookie!" Yana exclaimed with a happy smile as she headed for the kitchen.

MacGyver stood back and watched his wife greet each of the kids. She stopped what she was doing and got down on one knee to pay special attention to the younger ones. Ellory showed her the texts from Vogel, and MacGyver could tell that Addison wasn't thrilled that her ex and his daughter were texting, but she didn't let Ellory see her dismay.

After the kids had each been given a cookie and sent to their rooms to change, she looked over at him. MacGyver closed the distance between them and without hesitation, wrapped an arm around her and kissed her. Hard.

He was going to miss this. Coming home and seeing her interact with the kids. Smelling the food she'd been baking and cooking. Seeing the happiness in her eyes when she saw him. It sank home just then how much all this, *she*, meant to him.

"Hi," she said breathlessly when he finally broke the kiss.

"Hi," he returned with a small smile.

Then the kids were back, talking about their day, telling Addison about the fort they were going to make to sleep in.

MacGyver didn't get a chance to have his wife to himself until after the kids were in bed. She'd been busy reassuring them that they'd all be fine while Ricky was gone. That nothing in their routine would change. That Ricky would come back to them safe and sound. He couldn't tell them where he was going, or for how long, but with Addison's seeming lack of concern, the kids gradually relaxed and didn't seem as tense about his upcoming absence.

He and Addison were in bed, and he was holding her against him, when he told her, "You were wonderful with them tonight."

"They're going to miss you," she said quietly. "As am I."

"I know. This isn't going to be easy for me either. I've gotten used to the chaos that is our life."

She chuckled against him, then propped her chin on his chest so she could see his face. "It's a good chaos though, right?"

"Right," he agreed. "You get a chance to talk to Ellory about Vogel?"

"A little. Are you okay with her seeing him again?"

MacGyver wanted to say no. But he couldn't do that to Ellory. "Yeah. But if he's an ass, you get the hell away from him."

"I will. He's trying. I can tell from his texts that he isn't used to talking to a teenager, but he's making an effort. I'm not sure what else I can ask for."

MacGyver wasn't either. But he still didn't know what Vogel's angle was. It was too strange that he'd appeared out of the blue and immediately wanted to be best friends with his daughter when he hadn't given a rat's ass before seeing Addison at the hospital. "Just be careful," he warned.

"I will. I'm not going to let him fuck with my daughter. I'm cautiously optimistic," she told him. "But at the first sign of anything hinky, I'll call a halt to everything."

"Good. Now can we stop talking about your ex?"

Addison giggled. "Sure. What should we talk about then?"

"How about nothing," MacGyver said as he pulled her up so she was straddling his groin. She smiled down at him.

"No talking, got it," she said, before leaning down and covering his lips with her own.

Within moments, they were both frantically attempting to get their clothes off. Then MacGyver yanked Addison up his body so she was straddling his face. They hadn't done this yet, and he couldn't wait.

It didn't take long for her to start undulating over his face as he tongue-fucked her. His cheeks were covered in her juices, and all he could smell and see was her gorgeous pussy. It was pure heaven.

Right after she came, he eased her back down his body and she grabbed his cock, lining it up with her pussy before sinking down on him.

For a moment, they both stilled, each lost in the feeling of the other—then Addison began to fuck him. Hard. MacGyver held her hips, giving her stability, and he felt his heart swell in his chest at the sight of her bouncing up and down on his lap. His cock was shiny with her juices, and he'd never seen anything as erotic as his woman taking him.

When he felt her begin to tire, he took over, lifting her and slamming her down. His cock felt as if it was deeper inside her than he'd ever been. His balls began to tingle and he knew he was close.

On the next downstroke, he held her against him with one hand while the other went to where they were joined. As he exploded, he roughly strummed her clit. It didn't take long for her to come. She squeezed his dick, still deep inside her body, and MacGyver felt another spurt of come escape his cock.

"Holy shit!" Addison exclaimed as she dropped bonelessly onto his chest. They were both dewy with sweat, and MacGyver had never felt so drained as he did right that moment.

Seconds later, he felt a warm stream of their combined juices roll down his balls as he lay under his wife...and he tensed.

"Fuck."

"What? What's wrong?" Addison asked as she lifted her head to stare at him in concern.

"I forgot to put a condom on. I'm so sorry! I swear I didn't mean to forget, but having you come on my face made me block out everything except getting inside you."

To his surprise and relief, Addison didn't freeze against him. "I probably should be freaking out, but I can't muster the energy right now. I'll go see my gynecologist while you're gone. Sort out birth control."

"And if you're pregnant?" he couldn't help but ask, thinking about Preacher and Maggie. They hadn't planned on her getting pregnant so fast, yet she had.

"And if I am...?" she returned, turning the question back on him.

"If you are, then I'll be thrilled to give the others a little brother or sister," he said, meaning that with every fiber of his being.

"Five kids...it would be a lot."

MacGyver shrugged. "Like four isn't?"

"True."

"Look at me, Addy."

She lifted her head.

"I love you," MacGyver told her. "I know it's fast, but

then again, it's not. We got married for convenience, but how could I *not* fall in love with you after seeing what an amazing mother, businesswoman, and kind person you are?"

"Ricky," she breathed.

"You don't have to say it back, but I wanted you to know before I left."

"I love you too," she whispered. "And I'm not just saying that because you did."

Contentment spread throughout MacGyver. He had everything he'd ever wanted. A woman who loved him, kids who made him laugh and filled him with awe at the same time. A home. A job he loved. Friends. He was the luckiest son of a bitch in the world. He'd never take Addison or their life together for granted.

His cock twitched inside her, and he couldn't help but flex his ass. As she was soaking wet, his dick easily slid in and out of her well-prepared body.

"Again?" she asked with a grin.

"Again," he agreed, rolling over so she was under him. As he hovered over her, MacGyver memorized the face of the woman he loved, and who loved him back. Her red hair was in complete disarray around her face and shoulders, her green eyes sparkled as she stared up at him. Her chest was blotchy red, her freckles standing out in stark relief against the pale spots. Her nipples were hard on her chest and begging for his mouth.

She reached up and brushed a too-long piece of hair off his forehead. He needed a haircut, but because of the modified grooming options the SEALs enjoyed, it wasn't something he'd made a priority.

"Make love to me," Addison said softly.

"Gladly."

MacGyver loved his wife twice more that night, aware that with every tick of the clock, his time with her was coming to an end. Tonight was a gift, for both of them. Exchanging I love yous, agreeing that they both wanted another child, and vowing to do whatever it took to make their relationship work...it was exactly what MacGyver needed before heading out on his mission.

Later that morning, after eating breakfast with his family, reassuring each of the children that he'd be back before they knew it, and helping Addison drop them off at school, he stood back in his kitchen with his wife in his arms. She sniffed a little, obviously trying to hold herself together.

"Don't cry," he murmured.

"I'm trying not to," she told him as she dug her nails into his back.

MacGyver took her head in his hands and leaned down. He put his forehead against hers. "Call the other women if you get overwhelmed. They've already agreed to help with whatever you need. And they'll be more than happy to come over because they'll be feeling the same worry you are."

"Yeah," she agreed.

"And Caroline, Fiona, Alabama, and the others are also here if you want to talk. They've been through more deployments than you can count. And Jessyka would probably love for you to bring Artem, Borysko, and Yana over to hang with her kids."

"I'll call her," Addison told him.

It was time to go. MacGyver didn't want to, but dragging this out wasn't helping either of them. He kissed her one last time, long, slow, and deep. They were both breathing hard when he pulled back. "I'll call as soon as we're back."

"Okay."

"Try not to worry."

"Okay."

"If Vogel acts like an idiot, tell him to fuck off."

"Okay." This time she smiled when she said it.

"I love you," MacGyver told her. It felt good and right to say the words out loud whenever he felt the need now, rather than just thinking them.

"I love you too. Be careful. Kick some bad guy butt."

He grinned. "We will."

Turning, he went to the front door. He'd put his bag in Addison's VW Bug earlier. He was taking her car because she'd need his Explorer to fit all the kids in while he was gone. Leaving her was harder than he'd expected. Forcing himself to open the front door, MacGyver walked to the car. He hesitated, then turned around.

Addison was standing in the doorway, tears on her cheeks, but she was bravely smiling at him. "Love you," she called out.

MacGyver blew her a kiss, then got into the car. He backed out of the driveway and didn't dare look back as he drove down the street. If he did, it would hurt all the more. He rubbed his hand over his heart, wondering if leaving would get easier. He had a feeling it wouldn't.

CHAPTER TWELVE

Eleven days, four hours, and thirty-two seconds, that's how long Ricky had been gone. But Addison wasn't counting. Nope. Not at all.

But she had to admit that while it was extremely tough right after he'd left—she'd felt overwhelmed and underprepared to run the household by herself—it eventually got easier.

Except the nights. Those weren't easier. They were excruciating. She missed Ricky the most when she lay down in their bed alone. She didn't have much time to think during the day. She was busy with her job, chauffeuring the kids around, cooking meals, hanging out with Remi, Wren, Josie, and Maggie, not to mention deepening her friendships with Caroline, Jessyka, Cheyenne and the other SEAL wives.

She was surrounded with all the help she could ask for and couldn't be more thankful for her support network. Marrying Ricky had given her not only the man of her dreams, and three children who had quickly become the lights of her life, but a whole group of men and women who were now her rocks.

The only blight was her ex. Brady was still texting Ellory...which would've been fine, except it felt as if he was almost stalking her daughter. He wouldn't leave her alone, sent her messages all day and into the evening. Ellory had started leaving her phone out on the kitchen counter at night to keep it from vibrating on her nightstand with every text, waking her up.

Addison had asked Brady more than once to tone it down, but he'd ignored her, wanting to know what Ellory was doing almost every moment of the day. At first, Ellory was flattered. Had loved being the center of her dad's attention. But it quickly began to annoy her, and as a result, she'd put off meeting with him again.

But Brady was relentless. So eventually, she'd given in and agreed to a meet up—with Addison's approval of course. This time, Remi, along with Ricky's former SEAL friend Dude, were going with them to meet with Brady. Artem, Borysko, and Yana were also going, at Ellory's insistence. She wanted her dad to meet her brothers and sister, in the hopes they'd all become one big happy family. Addison had her doubts, but since they were meeting at the playground at Yana's elementary school, a nice public place where the younger kids would be entertained, it seemed harmless enough.

"Remi is going to meet us there, right?" Ellory asked when they were on their way.

"Yup. And Ricky's friend Dude will be there too."

"He's kinda scary."

"What? Dude isn't scary," Addison protested.

"Mom, he's big and muscular, with dark hair, dark eyes, and he's always...watching."

"True. But Ricky and the rest of the guys on his team are also big and muscular. As for watching, they've all learned to be extremely cautious because of their job. Besides, you've seen him with Taylor. He's a big marshmallow."

"Yeah, okay. He kind of is," Ellory agreed.

"Besides, you can't judge people on their looks. The nicest-looking person, the most good-looking, could be a bad guy, and the scariest could be an angel in disguise."

"Sorry."

"Don't be sorry, sweetheart. I'm glad you're cautious. But you know that Ricky wouldn't have suggested we invite Dude if he didn't trust him one hundred percent."

Addison had sent Ricky an email a few days ago. She was aware that it was unlikely he'd be able to respond, or even get the correspondence, but she'd really needed his advice about Brady. She'd asked Remi and the other women, but Ricky was the one she trusted fully since he'd already met her ex.

To her surprise, he'd responded. It was a short message, but he'd urged her to call Dude and see if he could go with them when they met with Brady. So she'd done just that and, to her relief, Dude was more than happy to meet them at the school.

"Borysko, it's your turn to keep an eye on your sister," Addison said, glancing into the backseat where the kids were sitting.

The boy frowned and tilted his head. "My eye? I do not understand."

"Sorry. Watch her. Make sure she's safe. That she keeps out of trouble."

"Yana good girl. She safe with us." Borysko sounded offended.

"Right, of course she is." Sometimes Addison forgot that these kids had lived a life that most children couldn't even comprehend. They'd been on their own in the middle of a war-torn country, having to scrounge for sustenance and stay hidden from soldiers and others who would do harm to a trio of young kids without a second thought.

"Artem? Are you all right? You've been quiet," Addison said as she pulled into the parking lot of the school.

"Is Ellory going to leave?"

"What? Where would she go?"

"Live with father."

"No. Definitely not. She's simply getting to know him. Remember how I explained she hadn't seen her father since she was a baby? Now that he's back, it's a chance for them both to get to know each other. She isn't leaving our house."

"Promise?" Artem asked.

It was Ellory who answered. "I'm not going anywhere," she told the little boy. "I don't want to live anywhere else except with my mom, Ricky, and you guys. Sorry, little man. You don't get my room." She smiled as she said that last part, teasing her brother.

"Okay," Artem said.

"Okay," Ellory echoed.

"I don't see Brady here yet, but I think it's fine if you guys all went and played. When you see him arrive, please come over and meet him though. All right?"

"Okay, Addy," Artem said politely.

"Swing!" Yana yelled, the sound echoing in the confines of the car.

Borysko took his sister by the hand and helped her out of the car, then he raced her toward the swing set. Artem followed behind at a slower pace. Addison watched as he looked all around, as if scoping out the area. It was obvious his past was sticking with him a little longer than it had his siblings.

Ellory's phone vibrated with a text, and she looked down at the screen. "Dad," she said with a roll of her eyes. "He says he's running late."

Addison held back her snarky comment.

Two cars pulled into the parking lot, and Addison saw Remi behind the wheel of one and Dude in the other.

When the retired SEAL got out of his car, Addison couldn't help but take a deep breath. Ellory was right. Dude *was* a little scary. He had some dark vibes. She wasn't scared of him, per se, but she was definitely glad he was on her side.

"Hi!" Remi said, immediately hugging both Addison and Ellory. "Are you nervous?" she asked the preteen.

Ellory shrugged. "No."

"Right, you've already met Brady and hung out with him. This'll be fun, I think. There are some benches over there, we could go sit?"

Addison nodded, but before she could walk in the direction of the seats, Dude caught her arm and said, "A word?"

"We'll just go on over there and hang out," Remi said cheerily.

Addison felt a little abandoned when both Remi and her daughter left her with the SEAL, but Dude dropped her arm and even took a step backward, giving her space. "I don't mean to frighten you," he said softly.

"You don't."

One of his brows lifted.

"Okay, you make me a little nervous. But that's not the same thing."

"You have nothing to fear from me."

"I know."

"I respect and admire MacGyver. We could've used someone like him on our team. Someone who can figure a way out of any situation. Your husband is a fucking—er... freaking genius. Smart as hell. His mind works in a way that few do. I just wanted to thank you for asking me to come with you today."

His praise of Ricky felt good, even if it wasn't *her* he was complimenting. Ricky was smarter than anyone she'd ever met. She loved that he spent time with Ellory in his garage, teaching her, tinkering with his electronics and other tools. And she loved even more that Ellory seemed to enjoy it just as much as he did. Artem and Borysko seemed more interested in toys and reading, and of course TV, more than using their hands. They might grow out of that, but in the meantime, she was happy that her daughter and husband were bonding.

"I appreciate you taking the time out of your day to come with us," Addison countered.

Dude nodded. "Anything you want me to know about Vogel...other than what MacGyver already told me?"

"Uh...I don't know what he said," Addison replied carefully.

"He doesn't like him," he said bluntly.

"Yeah, they didn't exactly hit it off."

"I think it's very magnanimous of you to agree to let your ex see his daughter. He certainly didn't earn that right over the last twelve years."

He hadn't. Dude wasn't wrong. "I feel as if it should be her choice if she wants a relationship with him. It's true that he disappeared without a word and never tried to get a hold of me, or her, but maybe he's changed. And I'd feel like the worst mom in the world if I didn't at least give them both a chance."

"I agree that a second chance is a good thing, but don't let your guilt put blinders over your eyes."

Addison frowned at the man. "What does that mean?" she asked, feeling a little defensive.

"Just that no matter how much you think a father and daughter should have a relationship, sometimes the best thing is to walk away."

He seemed to be talking in riddles, and it annoyed Addison. "Right."

Dude sighed. "I'm not saying this very well. Just trust your instincts. If they tell you that something is off, it probably is. Maybe Vogel actually had good reasons for staying away from his daughter for the first twelve years of her life. But why come back now? Why does he want to be in her life *now* when he didn't before?"

"I don't know," Addison said softly.

They heard a vehicle enter the lot, going a little too fast for the turn.

"He's here," she said unnecessarily.

Dude stepped toward her, took her arm again and backed her up a dozen or so steps, so they weren't standing in the middle of the parking lot.

Glancing pointedly at her arm, Addison said wryly, "You're very protective."

"You have no idea," he said, before giving a chin lift to the man walking toward them.

Brady looked good that morning. He had on a pair of jeans, a polo shirt, and his hair looked as if it actually had some sort of product taming it. As he got closer, Addison could also smell whatever cologne he was wearing. The difference between him and Dude couldn't be more obvious. Both men wore jeans, but Dude's T-shirt and black combat boots, messy hair, and smell of fresh soap seemed more...real...natural. Manly.

"Hey, Addison," Brady said as he approached. "Who's the dude?"

Addison couldn't help but laugh at that. "Actually, his name *is* Dude. He's a friend of my husband's."

"Dude? Really? That's your name?"

"Yes," he said, crossing his arms over his chest and staring stonily at Brady.

Addison was saved from the awkward moment by Artem, Borysko, and Yana running toward them.

"Oh, I didn't know you were bringing all the kids," Brady said. She knew Ellory had told him about her brothers and sister in some of the texts they'd exchanged. "Do they speak English?" he asked, right before the kids reached them.

His ignorant question irritated Addison. "Of course they do. They're still learning, but they've come an amazingly long way since arriving in the US. Artem, Borysko, Yana, this is Brady, Ellory's biological father."

She'd explained to the kids what biological meant, but for some reason felt the need to keep tacking that on when she talked to anyone about Brady.

"Hello," Brady said in an obnoxiously loud voice. "How. Are. You? I've. Heard. A. Lot. About. You."

Addison stared at her ex. "Why are you talking like that? They're right here, they can hear you just fine. And you don't have to speak so slow either. They understand you."

"Oh. Right."

Artem took a step toward Brady and held out his hand.

"I am Artem. Brother of Ellory, Yana, and Borysko. It is nice to meet you."

Brady looked down at Artem's hand. It was dirty and a little orange from the rust on the monkey bars, where he'd been playing. Instead of taking his hand, Brady simply nodded. "Hi," he said.

Artem stood there for a moment, clearly a little confused, only dropping his arm when Dude put a hand on his little shoulder and gently pulled him backward.

"I am Borysko."

"My name Yana."

Addison couldn't help but smile. The kids were on their best behavior, and they were so cute, formally introducing themselves as politely as they'd been taught.

"Right." Brady turned his head to look for Ellory. She and Remi were still sitting on the bench near the building. They were watching them but hadn't made a move to come over yet.

Just then, Yana said something to her brothers in Ukrainian. Artem answered her in the same language.

"I thought you said they spoke English," Brady said with a frown.

For the thousandth time, Addison wondered what she ever saw in her ex all those years ago. He was being such an ass...and that was probably what Artem was telling his sister. "They do," she said flatly.

"That's not English," he returned.

Addison rolled her eyes. When she realized what she'd done, she had the momentary thought that she'd obviously been spending a lot of time with her daughter, because the eye roll thing had rubbed off on her.

"Obviously," she told him, then turned to the kids. "Go

on and play, you guys. We'll all just be over there by the benches."

Borysko immediately took Yana's hand and led her away from them, back toward the swings. Artem glanced from her to Brady, then to Dude. He nodded at the large former SEAL, then followed his siblings back toward the playground.

Brady looked at his watch and said, "I don't have a lot of time. I got called into work unexpectedly. So if you'll excuse me, I'll just go talk to my daughter now."

Addison wished she was surprised that he wouldn't be able to stay long, but he used to do that with her too. Meet her for a date, then bug out early for one reason or another. She had no reason to think he was lying back then, or now, but her instincts were screaming that he wasn't being truthful. He looked awfully dressed up for someone who had to go to their janitorial job.

When Brady started walking toward Ellory and Remi, Addison and Dude followed.

He turned and stared at them with irritation. "Where are you going?"

"With you to meet with Ellory," Addison said.

"Come on, Addison. I want to talk to her without you hovering. She's not a kid."

"Wrong. She *is* still a kid. She's *my* kid. And honestly, you're still a stranger to her. So it's either have me 'hovering' nearby, as you call it, or you can turn around and get right back in your car and leave."

"And your bodyguard, does he have to be here too?"

"Yes," she said firmly.

"Fine. Whatever," Brady muttered.

By the time they reached the bench, Ellory and Remi had stood.

"Hi! I'm Remi," her friend said. She didn't offer her hand, just smiled at Brady with a friendly grin.

"Brady. Hi, Ellory."

"Hi."

There was an awkward silence as the five of them stood there. Then Addison suggested, "Why don't you two have a seat and chat and we'll just wait over here."

"At least that's something," Brady muttered as he stepped over to the bench.

He and Ellory sat, her daughter looking nervous and unsure as she scuffed her feet in the dirt.

"He's not what I expected," Remi said softly as they gave father and daughter a bit of privacy. Not so much that Addison couldn't hear what they were saying if she concentrated, but enough that Brady might relax a little.

"He's..." Addison struggled to come up with a good adjective.

"An asshole," Dude muttered.

Remi giggled. Addison struggled to keep the smile off her face.

"He's really not. Okay, sometimes he is. But he's trying. I have to give him points for that."

"No, you don't," Dude countered.

Addison was starting to feel stressed. And Ricky's friend wasn't really helping. Although he was probably being more diplomatic than Ricky would be. Her husband definitely didn't like Brady, and if he'd heard the way the man had spoken to Artem, Borysko, and Yana—as if they were all deaf and stupid—it would've rubbed him the wrong way too.

Addison did her best to keep one ear on the conversation between her daughter and Brady while paying attention to the other kids on the playground. She was watching Yana on the swing when she went to stand up and tripped over her feet, falling to the ground. She immediately let out a screech and began to cry.

"I've got her," Dude said, immediately jogging toward her.

"He has a soft spot for girls," Remi said. Then she whispered, "And I heard through the grapevine that he's a dominant."

"A what?" Addison asked.

"A Dom. As in, dominant and submissive? I bet that man is lethal in bed."

"Remi!" Addison scolded. "You're with Kevlar."

"I am. But that doesn't mean I can't look. And I can't help where my mind goes. When Vincent gets all bossy with me in bed, it's hot. *That* man being bossy in bed? I think I'd pee myself with fright...or pass out from lust."

Addison couldn't help but chuckle at that. And Remi wasn't wrong. Dude had a certain dangerous air about him. Even Ellory had picked up on it. It wasn't a stretch to believe that he was into the dominant aspects of BDSM. His wife, Cheyenne, was clearly a lucky woman.

They watched as Dude picked up Yana, then sat right there in the dirt and cuddled her. He kissed her little hand and brushed dirt off her knees. Addison glanced over at Brady, whose lip was curled in derision as he watched the same scene.

Both men were fathers, but one was obviously head and shoulders above the other.

She thought about what Dude had said and wondered why Brady was here. What his end goal could be. She wasn't sure he wanted to be a father, not a real one. So why was he going through the motions with Ellory?

She suddenly realized her daughter looked uncomfortable as she sat next to Brady. She wouldn't look at him and her body was twisted slightly away. Addison wondered what she'd missed. What had her ex said to their daughter while Addison and Remi were talking?

"Everything all right?" she asked, stepping closer to the duo on the bench.

"Of course, why wouldn't it be?" Brady asked gruffly.

"Ellory?" Addison asked, not caring what Brady said, needing reassurance from her daughter that she was okay.

"We're good," she said softly.

"We were just talking about her thing. You know, her disease. I did some research. Wanted to know what she could and couldn't eat, and what happened if she ate something like a fast-food burger."

Addison winced. First, fast food was horrible for Ellory. All the fat and grease didn't do her insides any favors. But secondly, the last thing her daughter would want to talk about was her Crohn's. It was hard enough that she had to deal with diarrhea, gas, enemas, laxatives, and everything else that came with the disease. Talking about all of it with someone else she didn't know well? No, not high on Ellory's list of what she wanted to do.

"Ellory, why don't you tell your dad about the play you're involved in."

"You're acting? That's awesome!"

"No, I'm the lighting director. I'm responsible for managing all the lights for the play."

"Oh," Brady said, his disappointment easy to hear.

Addison's hands fisted. Ellory had worked hard all semester to learn how to run the lighting board, and she'd been so proud of herself. As she watched her daughter's shoulders slump, Addison's anger at her ex grew.

"Got any dances coming up?" Brady asked. "They were

the highlight of my school years. You're too young for prom, but maybe some other formal thing where you can dress up? You could wear heels. That would give you a few more inches."

"She's only in seventh grade," Addison reminded him.

"So? I remember going to a few dances in middle school."

"I'm not interested in those," Ellory said.

"Right. Well, I need to get going," Brady said as he fake-looked at his wristwatch. "It was nice seeing you, Ellory. Maybe we can do this again soon without the watchdogs." Then he stood and headed for his car without a backward glance.

"Nice," Remi muttered.

But Addison's attention was on her daughter. Ellory hadn't even looked up when her father walked away.

"I'll just go see how Yana is," Remi offered, backing up and letting mother and daughter have a few moments alone.

Addison didn't say anything, just sat next to Ellory, letting her take the lead. If she wanted to talk, Addison would listen.

"That was...awkward," Ellory said after a minute.

Addison couldn't help it. She laughed. "Yeah."

"What did you ever see in him?"

Again, Addison found herself smiling. "I was young, sweetie. So was he. And I'd like to think he wasn't so... clueless back then." She leaned sideways and bumped shoulders with her daughter. "Hey."

"Yeah?"

"I love you."

"Love you too. Remember when I told Ricky that I was the lighting director for the show? He thought it was so cool. He brought me home a cake to celebrate. Even though I'd already been the director for a couple of months, he didn't know about it. He still wanted to do something to show me how proud he was."

"Yeah. That cake was horrible. He told me later that he didn't want to bother me by asking me to make something, that he wanted it to be something he took care of himself...to show you how important you were to him."

Ellory laughed. "Right? I only had one bite...because, well, you know. And yeah, yours are so much better. But it was the fact that he made a big deal out of something that was important to me. Brady...he just sounded disappointed."

She wasn't wrong. Addison let out a little hum. "Ricky has been trying really hard to be a positive male role model for you. Even if he makes mistakes—like bringing you a dessert you really shouldn't eat, when your mom already makes the best cakes in a hundred-mile radius. But his heart is in the right place, and it's sweet that he's always trying. I think you're right...Brady isn't really trying all that hard to truly understand you. To get to know you and what you like and don't like."

"Mom?"

"Yeah, sweetheart?"

"When is Ricky coming home? I miss him."

"Me too. And I don't know. Remember, he told us before he left that he never knows how long he'll be on a mission. Sometimes they last months, and other times they're faster, only a couple of weeks."

"Well...I'm not sure I want to see Brady again. At least not anytime soon."

It didn't escape Addison's notice that Ellory was now

calling him "Brady" instead of dad. "That's totally your choice, hon."

She nodded. "He doesn't make me feel very good about myself. But being around Ricky...he gets me. I like him a lot. I wasn't so sure about you getting married at first, but now I can't imagine him *not* being around. He listens to me. Lets me mess with his stuff in the garage with him. Doesn't push me to eat or tell me it's gross when my intestines do their thing. He's...nice."

Addison's heart swelled. Yeah, Ricky *was* nice. She kissed Ellory's temple. "You feel up to playing with the kids?"

"Yeah. You know when I said Dude was kind of scary?"

"Uh-huh."

"I take it back. He's not. I mean, he kinda still looks that way, but seeing him with Yana, and how he took your arm and made you step back when Brady drove into the parking lot like a bat out of hell? Protective isn't scary. It's comforting."

"Yeah, honey. It is. But I feel as if I have to say this... there's protective, then there's overbearing, psycho, stalker protective."

Ellory laughed. "I know. I've seen some of those crime shows you like to watch. It's okay for a boyfriend, or a girl-friend for that matter, to want to know where you are and if you're all right. It's another thing to call or text forty times, wanting to know when you'll be home. Or isolating you from friends and family, or making you feel like crap for wanting to hang out with them."

"Right. As long as you know the difference."

Ellory turned to look at her mom. "The way Ricky watches over the kids is protective. How his eyes watch you when you're baking in the kitchen, as if he can't believe you're there and he's counting all the ways he lucked out, is protective. How Dude immediately ran toward Yana when she fell, even though it was obvious she wasn't really hurt, just startled...that's protective. I know the difference."

Addison did her best not to cry. Her daughter really was growing up, and she both loved and hated it. Time went too fast. The next thing she knew, she'd blink and Ellory would be moving out, going to college. She wasn't ready.

"Jeez. Don't cry, Mom," Ellory said with a familiar roll of her eyes. "I'll go tire out the kids while you and Remi sit here and gossip."

"Sounds good. I'm ready to go when you guys are. Just let me know."

"I will." Ellory stood and headed for the playground. Then she turned and said softly, "You know? Sometimes what you don't have seems like the biggest prize. Something you want more than anything in the world. But then when you get it, you look around and realize you already *had* everything you've ever wanted."

As Ellory jogged over to where the younger kids and Dude were playing, Addison's vision blurred once again.

"You okay?" Remi asked, materializing as if out of nowhere.

"Yeah, I'm good," Addison said, wiping her eyes. "I just realized that my daughter is way smarter than I was at her age. Hell, than I was at twenty-one."

"She's a good kid. You've done an amazing job raising her."

That compliment meant more to Addison than she could put into words. All the sleepless nights, all the tears, the worries when the doctors were trying to figure out what was wrong with her medically, the trials and tribulations of navigating school and friends...knowing she'd done something right meant the world to her.

"Come on, you look like you need to swing. Or maybe go down that slide."

"Remember those old-timey merry-go-rounds they used to have in the seventies and eighties where kids would go flinging off them when it got going really fast?"

"Yeah?"

"We need one of those."

Remi laughed. "But we don't need the broken bones that come with them. We'll have to be satisfied with third-degree burns on our legs and hands from the million-degree metal slide."

"Except this one's plastic," Addison said with a grin.

"Darn it. That takes away all the fun."

"Thanks for coming today," Addison told her.

"Of course. That's what friends are for."

Addison knew she probably shouldn't ask what she was thinking, but she couldn't stop herself. "Do you have any idea when they'll be back?"

She didn't have to explain who "they" were. Remi knew. "No. But I'm hoping it's soon."

"Me too," she said quietly.

"It's crazy how much we miss them, isn't it? I mean, when they're home they can drive us crazy, but the second they aren't here, we'd do anything to get the crazy back."

"Yeah."

"I'll see if I can get Dude alone and ask him if he knows anything. Sometimes the other SEALs know stuff family isn't supposed to. Maybe he'll throw me a bone and let something slip."

"That man? Let something slip? You're dreaming."

"Wow. I could go so many X-rated places with that, but I won't. Because that would be wrong to lust over someone else's man," Remi said with a huge smile.

Addison barked out a laugh, then sobered. "Anything he could tell us would be a huge relief."

An hour later, the kids were tired and hungry and ready to head home. As it turned out, Dude hadn't known anything about the mission Ricky and the others were on, but he promised to see what he could find out. Which made Addison feel a teensy bit better.

That evening, after the kids all went to bed, Addison was sitting in the living room, feeling a little sorry for herself. She was lonely. Which always surprised her a little, because she'd spent plenty of nights sitting by herself watching TV. But that was before Ricky had come into her life. Before she'd said yes to a marriage of convenience that had somehow turned into the marriage she'd always wanted.

Ellory's phone vibrated for what seemed like the tenth time since she'd gone to bed. Picking up the cell, Addison saw it was Brady texting...*again*. Ellory had tried to be nice earlier, telling him she wasn't sure when they could get together again, since she was really busy with school. But Brady clearly hadn't gotten the hint. Or he'd simply chosen to ignore it. Now, Addison was officially done.

Ellory: This is Addison. You need to stop. Ellory is in bed.

Brady: Already? She's not a baby.

Ellory: Yes, already. And if you keep hounding her, you'll just push her away. Give her some space, Brady.

Brady: You're just trying to keep me from my daughter, and I won't have it.

Ellory: I'm not trying to keep you from her. I know her better than you do, and I'm telling you that you're smothering her. You need to cut back on the texts and calls and begging to see her.

Brady: That's what you want, isn't it? To keep me at arm's length.

Addison sighed and let her head drop to the cushion behind her. Brady was being an idiot. She was trying to help him, yet he was doubling down on playing the victim. And she was definitely tired of him texting at all hours and acting like a twelve-year-old shouldn't have a bedtime schedule. Their daughter was mature for her age, but she was still a kid.

Ellory: I told you, don't text this late again. Do not force this issue. If you do, I'll take you to court, and who do you think the judge will side with? Me. You haven't paid me a cent in child support and you haven't been any kind of father to her at all in her entire life. I will do whatever it takes to protect Ellory from anyone or anything that might do her harm, including her own biological father. Don't mess with me, Brady. I'm serious.

Brady: Don't fuck with ME, Addison. You don't want to know how far I'll go to see my kid.

Unease ran up her spine. She had no idea why Brady was being so insistent, but she was done trying to reason with him. She also wanted to leave the texts on the phone so Ellory could see them, but she wouldn't stoop to her ex's level. Besides, Ellory was a smart kid. She was already seeing her father for who he really was.

She deleted the texts and put the phone on Do Not Disturb. She could really use Ricky's levelheaded advice right about now. Although he was anything but calm when it came to Brady. Even bringing up his name could make the little furrow in his brow deepen.

For a moment, Addison wished she'd never run into her ex. He was a complication she didn't need or want. Her life was stressful enough as it was. Dealing with Brady —who it seemed more and more obvious had some sort of mystery agenda—wasn't something she wanted to even think about anymore. But she didn't have a choice. She'd have to ride this out until Brady got tired of playing the role of doting father and the real reason he was so insistent on getting to know his daughter came to light.

"Wherever you are, I hope you're all right, Ricky," Addison whispered into the quiet evening. "Come home soon. I miss you."

* * *

Brady slammed his phone down. His plan to get closer to his daughter wasn't going the way he'd expected. He'd had every intention of quickly sweet-talking the girl into liking him, then encouraging Ellory to ask her mother to spend time with him by herself. The moment that happened, he'd immediately take her to his contact, get his cut of the money, while she was shipped off to a dealer overseas. It was handy that Riverton was on the coast; his contact had perfected the art of quickly shipping bodies to various contacts in Asia. Of course, most bodies were already deceased. Having a live donor? That was better in every way, because the organs would stay fresh.

And Brady had already decided the con didn't have to stop there. He'd get his share of the money for bringing in Ellory...but he could also turn around and demand a ransom for the girl from Addison. She'd pay whatever was asked of her, Brady had no doubt. He'd hire someone to leave a note at their house or make a phone call, asking for ransom, complete with instructions on how and when to pay, all while he played the worried father.

He'd get double the money!

But first, he had to get Ellory to answer his goddamn texts.

The girl was weird. Sickly and pale and just fucking *odd*. It was embarrassing. And he had nothing in common with her; she didn't take after him in any way. He didn't even like talking to her. And the feeling was clearly mutual. It was obvious he'd have to come up with a new plan. One that still ensured he could get Ellory alone.

He didn't know how, but he'd figure it out. The amount of money she'd bring in was too great to just give up. No, he was in this now, he had to see it through. Especially after his associate had mentioned trying to cut out the middleman, since they were dealing with a rare live body. Instead of selling to one of his contacts, he was working on finding a buyer for her organs himself...which meant an even *bigger* payday. Brady couldn't back out now.

His daughter was a means to an end, and he would win. He always did.

CHAPTER THIRTEEN

MacGyver was exhausted. The mission had a few small glitches and had taken longer than they'd hoped. But in the end, they'd located the terrorist they'd been tasked with taking down and had stopped yet another plan to kill innocent US citizens. But eliminating terrorists was like playing Whac-A-Mole. They'd get one bad guy, then another immediately popped up to take his spot.

Being a SEAL was rewarding, but it was also a never-ending job. In the past, MacGyver had gotten depressed over the fact that there would always be humans trying to kill other humans, usually for no good reason. But today, even though he was tired, he was also filled with adrenaline.

They were almost home. They'd been debriefed in Germany, and back in Riverton, they'd have several meetings regarding the mission and what they could do better next time, but before that, MacGyver would get to see his family.

Even the thought was enough to make him feel buzzed.

"It's nice, isn't it?" Safe asked.

"What?"

"Having people waiting at home for you."

"Yeah, it is. How's Wren's job going with her father?"

"Great. She loves it. And finding her dad and her three half-brothers was such a blessing. How're things going with Ellory and her biological father?"

MacGyver frowned. "*Not* great. Vogel is nothing like Wren's father, that's for sure."

"That sucks. Is Ellory okay?"

"I don't really know. I hate that I missed this last meeting they had, but from what Addison told me, it didn't go so well. She said she'd tell me the details when I got home."

"Well, they're all lucky they have you. You're a great father, MacGyver. I have to admit when you said you wanted to keep Artem, Borysko, and Yana, I had my doubts. I mean, what do we know about raising kids? I want kids myself, but I'm also selfish enough to want to spend time with Wren before we go down that road. You jumped into fatherhood with both feet without any kind of life preserver."

"I can't tell you how I knew those three kids were meant to be mine. Something happened when we were skulking around that burned-out city in Ukraine. The thought of leaving them was so painful, I couldn't even contemplate it."

"Well, we're all very happy for you. And I meant what I said, you're a really good dad. The role suits you."

"Thanks."

By the time they landed, MacGyver was antsy as hell. All he wanted was to get home and see the people who'd become his whole world.

"You gonna call Addison and give her a heads-up that you're back?" Preacher asked.

"No, I think I'm just going to go straight home and surprise everyone. It's early enough that they should all still be awake."

"Not sure that's the best idea," Preacher replied with a frown.

"Why not?"

"I don't know. You might give them a heart attack if you just walk in."

MacGyver grinned. "I'm willing to risk it."

"Well, don't come crying to us if you get read the riot act for not telling Addison the second your feet touched the ground back here in the US."

MacGyver considered his friend's suggestion for a moment, but he really wanted to see Addy's and the kids' reactions when they realized he was home. Besides, he didn't want to waste any time on the phone when he could be on his way to holding his wife again.

The SEAL team scattered in the parking lot and MacGyver got into Addison's VW Bug, and thankfully it started right up. He couldn't help but smile at being in her car. She loved this thing. He hoped she didn't have any issues with his Explorer while he was gone.

A million questions were rolling around in his head. How was Ellory doing with her Crohn's? Was Yana talking more? Had Borysko learned a bunch of new words like he'd asked? Did Artem get a good grade on his most recent science homework? And Addison...was she completely frazzled? Had she been able to juggle everything all right? He worried about her most of all.

The lights were on in the house when he pulled into the driveway, and MacGyver couldn't stop smiling. This was like Christmas, Easter, and the Fourth of July all at the same time. He left his duffle bag in the car, deciding to deal with it in the morning, and headed for the front door. It was locked—thank goodness; he'd begged Addison to keep it locked anytime they were home—and after using his key to open it, he quietly stepped inside the house.

Taking a deep breath, MacGyver felt his chin quiver. He never thought a scent could bring him to his knees. But after spending weeks in dirt and grime, smelling his own and his teammates' body odor, the scent of freshly baked cookies had the power to bring tears to his eyes.

He heard the kids laughing, and it was just another layer of happiness that was almost too much for MacGyver. He walked silently toward the living room and saw his family lounging on the couches, covered in blankets he hadn't owned before marrying Addison. The scene was straight out of a Hallmark movie, except Yana's bangs had recently been cut haphazardly, Borysko had a bruise on his forehead, Artem's shirt had some kind of food stain, and Ellory was rolling her eyes at something one of her brothers said.

And Addison...she looked even more beautiful than she had before MacGyver left. She had dark circles under her eyes, her hair was in curly disarray, she was wearing one of his Navy T-shirts...and he couldn't stop staring at her.

This was all his. The mess, the chaos. The woman. The kids. They were *his*. It was so hard to believe. And it made what he did for a living completely worth it. The thought of any of these precious humans being caught in the crosshairs of a man like the one they'd just taken out was abhorrent.

"Ricky?"

Ellory's incredulous cry silenced the room for a split

second—then pandemonium broke out. The kids screamed and leaped up from the couches and ran toward him. Even Ellory. MacGyver went down on a knee and held out his arms. He was bowled over by his exuberant children as they practically tackled him.

"You home!"

"Ricky!"

"When you get here?"

"I can't believe you didn't let us know you were back!"

MacGyver couldn't stop smiling. He'd never been so happy in all his life. This was why those cheesy videos about soldiers surprising their families and kids were so popular. Why people cried when they watched them. He was experiencing that kind of emotion firsthand.

Looking up through his pile of children, MacGyver saw Addison standing above them with her hand over her mouth, tears running down her face. For a split second, he panicked, wondering if those tears were happy ones or not. But then she fell to her knees and joined the pile of bodies on the floor.

MacGyver laughed as he tried to wrap his arms around not only his kids, but his wife as well. Of course, that didn't work, partly because Yana came within two millimeters of kneeing him in the balls, Artem was practically yelling in his ear, asking him question after question, Borysko was lying like dead weight against him, and Ellory was kneeling right against his side, smiling like a loon.

It took a moment or two, but eventually MacGyver got everyone on their feet again and turned to Addison. "Honey, I'm home," he joked.

She let out an adorable mix between a snort and a laugh, then threw herself at him. MacGyver went back on a foot, but held steady as he hugged her tight. *This.* This was what he'd dreamed of. Waited for. Yearned for. Holding his wife.

But she didn't stay in his arms for nearly long enough. She pulled back and her gaze swept over him from head to toe. "Are you all right? You look like you've lost weight. Did you get hurt? Is everyone else okay?"

"I'm good, everyone else is fine, and I probably did lose a few pounds, but whatever smells so damn good I'm sure will put the weight back on me in no time."

"Mom made pound cake," Artem said, leaning against MacGyver as if he couldn't bear to be away from him for a second. "We never ate. But it is good."

"Strawberries!" Yana exclaimed from his other side.

"You had pound cake with strawberries?" MacGyver asked.

"Yes!" Borysko told him with a huge smile.

"And what happened to your hair?" MacGyver asked, brushing an uneven lock back from Yana's forehead.

"She got a hold of a pair of kitchen scissors," Addison said dryly, with a small shake of her head.

"And you, Borysko? That's a big bruise on your forehead."

"Fell at school." Then he clapped his hands together, obviously showing MacGyver how he'd hit the floor with his head.

MacGyver winced. "Ouch. But you're okay?"

"I am okay," he said with a smile.

"And how are you, Ellory? School going all right?"

"If you're asking about Chrys, she hasn't been bothering me. Well, she did once. Before school. She came up to me with some of her friends and started saying mean things, but I just stared at her with big scary eyes, like you suggested. When I didn't say anything or do anything, she got weirded out and left me alone."

MacGyver chuckled. "Good. And your theater work? How's that going?"

She beamed. It was the right question to ask, apparently.

"It's awesome! I love it. Before this year, I thought theater was only about acting, which I didn't want to do. But I love being behind the scenes. I was actually able to fix one of the lights last week. It went out and wouldn't work and no one could figure it out. But I channeled my inner MacGyver and tweaked this and turned that, wiggled a few wires, and it started working again!"

"That's my girl!" MacGyver praised.

It took over an hour to get caught up with each of the four kids and what they'd been doing while he was away. As he gave all his attention to the children, Addison quietly heated up some leftovers and brought him a fork and plate while he was talking. Then she took the dirty dishes away when he was done, bringing him a glass of water and a large chunk of pound cake smothered with strawberries.

The kids weren't wrong, it was one of the best desserts he'd ever eaten. His taste buds were tingling as he enjoyed every bite.

It took another forty-five minutes to get the kids into bed. They were keyed up because he was home, and they all wanted to talk to him at the same time. MacGyver read three stories to Yana, tucked the boys in and reassured them that he'd be home for a while. He had a quiet moment with Ellory to ask about her health. He told her that he wanted to hear all about her visit with her father when they had a bit more time and privacy, and to his relief, she simply nodded, didn't say she didn't want to talk about it.

MacGyver was exhausted—from the trip, the emotional reunion with his family—but he felt a contentment deep in his bones. This was what he'd been missing. Yes, it was tiring being a father to four children and making sure all their different needs were met, but extremely rewarding as well. Thinking about what Artem, Borysko, and Yana would be doing, where they'd be sleeping or what they'd be eating if he hadn't brought them to the States, was enough to give him an anxiety attack.

Now, finally, the kids were in bed and he could turn his attention to his wife.

Addison was waiting for him in the living room. She'd cleaned the kitchen, folded the blankets, and had started getting the kids' lunches ready for the next day. Once again, he was amazed at how good a caretaker she was.

Without a word, he walked over to her and took her in his arms. Neither of them spoke for a long moment.

"Welcome home," she murmured into his hair. "To the crazy."

"I missed it," MacGyver reassured her.

She chuckled against him, then pulled back, keeping her arms around his waist. "I can't believe you didn't call and warn me you were coming home," she said with a small frown.

"Didn't want to take the time. The only thing I could think about was getting here and seeing everyone."

"All right, I'll forgive you this time. But *next* time, you had better call me the second those wheels touch down."

MacGyver chuckled. "Yes, ma'am." He studied her for a moment. "You good? You look exhausted."

"I think that's my line," she joked.

"Addison," MacGyver warned.

"I'm fine," she said. "Just tired. I thought being a single mother to one kid was hard. Four is a whole new level."

MacGyver felt guilty for leaving her.

But she shook her head and said, "No."

"No what?"

"No, you aren't allowed to feel guilty. You're doing what you're meant to do. I can handle the kids while you're gone. But I did miss you. I thought about you every second of the day. Wondered where you were, what you were doing, if you were hurt...it wasn't fun."

MacGyver's heart skipped a beat. What was she saying?

"I understand what Caroline, Alabama, and the other women tried to tell me now. That while being a Navy wife isn't easy, it's damn hard at times, but it's also rewarding. Knowing that I'm taking care of things here while you're off doing your job...it makes me feel needed."

"Oh, you're needed, Mrs. Douglas."

She smiled a little at that. "Mrs. Douglas. I still haven't gotten used to that being my name."

"And speaking of names...don't think I missed Artem calling you 'Mom.' I didn't want to make a big deal out of it when he said it, because I didn't know if it was a regular thing by now or what. How do you feel about that?" MacGyver asked.

Addison smiled. "It's awesome," she whispered. "And that was the first time," she added, still grinning.

"This has been the best homecoming I've ever had. You, the kids, hearing Artem call you Mom...it's all more than I ever thought I'd get."

Addison hugged him tightly and MacGyver closed his eyes, appreciating the hell out of the woman in his arms.

He pulled back and slowly threaded his fingers through her auburn hair. The strands clung to him as if they were just as glad to have him home as he was to be there. "I'm dead on my feet," he admitted. "All I want is to sleep in my own bed and hold my wife."

"I think that can be arranged," she said with a smile. "Go on and shower. Wait, where's your bag? I can get that from the car while you clean up."

"Leave it. It's full of nasty-smelling stuff you don't want any part of. I'll take care of it tomorrow. I don't have to go in until noon. We have a debrief meeting with the commander and that's it. I'll pick up the boys tomorrow."

Addison sighed. "I missed you so much. I swear I've put at least a thousand miles on your car driving everyone around."

"I think it's about time we got the boys on board with taking the bus to and from school. They're more comfortable in their surroundings and their English is so much better."

Addison nodded. "I was thinking the same thing. It's a lot, dropping them off and picking them up every day, along with Yana and Ellory."

"Come on. No more shop talk. Our bed is calling our names."

Addison smiled and tilted her head. "Is that what that sound was? I thought it was a hallucination."

He loved this woman. So damn much. After making sure the house was locked up tight, MacGyver headed for the bathroom and a much-needed shower. By the time he was done, had scrubbed his teeth three times, and even put on some lotion—the heat in the Middle East was brutal on his skin—Addison was in bed and waiting for him.

Sighing in contentment at the feel of clean sheets and a comfortable mattress, MacGyver had barely settled onto his back before his wife was in his arms.

Closing his eyes, he did his best to control his emotions. His reunion with his kids had been poignant, but this...lying here in his bed, his wife in his arms, was overwhelming.

"Welcome home, Ricky," Addison whispered against his chest. "I love you."

"I love you too. So damn much."

MacGyver thought he'd lay awake for a while, enjoying the feel of being home, being clean, and having Addy in his arms. But instead, he fell asleep almost instantly. Feeling safe and loved—along with being up for almost thirty-six hours—served as a great sleep aid.

* * *

Addison was so tired, but she couldn't sleep. She'd dreamed of this every night since Ricky had left. Of lying in his arms. He smelled like lemons. He'd obviously used her lotion before coming to bed. The feel of his chest rising and falling as he breathed in and out was mesmerizing. He was back...and relatively unharmed. She hadn't missed the bruises on his chest and arms, but since he didn't even act like they hurt at all, she did her best to dismiss them.

Her husband was home. The time he was gone had been more difficult than she'd ever admit. She worried that she wasn't doing or saying the right things for the kids at every turn. Stressed about her ex and Ellory. Wondered how she was going to finish her baking jobs and get everything else done as well. The laundry was backed up, the house was a mess...but everyone was happy and healthy, so she was going to count that as a win.

She hadn't talked about tomorrow's schedule with Ricky, as was their usual routine when they went to bed, but he was obviously more than exhausted. He'd fallen asleep in seconds. They had time to talk about who had what activity and which chores needed to be done in the morning, during breakfast.

Sharing the first meal of the day with her husband wasn't something she would ever take for granted again. Nor all the things he did for their family. Yes, he worked during the day, but he still managed to do so many things that eased the workload on her shoulders.

Addison eventually fell asleep, one leg hitched over Ricky's thighs, her arm around his belly, clutching him to her tightly even as she slept.

She wasn't sure what woke her up, had no idea what time it was. It was still mostly dark in the room, except for the glow coming from the nightlights on the walls they'd installed in case one of the kids needed something in the middle of the night and came into the room.

In a flash, the evening before came back to her. Ricky was home.

"Sorry," he whispered, "my sleep schedule is whacked. I woke up, had my beautiful wife in my arms, drooling on me—but I won't mention that—and my cock, which has behaved itself for the last few weeks, suddenly developed a mind of its own."

Addison chuckled and looked up at her husband. Ricky was hovering over her, his weight on an elbow as his other hand was under her...his...shirt, playing with her nipple. She could feel his erection against her thigh.

Immediately, her libido switched on. She hadn't felt the

slightest urge to pleasure herself while he'd been gone. She'd been too busy, too worried to think about sex. But now that he was home, safe and sound and in bed with her...it was all she could think about.

Without hesitation, she sat up a little and whipped the T-shirt over her head. Then she shoved her underwear over her hips and kicked them away before lying back down and smiling at Ricky. "Hurry. Before the kids wake up and demand the foot-high stack of pancakes they eat every morning. I swear they have hollow legs. I don't know how they pack it all in."

Ricky smiled but did as she ordered, lowering his head to take one of her nipples into his mouth. Arching against him, Addison moaned softly. She'd missed this. Sex with Ricky was out-of-this-world amazing. He made her feel things she'd never felt before, and certainly couldn't duplicate with her own fingers and toys.

Feeling impatient, she reached down and shoved her hand inside his boxers, wrapping her fingers around his erection.

"Fuck, hon. Yes." His hips pushed into her hand, and Addison smiled.

Then he was a whirl of motion, pushing his boxers off and getting on his knees between her legs. He shoved his hands under her ass and lifted her hips off the mattress at the same time he lowered his head.

Addison jolted in pleasure at the way he literally attacked her pussy. There was no finesse in his actions. No gentle wooing. He went right for her clit and licked and sucked at her as if he was a dying man, and she was his only sustenance.

It had been long enough, and he was talented enough,

that it took only a few minutes before the telltale shaking of her thighs began as she approached orgasm.

The second she tensed around him, he lifted his head, dropped her ass back to the bed, and pushed her legs apart. She was still coming when he shoved his cock inside her in one quick thrust. The feel of him filling her to the brim prolonged her orgasm. As did the way he began to fuck her hard and fast.

He leaned over, bracing his hands next to her shoulders. His hips thrust powerfully as he took her. Addison reached up and grasped his biceps while staring into his eyes. Ricky didn't take his gaze from hers as he claimed her.

Every time he bottomed out, he pressed against her clit, making her twitch in pleasure. Had sex with him ever been *this* amazing? Probably. But it had been too long and she'd obviously forgotten.

"I love you," she breathed.

"Love. You. So. Much," he said in time with his thrusts.

It wasn't long before his rhythm began to falter and she knew he was close. Addison leaned up and took his earlobe between her teeth and sucked it hard. That was all it took. Ricky groaned and pushed deeper than he'd been before as he came, collapsing against her.

After a long moment, he went up on his elbows and said, "Holy hell, woman, you almost killed me."

"I didn't do anything but lie here," she teased.

"I know," he said seriously. "I love you so much. You're my everything. With you, I'm the man I always wanted to be."

"Ricky," she said, on the verge of tears. She'd missed him so much. Having him home safely was a dream come true. She refused to think about all the times in the future he'd be leaving for missions. She wanted to think that the first deployment would be the most difficult, but she had a feeling they'd only get harder and harder.

She shifted under him, and he asked, "Am I squishing you?"

"No, you feel perfect."

"Oh hell."

"What?"

"I didn't use anything...*again*. I'm sorry! I swear I'm not doing it on purpose. But all I could think about was your taste on my tongue, then getting inside you."

"It's okay."

He stared at her for a beat. "Are you on anything yet? Did you see a doctor while I was gone?"

Addison bit her lip, looking away. She'd meant to. It had been the perfect time to start birth control. But with everything going on with the kids and her job, she hadn't gotten around to it. She shook her head nervously.

"Look at me, Addy."

She raised her eyes and met his gaze.

"Four kids is a lot. More than you probably ever thought you'd have on your plate. Adding a baby into the mix would be crazy. Would ramp up our already jampacked lives to the max. With that said...the thought of you having my baby? A little red-haired boy or girl? I want that *so bad*."

She felt his dick twitch deep inside her body.

"Me too," she whispered.

"Fuck," Ricky sighed, lowering his forehead to hers. "You're killin' me, Addy."

"The timing isn't great. We don't even know if we'll get permanent custody of the kids as it is."

"We will," Ricky said with conviction. "Tex will come

through. The house isn't big enough for another, though. But we can probably get by with the baby in here with us for a little while."

Hearing her big bad husband talk about having a baby with her as if it was a done deal felt surreal. "It might not happen right away," she whispered.

"How long did it take you to conceive Ellory?" he asked.

"Um...one time. When the condom broke," she admitted.

Ricky chuckled, and Addison felt it from the inside. "Right. There's always the possibility that there could be a problem with my sperm, but we can play things by ear. So...is that it? Did we decide we aren't going to use birth control...that we'll let mother nature do her thing?"

Addison felt giddy inside. Jittery, but in a good way. "I think we did."

Ricky began to rock his hips slowly and sensuously, his cock moving in and out of her soaking-wet sheath. "This is gonna be fun."

Just then, the sound of Borysko's too-loud voice, yelling at his brother in Ukrainian, came from outside their room.

"Fuck," Ricky sighed with a grimace.

"Fun until our kids cock block us," Addison said with a giggle.

Ricky lifted his hips until his cock slipped out of her body, then he shifted to his knees. His erection brushed against her belly as he got up on all fours, leaning down to kiss her. "We'll just have to get creative. If we want Baby Douglas to join us anytime soon, that is."

"I have one request," Addison said as the voices outside their room got louder.

"Yeah? What's that?"

"We are not naming this baby, or any baby in our future, Doug."

Ricky chortled. "Doug Douglas. No way in hell. I'm going to shower, get myself off so I can be presentable to our children at the breakfast table. But...after the kids are at school? I want you back here. Under me. Taking my cock and my come. Now that you've said yes to a baby, I'm going to want to fill you every chance I get."

"I've created a monster."

"Yup," Ricky agreed. Then he kissed her once more before hopping off the bed and heading for the bathroom. His hard dick bobbed in front of him as he went, making Addison giggle again.

She quickly followed his lead, climbing out of bed, throwing back on the shirt she'd been wearing, a clean pair of underwear and a pair of sweatpants. Then she went to the door to their bedroom and slipped out. She'd use the kids' bathroom to freshen up. She had little ones to get ready for school, pancakes to make, laundry to do, cakes to bake...and apparently a husband to make love to. Life couldn't get any better.

CHAPTER FOURTEEN

"You look different," Maggie told Addison a few days later, when the entire team had gotten together at Safe and Wren's house. They were celebrating another successful mission, everyone coming home safely, and simply the joy of spending time with friends.

"I was thinking the same thing," Remi said.

"I'm just happy Ricky is home."

"Girl, we're all happy our guys are back," Wren said with feeling.

"No. I mean, yes, we are," Maggie said. "But Addison looks extra happy. Did Tex come through with the adoption approval yet?"

"Well, we got a call from our case agent and she said that she saw no reason why we wouldn't be approved. The kids are happy and their interviews went really well. All three said they wanted to stay with us, that they didn't want to go back to their country. Our home visits have all been good, and of course our background checks came back clean."

"That's great. And...?" Maggie pressed.

Addison knew she was blushing. She couldn't help it. "And...things with Ricky and I are going really well."

Everyone had huge smiles on their faces.

"We know what *that* means," Remi said with a little smirk.

"Is this when we get to talk about sex?" Wren asked.

Everyone giggled.

"I hate when Nate is deployed," Josie said. "Especially after what happened to him and his previous team, not to mention that little Iran thing. But, I have to say, I *really* like when he comes home. I swear a few weeks without makes him extra horny."

"Right?" Remi agreed. "I'm not complaining, but if I didn't know better, I'd think Vincent was a teenage boy again."

"Try mixing in pregnancy hormones and a guy who didn't have any experience before me," Maggie said dryly. "I'm surprised I can walk normally."

"Yup," Wren said.

"That's it?" Remi asked. "Just 'yup'?"

"Uh-huh. I'm in complete agreement with you guys. All of what you said and more."

"More?" Josie asked. "More would kill me."

"You're being awfully quiet," Maggie told Addison.

"I'm with Wren. I agree. But..." She hesitated, then decided to just go for it. If she couldn't talk to these women about her life, who *could* she talk to? "It's even more intense when you and your husband decide not to worry about birth control and let nature take its course."

All four of the other women squealed in excitement.

"I knew something was up!" Maggie crowed.

"Another kid? You're made of stronger stuff than me!"

"That's awesome."

"How are you not walking bowlegged?"

Addison couldn't keep the huge smile off her face. She loved these women and felt so blessed to call them friends. When she'd married Ricky, she'd not only gained a family, financial security, help with Ellory's medical bills, and a man she loved more than she'd ever thought possible... she'd gotten a group of friends who were the best support system she'd ever had.

"Calm down," she told them. "There's no guarantee we'll get pregnant anytime soon."

"That's what we thought," Maggie sighed.

"You aren't worried about how tough it'll be with the four you've already got?" Wren asked.

"Oh, I'm worried. Freaking out. But here's the thing—I raised Ellory on my own. That wasn't a walk in the park. Not at all. But now that I have Ricky, and you guys, and even Caroline and her crew, I feel as if I'm much more prepared this time around. I know it won't be easy. Starting over doesn't *completely* appeal. But...having Ricky's child? I can't stop picturing him holding an infant in his muscular arms. Just thinking about it makes my ovaries want to explode."

"Giiiiirl. Now I'm thinking the same thing," Josie whined. "Nate wants kids. No, that's wrong. He wants twins. Like him and his brother. And since they run in his family, with my luck, I'll probably have triplets or more."

"That would be awesome!" Remi breathed.

"That's because you wouldn't have to carry them around and squeeze them out your hoo-hah!" Josie countered.

Everyone roared in laughter.

"We want kids too," Wren said. "But we also both want some time with just us first."

"Well, you can practice with my baby when it arrives," Maggie said, rubbing her belly.

"And anytime you want to take Artem, Borysko, and Yana for an afternoon, just let me know," Addison threw in with a wink.

"Rent-a-baby! We can rotate them through our houses!" Remi exclaimed.

"If you guys would hurry up and get preggo already, our kids can all grow up together and have sleepovers and stuff," Maggie countered.

"That's not a bad idea," Josie mused.

"What's not a bad idea?" Safe asked as he and Blink approached where the women were sitting on the back porch. They'd been entertaining Artem and Borysko in the yard while the women chatted. Yana and Ellory were inside with the other guys, doing who knows what. Yana was probably watching a Disney movie and there was no telling with Ellory.

"Oh my, look at the time!" Josie exclaimed, looking at her wrist. A wrist that wasn't wearing a watch. "I forgot about that...thing...we needed to do at home," she told Blink.

He stared at her for a beat, then nodded as if he knew exactly what Josie was talking about.

"Have fun," Remi called out, when Josie stood to join Blink.

"Yeah, but not too much!" Wren added.

Josie smiled at everyone, then grabbed Blink's arm and towed him into the house.

"What the hell was that?" Safe asked.

Wren stood and hooked her arm through his. "Don't worry about it, hon."

"They're cool though?"

"More like red hot, I'd say," Wren answered with a smirk.

Safe had a confused look on his face, and Addison couldn't help laughing with the other women. Their men had no idea what they were in for tonight. All the talk about babies had obviously struck a chord, and Addison wasn't the only one who seemed to be eager for some alone time with her man.

"Addy. Cookies?" Borysko asked. He was sweaty and smelled like a little boy who'd been running around in the warm sun. Addison didn't hate it. Not at all.

"I think, yeah, we could all use some cookies about now. Run inside and wash your hands." The little boy turned to run into the house, but Addison stopped him by adding, "And take Artem with you."

Borysko made a U-turn and ran out into the yard to get his brother. Artem seemed to resist until he heard the word cookie, then he was chasing Borysko into the house, pushing him to try to get in front to beat him to the bathroom and wash up.

The women all went inside and Addison's gaze swept the room, looking for her loved ones. Yana was sitting on the couch staring down at her iPad, completely engrossed. Ricky was talking to Flash and Smiley. And Ellory...

Addison frowned. Her daughter was sitting in one of the chairs in the living room, her knees drawn up to her chest. She had her cell in her hand, and she was scowling at it even as her fingers flew over the screen.

She was so engrossed in what she was doing, she didn't

notice her mom standing next to her until Addison cleared her throat.

Looking up, Ellory seemed frustrated.

"What's up?" Addison asked.

In response, Ellory sighed. "He won't stop."

Addison's belly clenched. She knew who "he" was. "Did you tell him you were busy?"

"Yeah. He just tried to make me feel guilty."

Addison held out her hand. "Let me see, honey."

Without hesitation, Ellory handed her phone to her mom.

An arm wound around Addison's waist, and she leaned into Ricky. "Something wrong?"

"You want to go supervise the kids?" Addison asked her daughter. "Make sure they don't eat twelve cookies and throw up?"

"Okay."

As soon as she was out of earshot, Ricky said, "He's still texting her?"

"Apparently." Addison clicked open the messaging app and held it so Ricky could read over her shoulder.

Brady: Hey, whatcha doing?

    Ellory: Hanging out

    Brady: I'd love to see you again.

    Ellory: Yeah

    Brady: When?

    Ellory: IDK

    Brady: I'd love to just hang out with you on your own. Your mom tends to hover.

    Ellory: Maybe

    Brady: So when? What about this weekend?

Ellory: I have a play

Brady: Can I come watch?

Ellory: I don't think you'd like it. I'm not IN the play, just doing the lights

Brady: Oh yeah. How about lunch?

Ellory: I'm fasting right now

Brady: So when? Come on, El. I'm trying here.

Ellory: IDK I have to talk to my mom

Brady: If you don't want to, just come out and say it. I mean, I'm trying really hard to have a relationship with my daughter and it doesn't seem as if you're all that into it. Is your SEAL dad enough for you? You don't need your REAL dad?

Ellory: I didn't say that I just don't know

Brady: What are you doing right now? Maybe I can come over.

Ellory: I'm not home, I'm at a family thing

Brady: A family thing that doesn't include me?

Ellory: It's with Ricky's SEAL friends

Brady: I get it. I'm only a janitor. You're embarrassed to be seen with me.

Ellory: I didn't say that

Brady: Then agree to see me again. I want to get to know my daughter.

Brady: Ellory? Are you still there?

Brady: Don't ignore me. Your mom used to do that and it pissed me off.

Brady: I'm serious. Answer me.

Addison's fingers were moving before she thought about it. She vaguely heard Ricky growl into her ear, but she didn't need him to take care of this. She could handle her ex.

And this would be the last damn time he spoke like that to their daughter.

Ellory: This is Addison. Don't you *ever* speak to Ellory that way again. Don't try to make her feel guilty about spending time with her family. She'll see you on her own timetable, not yours. And I'm telling you right now, harassing her isn't making her want to see you at all. Back off, Brady. I mean it!

She was breathing hard by the time she hit send. Her ex was an idiot. If he couldn't tell that he was pushing too hard, was being a total ass, that was on him. But she'd be damned if Ellory suffered because of his stupidity.

Brady: I'm sorry. I don't have experience in being a dad. I just want to see her. To get to know her better. And since she won't answer my calls, texting is the only way I have to talk to her.
Ellory: If you don't want me to block you altogether, you'd better get your shit together. I'm serious.
Brady: Okay. I'll be better. I swear.
Brady: So...when can I see her again?

Addison groaned in frustration. He didn't get it. Not at all.

Ellory: We'll be in touch. Now don't text again, we're busy.

. . .

"What do you need from me?" Ricky asked, hugging her from behind. He put his chin on her shoulder as he tightened his arms.

"This," Addison said, leaning against him. "Why won't he get a clue?"

"I don't know."

That answer didn't make Addison feel any better. Even though Ricky was as in the dark as she was as to Brady's motives, she was still hoping for some sort of male insight.

Shoving Ellory's phone into her pocket, she turned in Ricky's arms. "If we ever get divorced and you want to see our kid...don't be an ass like Brady is being."

"First, we aren't getting divorced. I'm not an idiot like him. I know when I've got the best thing that ever happened to me, and I'm not going to do anything to fuck it up. Second, I'm going to have a close relationship with our children. I'm always going to support him or her, and you. So you don't have to worry about me ever not pulling my weight, emotionally, physically, or monetarily."

Addison took a deep breath and melted into her husband. She needed this. Him. Needed to be reminded that there were good men in the world. Good fathers. She didn't need Ricky to tell her that he would always be there for their kids. She knew that without a doubt.

"I'm sorry. I just...he's *so* frustrating!"

"I can have a talk with him if you want," Ricky said.

"No," Addison said immediately. "Your talk will just end up with him yelling and getting pissed off."

"All right. But if he has one more 'discussion' with El like he had today, I'm finding him and setting him straight. Just letting you know ahead of time so you don't get mad when he tattles to you like the baby he is."

Addison couldn't help but chuckle at that. Ricky had her ex pegged. He would absolutely bitch that her husband had searched him out and yelled at him. It wouldn't help sway her, not at all, but Brady was petty enough to try to get Ricky into trouble. As if.

"Your time with the girls go okay?" he asked.

Addison nodded, more than ready to change the subject. "Yeah."

"Everything good with Josie? She and Blink left pretty fast."

Addison smiled at her husband. "We were talking about babies. And making babies. And how cool it would be if our kids were all around the same age and could grow up together. Josie thought it was a great idea, and since Maggie has a head start on all of us..." She let her voice trail off.

Ricky smiled, and Addison could feel his cock growing against her belly. "So she took her man home to have wild monkey baby-making sex."

Addison laughed. "Pretty much."

"Kevlar?" Ricky called without pulling away from his wife.

"Yeah?" his teammate yelled back.

"Can you bring the kids home in a couple hours?"

"Ricky!" Addison exclaimed, trying to untangle herself from him. But he wouldn't loosen his arms.

"Sure. You good?"

"We're good. Just have some stuff to do at home that we can't manage with little people underfoot."

"Understood. The same stuff Blink and Josie suddenly remembered they had to do, huh? Sure thing."

Addison could feel that her face was bright red. But

she couldn't deny that the idea of a few hours alone in the house with Ricky was too appealing to pass up. They always had to be sure to be quiet so as not to wake the kids.

"Appreciate it," Ricky said, pulling Addison toward the front door.

"Wait! We need to say bye to the kids. Tell them what's happening."

"Kevlar and the others will let them know."

"Ricky!" she protested, letting him pull her out the door anyway.

She was laughing by the time they got to his car. He practically threw her inside before slamming the door and jogging around to the driver's side. "Time's a ticking," he told her.

Licking her lips in anticipation, Addison felt like a naughty teenager. She reached out and put her hand on his thigh, moving it up until she was cupping his cock. "I've never sucked a man off in a car before," she said suggestively.

"Fuck, woman. One, as much as I'd love for you to go down on me right here and now, you'd have to undo your seat belt, which is a hard no for me. Two...there's no way I'd be able to control this car and come down your throat at the same time. Three...if you want a baby, down your throat is *not* where I need to orgasm. Hold that thought, sweetheart. We'll be home in less than ten minutes."

"Ricky?"

"Yeah?"

"Make it eight."

She felt the car accelerate and smiled in satisfaction and anticipation.

* * *

"Fuck her!"

Brady was done. Done playing the role of doting father. Done trying to sweet talk his daughter. Fucking teenagers and their one-word answers. He'd made the right decision twelve years ago to walk away without a backward glance. He should've known taking a job back here in Riverton would eventually bring him face-to-face with his annoying fucking ex.

And seeing Addison again had made it impossible to avoid his daughter. At first, he'd actually had the fantasy that he'd meet Ellory and they'd get along great. That he'd easily charm her and she'd be thrilled to have a relationship with such a cool dad. But that idea died after their first meeting. The girl was exactly like her mom, just as uptight and annoying. Not to mention that disgusting disease. No smart man would deal with that shit—literally —for the rest of his life.

Once his plan for Ellory was done, he was moving away from this pissant town again. He'd go somewhere warm. Mexico...No, he didn't speak Spanish and had no desire to learn. Hawaii? Yeah, Hawaii was perfect. He'd have plenty of money to get there and set up a sweet place. Surely his associate would have plenty of use for him in a popular tourist destination.

And fuck Addison and her threats! He'd show that bitch what happened when she crossed him. If Ellory wouldn't spend time with him alone willingly, he knew exactly what to do. She was too old to fall for the "I've lost my dog" ruse that he'd used a couple times in the past to lure in children, but he knew what she loved most...

Her family.

She preferred that damn SEAL over him? Fine. He'd use that asshole against her.

This would be the first time he delivered a live body to his contact. The people they normally harvested from were already dead. He'd taken bodies and body parts from funeral homes...but he'd also been desperate enough a couple of times in the past to take someone against their will. Those had been extenuating circumstances. He'd been dead broke, had needed the money badly. And the fact was, kids were worth the most. Parents with children who needed a transplant were willing to pay whatever it cost to get a healthy heart, liver, lungs...

So Brady had gotten his contact what he'd wanted. A *donor*. On two separate occasions, he'd lured a kid into his car then smothered them. Fast and easy. And the payday was worth it.

This time was different. Since their buyer was overseas, they needed to keep Ellory alive until she got there. Keeping the organs fresh was key. The buyer was aware that she had shit wrong with her intestines, but since he was interested in her heart and brain, he didn't care that she was fucked up below the waist.

Ellory was a means to an end. Period.

He'd make his move soon. She could enjoy her fucking play this weekend, enjoy spending time with her SEAL dad and foreigner siblings. Because it would be the last weekend she'd get with any of them. Ever. Next week, she'd be on her way overseas. It wouldn't be a comfortable trip, stuffed into a Conex container, but Brady didn't care. His contact had already paid off the right dock workers, and he'd make sure she had water so she didn't die during the trip across the ocean.

But honestly, what happened to her after Brady handed

her over didn't matter. All that mattered was the payday he'd get after he made the drop.

Smiling, he threw himself down on the piece-of-shit sofa he'd dragged in from someone's trash pile. This time next week, he'd be in Hawaii, screwing some hot chick in a string bikini who he'd picked up on the beach, and he could forget all about his fucking ex and her whiny daughter.

CHAPTER FIFTEEN

MacGyver was in a good mood. A very good mood. Ever since he'd gotten back from his latest mission, things had been going very well for him. Artem, Borysko, and Yana were thriving. Every day they seemed to improve. With their weight, their English, their comfortability with their new lives. Yana had begun to sleep through the night in her own bed in the room she shared with Ellory, instead of waking up and going into her brothers' room.

The boys were less on alert all the time. They were more carefree, more playful, and the other day they both even got into trouble. Most parents would be upset if their kids backtalked, or refused to pick up the mess they'd made in the living room because they were more interested in going outside to play. But MacGyver took it as a sign they were becoming truly comfortable in their surroundings. They weren't afraid they would be sent back to Ukraine if they said or did the wrong thing.

And Ellory seemed to be managing her Crohn's better. The fasting was really working for her. He had to keep reminding himself that the things they did as a family didn't have to revolve around food. It was a difficult habit to break, as most get-togethers involved food of some sort. Food she couldn't eat. So they were taking more walks, trips to do things that didn't involve going out to eat all the time. The bullying at school seemed to have tapered off, and she was hanging out with two other girls who were involved in her theater class. So she was thriving, as far as MacGyver was concerned.

And his wife…

He'd never dreamed he could have a woman like Addison. He was so proud of her. He bragged about her baking business to anyone and everyone who would listen. He even kept some of her business cards in his pocket at all times, just in case someone showed the slightest bit of interest in a birthday cake or homemade goodies for one occasion or another. He'd also tacked a few up in the grocery store, and was pleased to see they were gone the next time he went in there.

Addison was also an amazing mother. The kids absolutely loved her. Most of their blossoming was because of her, MacGyver had no doubt about that. The best thing he'd ever done in his life was ask her to marry him.

Lately, he'd been thinking about having another ceremony. He felt bad that she'd been cheated out of the big wedding that most women seemed to love. None of their friends had been there, and he had no doubt a wedding and reception would be awesome. They could keep it small and intimate and—

His thoughts stalled at that idea. Small. Yeah, right. Even with just his team, it would be over a dozen people. Add in his parents, his four siblings, her parents, Wolf's SEAL team and their families…all of a sudden, there were at least fifty people. They'd need to rent a space on the naval base. Maybe they could do a combined beach ceremony and party.

But he was getting ahead of himself. First, he needed to ask Addison if that was something she'd want. If she said yes, the first thing he'd make clear was that she would *not* be making their wedding cake. He'd want her to relax and enjoy every moment, and not be stressed about something as simple as their cake. Of course, *she* wouldn't think it was simple, but he knew exactly how to convince her...

Distraction. Take her to their room and make love to her until she was putty in his hands.

Sex with his wife was...MacGyver couldn't even describe it. Being with Addison was simply *right*. And nothing between them was taboo. They'd experimented in bed with different positions, toys, and even a bit of role play, after she'd admitted to being curious as to Dude and Cheyenne's dominant and submissive lifestyle. It wasn't really for either of them, not as a permanent kind of thing...but MacGyver had enjoyed the hell out of being called "Sir" and having his wife at his mercy. Since he loved seeing her orgasm, forcing her to come four times before he finally entered her was also exciting. Almost intoxicating.

But what MacGyver loved most about his wife wasn't the sex. It was the way she looked at him. All the love she had for him shone in her eyes every time she so much as glanced his way. He appreciated how she loved with her whole heart. Him, the kids they were so close to finally adopting, her daughter.

And he loved her kindness. How she went out of her way to help anyone who might need it. The woman who couldn't afford to pay for a dozen cupcakes for her daughter's birthday, so she'd settled on six...Addison had thrown in six for free, just because. Another woman who was struggling to put her groceries in her car because she was on crutches...Addison crossed the parking lot to help her.

It didn't matter if she knew a person or not; Addison went out of her way to be kind to everyone.

Yes, MacGyver was blessed, and he knew it. And he'd do whatever it took to keep his wife happy. Happy wife, happy life. It was a corny saying, but he believed it down to his soul. And his goal in life was to keep Addison happy and healthy.

The time would come when he'd be deployed once more. And while he hated the thought of leaving his family, he'd do what needed to be done. He enjoyed any time spent with his SEAL teammates, but they were no longer his entire world. MacGyver felt as if he had more balance in his life now, and it felt incredible.

They'd actually recently begun the process of preparing for their next mission. It would be a doozy. More dangerous than the last, but just as rewarding. And there was always the chance something more imminent would interfere, and they'd be deployed elsewhere with little to no warning. Hostage situations were the main thing that derailed a planned mission. Or they could be needed as security detail for someone high up in political circles. He sometimes never knew where his job would take him.

But this morning, he was on the most important mission of all. MacGyver was making pancakes for his three little monsters. Addison had tried to get them to eat something else for breakfast, but from the first day they'd tried her pancakes, they'd been hooked and that was all they wanted. He'd left Addison in bed, sated and replete from their lovemaking. He'd skipped PT that morning just because, instead making love to his wife.

She wasn't pregnant yet but he wasn't worried. Was simply enjoying the journey to get there.

Yana was the first to arrive, looking sleepy but dressed for school. She sat at the table in the dining room and stared at MacGyver.

He raised a brow at her. "Good morning, Yana. You hungry?"

She nodded.

He smiled. "Then you need to come over here and get your plate and silverware. I'm not a waiter in this house. You can get your own dishes, then bring them to the dishwasher when you're done." Even though she was only five, she was perfectly capable of helping with simple tasks for breakfast.

She shrugged and slipped out of the chair and into the kitchen. She got a fork out of the drawer, took a plate off the stack waiting on the counter, then carried them to her seat at the table. She returned to the kitchen and got a cup and carefully filled it with orange juice from the refrigerator.

Artem and Borysko arrived a few minutes later and, without prompting, got their plates and forks. Ellory had just entered the room when MacGyver put a heaping pile of pancakes in the middle of the table.

All three kids stood up and reached for the stack.

"What do you say?" MacGyver warned.

They turned their heads toward him and said at the same time, "Thank you!"

"You're welcome. Enjoy."

They were like little jackals with a fresh kill. It didn't take long for the huge stack to become a tiny one.

"Morning," Ellory said quietly as she got her protein shake out of the fridge.

"Morning. How did you sleep?" MacGyver asked.

"Good. Where's Mom?"

"She'll be up soon, I'm sure. I let her sleep in a little this morning."

"Oh. Okay."

"I know I told you already, but I wanted to say it again. You were great this weekend. The lighting in the play was *perfect*."

"I messed up in the second act but recovered pretty quickly."

"I didn't even notice. But I *did* notice that you seem... happier lately."

Ellory leaned against the counter and took a sip of her shake. "I am. I love my mom and we had a good life. But having you and the kids here...I really love it. Spending time with you in the garage, and having you show me some of the stuff you've done on your missions, and playing with the electronics and stuff...it's fun. My mom is an amazing baker, but I've never really been into that. So it's nice to have something else to do with someone. And some of the things you've shown me have come in handy, especially in tinkering with some of the electronics in theater class."

"I'm glad," MacGyver said, feeling warm inside.

"And the self-defense stuff you've taught me and Mom has been both fun and makes me feel better in general. The world isn't safe, people can be awful, and I feel more confident knowing some things to help protect myself, and the kids too."

MacGyver hated that she felt that way about the world, but she wasn't exactly wrong. "Speaking of which, we need to have another lesson. Soon."

"Yeah. And lastly...things with Chrys have all but stopped. The brainstorming you did with me about smartass comebacks has really helped." She grinned at him. "She doesn't seem to know what to say when I come back at her, and she *hates* that. So she's stopped picking on me so much. All that to say...yeah. I *am* happier."

"Which makes *me* happy. And your mom talked to you about us having a baby?"

Ellory beamed. "Yes! Is she pregnant?"

"Not yet. But I wanted to be sure you knew that even if we had a hundred babies, you'll still always be your mom's first and favorite child."

She rolled her eyes. "Whatever."

MacGyver didn't want to bring it up, but he felt as if he needed to. "And your bio-dad? How are things with him?"

Ellory shrugged. "The same. He texted me this weekend after the play and asked how it went. I thought that was cool. He didn't push to see me, which was a relief. Does it make me a horrible person to say that I don't think I really want a relationship with him?"

"No, sweetie. It doesn't. He'll always be your dad, but sharing blood doesn't mean you have to be friends or anything."

"Yeah. Maybe things will get better as I get older. But right now, he just stresses me out."

"We'll play things by ear. But don't ever feel as if you *have* to have a relationship with anyone simply because you think it's the right thing to do."

"I won't. Thanks."

Then, without a word, the preteen surprised MacGyver by hugging him hard, before turning and heading to the table to entertain her siblings.

"Everything okay?" Addison said, walking into the kitchen and stepping into the space in his arms that her daughter had just vacated.

"Yeah. You're raising one hell of a woman, Addy."

"She's pretty awesome," she agreed. Then she took the spatula out of his hand. "Go sit with your kids. I'll make the next batch. You need to keep up your strength. You... exerted yourself quite a bit this morning already."

MacGyver grinned. "I did, didn't I?"

"Well, you skipped PT. I had to make sure that got *some* sort of workout."

He laughed, then kissed her forehead. "I love you."

"Love you too. Is my coffee ready?"

"Of course." MacGyver kissed her once more, not able to keep his lips off her, then picked up his own cup of coffee and headed for the table to find out what his kids had on tap for the day.

The mornings always went by too quickly and before he knew it, the kids were ready for school. He would drop off Yana and Ellory, while Addison waited for the bus with Artem and Borysko. Turns out, the boys loved taking the school bus. They felt so grown up, and not having to drop them off and pick them up saved Addison a ton of time each day.

"You gonna be okay picking up the girls this afternoon? I know you have six dozen cookies to make and decorate for that wedding," MacGyver asked her.

"I should be fine. I'll let you know if I'm not."

"All right. I can stop by the store and pick up the things on our list on my way home."

"Thanks. I'd appreciate that. We're running low on garbage bags too, and Borysko needs some new pants. I can't believe how much he's grown in the last couple of months. And, you should probably know, Ellory and I need to go shopping this weekend for bras for her," she added quietly. "She asked me last night if I'd go with her. I think she's finally starting to hit puberty."

MacGyver groaned. "I'm not ready. First it's training bras, then it's jeans with holes in them, then tampons, then giggling all the time and wanting to be on the phone with boys."

Addison burst out laughing. "It's good training for Yana. And if we have a girl in the future."

"Whatever," MacGyver said.

"Now you sound like Ellory," Addison said, still smiling.

"Love you, woman. So much."

"I love you too. Now get. I'll talk to you later."

"I'll call if I get a break around lunch."

"Sounds good. Drive safe."

"Always."

As MacGyver pulled out of the driveway, he couldn't help but smile at the sight of his wife's ass as she walked down the sidewalk with the boys, toward the bus stop at the end of the street. He was a lucky son-of-a-bitch, and he knew it.

He dropped Yana off at her school first, and when he pulled up to Ellory's a few minutes later, he felt compelled to reach out, stopping her from jumping out with a hand on her arm. "El?"

"Yeah?"

"I love you. I just thought you should know."

She beamed at him. "I love you too, Ricky."

"Have a good day. Kick some bully butt if necessary."

"I will. You kick some bad guy butt."

"I will."

They smiled at each other, and MacGyver stayed long enough to watch her walk into the school. He hadn't told the girl that he loved her before. Today just felt like the right time and place. He wasn't a mushy guy...Strike that, he hadn't been before he'd met Addison and her daughter, and before he'd started the adoption process for Artem, Borysko, and Yana. But he wasn't ashamed of letting those he loved know how he felt about them. Life was too short, he knew that better than most, and he didn't want another day to go by without his stepdaughter knowing how much he cared about her.

As he drove toward the base, MacGyver smiled. Today was going to be a good day. He had no doubt.

* * *

Today was going to be a great day. Brady felt energized. Jazzed. And it wasn't because of the few shots he'd taken before he'd left his crappy apartment.

Everything was in place. His contact was ready and the Conex was prepared. All he had to do was get Ellory and bring her to the dock. He'd pass her off to his associate, and then he'd play the concerned father when Addison called him to let him know that she was missing.

The only thing he needed to worry about was keeping his story straight when he was asked why he'd picked up Ellory from school. But he had a plan for that. He'd take her phone, change the time on both, then set up a fake text convo between the two cells, where she asked him to pick her up because she wasn't feeling well. He'd have to come up with a convincing reason why she'd get in touch with *him* and not her mom, but he'd figure that out.

First things first. Get the girl, take her to the dock without her realizing what was happening, then he'd figure out the smaller details.

Thinking about the money that would soon be in his

bank account made Brady almost giddy. He'd never made so much with one score; it would be life changing.

He pulled into a parking space at the middle school and took a deep breath. Then he let it out slowly before getting out of his truck.

"You got this," he muttered to himself as he walked toward the front doors. There would be cameras, Brady expected that. He did his best to look like a worried father as he stepped inside the building. Following the signs to the office, he went over his story in his head.

"Hi! How can I help you?" the woman behind the desk asked.

"I'm Brady Vogel. I'm here to pick up Ellory Wentz."

The woman clicked on a few keys on her keyboard, then frowned. "I'm sorry, I don't see that she's scheduled to be picked up early today."

"I know. I'm her father. Her biological father. Her mom and stepdad were in an accident. I'm here to bring her to the hospital so she can be with them."

"Oh! That's awful. Are they going to be all right?"

"The doctors aren't sure right now," Brady said with as much sadness as he could infuse into his voice.

"I'll check the list of approved people who can pick her up and get you guys on your way. If I can have your ID, please."

This was the tricky part. Brady pulled out his ID and gave it to the woman. "I don't think Addison has had time to put me on the list yet. You see, we just reconnected after years of being apart, and of course no one thought something like this would happen. But if you get Ellory, she'll tell you it's okay."

"Oh. I'm so sorry but…if you aren't on the list, we can't let her go with you."

"Right. So you're going to let her mother possibly die without Ellory being able to say goodbye? Because of a clerical error? I'm sure that'll go over real well. I'm generally not a sue-happy person, but in this case, I'd one hundred percent support a lawsuit. Look, I'm her biological father. I'm not lying. Just get Ellory and ask her. She's old enough to be able to say no to going with me. It's not as if I'm here to kidnap her. I just want to get her to her mom."

"I'm not sure...I'm new here and..."

Brady mentally rubbed his hands together in glee. He loved brand-new employees.

"Look. I don't want to get anyone in trouble. But the accident was horrible. There's a chance Ellory's stepfather will live, but her mom..." Brady looked down and tried to produce tears...with no luck. "She's bad," he said after a long pause.

"I'll send someone to get Ellory out of class."

Bingo.

"Thank you. I'm sure she'll appreciate being able to see her mother."

Ten minutes later—minutes during which Brady paced impatiently—Ellory arrived at the office.

She stopped in her tracks at seeing him. "Brady," she said, surprise evident in her voice.

"Hey, baby. I'm here to take you to your mom. She's been in an accident."

"Where's Ricky?"

"He was with her," Brady said.

"Is she...is she okay?"

"I'm afraid not."

"Ellory, Mr. Vogel isn't on your approved pick-up list. He says he's your biological father."

"He is," Ellory confirmed.

"Are you okay going with him?" the woman asked gently.

Ellory nodded.

Yes! Brady mentally counted the money that would soon be his. He stepped up to Ellory and put his arm around her shoulders and gave her a little side hug. "It'll be okay. Come on, I'll take you to see her."

The preteen nodded mutely as he steered her toward the door. She seemed shell-shocked, which was just how he wanted her. He didn't want her aware of her surroundings. Needed her to be hysterical and upset, so she wouldn't notice they weren't driving to the hospital.

By the time they got into his truck, she was crying, which pleased Brady to no end.

"Yana," Ellory said when he started the engine.

"What?" Brady asked, looking over at his daughter.

"What about Yana? And the boys? We're going to get them too, right?"

"The other kids are being picked up by one of your stepdad's SEAL friends. I offered to come get you so we could all get back to the hospital faster."

"But Yana is used to being picked up with *me*. She'll be upset if someone other than me shows up to get her."

Brady clenched his teeth and did his best to stay calm. This was a complication he hadn't anticipated. But then again...bringing *two* live specimens to his contact? Even if he didn't get more money, it would definitely raise his street-cred with the man.

"Of course we can go get her," he soothed.

Ellory nodded and looked down at the cell in her hand.

He had to get that phone from her. He didn't want it

leading the authorities straight to the docks, where the Conex was waiting for its special load—her.

"What are you doing?" he asked.

"Texting Mom," Ellory mumbled.

Brady reached over and put his hand across the screen. "Don't."

"Why not?"

"Because she can't answer. She's hurt bad, Ellory. She won't be texting anyone. Her phone might even still be in her Bug at the crash site." He deftly took Ellory's phone out of her hands as she burst into tears.

Perfect. He'd put enough of a traumatic image in her head to make her forget about anything but worry for her mom.

He drove to the elementary school, and this time Ellory came into the building with him. He went through the same process to get Yana, and having Ellory with him helped tremendously, especially with her red eyes and fresh tears.

Ellory explained to Yana what was happening, and soon Brady had *two* hysterical girls on his hands. Any other time, he'd be highly annoyed, but since their tears served his purpose and got them out of the school, he was thrilled.

The girls got into his truck, and he started toward the industrial docks where the huge container ships were loaded for transport.

Ellory's attention was on her sister, trying to assure her everything would be okay. Telling her that their mom was strong and she'd be fine...that Ricky was also hurt but she was sure he'd be all right too.

Everything worked exactly according to Brady's plan. He had Ellory's cell phone—which he'd turned off before shoving into his pocket—the girls weren't paying any attention to where they were going, and he was right on time. For once.

It wasn't until he'd stopped his truck that Ellory finally clued into the fact that they weren't at a hospital.

"Where are we? I thought we were going to the hospital to see Mom and Ricky."

"I just needed to make one short stop first. Don't worry, we'll leave here in a moment," Brady reassured her. "Stay here with Yana."

He got out and approached his contact, waiting nearby. The man was totally nondescript. He had brown hair, brown eyes, was average height, and he wore the same coveralls as everyone else who worked on the docks. Brady would be hard-pressed to describe him to the authorities. He didn't have any distinguishing features.

"I've got the merchandise for you. Safe and sound. Brought you a bonus too."

The man looked over at the truck, then back at Brady. "I'm not paying you more."

"Didn't expect you to," he told him, loving the look of surprise on the man's face. "Call it a present. A 'thank you' for doing business with me. One that'll bring you a good chunk of change. A live donor who's under five years old? Someone will also pay top dollar for her heart, I'm sure."

"She's healthy?"

"Yes." Brady didn't have access to the little girl's medical history, but she looked healthy enough to him.

"All right. The container's ready. You get them in and I'll do the rest. There's just a small space in the middle of other merchandise, so they can't bang on the walls of the Conex. The possibility that someone will hear them is low, but I didn't want to take any chances. The buyer for the teen is anxious to get her to Asia as soon as possible. His daughter's dying and he needs her organs. Pronto."

"Sounds good. My money?"

The man stepped to the right and leaned over to grab something behind a stack of boxes. He handed a gym bag to Brady. "I assume you aren't going to be so crass as to count it right here and now. We don't have time for that. It's all there."

Brady totally wanted to count it. But the last thing he needed was for Ellory to get any more suspicious than she already was. Time to get her and the brat put away in the box and be done with it. "I trust you," he told the man. It was a lie. He didn't trust the guy at all, but he had no choice at the moment.

"It was a pleasure doing business with you. Hopefully we can do something similar soon."

Brady nodded, then headed back to his truck. This next part would be tricky. He needed to get Ellory to go with him, but he wasn't sure how well that was going to go down. She wasn't stupid, she already had to be thinking something wasn't right.

Sure enough, when he opened the door, she asked, "What's going on? Who was that man? Why are we here?"

Brady secured the gym bag full of money behind his seat, then said, "Come here, Yana."

She'd been sitting in the middle, between him and Ellory. But now the little girl drew back and leaned against her sister.

Wanting to be done with this, Brady reached out and grabbed Yana's arm. He yanked her across the seat and out the driver's-side door. She wiggled and squirmed, trying to get away from him, but he held her tightly.

"Come here," he said, this time to Ellory, crooking his finger.

She quickly glanced from him to the passenger door.

"If you don't, I'll hurt her," Brady threatened.

If looks could kill, he'd be a dead man. Ellory went from sobbing her heart out to shooting daggers from her eyes. "My mom's not hurt, is she?"

"I said, *come here*," Brady demanded, lowering his voice and sounding as mean as he could. To give his daughter incentive, he squeezed Yana's arm until she squealed in pain.

"Don't hurt her!" Ellory yelled as she slowly scooted across the seat.

As soon as she was within reach, Brady reached out and grabbed her arm too. She almost fell out of the truck when he yanked her forward, but got her feet under her at the last minute.

"Stay quiet, or I'll leave you here and take Yana with me when I go. I'm sure I can find someone who would *love* to buy this beautiful little girl for his own pleasure."

It took a moment for his meaning to sink in, but when it did, Ellory gasped. "You're a monster!"

"You should've been nicer to me, daughter dear. If you had, you might not be in this position right now. But you blew it. And for the record, *you* were the one who insisted I pick up Yana. She wasn't supposed to be a part of this."

Ellory's mouth fell open, and Brady smiled in satisfaction. He'd rendered her speechless.

He dragged them across the blacktop filled with Conex upon Conex containers, all waiting to be loaded onto huge ships to be taken to the other side of the world. Brady went straight to the container his contact had indicated. The only one with an open door. Inside, there were boxes stacked from floor to ceiling except for a narrow passage down the middle.

The sound of an engine behind them startled Brady so badly, he almost lost his grip on the girls. When he turned around, he saw his contact sitting behind the wheel of a forklift. There was a stack of boxes ready to go on the lift. He suspected the guy was making sure he wasn't being double crossed, but Brady wasn't insulted. The man had just handed over a lot of cash. He wanted to make sure he got what was promised.

"In," Brady said, shoving Ellory toward the open container.

He wasn't surprised when she balked. "No."

"Right. Come on, Yana, let's go meet your new daddy. You have to do everything he says, even when he tells you to take off all your clothes and—"

"Stop it!" Ellory shouted.

"Then get inside. Now," Brady told her with zero emotion.

"How can you do this? She's just a little kid!"

"Money. It makes the world go 'round. And she's just another orphan no one wants. She's expendable."

"Wrong. *We* want her. And what about me?" Ellory asked. "Your own flesh and blood. Was it all a trick? Were you planning this the whole time? Did you *ever* want to get to know me?"

"In the beginning, sure. But I repeat—you blew it. You should be thanking me, Ellory. You're going to be useful for once. Your organs are gonna save someone else's life. Another girl. Someone who isn't disgusting, like you. Once she has your heart, she'll be as good as new."

Ellory gasped yet again.

"In," Brady said, squeezing Yana's arm once more. She

was screaming and crying nonstop now, and it was grating on his nerves. "There should be some water in there to tide you over, but I'd ration it, especially now that there are two of you. In a couple of weeks, you'll arrive at your destination and you'll meet your new owner. He'll take you to a facility, where you'll both be put to sleep and your organs harvested. You won't feel a thing, and you'll be saving the lives of who knows how many other kids."

"You aren't going to get away with this," Ellory whispered.

"I already have. Now hurry up, I've got to prepare for the role of a lifetime...that of a grieving and worried dad. When it's discovered that you and Yana are gone, Addison and your precious Ricky will freak out. I've already made arrangements for someone to call with a ransom demand. And I know they'll pay. So I'll get *double* the money for you and this little brat."

"There are cameras at the schools. They'll know you picked us up."

"Of course they will. And I'll show everyone the texts you sent me, begging me to pick you up because you were bullied by that chick again, and you just couldn't take it. But you were too embarrassed to tell your mom or anyone else, so you asked me to come get you. It was *your* plan to tell the school there was an accident, because you knew they wouldn't let me take you if it wasn't an emergency. You're a smart cookie; everyone will believe you're capable of coming up with something like that. And all I have to say is that you asked me to drop you off a few blocks from your house, so no one would see me with you. You were trying to protect me, after all...and apparently, someone snatched up you and Yana right after that."

Brady was feeling pretty proud of himself. This was

almost done. He just had to play a part for a little longer. "No more talk. Get in there. *Now!*"

Ellory took a step back, toward the interior of the container. Then another.

"Good girl," Brady praised sarcastically.

Without warning, he shoved Yana toward Ellory, hard enough that the little girl fell to her knees. She cried out and sobbed even harder. Then she got to her feet and ran toward her sister.

He motioned to his contact, and the forklift moved toward the opening of the Conex.

Brady's last view of his daughter was her backing up quickly as the stack of boxes on the forklift was fitted into place, blocked her from his sight.

Seconds later, his contact reversed and parked the forklift, and Brady helped him close and lock the doors of the Conex.

The man gave him a thoughtful look. "Is that really your daughter?"

"Unfortunately, yes."

"You're pretty damn cold-hearted. I think I like you."

Brady smirked. "Thanks for the opportunity. I'll give you a call once I'm settled in Hawaii."

"Hawaii's closer to Asia," the guy said with a grin. "I could definitely use someone in that part of the world to help me move product."

Brady shook his hand, then turned and headed back to his truck. He needed to get those text messages between his and Ellory's phones sorted. The same guy who was going to call and demand a ransom was going to help with that. He was pretty good with computers, and he swore when the cops got her phone records, they'd see a timestamp from before she was seen on the school cameras leaving the building.

This was going to work out, and Brady was more than thrilled.

* * *

Ellory sat on the floor of the container she and Yana had been forced to enter, holding her sister as the little girl cried hysterically. Brady was right—this was her fault. She'd insisted he pick up Yana before they went to the hospital. But then again, that was what any decent person would do.

She was extremely relieved that her mom and Ricky weren't hurt though. If there was anything good about this situation, it was that. Still, Ellory had to admit, she was terrified. She had no idea what to do. She didn't want to give her heart to anyone. She wanted to go home.

"Dark," Yana said between sniffs.

It *was* dark. Pitch black, in fact. Ellory couldn't tell the difference from when she closed her eyes to when they were open. She'd seen the little area they were in before the boxes were stacked in the passageway to their cubby, and before the door to the container was shut. It was probably around four feet by four feet and surrounded by boxes of whatever cargo was being shipped overseas. There was a bucket—she assumed for her to do her business in—and four small bottles of water. It wasn't nearly enough to last two weeks, if Brady was being honest about how long it would take them to get to wherever they were going.

She and Yana would die before they got there.

The thought made Ellory want to lay down and give up. But something Ricky said to her once sprang into her head. He'd been telling her about how hard Hell Week was for him. The infamous week-long training that movies and shows about SEALs liked to focus on. Ricky said he wanted to ring the bell that would get him out of the torture he was enduring. That he could hear it in his head, clear as day. Told her how jealous he was of his fellow sailors when they gave up and rang that bell. How the SEAL motto would go through his head over and over, making him want to quit even more. *The only easy day was yesterday. The only easy day was yesterday. The only easy day was yesterday.*

Ricky had admitted thinking that if *yesterday* was easy, he knew without a doubt that he wouldn't make it through the *current* day.

But as he lay in the sand after what seemed like a million pushups and sit-ups, or struggled to stay conscious while kneeling in the freezing surf...when his belly cramped from lack of food, and when his arms shook as he tried to hold up one of the big black rubber boats with his fellow wannabe SEALs...something hit him.

Yesterday was hell. He hadn't thought he could make it through...but he had. Now, there he was at today. And in fact, doing burpees in the sand and rolling around in the waves the day before *did* seem easy compared to how he felt doing his present task, when he wanted to tap out, to quit.

The motto was spot on. If he could stay strong and make it through the hell of today...tomorrow, it would be a memory. It would seem easy.

If Ellory could just stay strong, if she could use her brain and make it through this nightmare, soon enough, it would be just another "yesterday."

Everything she'd been through with her Crohn's seemed horrible at one point. The first endoscopy, the first colonoscopy, the first CT scan. But now those things weren't so bad. She'd gotten used to them. Those procedures seemed easy...now. It was like the motto Ricky told her about. Yesterday seemed easy, but that didn't mean she couldn't survive today. Ricky had; he'd made it through Hell Week and become a SEAL.

All she had to do was hold on until Ricky and his friends found her.

Brady sounded like he had everything all planned out—but he'd mess up somehow, she had no doubt. Ricky was a thousand times smarter than her bio-dad. Both he and her mom would figure out there was no chance she'd call Brady to come get her because she'd been bullied. Even if she *was* too embarrassed to call her mom or Ricky, she wouldn't call Brady. She'd reach out to Remi, or Wren, or even Caroline before she'd call her bio-dad.

There had to be some way to track where he'd taken her and Yana. Ellory just had to stay positive. They'd find them.

Something else occurred to her. The first time they ever met, Ricky had told her all about MacGyver, that guy on the old show who always seemed to be able to make things to get him out of bad situations. How Ricky had earned that nickname because he did the same thing. Figured out how to make cool stuff out of whatever he had on hand.

Ellory tilted her head back and envisioned the boxes upon boxes all around her. She had no idea what was inside them...but there had to be *something* she could use to try to get her and Yana out of this box, right? That was what Ricky would do. He wouldn't sit around feeling sorry for himself. He'd get off his butt and do what he could to save himself.

"Yana, take a breath. You're okay. I'm okay. We need to find a way out of here."

She felt the little girl do as she was told. She took a deep breath, and Ellory felt her wipe her face with her shoulder.

"Good girl," Ellory praised. "I know how much you like to open gifts. How about you help me open some stuff?"

"Like presents?" Yana asked in a small, wavery voice.

"Right. Remember when we came in here, all those boxes that were around us?"

Yana nodded against her.

"Well, how about we see if we can figure out what's inside them? I bet there has to be some good stuff. Maybe some blankets we can lie on. Or maybe, just maybe, there will be a box of cell phones ready to be used."

As far as she could tell, the container wasn't moving yet. The sooner they figured something out, the better. Once this box was put onto one of those huge ships, their opportunity for escape would be drastically reduced. They needed to get to work.

Standing up, Ellory helped Yana do the same. She had no idea how she was going to get into the boxes—she didn't have a knife, didn't have anything sharp—but like MacGyver, she would figure it out. She had no choice. If she didn't, she and Yana would disappear forever.

CHAPTER SIXTEEN

"What do you mean, she isn't here?"

"Ellory's father said you'd been in an accident, that he needed to bring her to the hospital to say her final good-byes to you."

Addison stared at the woman in disbelief. How could this have happened? Brady wasn't on the approved list to pick up her daughter.

"He was very convincing," the woman fretted, not impressing Addison at all. "And when we called Ellory in, she seemed all right to go with him. She wasn't afraid of him at all. In fact, when they left, he had his arm around her shoulders."

Addison was *furious*. So mad, she could barely see straight. Someone was going to pay dearly for this fuck-up. She was going to chew out the principal and call the cops and make a report—wasn't going to let *anyone* off the hook —but right now, she needed to find her daughter.

Spinning around, she left the office and sprinted for the parking lot. As soon as she was outside the building, she called Yana's school. A sick feeling was spreading in her gut, and she had a feeling she knew what she was going to be told when she got a hold of someone there.

She was right. Yana was gone too. Ellory and Brady had taken Yana out of school. And now she couldn't get a hold of either Ellory or her ex.

Suddenly feeling lost, not sure what to do or where to go, Addison did the only thing she could think of. She called her husband.

"Hey, you think of something I need to pick up on the way home?" Ricky asked in lieu of a greeting.

"Ellory and Yana are gone."

"*What?*" Ricky said, immediately all business.

"I arrived here at school to get Ellory and was told Brady picked her up earlier. He told them we were in an accident and in the hospital, and he needed to bring Ellory to see us."

"He's not on the list to pick her up," Ricky said, his voice hard and flat.

"I *know*," Addison practically wailed. "But the secretary is new—which isn't a fucking excuse and someone's head's going to roll once we find our kids. But she let him talk her into it. She said Ellory went with him without hesitation."

"If she thought we were hurt, of course she would," Ricky said. "Yana too?"

"Yeah."

"I'm on my way home right now. I'll get the boys before they can get on the bus and— Wait, did you call their school?"

"No." The sick feeling increased tenfold. What if Brady had taken Artem and Borysko too? She couldn't bear even the thought. It was too much.

"I'll call them right now. You go home, Addison. Drive

safely, I'll be there as soon as I can. I'm calling Julie Hurt. She's the closest to our place. You met her at Caroline's, remember?"

"Uh-huh." It hurt to think. All Addison could see in her head was Ellory. The day she was born. When she turned one, and stuffed a piece of cake in her face. At six, when she learned to ride a bike. The first time she had to take her to the emergency room because of pain in her belly. How she looked just that morning. The memories were painful.

Would that be all she ever had? Bittersweet memories?

And Yana. The little girl had to be scared out of her mind. She'd be so confused, unsure what was going on. At least Ellory was with her...Addison hoped.

"Addy!" Ricky barked, clearly realizing he'd lost her for a moment. "Listen to me. We're going to find them. No one is taking our girls from us. I'm sending Kevlar and Blink to find Vogel. They'll make him tell us what's going on. Where our babies are. Hear me?"

"Yeah." The world was coming back into focus.

"I'll have Smiley and Flash meet you at the house too. They'll probably beat me there, since I'm going to get the boys. Safe will meet up with Wolf and his team, and they'll start scouring the town to see if they can find the girls. Wolf will call Tex. Trust me when I say, Tex can find even the smallest trail. Okay?"

"Okay."

"Breathe, Addy. We're going to find them."

Knowing Ricky and his friends were on this made Addison feel much better. The sick feeling receded a fraction. She'd heard all the stories about the infamous Tex. Knew that he'd gotten Blink and Josie out of that prison in Iran. That he'd helped find countless others over the years.

The ass-kicking he'd clearly done when Artem, Borysko, and Yana had been taken by CPS. She had to believe he'd find her daughters too.

"Hang on just a little longer. For me."

"I'm better now. Knowing you're on this, it makes me feel not so alone."

"You aren't alone. You're *never* alone. I'll be home as soon as I can. Drive safe and lean on our friends. I love you, Addison. So much."

"I love you too. Drive safe yourself."

"Always."

The familiar back and forth went a long way toward snapping Addison out of the weird head space she'd been sucked into.

She hung up the phone and hurried to her Bug. Maybe by the time she got home, Ellory and Yana would be there.

Once more, hoping against hope, she clicked on Ellory's name on her phone, sagging in defeat when it went straight to voicemail. It was either off or dead...she'd hoped for a second that her daughter would answer and ask why her mom was freaking out so badly.

With nothing else to do but go home, Addison did just that.

* * *

MacGyver's head was spinning. He was furious that *both* schools broke protocol and allowed Vogel to take Ellory and Yana without permission. He was frustrated that Ellory's phone wasn't answering—the first thing he'd done was try to call her. He was terrified that Vogel had done something horrible to the girls.

The odd thing was...why? What did he have to gain?

Where would he take them? MacGyver had too many questions and no answers. Until Kevlar and Blink found Vogel and interrogated him, they'd have to be patient.

He'd call the police as soon as he got home, but he wanted to give his teammates a head start on finding Addison's ex. They would use techniques the cops couldn't to get answers. They'd get him to tell them everything about why he'd taken the girls.

He'd been unbelievably relieved when he'd called the boys' school and found that they were still there. He told the secretary that he'd be picking them up and sent a quick text to Addison, letting her know that Artem and Borysko were safe.

The boys were confused about why he was getting them from school, instead of letting them take the bus. After they'd stepped outside, MacGyver went to one knee in front of them.

"I have some bad news," he said solemnly.

Both boys stared at him with wide, worried eyes.

"Remember Brady? Ellory's biological father?" He refused to say "real dad" because that's who *he* was. He may have only known Ellory for a little more than a year, and he certainly hadn't been in any kind of fatherly role for long, but he still felt deep down that *he* was her real dad. It might've taken him twelve years to find her, but now that he had, he knew Ellory was his own. It was the same gut feeling he had when he'd met Artem, Borysko, and Yana in that fucked-up situation in Ukraine. Some inherent knowledge that they were meant to be his.

"Yes. She no like him very much," Borysko said.

"Right. Well, he picked up both Ellory and Yana from school today, and we don't know why. We also don't know where they are. We're looking for them now." MacGyver did his best to downplay the magnitude of what was happening.

But Artem's eyes widened in his little face, and he began to tremble. "He take them?" he asked.

MacGyver refused to lie. Not to these boys, who'd already been through hell and back. "Yes. But I swear that my friends and I are doing everything we can to find them and bring them home."

Artem turned to Borysko and began speaking urgently to him in Ukrainian. MacGyver didn't interrupt. Didn't ask what he was saying. There were times Artem seemed like the eight-year-old boy he was; other times, like now, he oozed vibes of someone ten years older.

Both boys seemed extremely worried and freaked out by the time Artem looked back at MacGyver. "Yana is scared. But Ellory is with her. She loves Ellory."

"Yes to all three things," MacGyver said.

"What we can do to help?" Artem asked.

"I need you to look after Addy. I also need you to trust my friends and me. We are doing *everything* in our power to find Brady and your sisters. The last thing I need is you two running off, thinking you can find her yourselves. This isn't that bombed-out city in Ukraine. There, you two were the experts. You knew where to hide, where to find food. But Riverton is *my* city. My friends and I will find Ellory's biological father and make him tell us what's going on. Okay?"

"Addy scared too," Borysko said. It wasn't a question.

"Yeah, she is, buddy. She's terrified. Not only for Ellory, but Yana too. Will you help me keep her calm? Hold her hand if she cries? Give her hugs?"

Both boys nodded solemnly.

The trip home was unnaturally quiet. MacGyver was

lost in his own head, worrying about what Vogel could possibly want with the girls. And the boys were most likely thinking about how scared Yana was. They'd been watching over her for quite a while now, and this had to be extremely difficult for them...not knowing what was happening or where she could be.

When MacGyver pulled up to his house, there were several cars already parked along the street. The three got out of the Explorer, and Artem and Borysko ran up to the door with MacGyver hot on their heels.

Addison stood when they entered, and the look on her face almost broke MacGyver. It was obvious she was hoping it was her daughter and Yana coming through the door. When she saw the boys, the control she was desperately holding on to broke.

Tears streamed down her face even as she held her arms open for Artem and Borysko. They ran to her and threw their arms around her. Addison rocked back on a foot, then sank to her knees so she could hold the boys better.

"Ricky's gonna find them," she told the boys. "We just have to stay strong until they come home. I'm sure Ellory is taking care of Yana, she's okay."

None of them knew what was happening with the girls, but MacGyver hoped like hell Addison was right. Love for this woman spread throughout his body like a warm blanket. She was devastated herself, and yet she was still doing her best to be positive for the boys. And the confidence in her voice, the absolute conviction that he would find Yana and Ellory, made him desperate to live up to every word that came out of her mouth.

Looking around, MacGyver saw that Julie Hurt had arrived, her husband, Patrick, at her side. Smiley and Flash were there as well. Flash was standing off to the side, looking frustrated and concerned, and Smiley had his cell up to his ear.

They weren't the only people who'd shown up. Abe, Benny, and Mozart were also there. As was Caroline. She was standing by the couch, where she'd been sitting with Addison when they'd arrived.

As he waited for Addy to be done reassuring the boys, the door behind him opened. Turning—and now fully understanding the hope and expectation he'd seen on Addison's face when *he'd* arrived—he saw Remi, Josie, Wren, and Maggie.

Addison and the boys were soon surrounded by the women. Everyone was hugging and crying, saying reassuring words to encourage their friend.

It made MacGyver feel incredibly grateful to have these people at their backs. Men and women who would drop everything simply to show their support. But he needed to talk to Addison. See if she could tell him anything else that might be useful in finding Ellory and Yana.

As if she could read his mind, Addison extracted herself from their friends and walked over to him. She practically collapsed into his arms, and MacGyver held her as tightly as he could. "Ricky," she whispered into his ear, as she held him with her own iron grip.

"I know. We're gonna get them back."

She nodded. And that small nod made MacGyver even more determined. His Addy trusted him with the most precious thing in her life...her daughter. And he wouldn't let her down.

He walked backward with Addison, putting a little space between her and the suddenly very crowded living room. He put his hands on her face and stared at her for a long moment. Her eyes were red, her skin was blotchy from crying, and her hair was mussed, but she wasn't broken. Not in the least.

"That asshole took our babies," she said, her voice trembling not with fear, but anger. "Why would he do that? He doesn't even really *like* Ellory."

"I don't know, but we're going to find him, and our girls, and make sure this *never* happens again."

Addison nodded.

Just then, Smiley announced, "They found him."

Addison spun around so fast, she would've fallen over if MacGyver hadn't grabbed her hips. "Where are they? Are they bringing them home?"

"They've found Vogel, not the girls," Smiley told her quietly.

"What?" Addison whispered, shock clear in her voice.

MacGyver's own stomach clenched. If Ellory and Yana weren't with Vogel, where were they?

CHAPTER SEVENTEEN

"I got this one!" Ellory exclaimed. It was way harder than she'd thought it would be to figure out how to climb the stack of boxes and break into one of the top containers. It was also one thing to maneuver in such a small space as this, but another in the pitch dark...and more difficult still with a very freaked-out little sister to look after.

But after several false starts, and after falling on her ass twice, she'd made it to the top of one of the stacks of boxes. Then she'd used her fingernails to pry up the tape on one side of the uppermost box. That took a while too. Whoever packed the boxes did an excellent job.

It was nerve-racking to reach into a box without being able to see what you were about to touch. It could be something sharp that would cut her, or something gross and slimy. But Ellory hoped to be able to use anything they found. Clothes could be used to cushion the floor beneath them, flashlights would be super helpful right about now, a box full of water bottles wouldn't be unappreciated. But of course, she was hoping for something like a bunch of guns or knives...or some sort of tool that could cut through metal.

Snorting at herself for such ridiculous thoughts, Ellory forced herself to concentrate on the task at hand. Reaching into the box, she braced for whatever she might find.

To her surprise, whatever she touched was soft. Furry. It wasn't alive—thank goodness—and it had both hard and soft parts. Moving her hand around cautiously, Ellory discovered there were a lot of whatever it was she was feeling. Frustrated at her lack of sight, Ellory turned her head to speak to her sister.

"Yana?"

"Ellory?" the little girl returned.

"I'm going to drop something down. I want you to move so your back is against the boxes. As far away from me as possible. Do you understand?"

"Yes."

"Do it now."

Ellory's limbs were shaking. She wasn't used to such strenuous exertion. Holding herself up by balancing on the tiny ledges of stacked boxes wasn't exactly something she did every day. If she made it out...no...*when* she made it out of there, she was going to ask Ricky if he'd help her get more in shape. She was skinny and short. Hopefully once she hit puberty that would change, but in the meantime, she wanted to be able to do physical stuff like this more easily in the future.

"I here," Yana said.

Ellory was proud of the little girl. This situation was scary as hell. But she was handling herself pretty well, all things considered. Maybe it was because of where she'd come from. Of everything she and her brothers had to do to survive in their home country. And that made Ellory a little sad. Proud, but sad.

"Okay, I'm throwing down whatever this is. Stay where you are until I climb down. Understand?"

"Yes."

Ellory shifted her balance on her toes and picked up whatever was in the box. She held it over the small space they'd been allotted and dropped it. There was a soft thud when it landed. "Okay?" she asked Yana.

"Okay!" the little girl said immediately.

Ellory picked up another one of whatever was in the box and dropped that too. Then did it one more time. She wasn't sure when she'd have the strength to climb back up the towering boxes of doom, so if she'd found something they could use, she wanted to be able to have a couple of them...whatever it was.

"I'm coming down now. Stay where you are, Yana. You're doing so good."

"Ellory care."

"I'm being careful," she reassured the little girl. With her muscles shaking, Ellory carefully made her way back down the stack of boxes. When she reached the bottom, she couldn't help but be pleased that she'd made it.

Feeling around, she found the items she'd thrown to the floor.

"Yana go you?"

"Yeah, it's safe. Come here," Ellory told her. Within seconds, she felt Yana's outstretched hand, looking for where she was standing. Taking it, Ellory sat on the metal floor of the container with a small sigh. It felt good to sit. To rest her legs. Her thighs and calves were going to be very sore from balancing on the small lips of boxes she'd used as a ladder.

Yana settled into her lap as if she'd done it a thousand times. Ellory couldn't help but be glad she was there, which immediately made her feel guilty as hell. She didn't want her sister to be here, no way in hell, but having her there made everything feel a little less scary. She couldn't break down. Had to stay in control to look after Yana. If she'd been by herself, she would probably be in a heap on the floor, sobbing. She wouldn't have found the energy or bravery to climb up those boxes in the dark.

"Let's see what we have here," she said, as she reached for one of the objects. Ellory turned it over in her hands and tried to picture in her mind what she was holding. After a moment, she realized it was a stuffed animal of some kind. The hard spots were probably the plastic eyes and nose. There was something between the paws of the thing, but Ellory couldn't figure out what it was. She turned it over and over, running her hands along every inch of the toy.

Just when disappointment was setting in that she'd found a box full of stuffed animals that would be absolutely no help whatsoever in getting them out of their prison, she touched what felt like a button hidden in a seam of the fur along the stuffed animal's back.

Without thinking, she pressed it.

The thing came to life in her hands, scaring the crap out of Ellory and making her throw it across the small space. Yana jerked in fright and hit her head on Ellory's chin in the process.

Blinking, Ellory couldn't believe what she was seeing. The stuffed animal was a bear holding a present. It wore red and green overalls, and what scared her and Yana so badly was a string of tiny lights, flashing around the gift in the bear's hands, and the song "Jingle Bells" that immediately started playing.

Ellory stared at it for a moment—then smiled. Huge.

She could see! The bear had *lights*, and even though they were flashing, they were shockingly bright in the pitch-black space, lighting up their small prison as easily as if she'd flicked on the light to her room back home.

Ellory eagerly reached for one of the other bears she'd thrown out of the box and quickly found the button at the back, turning that one on too. It also flashed its colorful lights and began playing "Jingle Bells." She did the same with the third.

The bears threw off enough light that she could easily see the boxes stacked around them. Shaking her head, Ellory was amazed that she'd done what she had...climbed up about ten feet or so to the top box. It looked scary as hell, and she probably never would've attempted it if she could see what she was doing.

But it was worth it. They had light! Now that she could see, maybe she could make some sort of steps out of the boxes. If she could get back up to the top once more, throw down the top box, then the next, she could create a stairway, making it easier to examine what was in the other boxes around them. Surely they weren't *all* full of stuffed animals.

A particular memory from hanging out in the garage with Ricky, tinkering with his stuff, came to mind. One of the first things he'd taught her was how useful a battery could be. Hand warmer, lighter, electromagnet for a compass, fire starter...there were a ton of things he'd shown her. A fire inside this container was a horrible idea...but maybe she could MacGyver something else that would help them.

She grinned. MacGyver. She just had to channel Ricky. If he and his SEAL buddies were stuck in here, what would they do? Her mind spun, and suddenly she was anxious to see what else she had to work with. Brady might think she was useless because of her disease—he'd never said it, but she wasn't dumb; she could see in his eyes that he thought she was pathetic—but she'd show him.

"Yana, can you hold this guy—I think we'll name him Fred—and if his lights stop, can you push this button so he starts up again so I can see?"

"Yes," Yana said, grabbing the bear and holding him to her chest.

Ellory stood and did a few stretches. She felt energized. "One box down, ninety-hundred to go," she muttered, before helping Yana stand off to the side where she wouldn't get hit by the box Ellory planned to shove off the top of the stack. Then she took a deep breath and began to climb once more. Time was of the essence. She had no idea how long it would take for the container they were in to be put on whatever ship would take them across the world. The faster she could work, the sooner she MacGyvered a way out of here, the better.

* * *

MacGyver glared at Brady Vogel. As soon as he got word that Kevlar and Blink had Ellory's biological father in their grasp, he'd left the house to meet up with them. Smiley and the older SEALs had stayed behind to make sure the boys and Addison were all right.

Addison wasn't happy with him at the moment. She'd wanted to come with him. To face her ex. To demand to know why he'd kidnapped her girls and where he'd taken them. But MacGyver had begged her to stay home. He'd finally gotten through to her by saying that if something happened to her, he wouldn't be able to live with himself.

Their parting was extremely painful. MacGyver wanted to stay home with her, hold her, comfort her. His team-mates could get the information they needed from Vogel, of that MacGyver had no doubt. But he needed to confront the man. Get answers.

He and Flash had met up with Safe and Preacher at Wolf's house. Surprisingly, the older SEAL and former team leader had offered up his basement as a perfect place to interrogate Vogel.

When MacGyver arrived, the furniture in the base-ment had been pushed to the side and Vogel was sitting in a chair, his hands cuffed behind him, his face sporting two very painful-looking black eyes. He had blood coming from a split lip, but he wasn't cowed. Not in the least.

"I told you what would happen when MacGyver got here," Kevlar said. "He's not going to be as nice as Blink and I were. If I were you, I'd start talking. And not the bullshit you've been spouting so far," he growled.

"I've been telling you the truth. Ellory texted me and said she was sick of being bullied and didn't want to tell her mom, since she'd told her the bullying was done. She was embarrassed. So she asked if I would come pick her up. It was *her* idea for me to say that you and her mom were in an accident. She's smart! She knew I wasn't approved to pick her up. Check my phone. The texts are there. She begged me to get her out of school. It wasn't *my* idea!"

MacGyver listened without expression. He didn't believe Vogel's story for a second. "And Yana? Why did you pick her up?"

"Again, Ellory told me to. Said her mom always picks up her and Yana together. Said the little girl would be afraid if Ellory wasn't there to get her. She went in with me and pretended to be upset so we'd be able to sign her out too. Check the school cameras, man! They'll show you I'm not lying."

"Where's his phone?" MacGyver asked.

"Here," Kevlar said, chucking it over to him.

MacGyver caught it and turned it over.

"Code is one-two-three-four-five," Kevlar added, without the smallest hint of amusement on his face.

"Of course it is," MacGyver muttered, before unlocking the phone and opening the text messaging app. There were texts from Ellory, begging him to come get her from school. Suggesting that he tell the secretary that he and Addison had been in an accident. On the surface, they seemed to prove the man wasn't lying—but MacGyver's bullshit meter was still pinging like a motherfucker. Especially after the conversation he'd had with Ellory that very morning at breakfast.

"Where are they now then? Where did you take them?" he asked the man.

"I dropped them off a few blocks from your house. Again, it was Ellory's suggestion. Since Addison works from home, she didn't want her mom to see them getting out of my car. Thought Addison would be hurt or something, since Ellory didn't call her to get her from school. I don't know, man. She's a teenager. They make no sense."

"She's only twelve," MacGyver said, feeling annoyed. For some reason, he wanted to make it clear that Ellory wasn't yet in her teens. It made a huge difference in his eyes.

"Whatever. Look, man. I was trying to do the right

thing. My daughter was in distress and I wanted to help. That's it. I have no idea what happened to her and the other girl after I dropped them off."

Everything within MacGyver was screaming that Vogel was lying through his teeth. It would be an easy thing for Tex to check the cameras at the schools and the time-stamps on the texts. They didn't have Ellory's phone, but Tex could also look into her phone records and make sure Ellory really did send the texts. He could ping the locations and see where the texts were made from. Her phone was off right now, so they couldn't track her or Yana that way.

Frustration ate at him. He thought for sure once they had Vogel, they'd have the answers they needed. But Yana and Ellory could be anywhere.

Just then, Preacher's phone rang.

"Preacher. *What?* Fuck. Right. Hang on, let me put my phone on speaker...okay...we can all hear you."

"MacGyver?" It was Smiley.

He stepped closer to Preacher. "Here," he said.

"Addison just got a ransom call."

MacGyver's world spun. "What?"

"Yeah. The guy said he has Ellory and Yana. Said he wants two hundred and fifty thousand for their safe return."

MacGyver couldn't speak. He was literally frozen.

"When did the call come in?" Safe asked.

"Just now. Less than two minutes ago."

"I told you I wasn't involved in this!" Vogel crowed from where he sat.

MacGyver blocked him out.

"We didn't get the entire thing recorded, but we got most of it," Smiley said.

"Play it," Kevlar ordered. "Maybe we'll recognize the voice."

There was some shuffling on the other end of the line, and then a voice MacGyver had never heard before in his life spoke on the recording.

...fine now, but if you don't get two hundred and fifty K to me by tomorrow night, they won't be fine any longer. Don't call the cops, and the money should be in fifty- and twenty-dollar bills. Don't try anything funny or you'll never see the girls again. Put the money in a cardboard box and leave it behind the gas station on Fourth and Aspen, by the dumpster, at ten o'clock sharp tomorrow night. Then drive away. This will be your one and only chance to get them back.

Everyone was silent for a moment.

Then Wolf asked, "Anyone recognize the voice?"

MacGyver shook his head, along with the rest of his team.

"Fuck," Kevlar muttered.

"He's going to kill my daughter! What are we gonna do?"

Everyone turned to stare at Vogel. This was the first time he'd shown any emotion other than desperation for them to believe him, so they wouldn't continue using him as a punching bag...and it didn't seem genuine.

Why was he so concerned *now*? Shouldn't he have been freaking out the entire time, from the moment he realized his daughter was missing?

The man knew where the girls were. MacGyver would bet his Budweiser pin on it.

"Let him go," he said in a low, controlled tone.

"What?"

"Are you fucking kidding?"

"Have you lost your mind?"

MacGyver ignored his friends' exclamations. "You're coming with us back to the house. You're a witness. You were the last one to see Ellory and Yana. Any scrap of information you know, we need to hear. Cars you passed, people you saw, things Ellory said. You're her father, so you deserve to be a part of this as much as we do."

To his relief, no one questioned him further, and MacGyver ignored the speculative looks his teammates were giving him. He turned to Preacher, who was still holding out his phone. "Smiley?"

"I'm here," his friend said.

"Tell Addison and the others we're on our way back to the house. We'll figure out a way to get the money one way or another. Even if I have to sell everything I own, I'm getting our girls back."

"Will do. Later."

MacGyver didn't have time to discuss what he was thinking with his friends, and in any case, he certainly wouldn't do so in front of Vogel, but they knew him well enough to know he had a plan. They would go with the flow until he could tell them what he was thinking.

Vogel knew something. The girls' disappearance started and ended with him. He may not have made that ransom call—but he also didn't seem surprised by it. And his emotions definitely weren't genuine.

Sometimes keeping your enemies close was the best way to gather intel. And that was exactly what MacGyver was going to do. He wasn't going to let the man out of his sight. He was the key to finding Ellory and Yana, of that MacGyver had no doubt.

CHAPTER EIGHTEEN

Ellory studied the random pile of items around her, frustrated. She'd built the staircase of boxes easily enough, but had been disappointed by what she'd found in the first dozen containers she'd opened. They were full of the same Christmas toys as she'd already discovered. They definitely had plenty of light now, but the repeating "Jingle Bells" song was starting to get to her. She wanted to rip the heads off the bears to shut them up, but she didn't dare since that might mean they'd lose the light they provided.

She'd refused to give up, knowing there had to be *something* she could use to help her and Yana escape.

She was excited when she'd opened the thirteenth box and found dozens of travel packets of tools. A tiny hammer, two screwdrivers, and a pair of pliers were inside each folded piece of plastic. There were nails, screws, and even a couple of thumbtacks in each, as well. Then she felt stupid. The tools were pretty much useless unless someone was doing something as simple as putting up a picture frame. They were obviously made by some company thinking it was a cute thing for women or children.

But her dismay didn't last long. Even if they were tiny and cheap, she had tools. They were still items she could use. Maybe.

Other boxes held things that weren't as useful. Plastic flip-flops, tiny squishy frogs, and even a box full of sex toys, which grossed Ellory out.

There hadn't been clothes of any kind so far, which was disappointing, as she wanted something softer than the metal floor of the container for Yana to lie on. She glanced at her little sister and wanted to cry. There were· tear tracks on her cheeks, and she was lying on her side, holding one of the stuffed bears in her arms, sound asleep.

The pressure she was under hit Ellory hard then. If she didn't find a way out of this box, they would both end up dead. Remembering what Brady had said, about how he'd sold her for her organs, made Ellory panic. She had to get out of here. *Now*. Before it was too late.

She'd thought about climbing over to the door, but after seeing how tightly packed the boxes were in the space, she didn't think there was any way she could remove enough of them for her and Yana to be able to make it to the door. And even if they did, she wasn't sure how they'd get out. She'd heard the padlock click closed even from where they were three quarters of the way inside the container.

She was still staring at Yana, trying to think of some way to use the batteries, tools and plastic frogs to escape, when something caught her eye behind Yana's head.

Moving slowly, Ellory crawled over to her sister to see what it was that she'd noticed. The color of the floor was different in one spot. It was...orange. At least, she thought it was; it was difficult to tell with the flashing colorful lights from the stuffed bears.

Moving Yana slowly and carefully, so the little girl didn't wake up, Ellory brought one of the bears closer so she could examine the spot on the floor. She touched it, and was surprised when it seemed...spongy.

"Holy shit!" she exclaimed, feeling a little guilty for swearing but she figured if there was ever a time to use a bad word, this was it. "It's rusted. The floor's rusted!"

Excitement spread through her body as she picked at the flecks on the floor. When a piece of rusted metal came up, Ellory gasped. She wasn't going to get too excited yet. Just because there was a little rust on the floor didn't mean it was anything like a trap door they could escape from. But the hope that swam through her bloodstream couldn't be stopped.

She began to poke and prod at the rusty spot, thrilled when more and more pieces of the metal broke off in her hand. Spinning around, she grabbed one of the useless little travel packs of tools and pulled out the hammer.

Slamming it down onto the weak part of the floor, Ellory winced at the loud sound that echoed in the small space.

Yana jerked awake and whimpered.

"I'm sorry, Yana. I didn't mean to scare you. But look! The floor is weak here. Maybe we can bust through it and get out."

"Good?" Yana asked.

"Yeah, this is good," Ellory said. Of course, the floor being weak was one thing, making a hole big enough for her and Yana to get out of was another. And it didn't matter *how* big a hole they made if the container was sitting on the ground. They could get through rusted metal, but they couldn't tunnel through concrete or asphalt or whatever was under the container they were in.

And if their Conex got stacked onto another, they were equally screwed.

They would have one chance to get out of here—when the container they were in was moved. And it was likely they'd be caught. But Ellory wasn't ready to give up. She had to try.

"Come on, Yana, take this." She handed her one of the little screwdrivers. "See if you can pry up the metal." Demonstrating what she wanted the little girl to do, Ellory watched with pride as her sister didn't even hesitate.

As Ellory hammered at the rusted metal, and Yana did what she could to pry up the loose parts, Ellory prayed as hard as she could that Ricky and her mom were on their trail. Because getting out of this box was only the first step in rescuing themselves...she couldn't drive, had no idea where they were, and she didn't want to run into anyone else who might be in cahoots with Brady.

Ellory smiled. Cahoots. She hadn't ever had a chance to use that word in a sentence in everyday life. Her English teacher would be so proud. Then she sobered. Her English teacher wouldn't know about the word usage if Ellory didn't get out of here.

"Keep going, Yana. This is going to work."

One thing Ricky always emphasized was the power of positive thinking. He told her that anytime he was in a situation that looked bleak, he and his SEAL teammates would never ever talk about the bad things that could happen. They knew about them, but they didn't voice them out loud. He said that gave the bad energy in the world power to outweigh the good.

Taking that advice to heart, Ellory began to talk to her sister about all the things they were going to do when they got home. About how happy Artem and Borysko would be to see them. About how their mom would cry. Maybe Ricky too. How they'd get to eat whatever they wanted, sleep in their own beds, put on some clean clothes.

She babbled on and on as she and Yana worked, hoping against hope with every strike of the hammer that she'd be able to break through this stupid metal box before the huge cranes came to haul them away.

* * *

Addison had no idea why Ricky had brought Brady to their house. She was *furious*. At Ricky. At her ex. At everyone and everything. She was at the end of her rope, and all she wanted was for everyone to get out of her house and leave her alone.

But as soon as she had the thought, she felt guilty. Everyone was there because they were trying to help. The women were keeping Artem and Borysko distracted in their room, the men were doing everything in their power to gather the ransom money—and to hopefully find Ellory and Yana before they had to *use* the money.

A few of the SEALs were on the phone, talking to the Tex person she'd heard so much about, their commander, and Wolf and the men on his team who weren't already at the house. Their women were actually out driving around, physically looking for any signs of the girls.

Everyone was helping—and all Addison could do was stand around helplessly.

Ricky hadn't left her side. When he'd come back to the house with her ex in tow, he'd come straight to her and hadn't moved since. It was as if he was...guarding her? That couldn't be right though. Ricky wouldn't have brought her ex here if he thought he'd hurt her...would he?

For the first time in what seemed like forever, Addison's brain kicked into gear. Why *was* Brady here? He was the one who'd taken Ellory and Yana out of school without permission.

"Ricky? Can we talk?"

"Sure."

"Alone?"

He looked around at all the people in their house, and then down at her with one brow cocked. She wanted to laugh, but she felt as if that would somehow be inappropriate considering all that was happening.

"Why is Brady here?" she whispered.

Ricky looked around, then with an arm around her waist, he pulled her down the hall toward their room. He ushered her inside and shut the door. "Are you all right? Hanging in there?"

"No, and yes. Why is he here?" she asked again, looking her husband in the eye. "I hate him. I don't want him here."

"I hate him too," Ricky said, surprising Addison. "And he's here because he knows something. I don't know what, and he's putting on a decent show of being a concerned father, but something's off about him. And the only way I know how to find out what he knows is to keep him close."

A light bulb went off in Addison's head. "You think he might say or do something that will lead us to the girls?"

"Maybe. But I'd rather know where he is than have him out there doing God knows what."

Addison nodded. That made perfect sense to her. "Maybe I can help. Irritate him. Get him riled up. Maybe he'll slip up and say something useful."

"I don't want you to do anything that will cause you pain," Ricky said.

Addison blinked at him. "Not knowing where my girls are is causing me pain. Not knowing if they're hurt, or if someone is scaring them, or even if they're..." she paused and took a deep breath before continuing, "*alive*, is causing me pain. If I can antagonize Brady enough that he breaks, I'll do it. I can't hit him physically, like you guys obviously got to, but I can hit him with words."

"I love you," Ricky whispered, putting his forehead against hers.

"I love you too."

"I've been scared while on a mission. When things went south and I thought I might die, or my friends might die. But I've never been as terrified as I am right this moment. Not knowing where our kids are? I feel as if I can't function. I can't think."

"I know," Addison soothed. Amazingly, knowing he was as scared as she was kind of steadied her. Made her feel not so alone. "Do you think he did it?" she asked.

Ricky obviously knew the "he" she was talking about. "Yes."

"He wasn't the guy on the phone. The ransom guy."

"Nope," Ricky agreed, taking a deep breath. "But that doesn't mean he didn't hire someone to make the call."

"And the texts? Could those be faked?"

"I think they could. That's not my area of expertise, but Tex is doing what he can to try to figure it out."

"So you think he took them and put them somewhere," Addison concluded.

Ricky stared at her for a long moment. "Yeah, sweetheart. I do."

"Why?"

"*That*, I don't know for sure. We've got a whole house full of people who won't rest until they figure it out. But I'm thinking that ransom money has a lot to do with it."

Her eyes narrowed at that. "Right. So...can I go and piss off my ex now? I've waited a long time to tell him off."

Ricky's lips twitched, but he didn't manage a full smile. He nodded then turned to the door.

Addison didn't waste any time. She waded through all their friends, passing Wolf, who'd obviously arrived while they were in the bedroom. Made sure Artem and Borysko weren't in earshot—they weren't; Remi and Maggie still had them back in their room, playing cards—and walked straight up to Brady.

"Why are you here, Brady?"

"Why? Because my daughter is missing," he said.

"Not good enough. Why do you even care? You went almost twelve years without giving one little shit about her. You didn't call. You didn't contribute to her upbringing in any way, emotionally or monetarily. *Nothing*. So why now?"

"I've changed," he retorted.

"Have you?" she challenged. "The first time you watched me change her diaper, your forehead crinkled and you made a face that communicated just how gross you thought it was. And when you found out about her Crohn's, you made the exact same face."

"Cut me some slack, Addison, it was a surprise."

"It wouldn't have been if you were there for her."

"What do you want me to say?" he asked belligerently.

"I want you to tell me why the hell you went behind my back and lied to pick up my daughter!"

"She's my daughter too. I should've been on that list in the first place!"

"Wrong. She's *not* your daughter. Biologically, yes. But in every other way, no. Ricky's done more to raise that girl than you ever have, and he's only known her for little more than a year."

That seemed to get to him.

"He's not her father," he growled.

"The hell he's not. He's spent countless hours with Ellory, talking to her, bonding with her, teaching her things. He listens to her. He gets her blankets and heating pads when her belly hurts. He's more of a father than you've ever been in her entire life."

"That's not my fault!"

"Yes it is!" Addison yelled back. "You had every opportunity to be a dad. But instead, *you left*. Without a word. Without looking back. And now that you're in Riverton, you think you can just step into the role of dad? You can't. It's not that easy."

"That's because you've been telling her lies about me. Turning her against me!"

Addison laughed, but it wasn't a humorous sound. "No, I haven't. Believe it or not, we don't talk about you when you aren't around, Brady. The entire world doesn't revolve around you. No. You've turned her against you all on your own. With your incessant texts and calls. Your insensitive remarks about her Crohn's and her size. There's *no way* that Ellory would've contacted you if she was being bullied —and you and I both know it. So why don't you just tell me what you did with her and Yana and this whole damn farce can end!"

She'd stepped forward and was yelling in Brady's face by the time she was finished, but she could still feel Ricky's hand at her back. He was letting her say what she needed to say while still right there, ready to step in if things went sideways.

And she could feel the rest of her friends there too. They had everyone's attention in the entire room.

As if he could feel the animosity coming from each and every person staring at him, Brady began to sweat. "You've always been so goddamn overbearing," he sneered. "So controlling. It's about time you learned that you can't control everyone and everything around you. About time it came back to bite you in the ass! You've always had *everything*. You have no idea how it feels to have to clean up after everyone. People throw shit on the floor and don't think twice about who has to pick up their trash. You've never struggled, Addison. *Ever*."

"That's such bullshit," she told him. "I've done nothing *but* struggle. You think it's been easy, being a single mother with a kid who has a chronic disease? It hasn't. It's never easy—but it's still a privilege. And everything I have, I've worked my ass off for. *Life* isn't easy, Brady. That's some-thing you've never managed to learn because you've been too busy playing the victim. You've been looking for the easy way out your entire life!"

"Well, you won't have to worry about me for much longer," he told her, not backing down.

"Yeah? Why this time?" Addison pushed.

"Because I'm leaving this shit hole! I'm going to go to Hawaii to sit in the sun and sand and enjoy myself for fucking once!" Brady's face was bright red at this point. He was breathing hard, and he looked as if he wanted to haul off and hit her.

Addison laughed. "And how are you going to afford that? Hawaii's expensive, dumbass. Milk costs triple what it does here. And an apartment? At least double."

"I have money," he insisted.

"Yeah? Then how about giving us some to help get *your* daughter back safe and sound, since you're so concerned? Don't think I haven't noticed you aren't offering a single dime toward the ransom!"

"She's not coming back!" he yelled. "Why would I pay to get her back when she's already gone?!"

The words exploded into the room—and Addison instinctively took a step back as she gasped in shock.

"I-I mean..."

But it was too late. He'd said the words, and everyone heard them.

It was Blink who swiftly grabbed Brady in a chokehold from behind and leaned down to whisper in his ear. Addison was standing more than close enough to hear what the usually silent SEAL said to her ex.

"We knew you had more intel than you were sharing. You're surrounded by men who know ten ways to kill and hide a body that'll never be found. Time to start talking, Vogel. Unless you want to spend hours being tortured for the information. Because right now? Each and every one of us would love to take a turn."

Addison held her breath.

It felt as if the *entire room* held a collective breath.

Brady flicked his gaze around the space frantically, as if looking for some sort of escape. But there was none.

With his left hand, Blink reached into his pocket and took out a KA-BAR knife. The folding one all the SEALs carried with them at all times. He expertly flicked it open but instead of holding it to Brady's neck, as Addison might've expected, he reached between the man's legs and pressed the tip against his dick.

"I spent plenty of time being tortured in an Iranian

prison. If you think I don't know what I'm doing...think again."

"Okay okay! Don't cut my dick off! I'll tell you where they are! But it doesn't matter. It's too late!"

Addison's blood ran cold. She'd done it. She'd egged on Brady enough to break him. But hearing that it was too late? That almost broke *her*.

Ricky's arm went around her waist, holding her up as he backed farther away from Brady and Blink.

"Get the women out of here," Kevlar ordered as the men closed ranks on Brady. The table was moved to the living room, and a chair was placed in the middle of the tiled dining room floor.

Addison was aware of people moving around her, but she couldn't take her eyes off her ex. He was going to tell them where Ellory and Yana were. What he'd done with them. She was elated and terrified at the same time.

"Come on, Addison, come with us into your room," Julie Hurt said quietly.

"No, she stays," Ricky said, tightening his arm around her.

Addison sagged into him. She was more thankful than she could say that he wasn't going to make her leave. She didn't really want to stay to see Brady tortured, but no way was she going anywhere until she had the information on her babies.

Brady was sitting on the chair now, slumped over, surrounded by big bad Navy SEALs.

"Talk, Vogel," Safe ordered.

And he did. Without prompting, he spilled his guts. Explained everything.

When he was done telling them what he'd done, how he'd *sold* Ellory's body parts and arranged for her to be shipped overseas alive, to a buyer who wanted the organs as fresh as possible, Addison wanted to vomit.

And when he admitted to hiring someone to make the ransom call, because he wanted to throw suspicion off of himself by acting like a worried father—and because he wanted to double his money—Addison wanted to kill the bastard herself.

But it wasn't until he told them where he'd left little Yana and Ellory that true fear hit.

They'd been locked inside one of those huge metal containers, scheduled to be loaded onto a ship.

No, he didn't know which one, only that it was blue. No, he didn't know when the ship was scheduled to leave, only that it was soon. Yes, he'd tell them the name of his contact, but it was probably a pseudonym.

The more he talked, the more horrified and scared Addison became. This man, the father of her child, had kidnapped, sold, and as good as murdered her. And there he sat, obviously feeling more sorry for himself than worried about the life of his own daughter.

"We'll call the cops, you guys go to the shipyard," Wolf said.

Without a word, Ricky turned toward the door, pulling Addison with him. Once again, she was thankful he didn't try to talk her into staying home. She needed to be where her girls were. She just prayed that they weren't too late. That they wouldn't see a huge container ship pulling out of its dock on its way to Asia. If that happened, she had no idea how they'd find Ellory and Yana. The clock was ticking, and she was deathly afraid it was too late.

CHAPTER NINETEEN

Ellory grinned. They'd done it! She and Yana had used the stupid tiny hammer and cheap screwdriver to make a large enough hole in the floor of the container that they could both fit through. Of course, there was nothing underneath but the concrete the box was sitting on top of. But eventually it had to be moved, and that's when they could make their escape...she hoped.

"Good job, Yana!" she told her little sister. Staying busy had done them both good, taken their minds off of their current situation. Thank God the container they were in was old and crappy.

"Come here," she told Yana, pulling her back into her lap. It made Ellory feel better to have her near, as much as she hoped it comforted the little girl.

"Bad man. Father," Yana said.

"Yeah," Ellory agreed. "Brady is not a good man."

"Why?"

She sighed. "I don't know. He can't have always been that way, because our mom is smart enough not to be with someone who treats her badly."

"Ricky good," Yana said.

"He is," Ellory agreed.

"In Ukraine, he help. Good. Food, water. Hide." Then the little girl sighed and said something in Ukrainian. Ellory assumed she was explaining in a language she knew why she thought Ricky was a good person.

She looked up at Ellory. "He find. Save. Like in Ukraine."

"I hope so," Ellory said, with a deep sigh of her own. The Christmas song was making her head feel as if it was going to burst like a watermelon hit with a sledgehammer. She busied herself turning off all of the toys except for the one Yana was clutching. The decibel level of the sound was immediately much more manageable. The lighting wasn't as good, but now that they'd done what they could to rescue themselves, their only option now was to wait. Might as well wait in the light coming off one bear rather than ten.

She picked up one of the toy frogs and put it in her pocket. It was silly. But maybe, just maybe, it'd be good luck. While Ellory felt good about what they'd done, it was still a long shot that they'd be rescued. And getting out of this container while it was being moved would be dangerous and tricky. They'd have to get out fast, because if they went out the hole when the container was too high, they could be hurt or even die by falling to the ground. Even if they managed to get out, they had to worry about someone seeing them and taking them captive again.

The truth was, Ellory was terrified. Not only for herself, but for her little sister. Yana didn't deserve to be here. She'd already been through so much in her short life.

Not wanting to cry and let the little girl know how scared she was, Ellory pressed her lips together tightly. She wanted her mom. Wanted to feel her arms around her. Her mom's hugs always made her feel better.

Ellory had no idea how much time had passed since they'd made the hole in the floor of the container, how long she and Yana had been sitting in the semi-dark, quietly waiting...when suddenly, the container jerked.

It was time! They were being moved.

Yana scrambled off her lap and looked at Ellory with wide eyes.

"This is it. We'll have to move fast. I'll go first and as soon as I'm out, you follow. I'll help you. Okay?"

"Okay," Yana echoed. She looked terrified but she wasn't crying, which Ellory was taking as a good sign. Reaching out, she turned off the stuffed bear, and the sudden darkness was almost as jarring as the abrupt cessation of sound.

Ellory hesitated, then stuffed the toy down her shirt. The bear had saved their lives, and Yana seemed attached to it. She didn't want to leave it behind.

The container swayed back and forth slightly as it slowly lifted off the ground. Ellory stared down at the hole and blinked, the sudden light making her squint. It was still light outside, but not terribly bright. She guessed the sun was about to set, and she couldn't decide if that was a good or bad thing. Good because it would let them see where they were, where to run...but probably bad because it would allow others to see them more easily too. If the man Brady had met at the docks was the one moving the container, he'd obviously know who they were, and he'd do whatever it took to get them back.

Ellory *wasn't* going back. No way. Brady had been dumb enough to tell her their entire plan. She was still using her organs, thank you very much, and she didn't want to give them to anyone else.

Seeing the concrete slowly getting farther away as the container rose, she decided now was the time.

Moving quickly, praying the container wouldn't suddenly get lowered back to the ground—because she'd be squished like a pancake if it was—she lay down and stuck her arms out first, then her head. It was a tight fit, the rough edges of the metal bit into her shoulders, but Ellory barely felt them. Her adrenaline was sky-high and all she could think of was getting out.

The container was getting higher and higher and if she didn't hurry, there was no way Yana would be able to get out without getting hurt.

The second she had the thought that she wasn't going to make it, that she wouldn't fit through the hole after all, that they hadn't made it wide enough, her body popped out.

Ellory was glad her arms were already over her head to keep her from cracking her skull when she landed. Freedom had never felt so good! But she had no time to appreciate it. Springing to her feet, she turned and looked up. The container was five feet above the ground. Then six. Whoever was moving it wasn't messing around.

"Yana! Jump!" she ordered urgently as she held up her hands.

She saw Yana's terrified face for a moment before her legs appeared through the hole. The little girl had no trouble slipping out. One second Ellory thought it would be too late, that the container was too high, and the next, Yana was in her arms.

They both crashed to the ground in a heap of arms and legs. Ellory hit her tailbone when she landed on her butt, but she wrapped her arms tighter around her sister, trying to protect her from injury.

It took a second for the realization to hit that they were both free. That they were out of the box. But as soon as it did, the man operating the crane yelled something, and Ellory realized that they *weren't* free. Not yet.

"We have to get out of here, Yana!" she said urgently, getting to her feet and helping her sister stand.

Looking toward the man who was yelling, Ellory followed his line of sight—and saw her worst nightmare. The guy her father had sold them to was climbing out of the cab of a truck parked nearby, and the look on his face was one of pure fury and disbelief.

"Run!" Ellory yelled, pushing her sister toward the countless containers stacked up around them. They'd have to hide within the maze of huge metal boxes. They'd wait until it was dark, then try to sneak out and find help.

With the man's threats echoing in their ears, the girls ran.

* * *

MacGyver drove like a bat out of hell. He couldn't believe what Vogel had done. He'd *sold* Ellory. Knowing full well that she'd suffer while being shipped overseas in a fucking Conex container. And he'd left Yana there too, even though she hadn't been a part of the deal. She was collateral damage—Vogel's words, not his.

Fuck him. Fuck his contact. They'd figure out who that was and take him down too. Right now, the most important thing was finding which of the hundreds of containers Ellory and Yana had been stashed in.

Refusing to let doubt creep in, MacGyver did his best

to stay positive. Failure wasn't an option. They'd shut down the entire shipyard and search every single damn Conex. They'd find the girls. They'd be scared out of their minds and freaking out, but they'd find them.

The line of cars following him gave MacGyver the confidence to make those claims in his head. He had some of the best SEALs the Navy had ever trained at his back. No one was going to give up until they'd found his daughters.

"I can't fucking believe this! What an asshole! A fucking *douchebag*. I wish Blink had cut his dick off. Is Wolf gonna kill him?"

MacGyver glanced at his wife. By all rights, she should be a mess right now. But anger had taken over and when he looked in her eyes, he saw the same determination he felt. "No," he said. "But the man's gonna wish he'd never messed with us."

"I can't believe he set all this up! That he pretended to be worried about her. His own flesh and blood!" Addison said, with only a little less heat than before.

MacGyver couldn't afford for her to slide into hysteria or worry. "He's not the man you knew twelve years ago."

"Actually, he is. He's exactly the same. Selfish and only out for himself. What's the plan? Where are we going to start looking when we get there?"

"At the containers closest to the ships. Any blue ones. I have no idea if enough time has passed for the Conex to be loaded onto a ship already or not, but I have no doubt Tex is already on this. He'll block any ships from leaving until we find the girls."

Taking a deep breath, Addison nodded. Her hands were clenched in her lap, but beyond that, she suddenly looked amazingly calm.

"Are you...are you all right, sweetheart?"

"Yes," she said with another nod.

"Because it's okay if you aren't."

At that, she turned to him. "Ellory is smart. And you've been spending all your free time with her out in your garage, teaching her exactly how you got your nickname. If there's any way to escape, she'll find it. Because she learned from the best. *You*, MacGyver."

It was one of the very few times his wife had used his SEAL nickname, and the timing, the reason she was using it now, meant more to him than he could put into words.

Despite that, he was filled with doubt. Ellory was still a little girl. There was almost no way she'd be able to find her way out of a metal container. Not without a blowtorch and a hell of a lot of luck. But his wife's praise and belief in both him and her daughter made him want to weep, and he'd never say anything to kill Addison's hope.

"She's brave, she'll get through this. And Yana...she might be five, but that girl has already been through hell. Literally. She'll stay strong too. Our girls are going to be all right." His words were more for his benefit than Addison's, but MacGyver wasn't surprised when she nodded firmly in agreement.

She reached out and put her hand on his thigh. "I love you. I'm terrified and pissed and a hundred other emotions. But knowing you're here...that you won't rest until you find our girls...it's what's keeping me going."

"I feel the same, hon," MacGyver admitted. "I've been through hundreds of missions, but this one is personal. If I'd had the strength, I would've left you back at the house with Artem and Borysko. But I need you, Addy. You're the incentive I need to keep going, to not fall to my knees in frustration, fear, and anger. You're also the reason that asshole is still breathing, because if you weren't there, I would've killed him without a second thought."

"Well, I need you. Ellory and Yana are going to need you to help them work through their feelings when we find them. And Artem and Borysko need you to show them how to be good men. So I'm glad you didn't kill him... because visiting you in the penitentiary wouldn't have been the same."

To his amazement, MacGyver chuckled. Then he sobered. "Vogel will get what's coming to him. For now, we just need to concentrate on finding a needle in a haystack."

"We can do this," Addison said. "After all, the Myth-Busters were able to find four needles in their haystack. All we need is to find one."

MacGyver wasn't surprised his wife enjoyed the old science TV show. It was a shame it wasn't on anymore, but he made a mental note to have a marathon *MythBusters* watching session with his family in the not-too-distant future.

As they neared the shipyard, tension returned to MacGyver's shoulders. Looking at the sea of shipping containers was daunting. But they had a place to start. Vogel claimed the one holding Ellory and Yana was blue. They'd start with the ones closest to the ships and work their way back from there.

Patrick Hurt put out a call for all SEALs, active duty or not, anywhere near the shipyard to come out and help search. MacGyver had no doubt his brothers-in-arms would show up in force. They'd find his girls. He couldn't imagine any other outcome.

* * *

Bree Haynes was a stalker. At least, she was acting like one. When she'd fled Las Vegas, and the men who were searching for her, she didn't really have a plan. All she knew was the man who'd helped her at the lowest time in her life—Jude "Smiley" Stark—was a Navy SEAL stationed in Riverton, California.

Even though she'd only met him briefly, he'd made her feel safe. Secure. So when her ex was pulling out all the stops to find her—so she could be shipped off to some foreign brothel as a sex slave—she could only think of one place to go.

And here she was.

In Riverton.

She was living out of her car, a Subaru Outback, and when she'd first arrived, she'd parked near one of the entrances to the naval base. To her amazement, it had only taken three days for her to recognize Jude Stark as he'd entered the base early one morning.

Since then, she'd been following him. She knew where he lived, where all of his teammates lived, and where he spent his nights. Usually at his condo. He also frequently went out of town. She'd followed him to the interstate more than once, but Bree always turned back before reaching the city limits, too afraid to leave Riverton, now that she'd made the journey here. She had no clue where Jude went so frequently, but she supposed it didn't really matter one way or another.

Tonight, however, when she'd spotted him leaving the base, he'd been hauling ass. She'd discreetly followed him to one of his friends' houses, where there were a ton of other cars parked.

More people arrived, and after a while, a bunch of them—including all of his teammates—came running out of the house, and she literally couldn't stop herself from following the caravan.

Her curiosity was out of control. She supposed it came with the boredom of her current situation. She spent all her time hiding out in her car, making up stories for the people she saw walking past her night and day.

She didn't sleep well, was always expecting the worst, like her ex tracking her down, or her new "owner" popping up and grabbing her at any time. And she had to admit... she'd become somewhat obsessed with Jude's friends. The women were always smiling and laughing, and the kids at the house everyone had just left were adorable.

But today, the tension coming from that house was palpable, even from her vantage point down the street, parked well away from the commotion.

Following the caravan at what she thought was a safe distance, she saw everyone pull into a huge shipyard. She itched to know more. To get closer. To find out what was happening. But Bree knew it wasn't a good idea. She should leave the area. The *state*. Go east, far away from Vegas to start a new life. She had money, although it was stuck in her bank account at the moment. If she tried to withdraw any of it, she'd probably be traced, and then she'd *really* have no choice but to leave the area.

But something...no, *someone*, was keeping her here. Jude. It was ridiculous, this pull he had on her.

Shaking her head to clear it, Bree parked about a block down from the entrance to the shipyard. She'd figure a way to get in, to find out what was happening. She may not be able to help...but then again, she might. She could be an innocent bystander who just happened on the scene.

There was no way Jude would recognize her. After all, he'd only seen her once, late at night, and she definitely wasn't looking her best at the time, all trussed up and bruised in the backseat of her kidnapper's car.

The fantasy of being able to integrate herself into the lives of the men and women she'd basically been stalking flared. Then died almost immediately.

She couldn't do that. It would be dishonest. Besides, why would they want to hang out with a homeless woman they didn't know, who had no ties to the Navy? She also didn't want the danger she was in to touch anyone else. Not the women she'd watched from a distance, not their children. And especially not Jude Stark.

This had to stop. Her stalking. Her obsession. She'd find out what was happening, assuage her curiosity, then leave. Head east. Or north. Whatever. Get as far away from California, Las Vegas...and the man who'd sold her to a sex trafficker. She'd start over somewhere. Figure out how to change her name, get her money from the bank, and *live* again.

Closing her car door quietly, Bree tried to look as casual as possible as she walked down the sidewalk. She was an ordinary citizen who just happened to be walking by.

As she headed for the entrance to the shipyard, she glanced to her right, toward the fence. Stopping in her tracks, she stared at the way the fence was pulled up out of the ground in one spot. It would be easy to slip under. She was small enough. At only five foot five, and after losing at least twenty pounds in the last few weeks because of her situation, Bree knew it would be a simple matter of getting on her belly and slithering under the fence. Hell, that's probably how the other local homeless men and women got in and out. There were probably lots of empty containers that would make excellent shelters from the sun, rain, and wind.

She considered her options for a heartbeat before glancing around. Seeing no one, she moved without thinking any more about it. She dropped to her belly and crawled under the fence. Once on the other side, she quickly ran behind the closest container.

Smiling, Bree couldn't believe she'd done it. She'd gotten in without having to make up some lie and without coming face-to-face with the people she'd been semi-stalking for what seemed like forever, but in reality was only a few months.

Moving stealthily through the shadows, Bree made her way in the direction the cars had gone. She would get close enough to hear what was going on, then she'd leave. For real.

She'd walked about half the length of the shipyard when she heard something odd. Pausing, Bree tilted her head to listen carefully.

The sound of someone crying was unmistakable.

It was quiet, hushed, but she'd done the same so often, sobbed hysterically but tried to do so quietly, so her hiding place wouldn't be discovered, that she easily recognized the sound.

Turning in a circle, she tried to figure out which direction the sound was coming from. The sun had dipped below the horizon now and it would be dark soon.

Pinpointing what she thought was the right direction, Bree began walking. Around one Conex, then another. She glanced to her left just as she was passing a tiny little space between two containers—and stopped abruptly.

There, smushed together, were two of the girls she'd seen around the house where everyone had been earlier.

They'd somehow managed to squeeze themselves into a space that was only about twelve inches wide.

Instinctively, she crouched down so as not to look so threatening. She wasn't the tallest woman in the world, but to two scared kids, she probably looked huge and terrifying.

It hit her like a ton of bricks—these girls must be the reason why everyone had left the house earlier like a bat out of hell. And since they'd come straight to the shipyard, they had to know they were here somewhere. Bree had no idea *why* they were here, or what was going on, but they were in trouble, of that she had no doubt. Why would they be hiding otherwise?

"Hey. My name is Bree. Bree Haynes. I'm a...friend of Jude Stark's," she said softly.

"I don't know who that is," the older girl said. "Go away! Leave us alone!"

Of course she didn't know him as Jude. The SEALs who'd saved her had called each other by their nicknames. "Smiley. He goes by Smiley."

It seemed like a weird name to Bree, as she hadn't seen Jude smile even once when she'd met him. Or even much since she'd been following him. He was as serious a man as she'd ever met...which weirdly made her more comfortable. Too many people—her ex and the man he'd sold her to included—smiled all the time. Maybe assuming that would make people relax around them. As if.

"Smiley?" the girl said.

"Uh-huh. And he's here. Along with the others."

"Others who?"

"Um...everyone? There were about a half-dozen cars that entered the shipyard just minutes ago. I bet they're here looking for you."

For a moment, Bree thought that would make the girl come out of her hiding spot, but as soon as she started to straighten, she slumped back down, holding onto the younger girl even tighter.

"He's looking for us," she whispered.

"Who is?" Bree asked.

"The guy my dad sold me to. *Us* to."

Bree was so confused, but now wasn't the time to ask questions. The girl was old enough to know what she was talking about. And the fact that she'd been sold to someone, just as Bree had, was enough for her to want to do anything in her power to protect her. *No one* should have to deal with what Bree herself was going through.

"Where is he? When did you see him last?"

"I don't know but it wasn't long ago. Yana was tired and couldn't run anymore, and everywhere we hid, he found us. I don't know how."

A noise nearby had the girl whimpering and lowering her head toward the smaller girl in her arms.

"Want Ricky," the little girl said between sobs.

Determination rose within Bree. "I'll distract him. Lead him away. Then you and the little one can get to Ricky." She wasn't sure which of the guys was Ricky, but if these kids wanted and trusted him, she'd do what she could to help them get to him. "Stay here until you can't hear anything anymore, then go back the way you came. Toward the cars and lights. They're looking for you."

"What if he gets you?"

"I'm not who he wants, so it doesn't matter. He'll realize I'm not you and let me go." Bree wasn't so sure that was the case, but the little girl didn't need to know that.

The sound of footsteps was louder now, and Bree was out of time. "Be safe. You can do this." Without waiting for a response, she stood and ran as quietly as she could past a row of containers. Then she smacked her hand against one of them, hard, and let out a fake pained cry.

Pausing for a moment to make sure the guy chasing the girls took the bait, she took off running in the opposite direction the girls were hiding, but not too fast that the man would lose her. She raced toward the far corner of the shipyard. Away from the SEALs she'd been stalking... er...following.

The man was faster than she'd given him credit for. Even in the semi-dark. Bree did her best to lead him as far away from the girls as she could, but it was only a matter of time before he caught her, especially when Bree realized she'd run out of shipyard. She ran around a Conex and barely caught herself from slamming into the perimeter fence.

Spinning around to run in a different direction, she came face-to-face with the man who'd been chasing her.

He was nowhere near the size of Jude or his friends, but he was still a few inches taller than Bree and probably a hundred pounds heavier. His brown hair was cut close to his head, and he had on a black shirt and dark jeans.

"Who the fuck are you?" he growled menacingly.

"Don't hurt me! I was just looking for a safe place to sleep tonight," Bree lied.

"*Fuck*! Damn it!" the man swore. Then he lunged forward and punched her in the face. *Hard*.

Bree's ex had hit her before, but the pain still took her by surprise. She went down, and the man didn't waste any time using his steel-toed boots to kick the shit out of her, even as he continued to use his fists. At first she tried to fight back, but after painfully ripping off a fingernail while clawing at him, trying to get him to stop, Bree curled into a tight ball, attempting to protect her head and kidneys at the same time.

Strangely, the man was silent as he hurt her. It was almost more terrifying that he wasn't speaking while he did his best to beat her into unconsciousness.

"Fucking homeless trash," he said after he finally seemed content with the damage he'd done. He spit on her and turned to walk away.

Bree lay on the concrete for a long and agonizing moment. Everything hurt. But she'd done it. She'd led him away from the two girls. She only prayed they'd taken the opportunity to run as hard and fast as they could toward Jude Stark and his friends.

CHAPTER TWENTY

MacGyver kept Addison at his side as he made his way toward another blue Conex. With every container they opened without finding Ellory and Yana, his confidence took a hit.

But there were cops and current and former SEALs all over the shipyard. At least twenty men he didn't know had shown up, along with his own circle of friends, and more were apparently on their way. If Yana and Ellory were here, they'd find them.

It was the *if* that had MacGyver feeling antsy and a little worried.

The men had fanned out, covering as much ground as they could. The only sound in the night was the squeaking of hinges as containers were opened and closed. The lights in the yard had been turned on in the area they were searching, making it seem more like day than night. But even with the enhanced brightness, the search was slow-going.

He and Addison were working mostly in silence. What was there to say? He couldn't give her false hope, and they both knew the clock was ticking. The longer it took to find them, the more worried they both were that they were too late. That the container had already been loaded onto a ship and was even now chugging its way across the ocean.

There was also the matter of the man who'd taken them. They had no way of knowing if he was still on the premises. For that reason, no one called out for the girls. On one hand, they wanted Ellory and Yana to know that people were looking for them. On the other, they couldn't afford to alert Brady's associate. If there was any chance at all that he still had access to their girls, he might hurt them...end things right here and now.

It was impossible to know what was the right thing to do in this situation.

They were opening what seemed like the hundredth container when there was the sound of a commotion behind them. Turning, MacGyver saw about four men running toward something. No, some*one*.

Two someones.

He was moving even before he thought about what his feet were doing.

He'd recognize Ellory and Yana anywhere.

"Mom!" Ellory yelled.

"Ricky!" Yana called out at the same time.

MacGyver had no idea how he covered so much ground so fast, but before he knew it, he had one of his daughters in his arms. He went to his knees, and Yana threw herself at him, sobbing so hard he could feel her little body hitching against his own as she held him with all the strength she had.

Addison was right there at his side, with Ellory in her embrace.

MacGyver had never felt like this before. The relief was overwhelming. Tears sprang to his eyes. He'd come so close to losing part of his family. He needed to talk to the girls. Get their stories. Figure out what happened so it would never happen again. Yes, he'd heard Vogel's side of the situation, but he had no doubt that the man had downplayed the events.

"Are you all right?" he asked, pulling back and putting his hands on Yana's cheeks, running his gaze up and down her body, checking for injuries, for anything that looked out of place. Her hair was in disarray, she was dirty, there was a small scrape on her face, and she had a stuffed bear in her arms that MacGyver had never seen before...but otherwise, she looked remarkably whole.

"I am okay," Yana said clearly. "Ellory here. She help. Safe."

He interpreted his daughter's words easily. She was learning English so quickly...Tears sprang to his eyes again. "Ellory?" he asked, looking over at the preteen and his wife. "Are you good?"

"Yeah."

"Not hurt?" MacGyver clarified.

"No. I think I scraped my side getting out of the container, but otherwise I'm okay. Scared and so glad to see you and Mom, but okay."

MacGyver held out an arm, and both Ellory and Addison leaned into him. The four of them knelt there on the ground and held each other. Thanking their lucky stars that they were together again.

Ellory lifted her head and looked at MacGyver. "He was here just a few minutes ago, still looking for us. Black shirt, jeans. He has brown hair and it's cut real short. He's not too tall. And not fat but...thick."

Once again, MacGyver was amazed by Ellory. She had every right to be hysterical, and yet she was doing her best to help catch the guy who'd sold them.

"On it," Kevlar said from behind MacGyver. He turned to the dozen or so men who were standing around and ordered, "Fan out. Find him. *No one* leaves this yard without being questioned."

Immediately, the SEALs who'd come to find the girls disappeared behind Conexes, looking for the man Ellory described. Everyone except for MacGyver's team. They were all surrounding the family. Protecting them.

Ellory stepped back from her mom, and Yana pulled away from MacGyver to hug her, holding on to her sister just as tightly as she had to him. The girls had been through something that had obviously strengthened the bond between them.

Looking around at MacGyver's teammates, Ellory gave them a small smile. "You're all here. Wait, where's Artem and Borysko? Did he take them?! It was Brady!" she blurted, looking at her mom in a panic.

"Shhhh, we know. Your brothers are safe. Wolf is back at the house with them, along with Remi, Wren, Josie, Maggie, and a few others. And Brady's in custody. He admitted what happened."

"*His* story about what happened," MacGyver interrupted. "Can you tell us your side?"

"I was called out of class. He told me that you were both hurt, that you were *dying*, and he was there to pick me up and bring me to you. I asked him to pick up Yana too, because I know that's what you always did, Mom, and I had no idea how long I'd be at the hospital and I didn't want her to be left at school. Then he brought us here instead of the hospital, took my phone, and he hurt Yana to make me get out of his car. Then he and the other guy locked us in the container. He said he sold my organs! That my heart was going to go to some girl overseas."

Ellory's eyes filled with tears as she leaned into Addison. Yana's arms were still around her sister, trying to offer her support.

"Why would he do that?" she asked quietly. "I thought he wanted to get to know me."

"I don't know, sweetheart," Addison said. "Some people are just..."

As she searched for the right word, MacGyver finished for her. "Evil. Some people are just evil, El. Vogel is more interested in money than anything else. It has nothing to do with you, sweetheart. If he could get money out of his own mother, I'm sure he would've tried."

The preteen took a deep breath then nodded. She wiped her face with her shoulder and stood up straighter. "He said he was going to blame *me*. That he could do something with my phone to make it look like I texted him and asked him to pick me up. That it was my idea to say you guys had been in an accident. But I didn't! I *wouldn't*."

"We know, El. We have a guy looking at your phone records, he'll be able to prove that the texts were fake and the timestamps were manipulated," MacGyver soothed. He stood and picked up Yana, wanting her in his arms.

She held out the bear she was holding. "Beary!"

MacGyver smiled. "He's very cute."

"Song. Lights!"

"It plays 'Jingle Bells' and has flashing lights," Ellory said. "There were boxes of them in the container we were in. I found them, and we used them for light to see what else we could find."

MacGyver had never been so proud of anyone in his life. "And? What else did you find?"

"Well, no cell phones to call for help, but there were these ridiculous little tool sets. With these tiny hammers and screwdrivers in them? I saw that the bottom of the container was rusted out, so we used the tools to make the hole as big as we could. Then when the Conex was lifted, we dropped out the bottom and ran."

Ellory turned toward his teammates, who were listening intently even as they watched for anyone who might spring out from behind one of the containers to attack the girls. They had no indication that would happen, but no one was taking any chances.

"Smiley?" she asked.

"Yeah?" the gruff-looking SEAL said.

"Is your name really Jude? Jude Stark?"

He frowned in confusion. Even MacGyver wondered where in the world the question had come from.

"Yes. Why? How did you know that?"

"Your friend told me."

"My friend? What friend?" Smiley asked.

It was Ellory's turn to look confused. "The girl. Um... she told me her name, but I forget it now. She was here. She found me and Yana hiding. Said she'd lead the bad guy away and for us to run here, toward where everyone was searching for us."

As far as MacGyver knew, other than Addison, there weren't any women who'd come to search. He supposed it wasn't outside the possibility that there was a woman who'd arrived after everyone had split up, but he wasn't aware of any.

"Bree," Yana said suddenly.

"That's it!" Ellory said with a smile. "Good job, Yana.

She said her name was Bree, and you were her friend. She made some noise and got the guy to chase after her. That's when we ran back here to you guys."

"Are you *sure* that was her name?" Smiley asked, clearly stunned.

Now *MacGyver* was confused. They all knew about the woman from Vegas, the one Smiley had been searching for desperately. The one who'd been sold along with Josie. But his teammate hadn't been able to find any sign of her. How could she be in Riverton? Let alone here, at this shipyard, while they were looking for Ellory and Yana? It seemed like too much of a coincidence.

Smiley anxiously glanced around the shipyard.

"Go," Preacher said.

"Are you sure?" he asked.

"Yes," Kevlar answered for all of them. "If that was your Bree, you have to go."

"Not to mention, if she led the perp away from the girls, she's put herself in danger," Safe added. "Now that we've found Ellory and Yana, a couple of us can go with you. See if we can find her."

"No. We don't know where this guy is, or if he's got help. Stay here and make sure the girls remain safe. If Bree's still here, I'll find her." Smiley quickly turned away and ran toward the direction the girls had come from.

Almost as soon as he was gone, there was shouting from the opposite direction. From the entrance to the shipyard.

"Come on. Let's get you guys somewhere safer," Flash said, gesturing toward the command center that had been hastily set up.

Addison maneuvered them so that Ellory was between her and MacGyver. He put his arm around his stepdaughter's shoulders as he held Yana and walked toward where people were congregating.

They arrived at the same time as two former SEALs. They had a man restrained between them. He looked exactly as Ellory had described. He was cursing at the men holding him, shouting at them to let go, claiming he was just a dockworker trying to do his job. He threatened to call the police and have them all arrested for trespassing.

"Is that him?" Kevlar asked Ellory.

She nodded, her eyes huge in her face as she stared at the man with fear.

He suddenly wrenched his right arm upward, obviously surprising the man holding it, allowing him time to pivot and slam his fist into the crotch of the guy on his other side. Unprepared, the former SEAL let go. It all happened in a matter of seconds.

Instead of making a run for freedom, the asshole came straight at Ellory.

The look on his face was pure evil. Fury. Resentment.

MacGyver had put Yana down the moment the man yanked his arm free, lunging in front of Ellory and his family. He had no weapons but that didn't matter. He'd always stand between his family and any kind of danger.

The SEALs who'd restrained him recovered immediately and sprang forward, but the man had desperation on his side. As he ran toward them, he pulled a gun and aimed.

Pandemonium broke out all around them. The man didn't say anything, all his attention on Ellory, who MacGyver prayed was sufficiently out of gunshot range behind him.

He managed to get off one shot before he was literally tackled by half a dozen men, disappearing under a pile of bodies. MacGyver recognized Dude and Abe, two of Wolf's former teammates, as well as Flash and Blink. The other men who'd taken down the kidnapper, MacGyver didn't know, beyond the fact they were SEAL brothers.

Quickly turning, he held out his arms to further protect his family and urge them backward, away from the altercation.

Addison inhaled sharply. "You're bleeding!" she exclaimed.

"Ricky, your arm!" Ellory shouted at the same time.

Yana's lip quivered as she stared at the blood.

Looking down, MacGyver saw blood oozing from under his shirt sleeve. He flexed his biceps and winced, but he could move his arm and the blood wasn't pumping out rhythmically, indicating a major artery was severed. He was good. His main concern at the moment was getting his girls away from the asshole who'd dared point a fucking weapon at them.

"I'm fine. It's just a graze. We need to move away. Come on, back up."

But his girls weren't having it. Addison stepped into his space and put her hand over the wound on his upper arm, pressing hard. Ellory put a hand over her mom's, and Yana grabbed his other hand, holding onto it tightly as she stared up at him.

"I'm fine, I promise," he said, feeling overwhelmed with emotion.

"You were *shot*," Addison whispered.

"He was trying to shoot me," Ellory said, her voice trembling, "and you stepped right in front of us. Like you weren't concerned at all that he was pointing a *gun* at you!"

Somehow, MacGyver managed to maneuver his family backward, away from the pile of bodies behind him. Did he want to be involved in beating the shit out of the man who dared threaten his family? Yes. But he needed to reassure his girls more.

He got them to move at least thirty more feet away from the man who'd tried to kill one or all of them, then he sat on the ground. Yana immediately crawled into his lap, while his wife and stepdaughter did their best to give him first-aid. They lifted his sleeve and insisted on pouring a bottle of water over the wound that Preacher had given to Ellory earlier.

MacGyver was vaguely aware that the man who was obviously the mastermind behind Ellory's kidnapping was now lying motionless on the ground, SEALs standing guard around him. He had no idea if he was dead or not, but for the moment, he didn't care.

It took another hour for things at the shipyard to calm down.

The paramedics arrived, the man's body was covered with a sheet—which answered the question about whether he was alive or dead—and MacGyver's arm was taken care of. He refused transport to the hospital after seeing for himself that the bullet had merely taken a chunk of flesh out of his arm. He'd definitely suffered worse while on missions.

Ellory had been questioned by the police and was going to have to go in the next day for a more extensive statement. Tex was working on getting data off her phone to send to the detectives, and they would be getting the videos from the schools to review as well. And Addison had already demanded meetings with the principals, vice principals, and resource officers at *both* schools to make sure someone was held accountable for what had happened.

The men who'd been holding on to the kidnapper—whose identity was as of yet unknown—apologized profusely for letting down their guard, and after personally thanking each and every person who'd shown up to search for the girls, MacGyver and his family were finally on their way home.

Artem and Borysko were overcome with emotion at seeing their sisters safe and sound, as were the other women and Wolf. It took another hour and a half for things to calm down at the house, and when all the kids decided to sleep together in the girls' room, neither MacGyver nor Addison protested.

Everyone was feeling a little off-kilter. It would take a while for things to go back to normal, but MacGyver could only be relieved that everyone was home. Safely.

Addison clung to him a little harder when they finally settled into their bed. They'd left their door open in case any of the kids woke up frightened in the night.

After a few long moments, she looked up at him. MacGyver expected her to tell him she loved him. Maybe how relieved she was that they'd found Ellory and Yana. What *he* didn't expect was the look of anger on her face or the way she was glaring at him.

"What?" he asked, his brow furrowing.

"If you ever do that again, I'll shoot you myself," she honest-to-God growled.

"Do what?" MacGyver asked, honestly confused.

"Put yourself in the direct line of fire of a freaking bullet!" she hissed. "I mean it, don't do that shit. You could've *died!*"

MacGyver relaxed, now that he knew what she was so upset about. "I'm sorry, I can't agree to that."

Addison came up on an elbow and glared down at him.

"There is *no* situation where I would not put myself between you or my children and any danger. That's not how I'm wired, Addy. I will do whatever it takes to make sure you're safe. That Ellory is safe. That Yana, Artem, and Borysko are safe. Yes, even if that means stepping in front of a bullet. Because I wouldn't be able to live with myself if I stood by and did nothing and any of you were hurt."

"You think I'd be able to live with *myself* if you died protecting me?" Addison asked just as passionately.

MacGyver rolled until his wife was on her back beneath him. He hovered over her, careful not to put too much weight on his injured arm, willing her to understand. "You married a protector," he told her seriously. "I'll protect my teammates, their families, my country, and anyone else who needs it to the best of my ability. But you? And my children? I will go to the ends of the earth to make sure they have everything they need and want in their lives. I will teach my girls self-defense, my boys to stand up for the rights of anyone being discriminated against, and I will always, *always*, stand between danger and those I love. Besides, don't think I didn't see you do the exact same thing. You stepped in front of Ellory and Yana as if *you* were prepared to take a bullet for them. You know exactly how I feel—because you felt it too."

Addison stared up at him, and MacGyver saw tears fill her eyes. He didn't think she even knew she was very gently caressing the bandage over the wound on his upper arm. "I love you," she whispered as the tears overflowed and fell down her temple into her hairline. "So much it scares me. I can't do this without you."

"This?"

"This parenting thing."

"Wrong. You've been doing it for years with Ellory, and

you didn't miss a beat when you had three more kids added to the one you already take care of."

"Fine. Then I can't do the parenting-a-baby thing without you."

MacGyver froze. "What? Are you saying..." His voice trailed off.

"No. I mean, I don't think I'm pregnant yet, but with the way you're taking the impregnation job so seriously, it's only a matter of time. It's been a long time since I've had to deal with an infant. I can't do the feedings, the diapers, the crying...all of it, and work, and take care of the other four kids we have, all by myself. And I can't have you throwing yourself in front of bullets all the time. I need you, Ricky. I love you so much it's almost scary."

He was both relieved *and* disappointed she wasn't already pregnant. "No more bullets," he agreed, although silently, he knew down to his soul that if they were ever again in any kind of situation like they were in today, he'd do the exact same thing.

"No more bullets," she echoed.

MacGyver eased down and pulled his wife into his arms once more. Looking over at the clock, he saw it was almost two in the morning. The kids would be exhausted tomorrow. Crabby. Ellory had to go to the police station to make her statement. He needed to talk to Smiley—no one had seen him again after he'd learned Bree was at the shipyard, that she'd essentially saved Ellory and Yana from being recaptured. He wanted to thank Wolf and his team once more, Addison needed to spend some time with the other women, have some girl time to reassure them, and herself, that everyone was all right.

They all had a busy day tomorrow. It would be difficult, but they'd get through it...as a family.

It was hard to believe that such a short time ago, he was living a solitary life. He wouldn't trade the chaos he now lived in for anything. Some people thought it was crazy for him to want to adopt three orphans from a war-torn country. But it had brought him the woman of his dreams, a stepdaughter, and the life he'd always dreamed of but had almost come to terms with never having.

And they were going to have a baby. Maybe not tomorrow or the next day, but eventually he'd knock up his wife. She'd grow huge with his flesh and blood, and his family would lose their minds with another grandbaby and niece or nephew to love on.

Speaking of which, it was past time for him to introduce his children to their grandparents. Addison's parents needed to come visit as well.

When he'd gotten married, he'd been reluctant to involve either of their families in their lives because it had been a marriage of convenience. A fake marriage. But now? There was nothing fake about their love for each other.

"What are you smiling about? Why aren't you sleeping?" Addison asked sleepily as she lifted her head to try to see his face better. "Does your arm hurt? Are you thinking too hard about what happened?"

"I'm smiling because I've never been happier. I'm not sleeping because I'm lying here thinking about the future. Our future. No, my arm doesn't hurt."

"Okay. Ricky?"

"Yeah, Addy?"

"Saying yes was the best decision I've ever made in my life."

The smile on MacGyver's face grew. "Asking you to marry me was the best decision *I* ever made."

She lowered her head back to his chest and snuggled closer to him. "Love you."

"And I love you," MacGyver echoed.

It took quite a while for him to fall asleep. Visions of the future wouldn't stop rolling through his brain. Their life wouldn't be easy or calm. Chaos would be something they'd just have to get used to. But that was perfectly all right with MacGyver. With Addison by his side, they'd be able to make it through anything.

CHAPTER TWENTY-ONE

Addison was so grateful for the help she got from her friends in the days after the girls' kidnapping. Wren took Yana to school and picked her up. Remi took over carpool duty for the boys, taking them to and from school when they said they didn't want to take the bus anymore. They were worried someone would try to steal them away, which was a fear Addison and Ricky hoped would fade. They'd enjoyed riding the bus, and she hoped they'd relax enough to love it again soon.

And the day after the abduction, Addison and Ricky accompanied Ellory to the police station.

Sitting there and listening to her daughter tell the detectives everything her own father had done made Addison sick to her stomach. She wondered if he ever had any desire to get to know his daughter, but in the end, she decided it didn't matter. He was where he deserved to be, behind bars. She had no illusions though—he'd eventually get out. But he was barred from ever contacting his daughter again, and if he did, Addison had no doubt Ellory wouldn't hesitate to let the authorities know.

Now, a few days later, Addison wanted to see where her daughter's head was at. Make sure she was dealing with everything that had happened. Ricky was at the base, the younger kids were at school, and Addison had taken some time off from work. She needed to spend time with Ellory.

"How are you doing, El? Really?"

"I'm okay, Mom."

"You know you can talk to me about anything."

Ellory rolled her eyes, which surprisingly made Addison relax a little. Her daughter was getting back to normal, and nothing felt better.

"You sleeping all right?"

"Uh-huh."

She was playing with a little frog, rolling it around in her fingers as they spoke. She'd gotten it from the container where she'd been held hostage. It was in one of the many boxes she'd opened.

"I'm worried about you."

At that, Ellory looked up. "Why?"

"Because you're my daughter, and I love you. And you went through some pretty awful things. I'm concerned about that frog," she admitted, nodding at the little toy Ellory was playing with. "Why did you keep it? Doesn't it remind you of being stuck in that box?"

Ellory stared at the toy for a long moment, then met her mom's gaze. "It reminds me of what happened, but not in a bad way. I was scared, that's not a secret. But when I found that box of stuffed bears and realized they were flashlights of a sort, it gave me a kind of confidence I'd never felt before. *I* had done that. I climbed to the top of those boxes and found something useful to the situation. The box of frogs wasn't useful at all, except it gave me the drive to keep searching. That's when I found the tools."

She shrugged. "Looking at this frog reminds me that I'm more than just what people see. More than the sick kid. The puny one who hasn't grown any boobs yet. More than the disgusting daughter that Brady saw. I'm resourceful and smart. *I* got Yana and myself out of that box. *I* saved us. The bad guy didn't win. That's what I see when I look at this frog."

Addison pressed her lips together hard, attempting not to cry.

"Jeez, Mom. You aren't going to cry again, are you?" Ellory asked with another roll of her eyes.

That was what Addison needed. She laughed. "Maybe. And you'll just have to get used to your mama crying now and then."

Ellory smiled at her and put the frog back into her pocket. "Ricky told me he was proud of me," she said out of the blue.

"He is," Addison agreed.

"When he saw how that stupid 'Jingle Bell' song in Yana's bear bothered both of us, he took me to the garage and we figured out together how to turn it off. We did a bear-ectomy." She grinned. "Took out the box that played the song, then rewired it so the lights still work. I love how he doesn't offer to play dolls and talk makeup with me just because I'm a girl. He also told me that his team gave me a nickname!"

"They did?" Addison asked, knowing all about her daughter's new nickname. Ricky didn't keep anything from her. They talked every night when they went to bed. About the schedule for the next day, school, the adoption process, and about his work—what he could share, that was. He'd let her know that his friends now called their daughter "Little Mac"—impressed by how she'd used the

343

skills he'd taught her to MacGyver her way out of the Conex container.

"Yeah. Little Mac. Like little MacGyver."

"How do you feel about that?" Addison asked.

Ellory smiled again. "I cried when he told me. I can't think of anything better than being MacGyver's daughter. Of being a little MacGyver. Of him being my dad."

"It's a high honor for sure," Addison told her, hanging on to her control by a thread.

"He said he wanted to adopt me...if I was okay with it."

Addison couldn't stop the tear that fell down her cheek. "And you said?" she managed to croak.

"Oh Lord, there goes the crying again," Ellory said with another roll of her eyes. "Of *course* I said that would be awesome. I asked if I could call him Dad, and he got all emotional and said he'd love that...if it's okay with you, of course."

"There's nothing I'd like more. Ricky and I talked about it already, and we both agreed that it would be up to you. But I'm so happy that you're open to it."

"Why wouldn't I be? He's awesome," Ellory said. Then her smile faded, and she said in a very serious tone, "Can I ask you something?"

"Of course. You can ask me anything."

"Are the SEALs going to get in trouble for killing that guy?"

Addison stiffened. She really didn't want to talk about this with her twelve-year-old. But she couldn't hide it from her. She'd been through hell, and she wanted to be as honest as she could be. Wanted to respect her need for answers.

"No."

"I overheard the detectives talking about it. They said

he was stabbed. In the heart. That it happened when everyone tackled him but they don't know who did it."

Every time Addison thought about that day, it made her feel sick, but Ellory was growing up quickly. It was her right to know about the man who'd tried to kill her, the man who'd shot Ricky.

"That's true. Somehow, when the guys were trying to disarm him, he was stabbed."

"I'm glad," Ellory said bluntly. "I know that probably makes me a horrible person, but I don't care."

"It doesn't make you a horrible person, it makes you human. He wasn't a good man. He did very bad things, all in the name of money."

"He shot Ricky."

"Yeah."

"He was aiming for *me*."

Addison didn't agree. Even if it was true, she couldn't bring herself to admit it.

"He wasn't even beat up or anything. Just had a knife sticking out of his chest, right over his heart. Those SEALs...they're pretty badass," Ellory said.

"Yeah, they are." Now *that* was something Addison could agree with.

"Mom?"

"Yeah, sweetie?"

"I love you. I think you're pretty cool."

That was high praise coming from a preteen. She was wrong, Addison wasn't cool at all, but she wasn't going to contradict her daughter. "I love you too, and I think you're pretty cool yourself."

Ellory rolled her eyes yet again. "I'm not. But I don't care. I am who I am. Crohn's patient, nerd, theater geek, and Little Mac."

"Yeah." The stupid tears were back.

"Seriously, Mom? You're *so* hormonal."

Addison frowned. She *had* been crying more than normal lately. It was true, her daughters had been through something horribly traumatic, but still...

Could it be because she was pregnant?

She had no idea, and as much as she wanted a baby with Ricky, things were so darn chaotic right now. It wasn't the best time. But then again, was *any* time ever going to be the "best time?" Things with the kids would only get busier as they grew up. And she wanted Ellory to have some time with her new little brother or sister...didn't want to wait until she'd gone off to college before having a baby.

"Mom? You okay?"

"I'm okay," Addison reassured her. "Just thinking."

"I'm ready to go back to school," Ellory said, seemingly out of the blue.

"Are you sure?"

"I'm sure. What happened sucked, and I learned my lesson. Never go with anyone who isn't on the official pick-up list. Which now includes many more people," Ellory said with a laugh.

It was true. She and Ricky had added his entire SEAL team, all their women, Wolf, Caroline, and even Julie and Patrick Hurt.

"I told you before, it's your decision on when to go back. I know you've been keeping up with your schoolwork."

"Yeah. But my theater teacher is going to announce the new play we'll be doing tomorrow. I want to be there. I think I'm going to try out for stage manager this time."

Addison was so proud of her daughter, she could burst.

She was strong as hell, something she'd always known based on how she dealt with her Crohn's diagnosis and the symptoms that still flared up from time to time. But now, seeing how she'd bounced back after such a terrifying experience as being kidnapped and sold for her organs was almost humbling.

"Okay, hon."

"I'm gonna go to the garage and work on that thing Ricky and are doing together. I want to show him how much I got done when he gets home tonight." And with that pronouncement, Ellory stood and headed for the garage with a smile.

Addison sat on the couch for a long moment. Ellory was moving on from what Brady had done; it was time for her to do so as well. She had plenty of people emailing and inquiring about cake and cookie orders. Life was officially back to normal.

That night, when she and Ricky were in bed after a chaotic evening with the kids, Addison rolled toward him and straddled his hips.

He looked up at her with so much love in his eyes, she could've melted on the spot. She was the luckiest woman in the world, and she was suddenly speechless. Didn't have the words to tell this man how much she loved him.

So she showed him instead, peeling her T-shirt over her head and smiling when his hands immediately lifted to cover her breasts. She leaned down and fed him a nipple. He took it into his mouth, sucking hard, making her pussy gush with need.

It didn't take much foreplay for her to be ready for him. It was a little comical, the contortions they both had to endure in order to get the rest of their clothes off, but before long, she was once again straddling Ricky, this time with both of them completely nude.

Lifting up, she took hold of his hard cock and lined it up with her pussy, sinking down in one quick movement.

They both gasped at the feeling of bliss when he bottomed out. Their lovemaking was hard and fast. Ricky helped by grasping her hips and lifting and slamming her down on his cock. Then he moved a hand between her legs and firmly stroked her clit as she took him.

After she exploded in ecstasy, he rolled them until he was on top. He put her ankles on his shoulders, leaned in, and fucked her hard, fast, and deep. Addison loved seeing the expression on his face as he took her. The intensity in his eyes. He never looked away as he made love to her, which made what they were doing all the more intimate.

She squeezed her inner muscles around his cock, loving the moan that escaped when she did it. He pushed himself as deep inside her as he could get, then ordered, "Do that again."

She did.

He twitched deep inside her body.

So she did it again. And again. Fucking him solely from the inside. She reached down and began to masturbate as he held himself still inside her. She always thought men needed the friction of movement to come, but her husband proved her wrong.

When she flew over the edge for a second time, every muscle in her body tensed, especially those in her pussy.

He grunted and shoved his hips against her, obviously coming hard inside her. And the satisfaction Addison felt was overwhelming. The love she had for this man all-encompassing.

When he was finished, he lay over her, not pulling out.

Staying deep inside her body. He'd eventually slip out when he softened, but she enjoyed the feeling of being full of him as long as she could.

"Ellory accused me of being extra hormonal today," she said quietly.

Her husband wasn't a stupid man. His head flew up, and he looked down at her with an inquisitive stare. "And?"

"And nothing."

"Did you take a test?"

She wanted to make a joke about a math test or something, but didn't. "No. I don't want to be disappointed if it's negative."

"So you're what...? Just going to ignore it? Be surprised in nine months when you suddenly go into labor?"

Addison chuckled. "No. But...it's so early. I just...I want to wait for a while. Enjoy you. My family. Get back into the swing of things."

"What if you pee on the stick and don't look at the results? Only I will."

Addison burst out laughing. "As if you'd be able to keep a secret like that."

"Hey, I keep secrets all the time," Ricky protested.

"I know you do. But you wouldn't last a day with this. You'd be all like, 'I think you should start taking some vitamins, hon,' or, 'Are you tired? Maybe you should sit.' I'd know in a heartbeat if you knocked me up."

Ricky smiled sheepishly. "Okay, you might be right."

"I *am* right," she countered.

"I hear what you're saying, but I want to make sure you're healthy. That everything is okay with our baby. What about this—one month. We'll carry on as normal for a month. Then you'll do the test and we'll go from there."

Addison thought about that for a moment, then nodded. "Okay."

Ricky leaned in and kissed her. His hips flexed, then he rocked them a fraction. "A baby. I never dreamed asking you to marry me would make me the happiest man on earth."

"We don't know if there's a baby yet," she warned.

"We don't," he agreed. "But I have another month to do my best to make sure there is."

"Again?" Addison asked, as he began to slowly move in and out of her body.

"Again," he confirmed. "I'm going to want to come inside you as much as I can in the next month. Make *sure* my seed takes root."

She giggled. "Who says that?"

"Me," Ricky said with a huge grin.

He was a dork, but he was *her* dork. Addison wouldn't want him any other way. "Then you better get on it, because there's no telling when one of our kids is going to knock on our door and want something."

"Yes, ma'am," he said with a smile. Then proceeded to make Addison forget everything except the way her husband made her feel.

EPILOGUE

"What is *up* with you?" Safe asked Smiley. "You're an asshole, but lately you've been even *more* of an asshole."

"Leave him alone," Kevlar said in a tone the team rarely heard.

Safe looked at his friend in surprise. "I'm not trying to be mean, I'm trying to understand."

Smiley stared at his teammate. He was well aware he was being an asshole to the people who meant the most to him. But he couldn't help it. He was frustrated and worried.

And Jude Stark wasn't the kind of man who worried. Life happened. You couldn't control it, you could only ride the wave as best you could. But ever since the events with Ellory and Yana, he'd been on edge. The woman he'd been desperately searching for in Las Vegas was *here*. In Riverton. She'd been so close—and yet once again, she'd slipped through his fingers.

And once again, she'd been hurt.

He'd found a spot in that shipyard, way back in a corner near the fence line, that had a sizeable puddle of blood. He could easily envision what happened, especially after seeing the bruised knuckles of the asshole his SEAL friends had killed.

Bree had led the kidnapper away from the kids, allowing them to escape, and she'd found herself cornered. She might have fought back, but it would have been no use. The woman he remembered was small and slight...and she'd had the shit beaten out of her. Enough that he'd found a fucking *fingernail* on the ground.

Closing his eyes, he could picture what happened as clear as day.

Bree, lying on the ground, curled into a ball trying to protect herself, while she was kicked and beaten to a pulp.

The only consolation Smiley had was the trail of blood that led him to a spot in the fence, where she'd clearly crawled under and out of the shipyard.

He had so many questions. Why was she here? How had she gotten involved in Ellory and Yana's rescue? Was she *still* here? Did she need help? And if she did, why didn't she make contact with him?

He had no answers—and it was driving him crazy.

"Smiley?" Kevlar said his name quietly. "What do you need from us?"

Deciding if he was ever going to find Bree Haynes, he had to admit he needed assistance, Smiley turned to his team.

They were standing on the beach near the naval base. They were supposed to be working out, but in an extremely rare occurrence, Kevlar had stopped them after only three miles of running, saying it had been a long time since they'd really appreciated a sunrise. It was a ruse, of course. For Kevlar to talk to his team, to put his finger on the pulse of the men who were not only his friends, but who he felt were his responsibility.

They all had a lot going on, and Smiley actually appreciated being able to get caught up with everyone's lives. He didn't love being the current center of attention, but since he needed a sounding board, and help, he'd suffer through it.

"She's close," he told his friends. "I can feel it. I don't know why she hasn't reached out. But she needs help. That has to be why she's here. And she somehow knew we were at that shipyard...which means she's been following us. *Me.* I need you all to be on the lookout. For a car that's hanging around, for a woman in places you wouldn't expect. And if you see a woman who looks the way I described Bree, detain her."

"I'm not sure—"

"I'm not saying slap a pair of zip-ties on her and throw her to the ground. But...talk to her. See if you can get her to stay close by until I can get there. I have no concrete evidence, but this woman is in trouble. She wouldn't be working so hard to stay under the radar if she wasn't. And I haven't been able to find any info on her ex, the asshole who sold her into sexual slavery."

"Tex hasn't come through?" Preacher asked in surprise

"I haven't asked him to look into that part," Smiley admitted. "Just asked him to let me know if she uses a bank card or credit card anywhere."

"Why not?" Blink asked. "I bet he could have all the info you need in less than twenty-four hours."

Smiley wasn't sure how to answer that. Except...*he* wanted to be the one who saved the day. It was stupid. But all his life, he'd been the grunt. The guy who did what was asked of him and followed everyone else. One of the team.

Just once, he'd wanted to be the savior. The guy who swooped in with the red cape.

"Because I'm an idiot?" he said with a self-deprecating shrug.

"No, you're not...but you *are* kind of being one in this case," Kevlar told him honestly. "And of course we'll be on the lookout for you. If we see anything or anyone who looks like the woman you described, we'll get in touch with you immediately. Believe it or not, we all want to find this Bree person."

"Especially me," MacGyver said. "I owe her everything. Without her..." His words trailed off. They were all well aware of what might've happened to Ellory and Yana without Bree's sacrifice.

"How are they?" Preacher asked. "The girls?"

"Surprisingly good. Ellory had a pretty intense Crohn's flare, and we had to go to the emergency room, but she's feeling better. And Yana has been speaking a lot more. They were lucky. *We* were lucky."

"And Addison? She coping all right?" Safe asked.

"She's good. And...there's a chance she might be pregnant."

All the men smiled and congratulated MacGyver.

"Maggie's gonna be thrilled. Having a cousin born so close to our kid would be awesome," Preacher said with a shit-eating grin on his face.

"I think that's what convinced her not to use any birth control," MacGyver admitted. "She liked the thought of our kid having a friend close to his or her age to grow up with."

"Yeah, that's what Josie said too," Blink mused, staring over the water as if remembering a particularly good moment between him and his girlfriend.

Everyone stared at the taciturn SEAL.

"What?" he asked with a small grin. "There's nothing I can think of that would be better than our kids all causing havoc in the same class at school."

"What are the odds of you having twins?" Flash joked.

"Well, since I'm a twin, my mom was a twin, and *her* dad was a twin, I'd say pretty good."

"Right, so two of our women are knocked up, Blink's gonna see what he can do about giving Josie a pair of little red-haired babies...what about the rest of you?" Preacher asked.

"Don't look at me," Smiley said in a rush.

"Me either," Flash added. "I don't even have the possibility of a girlfriend on the horizon."

"Aren't you heading to Jamaica?" Safe asked.

"Yeah. What does that have to do with anything?"

"I'm just sayin'...bachelor party, men being men... there are bound to be some hot chicks on the beach. Maybe you can turn on the charm and see what happens."

"I still can't believe you're going to Jamaica, of all places," Kevlar bitched.

"Come on. My sister begged me. You guys know she's a decade younger than me, was a surprise baby for my parents. We're also really close. I've been looking out for her since I was a kid. And when she got engaged, I wasn't exactly thrilled, since her fiancé is kind of a player. When he said he wanted to go to one of those expensive resorts for his bachelor party, she said she'd support it only if her big brother was invited."

"So you're the voice of reason, huh?" Safe said with a chuckle.

"Pretty much. The guy knows if he does *anything* out of

line, I won't hesitate to tell my sister. So he'll be on his best behavior."

"But Jamaica?" Kevlar repeated. "I'm surprised the commander approved your leave request."

"Right now, the state department's travel advisory is only at level two," Flash argued.

"Yeah, but a month ago it was level three, 'reconsider travel.' Crime is still a big problem there. The police aren't very effective in responding to incidents, and the homicide rate is one of the highest in the Western Hemisphere," Kevlar retorted.

Flash sighed. "I know. I argued against Jamaica for the same reasons...with no luck. My only consolation is that, again, we'll be in one of those fancy resorts with security."

"You know as well as I do that's no guarantee that nothing will happen," Kevlar said.

"Yeah. I'll be careful, all right? We'll only be there for three days. If I didn't go, and anything happened to my sister's fiancé, I'd never forgive myself because it would break her heart. I'm going to make sure he gets home safe and sound, as much as I am to keep an eye on him."

Kevlar grunted, but nodded.

"So...Blink...you're going to convince Josie to have your babies...you gonna marry her?" Preacher asked with a grin.

"Yes."

"Sometime this century?" he joked.

To everyone's surprise, he looked over at Kevlar. "You think Remi will stand up with me? Be my best man, so to speak?"

Kevlar's eyes widened. "Seriously?"

"Yeah. She's the sister I never had, and after everything that happened with us...I'd be honored to have her at my side when I marry the most important person in my life."

"Of course she will!" Kevlar blurted. "She'll be honored. Will probably cry. What about your brother?"

"Oh, I want him there too. Can't get married without my twin and the rest of the family. And probably his Night Stalker friends. Josie and I have already talked about it, we want a big party with all our friends and family."

"Sounds perfect," Kevlar said with a small smile.

"I want to know when our esteemed leader is going to make an honest woman out of Remi," Flash asked.

"You know how offensive and out-of-date that saying is, right?" Kevlar asked with a roll of his eyes.

"Whatever, you know what I mean."

"I do. And the answer is...soon," he promised.

"Good. And what about you, Safe? You gonna marry Wren?" Flash asked.

"We aren't in a rush," he replied.

MacGyver frowned at his friend. "What are you waiting for?"

"I don't know. I love her, she loves me, we don't feel the need to be married. The thing between us is real, solid. A piece of paper isn't going to change that."

"Trust me, there are benefits to being married," MacGyver said. "What if she gets sick? Or there are issues with a pregnancy? Or she's in a car accident? We're all one medical emergency away from going bankrupt. There are some protections she'll have automatically if you guys are married."

Safe thought about his friend's words for a moment. "I'm not going to ask her to marry me simply as a 'just in case' kind of thing."

"Then marry her because you love her. Because you can't imagine spending the rest of your life without her. Because if something happens to you on a mission, she'll have the support and backing of the Navy. Life insurance. Health insurance. She's not going to think you're marrying her simply because she'll get money when you die. She loves you. It's obvious to all of us." MacGyver turned to Kevlar. "Same goes for you."

"What if you two had a double ceremony?" Flash suggested to Blink and Kevlar. "Blink wants Remi to stand up with him...what if she was literally standing next to him while getting married to her man, at the same time he was marrying Josie?"

Kevlar looked at Blink. "It's not a horrible idea."

Blink smiled. "It's not. But it means that you need to get off your ass and get a ring and ask her."

"I have a ring," Kevlar protested. "I was just waiting for the right time to ask."

"No time is the right time," MacGyver protested. "Just do it."

"What is this, a Nike commercial?" Smiley muttered.

"We could make it a triple ceremony," Kevlar suggested, looking at Safe.

"Nope. No way. I love you guys, but I want my wedding day to be just about me and Wren. Probably won't be a huge shindig or anything, but even if it's at the courthouse, I want it to be about us."

"So...once you three make things official...it'll just be Flash and Smiley we need to get married off," Preacher said with a chuckle.

"What happened to us?" Smiley asked with a shake of his head. "We were all badass Navy SEALs. Now we're sitting on our asses instead of working out, talking about fucking weddings. It's a disgrace."

"You'll understand when you meet the woman you can't imagine living one more day without," Safe said.

"Whatever," Smiley bitched.

"So...Addison is good, the kids are good; Maggie and Addison are knocked up; Kevlar, Safe, and Blink are getting married; Blink is going to spend all his free time trying to continue the family tradition of having twins. I'm going to fucking Jamaica to make sure my little sister's fiancé keeps his dick in his pants during his bachelor party weekend. And Smiley is his usual asshole self, but we're all going to help him anyway by being on the lookout for the mysterious Bree, so he can finally figure out what the hell is up with her and *stop* being such an asshole. Did I cover everything?" Flash asked.

"Pretty much."

"I think so."

"Sounds about right."

"Good. So, since we chatted through the sunrise and covered all our bases, can we get the hell out of here? I need to pack, and I'm sure all of you want to go home and see your wives, girlfriends, and soon-to-be fiancées," Flash said.

Everyone laughed but turned to head back down the beach.

Smiley held back when everyone began to jog toward the parking lot. He was blessed to have such good friends. He was happy for them, between all the babies and marriages. Deep down, he wanted that too. But the hard crust around his heart and his bad experiences growing up were both huge roadblocks to him ever enjoying what his friends had.

But if he could find Bree Haynes and make sure she was safe, it would go a long way toward making him feel as if he'd finally done something good in his personal life.

That he hadn't sat back and allowed another woman to suffer...the way his own mother had.

Shaking his head, not wanting bad memories to overwhelm him, he quickly jogged after his teammates. He would find Bree. One way or another. Then move on with his life with a clear conscience.

Even as he had the thought, the image of the dark bloodstain on the ground at the shipyard flashed in his brain. He hadn't saved Bree from that beating...and it was possible he wouldn't be able to save her from whoever was after her.

But he wasn't going to give up.

He couldn't stand back and do nothing. Not again. Not ever again.

* * *

Kelli Colbert didn't want to go to Jamaica. She'd done her research. It wasn't safe. Besides, the only reason she was going was because her cousin had been forced to invite her. She was an old, unwanted, weird, short and stumpy, unfashionable spinster.

At least according to Charlotte.

Kelli was well aware that she wasn't what the media considered ideal when it came to her looks. She was only five foot two. Her shoulder-length dirty-blonde hair wasn't trendily styled, and it boasted no highlights, no layers. She was twenty-eight to Charlotte's twenty-two, and she'd never really had a steady boyfriend.

Charlotte was the complete opposite. Tall, slender, long blonde hair, beautiful big blue eyes. She'd been a cheerleader in high school and college, and had finally gotten her boyfriend, the quarterback on the college football team, to propose.

Of course, he was just the reserve quarterback, Kelli thought to herself with a small snort. From what she'd heard, he'd barely graduated. He was working for his father in his insurance business. Which was fine, but again, she'd heard through the family grapevine that he sucked at sales. That his daddy was financing the entire wedding.

It was safe to say Kelli didn't get along that well with her cousin, so when she was invited to Jamaica, she was surprised. She'd tried to politely decline, but her mom had sat her down and told her that it was important she go. To try to deepen the friendship between her cousin and herself. Kelli tried to explain that they were *never* going to be close but, not wanting to disappoint her mom, she'd finally agreed to go.

She'd regretted saying yes ever since.

Charlotte had sent her an email of "rules" she'd be expected to follow. She was acting like a total bridezilla, even though there were still months to go before she and Kolson got married.

Kolson. He was as obnoxious as his name. Kelli felt bad for having such mean thoughts about someone who would eventually become a part of her family, but the entire bridesmaid trip was making her feel entirely unlike herself.

Kolson would be taking his groomsmen to Vegas the same weekend she and Charlotte would be in Jamaica with her bridesmaids. The three A's, as Kelli called them—Afton, Alice, and Ava—were mirror images of Charlotte. Tall, skinny, blonde. She was going to stick out like a sore thumb, and Kelli had a feeling her role would be to fetch and carry for the others.

Screw that.

She would go to Jamaica, but her ass was going to sit in a chair on the beach for the entire weekend. She wasn't much of a drinker, so she'd be content with her nonalcoholic frozen drinks and her ebooks.

It would be a nice vacation from her stressful job as a travel agent. Some people—meaning Charlotte—didn't think her job was all that difficult. But dealing with airline changes, asshole clients, and the stress of trying to make sure trips of a lifetime went off without a hitch had finally left Kelli looking for something else to do with her life.

The topping on the shit cake that was this whole trip to Jamaica was the fact that Kelli had planned the entire thing. Charlotte was *crazy* demanding, and she'd changed her mind half a dozen times over the last few weeks as to where she'd wanted to stay. But the trip was finally planned, and even though it wasn't the smartest place to go, Kelli was done arguing with everyone.

She'd attend, keep her head down, and breathe a sigh of relief when she arrived back home. Nothing was likely to happen in a resort filled with tourists. As long as she didn't step foot off the property, she'd be fine. Her biggest concern would probably be trying to ignore the constant digs Charlotte made about her lack of a love life, and spending as much time as possible away from the three A's and her bridezilla cousin.

She could do that. Piece of cake.

But no matter how much of a pep talk she gave herself, Kelli had a feeling this trip would change things. How? She had no idea, but she couldn't shake the thought that by the time she returned from the tropical paradise, her life would take a drastic detour from the slightly stressful, yet boring existence she lived now. But good or bad, the decision was made.

She was going to Jamaica with her cousin and the three A's.

* * *

I know you are all wondering about Smiley and Bree...but first up is Flash and Kelli's story! You *know* things aren't going to go smoothly in Jamaica...but how bad could things get? You'll have to read their story to find out! Get *Protecting Kelli NOW!*

Scan the QR code below for signed books, swag, T-shirts and more!

Securing Zoey
Securing Avery
Securing Kalee
Securing Jane

Delta Force Heroes Series
Rescuing Rayne
Rescuing Aimee (novella)
Rescuing Emily
Rescuing Harley
Marrying Emily (novella)
Rescuing Kassie
Rescuing Bryn
Rescuing Casey
Rescuing Sadie (novella)
Rescuing Wendy
Rescuing Mary
Rescuing Macie (novella)
Rescuing Annie

SEAL of Protection Series
Protecting Caroline
Protecting Alabama
Protecting Fiona
Marrying Caroline (novella)
Protecting Summer
Protecting Cheyenne
Protecting Jessyka
Protecting Julie (novella)
Protecting Melody
Protecting the Future
Protecting Kiera (novella)

ABOUT THE AUTHOR

New York Times, USA Today and *Wall Street Journal* Bestselling Author Susan Stoker has a heart as big as the state of Tennessee where she lives, but this all American girl has also spent the last fourteen years living in Missouri, California, Colorado, Indiana, and Texas. She's married to a retired Army man who now gets to follow *her* around the country.

She debuted her first series in 2014 and quickly followed that up with the SEAL of Protection Series, which solidified her love of writing and creating stories readers can get lost in.

If you enjoyed this book, or any book, please consider leaving a review. It's appreciated by authors more than you'll know.

www.stokeraces.com
www.AcesPress.com
susan@stokeraces.com

f facebook.com/authorsusanstoker

X x.com/Susan_Stoker

instagram.com/authorsusanstoker

g goodreads.com/SusanStoker

BB bookbub.com/authors/susan-stoker

a amazon.com/author/susanstoker

Made in the USA
Middletown, DE
04 May 2025

75103936R00227